I know John Charming is an unfortunate name.

Believe me, I've heard them all. No, I've never been turned into a frog. No, I haven't slain many dragons lately. How could I? They've been hibernating close to the Earth's core for over a thousand years. No, I don't have any unusual shoe fetishes, glass slipper or otherwise. No, my kisses won't bring women out of any comas, though I hope they might perk them up a little.

But make no mistake: the reason there are so many stories about "Prince" Charming is that there was never one man— the Charmings were an entire family line standing between humanity and all other for generation after generation, and in the old days it was common to give any monster killer in a story royal status. That is a heavy burden, but I carried my name proudly for as long as I was able. And I am still that man. No matter what else is in my DNA, no matter what my old order says, no matter what titles have been stripped from me or how long I am forced to run and hide... I am still that man.

I think.

By Elliott James

Pax Arcana
Charming

Pax Arcana Short Fiction
Charmed I'm Sure
Don't Go Chasing Waterfalls
Pushing Luck
Surreal Estate

ELLIOTT JAMES

www.orbitbooks.net

Orbit
Hachette Book Group
237 Park Avenue, New York, NY 10017
HachetteBookGroup.com

First Edition: September 2013

Orbit is an imprint of Hachette Book Group, Inc. The Orbit name and logo are
trademarks of Little, Brown Book Group Limited.

The Hachette Speakers Bureau provides a wide range of authors for speaking
events. To find out more, go to www.hachettespeakersbureau.com or
call (866) 376-6591.

The publisher is not responsible for websites (or their content) that are not owned
by the publisher.

The characters and events in this book are fictitious. Any similarity to real
persons, living or dead, is coincidental and not intended by the author.

Library of Congress Cataloging-in-Publication Data
James, Elliott.
    Charming / Elliott James. — 1st ed.
        p. cm.
    Summary: "A fascinating twist on the Prince Charming fairy tale with a modern
twist and a hunt for monsters—both within and supernatural." —Provided by
publisher
        ISBN 978-0-316-25339-0 (trade pbk.) — ISBN 978-0-316-25338-3 (ebook)
    I. Title.
    PS3610.A4334C43 2013
    813'.6—dc23
                                    2013004664

10 9 8 7 6 5 4 3 2 1

RRD-C

Printed in the United States of America

This book is dedicated to my grandmother,
who taught me to love words.

HOCUS FOCUS

There's a reason that we refer to being in love as being enchanted. Think back to the worst relationship you've ever been in: the one where your family and friends tried to warn you that the person you were with was cheating on you, or partying a little too much, or a control freak, or secretly gay, or whatever. Remember how you were convinced that no one but you could see the real person beneath that endearingly flawed surface? And then later, after the relationship reached that scorched-earth-policy stage where letters were being burned and photos were being cropped, did you find yourself looking back and being amazed at how obvious the truth had been all along? Did it feel as if you were waking up from some kind of a spell?

Well, there's something going on right in front of your face that you can't see right now, and you're not going to believe me when I point it out to you. Relax, I'm not going to provide a number where you can leave your credit card information, and you don't have to join anything. The only reason I'm telling you at all is that at some point in the future, you might have a falling-out with the worldview you're currently enamored of, and if that happens, what I'm about to tell you will help you make sense of things later.

The supernatural is real. Vampires? Real. Werewolves? Real.

Elliott James

Zombies, Ankou, djinn, Boo Hags, banshees, ghouls, spriggans, windigos, vodyanoi, tulpas, and so on and so on, all real. Well, except for Orcs and Hobbits. Tolkien just made those up.

I know it sounds ridiculous. How could magic really exist in a world with an Internet and forensic science and smartphones and satellites and such and still go undiscovered?

The answer is simple: it's magic.

The truth is that the world is under a spell called the Pax Arcana, a compulsion that makes people unable to see, believe, or even seriously consider any evidence of the supernatural that is not an immediate threat to their survival.

I know this because I come from a long line of dragon slayers, witch finders, and self-righteous asshats. I used to be one of the modern-day knights who patrol the borders between the world of man and the supernatural abyss that is its shadow. I wore non-reflective Kevlar instead of shining armor and carried a sawed-off shotgun as well as a sword; I didn't light a candle against the dark, I wielded a flamethrower... right up until the day I discovered that I had been cursed by one of the monsters I used to hunt. My name is Charming by the way. John Charming.

And I am not living happily ever after.

1

A BLONDE AND A VAMPIRE
WALK INTO A BAR…

Once upon a time, she smelled wrong. Well, no, that's not exactly true. She smelled clean, like fresh snow and air after a lightning storm and something hard to identify, something like sex and butter pecan ice cream. Honestly, I think she was the best thing I'd ever smelled. I was inferring "wrongness" from the fact that she wasn't entirely human.

I later found out that her name was Sig.

Sig stood there in the doorway of the bar with the wind behind her, and there was something both earthy and unearthly about her. Standing at least six feet tall in running shoes, she had shoulders as broad as a professional swimmer's, sinewy arms, and well-rounded hips that were curvy and compact. All in all, she was as buxom, blonde, blue-eyed, and clear-skinned as any woman who had ever posed for a Swedish tourism ad.

And I wanted her out of the bar, fast.

You have to understand, Rigby's is not the kind of place where goddesses were meant to walk among mortals. It is a small, modest establishment eking out a fragile existence at the tail end of Clayburg's main street. The owner, David Suggs, had wanted a quaint pub, but instead of decorating the place with dartboards or Scottish coats of arms or ceramic mugs, he had decided to celebrate southwest Virginia culture and covered the walls with rusty old railroad equipment and farming tools.

When I asked why a bar—excuse me, I mean *pub*—with a Celtic name didn't have a Celtic atmosphere, Dave said that he had named Rigby's after a Beatles song about lonely people needing a place to belong.

"Names have power," Dave had gone on to inform me, and I had listened gravely as if this were a revelation.

Speaking of names, "John Charming" is not what it reads on my current driver's license. In fact, about the only thing accurate on my current license is the part where it says that I'm black-haired and blue-eyed. I'm six foot one instead of six foot two and about seventy-five pounds lighter than the 250 pounds indicated on my identification. But I do kind of look the way the man pictured on my license might look if Trevor A. Barnes had lost that much weight and cut his hair short and shaved off his beard. Oh, and if he were still alive.

And no, I didn't kill the man whose identity I had assumed, in case you're wondering. Well, not the first time anyway.

Anyhow, I had recently been forced to leave Alaska and start a new life of my own, and in David Suggs I had found an employer who wasn't going to be too thorough with his background checks. My current goal was to work for Dave for at least one fiscal year and not draw any attention to myself.

Which was why I was not happy to see the blonde.

For her part, the blonde didn't seem too happy to see me either. Sig focused on me immediately. People always gave me a quick flickering glance when they walked into the bar—excuse me, the pub—but the first thing they really checked out was the clientele. Their eyes were sometimes predatory, sometimes cautious, sometimes hopeful, often tired, but they only returned to me after being disappointed. Sig's gaze, however, centered on me like the oncoming lights of a train—assuming train lights have slight bags underneath them and make you want to flex surreptitiously. Those same startlingly blue eyes widened, and her body went still for a moment.

Whatever had triggered her alarms, Sig hesitated, visibly debating whether to approach and talk to me. She didn't hesitate for long, though—I got the impression that she rarely hesitated for long—and chose to go find herself a table.

Now, it was a Thursday night in April, and Rigby's was not empty. Clayburg is host to a small private college named Stillwaters University, one of those places where parents pay more money than they should to get an education for children with mediocre high school records, and underachievers with upper-middle-class parents tend to do a lot of heavy drinking. This is why Rigby's manages to stay in business. Small bars with farming implements on the walls don't really draw huge college crowds, but the more popular bars tend to stay packed, and Rigby's does attract an odd combination of local rednecks and students with a sense of irony. So when a striking six-foot blonde who wasn't an obvious transvestite sat down in the middle of the bar, there were people around to notice.

Even Sandra, a nineteen-year-old waitress who considers customers an unwelcome distraction from covert texting, noticed the newcomer. She walked up to Sig promptly instead of making Renee, an older waitress and Rigby's de facto manager, chide her into action.

For the next hour I pretended to ignore the new arrival while focusing on her intently. I listened in—my hearing is as well developed as my sense of smell—while several patrons tried to introduce themselves. Sig seemed to have a knack for knowing how to discourage each would-be player as fast as possible.

She told suitors that she wanted to be up-front about her sex change operation because she was tired of having it cause problems when her lovers found out later, or she told them that she liked only black men, or young men, or older men who made more than seventy thousand dollars a year. She told them that what really turned her on was men who were willing to have sex with other men while she watched. She mentioned one man's wife by name, and when the weedy-looking grad student doing a John Lennon impersonation tried the sensitive-poet approach, she challenged him to an arm-wrestling contest. He stared at her, sitting there exuding athleticism, confidence, and health—three things he was noticeably lacking—and chose to be offended rather than take her up on it.

There was at least one woman who seemed interested in Sig as well, a cute sandy-haired college student who was tall and willowy, but when it comes to picking up strangers, women are generally less likely to go on a kamikaze mission than men. The young woman kept looking over at Sig's table, hoping to establish some kind of meaningful eye contact, but Sig wasn't making any.

Sig wasn't looking at me either, but she held herself at an angle that kept me in her peripheral vision at all times.

For my part, I spent the time between drink orders trying to figure out exactly what Sig was. She definitely wasn't undead. She wasn't a half-blood Fae either, though her scent wasn't entirely dissimilar. Elf smell isn't something you forget, sweet and decadent, with a hint of honey blossom and distant ocean. There aren't any full-blooded Fae left, of course—they packed their bags and went back to Fairyland a long time ago—but don't mention that to any of the mixed human descendants that the elves left behind. Elvish half-breeds tend to be somewhat sensitive on that particular subject. They can be real bastards about being bastards.

I would have been tempted to think that Sig was an angel, except that I've never heard of anyone I'd trust ever actually seeing a real angel. God is as much an article of faith in my world as he, she, we, they, or it is in yours.

Stumped, I tried to approach the problem by figuring out what Sig was doing there. She didn't seem to enjoy the ginger ale she had ordered—didn't seem to notice it at all, just sipped from it perfunctorily. There was something wary and expectant about her body language, and she had positioned herself so that she was in full view of the front door. She could have just been meeting someone, but I had a feeling that she was looking for someone or something specific by using herself as bait... but as to what and why and to what end, I had no idea. Sex, food, or revenge seemed the most likely choices.

I was still mulling that over when the vampire walked in.

THE LAST INTERLUDE, I PROMISE

This is how the Pax Arcana works: if one night you couldn't sleep and wound up looking out your window at three in the morning, and your next-door neighbor was changing into a wolf right beneath you... you wouldn't see it. Don't get me wrong, the image would be refracted on a beam of light and enter your optic nerves and everything, but you would go on with your life without really registering that you'd seen a werewolf any more than you noticed or remembered a particular leaf on a tree that you'd seen that morning. Technically seen anyway.

This is not a dramatic spell... it is simply an extension of how the human mind already works. If our brains didn't dump most of the massive amounts of sensory information that they take in every second, they wouldn't be able to function. We wouldn't be able to distinguish the present from the past, and our brains would overload like crashing computers.

This is why you occasionally see something strange or disconcerting in the corner of your eye, but when you whirl around, there's nothing there. The reason these experiences are so unsettling is that what you're really experiencing is an afterimage. Something you saw five seconds or five minutes or five days ago, without really registering it, was so disturbing that once the danger was gone, the subconscious memory briefly fought off the effects of the Pax Arcana and resurfaced like a drowning person breaking water... before getting pulled under again.

But just suppose that you looked out your window and did register the werewolf. Let's imagine that you are unusually sensitive, or you have a head injury, or a dog attack traumatized you as a small child. For whatever reason, assume something went wrong with the spell, and you actually saw the werewolf even though it wasn't directly threatening you. Such incidents are rare, but they do happen.

Ask yourself this question: if you actually did notice your neighbor changing into a wolf, would you believe what you were seeing with your own two eyes? Seriously? I don't think you would.

I think you'd imagine you were having a lucid dream. Or you'd think your neighbor was playing some kind of elaborate prank with high-tech special effects. You might come up with increasingly far-fetched and paranoid theories about how drugs got into your system. Lacking a more rational explanation, you might even become convinced that you were losing your mind. Perhaps you might go to a therapist later or attempt to self-medicate. Most likely, you'd go back to your normal life the next day and wait cautiously for any further signs of mental breakdown, and as long as nothing else happened, you wouldn't say anything about it. To anyone. Ever.

Be honest. Am I wrong?

There are tens of thousands of people, all around you, maybe hundreds of thousands, who at some point have experienced something that they can't explain. And these people are silent. They are ashamed. They are afraid. They are convinced that they are the only ones, and so they say nothing. That is the real reason the Pax Arcana is so powerful. Rationality is king, and your emperor isn't wearing any clothes.

2

IF SHOVING YOU IS WRONG,
I DON'T WANT TO DO RIGHT

The vampire didn't walk into the bar so much as flow. Like water. Like night. He was wearing a tight black T-shirt and dark jeans over muscles that seemed to have been sculpted from ivory. His hair was black and tousled, framing piercing green eyes that burned with banked passion in spite of the cold smile on his cruel slash of a mouth.

OK, just kidding. Sorry. That whole thing about vampires being übersexy Euro-trash? It's a myth. Vampires project a low-level mental command called a glamour that makes any mortal who meets them see them in the most attractive light possible. Personally, I'm immune to this kind of glamour—it's part of what I am. When I look at vampires, I see what's really there: walking corpses with pale white skin the color and texture of worm flesh, lank greasy hair, bad teeth, and breath that smells like a butcher shop.

Popular young adult novels notwithstanding, vampires only sparkle when they burn.

This particular vampire was wearing a T-shirt that was

green, not black, and it was faded. There were indeterminate stains on the shirt where bleach had been applied to something that didn't want to come out—I'm assuming blood, although I might be stereotyping. His jeans were blue and showed signs of wear in the usual places, and like a lot of vampires he had shaved his skull completely bald. Unwashed hair gets grody fast, and most vampires have an innate phobia about being submerged in running water—anything even remotely symbolic of baptism or birth makes them extremely uncomfortable. Only the strongest-willed vampires force themselves to clean up regularly, and I could smell that this guy wasn't one of them. His eyes were close-set and his nose was bony, and they looked out of place on a face as broad as his was, as if his features had been pinched by a giant index finger and thumb.

What was really disturbing about the vampire was that those same eyes were bloodshot, his fangs were bared, and he was radiating hostility. He was so beyond normal, in fact, that he actually triggered the Pax Arcana.

Which was why no one was paying any real attention to him at all, at least not on a surface level. A few people who were texting frowned as the spell surge disrupted their signals, but that was about it. That's one of the things that sucks about magic: it moves molecules around; and when molecules move, electrons shift; and when electrons shift, the air becomes electromagnetically charged. This is why all of those reality shows about ghost hunters basically amount to a bunch of guys with science degrees getting excited while they talk about energy readings, and you're just sitting there bored watching a TV screen fill up with fuzz and static before the cameras go off-line.

This is also where all those old expressions like *hair-raising* and *spine-tingling* come from. They were coined centuries ago by people who didn't have the scientific terminology to describe air saturated with a low-level electrical charge.

Anyhow, the reason the vampire's behavior was self-destructive was that the Pax Arcana may be powerful, but it has limits. All acts of magic require energy, and if every supernatural creature on the planet behaved the way this vampire was behaving, the Pax would become overtaxed. Or, I suppose, overPaxed.

If the vampire persisted in this kind of reckless behavior, he was eventually going to attract the attention of a knight, or a supernatural being who didn't want his or her or its way of life disrupted. Some supernatural being like...the blonde.

Which is why I said, "Oh shit." I had finally figured out what Sig was doing there.

Being a vampire, he heard me curse even though it was under my breath and across a bar. Being a vampire, a species that's only slightly less territorial than junkyard dogs or evil stepmothers, he took it as a challenge. And, being a vampire, he stopped staring at Sig and looked at me.

Being me, I returned the look. I didn't put anything overt into it, but just the fact that he could tell I was really looking back at him was significant. I held his gaze and let my body go completely still, which all animals recognize as a sign that someone is ready to either fight or flee...and I wasn't going anywhere.

I'm kind of territorial myself. Granted, it wasn't my bar, but I was tending it. I was tending the hell out of it. And I wanted the vampire and the blonde to take it somewhere else, and fast.

He walked toward me, not stopping until he was at the bar directly across from me. "Give me whatever you have on draft," he rasped. Of course, he wasn't really ordering a beer. Vampires can eat or drink normal food, but they can't metabolize it, which means one way or another their bodies later wind up expelling their food or drink undigested.

No, when the vampire demanded I serve him, he was establishing a pecking order. Me badass. You Jane.

"Smell me," I invited quietly.

This guy was a newbie. For a second he thought this was some strange kind of insult, but he still hadn't gotten a good whiff of me, and when he realized that, his nostrils dilated. A vampire's sense of smell isn't as good as mine—he still hadn't smelled the blonde yet—but it's close.

"What the hell kind of a thrope are you?" he asked.

In the supernatural community—if you can call such a scattered and mismatched assortment of predators, refugees, and outcasts a community—*thrope* is a catchall phrase for beings who are humanoid but can change into another form.

What the vampire was saying was that he'd never smelled anybody exactly like me before, but he was pretty sure that I changed into something else. He wasn't right, but he wasn't wrong either. I'm complicated.

"All you need to know is that you're not welcome here," I said evenly.

By the way, that whole thing about vampires needing to be invited into a place? That was only true centuries ago when even peasant huts were routinely blessed by the village priest. Nowadays, the only sincere prayer being uttered over most buildings is the one where their contractor hopes a hurricane won't expose the safety shortcuts he took to lower his construction bid. And that rule never applied to bars anyhow, except in cultures where beer halls were sacred.

But if my comment didn't cause the vampire to be magically bull-rushed out of Rigby's, it still threw him a little.

"Go suck somewhere else," I added.

The vampire snarled and threw a right punch that was almost fast enough to break the sound barrier. It was definitely powerful enough to break a brick wall or my jaw. I knew from experience that the vampire was stronger than I was, so I didn't try to catch his fist in my palm like they do in the movies; instead, I grabbed his wrist while it was still moving and stepped back, adding my weight and muscle to his. He was surging forward, so it was easy to use his own momentum to yank him in the direction he was already going and pull him off the balls of his feet.

I took advantage of his momentary loss of balance and kept guiding him until his midriff smacked into the bar and his feet scrambled for purchase. I snaked my fingers around the broad base of his right thumb and twisted his entire hand in a quick, sharp, and painful movement that locked his right arm and lifted him farther off of his feet as I continued to guide him over the bar top. The tips of his toes were now off the floor so that they couldn't give him any leverage. He couldn't get at me with his left hand without breaking the right arm that I was now hiding behind, holding it twisted and hyper-flexed from above. Breaking your own arm takes a certain amount of willpower and leverage, whether you regenerate or not. Vampires don't have much of a nervous system left—it takes a pretty big jolt to make them feel pain or pleasure—but every half-remembered reflex and instinct their bodies still have makes their muscles tense and fight them when they attempt self-harm.

Showing my teeth, which were standard human size, by the way, I moved my face closer down to his. "If you push this, I'll end you and to hell with the consequences."

The vampire and I had both moved faster than was humanly possible, and because the Pax was already in play, none of the normal customers were noticing anything although some of them would be having nightmares and odd shivers and twitches for the next few days. The blonde was watching us, and she seemed both outraged and stunned, but she stayed seated. Even among supernaturals—hell, especially among supernaturals—there are rules: rules about hospitality, rules about mating, rules about territory, rules about oath-taking, and rules about oath-breaking. One of the most basic rules is that you don't step into the middle of someone else's fight.

As for the fight itself, people who specialize in Brazilian jujitsu or aikido will talk about different kinds of submission locks and choke holds and so on, but I generally don't try to immobilize anyone who's truly dangerous for longer than it takes to disable or kill them. I released the vampire's hand and shoved him off the bar in the same motion. He traveled a few feet but quickly regained his footing with insect grace. We locked stares again, and he attempted to hypnotize me. I could tell because I got a little itch right behind my forehead.

The vampire's bloodshot eyes widened when he realized that his mental compulsion wasn't going to work, and my hand came up from behind the bar holding the baseball bat Dave keeps there. He wasn't wearing a bulletproof vest the way a lot of your more savvy vampires started doing after they became available online; one quick smack against the side of the bar and the bat would do for a stake. It was only a few nights until a full moon, and my heart was pumping blood and adrenaline through my body several times faster than a normal human's; God help me, I wanted him to try something.

But the vampire wavered, smelling something new that made him hesitate, probably the blonde. His nostrils puckered, his body stiffened, and then he took a step back, physically and symbolically.

"Get your hunger under control," I whispered, knowing he

would hear me. "Figure out a way to get what you need, but if I hear about any strange deaths in the next few days, I will find you."

He abruptly turned and walked toward the restrooms at the side of the bar. Becoming supernatural doesn't magically make you braver in the face of danger—it just means that there are fewer things that are dangerous to face. Vampires don't have any moral qualms about coming back with friends if they meet someone powerful enough to be a threat either, but vampires don't often have friends. They sometimes have hive mates, but even then they're hesitant to ask those hive mates for help because vampires are very image-conscious and cruel to one another. I doubted that someone like Baldy had any hive mates in any case.

I was wrong, of course.

The blonde sprang to her feet and moved to follow the vampire.

"You. Vampire Hunter Barbie. Hold it." I pitched my voice so that she could hear me even with normal human hearing, but nobody else could.

Sig adjusted her path and stalked toward the bar, moving at an angle that put me between her and the direction the vampire was moving in. When she spoke, her voice was low and strained. "You still have a chance to avoid getting tangled up in this. I suggest you take it."

"I don't care what you do," I assured her. "Just do it away from my bar."

Sig gave me her full attention. I didn't know it then, but she always became calmest at the prospect of imminent violence, a kind of awful and solemn calm that didn't fool anyone. Her eyes became large and serious, her voice soft. "And how are you going to stop me?"

"You just have normal human hearing, don't you?" I asked.

"Why?" she asked suspiciously.

"Because," I said, "I've already stopped you."

The bathrooms had windows facing out on a side alley, and vampires move fast.

With a curse, the blonde rushed toward the restrooms, shooting me a look that left blister marks. I raised my hand and sarcastically waggled my fingers at her. Goodbye, whatever you are. Forget to write. Nice ass.

Wait...did I write that last part out loud?

As soon as it was clear that the blonde wasn't coming back, I scrounged behind the bar counter until I found a bottle of olive oil. Just to be safe, I sprayed myself a glass of water and then dribbled a drop of olive oil into it. The drop floated there on the surface of the water just the way it was supposed to. She hadn't really tried to give me the evil eye after all, at least not literally.

You can't be too careful.

~3~

BACK TO OUR REGULARLY SCHEDULED DEPROGRAMMING

There were some very good reasons to be concerned when Sig stormed back into the pub ten minutes later, from the murderous frustration written all over her face to the fact that I still didn't know what she was or even what her name was yet. Another excellent cause for anxiety was that Sig had discarded her ignore-the-bartender policy and was headed straight for the countertop I was working behind. But the main reason I should have been worried was that I wasn't worried. When I saw her, my chest felt inexplicably lighter. I'm a little stubborn about some things, and it was only then that I admitted to myself that I had been hoping to see her again, common sense to the contrary.

A few people had come to sit at the bar while the blonde was gone, so I slid farther down to a spot where we could talk with some degree of privacy. This also put me closer to the special knife I keep hidden behind the bar. I grabbed a pot of coffee so that I could throw hot liquid into her eyes and dive for the knife if she tried anything.

"Can I help you?" I asked, reaching for a mug—I had to have some excuse for the coffeepot.

The blonde made a noise from the depths of her throat that was hard to identify. It was half a growl and half something that sounded like "You'd better be right."

I didn't see a Bluetooth device or a cell phone. On the other hand, talking to invisible people isn't necessarily a sign of insanity in my world.

Sig didn't sit down. Instead, she rested her fingertips on the edge of the bar that separated us and stood on the balls of her feet so that she could vault over or push herself off the counter as quickly as possible. Forgoing any social pleasantries she said, "If a woman dies tonight, I'm holding you personally responsible."

I thought this over while I poured coffee into the mug and slowly slid it over to her. "Millions of women die every night," I pointed out. "You're not giving me very good odds. Cream or sugar?"

She had a very expressive face, and I watched her consider doing something violent with the coffee cup, then watched her wrestle the anger down and decide to try to communicate again. It was a close call. "Both," she finally said grudgingly.

I provided her with the cream and sugar. When I was growing up, me and the other squires—aspiring tough guys each and every one of us—used to call any coffee that wasn't black *commie coffee*. But that was back when everybody liked Ike and loved Lucy. God knows what we would have called decaf. "I take it you lost him," I said.

The knives her eyes were throwing at me became chain saws. "He. Is. A. Vampire." Her teeth were clenched.

She had a point. "I know," I said.

"You also knew that he was heat seeking!" she accused in a low, throttled voice. "And you let him go."

In answer, I pointed to the white dry-erase board that nobody ever reads. I had known that either she or the vampire might return, and I had taken a red marker and hastily scrawled the words NO SOULS, NO SERVICE upon it.

Sig closed her eyes and took a deep breath. I struggled heroically not to steal a glance at her chest. Like all heroic struggles, it was a losing battle against overwhelming forces.

Her eyes were still angry when they opened again. "You're not being charming," she said, and I tried not to give any sense that my blood had just gone cold. Had her use of my name been an accident? "You sent a vampire off to find a new hunting ground!"

"No," I said without inflection as I erased the red marker with a swipe of a bar rag. "Vampires don't have to kill to feed. I reminded him that there were risks involved with the kind of choices he was making."

"People in this area have gone missing recently," she informed me. "All female."

"It hasn't been in the paper," I said.

"The *Tablet*?" she exclaimed derisively. This was the name of Clayburg's local rag, and again, she had a point. I've moved around enough to know that there are two kinds of small-town papers—the ones that aspire to be bigger than they are and aggressively report on local news as if every house fire and high school game were a matter of national importance, and the ones that are little more than brochures designed to attract tourists and textile companies. Despite Clayburg's being a college town, the *Tablet* was of the latter variety.

"The police haven't said anything either," I pointed out.

"When they start making public warnings, bars are right up there with schools, churches, and hotels on their visiting list."

She looked at me more carefully.

"That's right," I said. "I'm pretty *and* smart."

Her lips pressed together even more tightly. I couldn't tell if I'd annoyed her further or almost amused her. I'm not sure she knew.

"These aren't the kind of women who have a stable lifestyle," she said by way of an answer. "They're the kind who move from loser to loser or pimp to pusher because they don't have steady jobs and their kids are in foster homes. The ones who have been kicked out of their families and are hard to contact because their names aren't on any rent leases and they keep changing their phone service instead of paying their bills."

"Then how do you know they're missing at all if the police aren't taking it seriously?" I asked.

"I've seen their ghosts wandering around town," Sig said simply, and for a moment she looked sick. Something I didn't have a name for seemed to drain out of her then. There's a reason we refer to having bad memories as being haunted. "They all died recently, naked, with their throats ripped out."

I nodded soberly. I won't lie, a part of my mind was busy running through a list called "Clues to What the Blonde Is" and checking a box that said "Sees dead people"—but I was genuinely disturbed by her words.

The thing about the women being naked...vampires generally don't have sexual feelings, at least not the kind involving genitals. They're dead. Well, OK, they're undead, but the point is, they're not alive. Their bodies don't produce sperm or viable eggs, and while they do have a biological urge to reproduce, the method involves their fangs, not their crotches.

On the other hand, sex isn't just about reproducing, and psychologically, vampires still remember parts of their former existence, and they still have emotional needs although most of these are submerged by the one great need that defines their existence. Because of this, the taking of blood occasionally becomes a kind of psychosexual thing with some of them, particularly the males who spent their whole life defining themselves by their ability to get an erection. The rush of blood through their body can...well...send blood rushing through the part of their body that used to experience this as a form of arousal. This is why some vampires will have sex the old-fashioned way directly after feeding. It's a case of striking while the iron is...hard.

These sexual predators are the sorts of vampires who begin actively targeting people who they might have found attractive in their former life. The ones who only view humans as takeout couldn't care less about things like appearances—all they care about is whether or not their victim has the right blood type. And yes, while it is true that vampires' bodies convert the blood they feed on into something else, something with more antibodies and a higher degree of oxygenation, something colder that goes further but can't replenish itself—it is also true that the rules of blood transfusion still apply. Vampires can accept blood only from someone who matches their original blood type (unless the victim is a universal donor or the vampire was AB positive when he or she was mortal). Vampires can also identify blood types by smell. That's not something you generally see addressed in movies and legends because it would make for some inconvenient plot maneuvering, but it's true.

From what Sig was saying, Baldy was one of those vampires who invest the taking of blood with a sense of sexual intimacy. The fact that he was choosing the kind of women who wouldn't soon be missed also suggested that his acts were premeditated, not sudden surrenders to an overwhelming compulsion.

Even for a vampire, it takes a certain kind of sick mind to have sex with the buffet table.

On the other hand...I had no idea what drove Sig or any proof that what she was saying was true.

"So how did you know he was going to be at a bar tonight, much less here?" I demanded. "And why do you even care? What exactly are you?"

Most supernatural beings don't much care about what happens to normal humans as long as it doesn't significantly affect their way of life. Even the ones who enjoy living among humans and have human friends usually accept that humans are part of the food chain and don't get more than upset in an abstract way when bad things happen to food people. They might think it's a sad event, but they don't cry about it, any more than most people cry when thousands of deaths occur in a foreign country.

It was odd that Sig cared, and it was even odder that she assumed I would share this character flaw.

"I'll trade you answers for answers," she said. "If I ask the first question."

I didn't agree right away. Trades, like riddles and true names, are still taken very seriously in the supernatural community. There were things I was not willing to tell her under any circumstances. On the other hand, as long as she asked first, I could just end the game by refusing to answer. If I asked first and she gave me information in trade and *then* I refused to answer, all heads were off. I mean bets were off. Maybe.

While I was mulling her offer over, Mike Spraker ignored Renee, who was waiting on his section, and made a point out of coming up to the bar. He only wobbled slightly.

"Howdy," Mike said. He was a regular and looked it, a skinny but paunchy stick of a man with graying brown hair and a scraggly-ass beard. He smelled of sour sweat, beer, and failure. His voice was jaunty and a little too loud as he ordered a Rob Roy.

I made the drink without comment, though it was a little more exotic and expensive than Mike's regular beer and chaser. He tried to look casual as he put his elbows carefully on the bar and turned his head sideways and, oh, look at that, just happened to notice the attractive woman standing there.

"Damn," Mike said loudly, going for a breezy attitude but trying a little too hard. "What's the point of comin' to a bar if the only good-lookin' woman in it is going to spend all night talkin' to the hired help?"

Mike didn't see the looks being shot at him by two apparently unattractive women who were close enough to overhear him. He was too busy avoiding my eyes.

"There isn't one," Sig said. "Go away."

I put Mike's drink in front of him while he tried to think of the wrong thing to say. "Mike," I called in a tone that cut through the fumes and made him look at me.

"It's on the house," I said deliberately, holding eye contact. "Last one."

Don't make me take away whatever dignity you have left, my expression added.

After a moment Mike nodded and skulked off.

Sig looked at me exasperatedly. "So you get all up in a heat-seeking vampire's face, but with Mr. Lonesome Loser there you show diplomacy?"

I shrugged. "Mike's harmless."

"No," Sig corrected. "He's powerless. There's a difference. If there was anyone left who trusted him, he'd use them horribly. That man's a bottomless pit of selfish need."

I looked at her speculatively. Maybe she had a gift for seeing deeply. Then again, maybe she'd just loved an addict before. "All right," I agreed. "Answer for answer. You ask first."

"What are you?" she asked.

I hesitated. That was fast. "I'm the child of a werewolf."

She didn't hesitate at all. "Bullshit."

Like vampires, werewolves can't reproduce the old-fashioned way, although they are living beings and fully capable of having sex. The complication is that transforming into a wolf is one hell of a shock to the system, and most people who have been bitten by a werewolf don't survive their first full moon—their heart stops before their new body fully develops the ability to regenerate. Anyone who is too old or too young or too unhealthy doesn't stand a chance, and the effects of all that tissue-tearing and muscle-ripping and stepped-up cellular production and electron-shifting are especially brutal on a fetus and the surrounding sac it needs to survive.

"It's true," I said. "My mother was past due with me when she was bitten by a wolf, and she delivered me soon after... before the next full moon. She died during her first transformation. I didn't change."

Her eyes narrowed. "This isn't another question. This is clarification. Are you a werewolf or not?"

I shrugged. "That depends on who you ask. I don't shift shape. I don't have infra-vision. Silver only gives me a mild rash after several hours of contact, and human flesh gives me indigestion."

Silence.

"Sorry, that last part was a bad joke," I said. "I've never had any urges in that direction."

"I saw you deal with that vampire," she said. Again, not quite another question.

I nodded. "I'm stronger and faster than your average human."

"You also knew there was something different about me as soon as I walked into the bar," she persisted.

Was I really obligated to give this specific an answer? I sighed. A trade is a trade, and I didn't have a convenient label to toss her way. A half-human vampire is called a dhampir. What I am is so rare that there's not even a word for it. "My senses of smell and hearing are also acute. Also, my hobbies include hiking and scrapbooking, and I like long walks on the beach, sunsets, foreign films, and hot fudge sundaes. Is it my turn yet?"

She could figure out by herself the part about me healing fast and not aging. None of that even started until I was in my late twenties.

At which point the knights who had reluctantly trained me and educated me and finally, grudgingly, accepted me as one of their own because of my family name...turned on me and tried to kill me. They're still trying. But Sig's question definitely didn't demand that specific an answer.

"So you don't change form," she mused. "I guess that makes you some kind of a neuter."

"That's not what your mom said," I replied.

She grinned for the first time. "That doesn't really work with females."

"That's not what your mom said."

Sig took a sip of coffee and made a pleasantly surprised face. I make a good pot of coffee. "Ask me a question," she commanded.

I obliged and picked up where I'd left off. "How did you know to be here tonight?" I wanted to know what she was, but if the bar had a big target painted around it and was likely to draw attention from any nearby knights, I wanted to know that more. And I thought there was a pretty good chance that one question would answer the other.

She grimaced. "I have a friend with a gift for precognition—don't ask me for a name because that's not mine to give. This individual had a vision of a vampire in a bar. I pestered my friend until I got a few more details." Her eyes narrowed. "I was told to look for a place with an idiot for a bartender."

"I can't believe this," I said, careful to make it a statement. I didn't want to waste a question on something of the are-you-kidding or what-the-hell-is-your-problem variety. "You're pissed because I didn't know about missing women who the police haven't announced yet. Because I'm not assuming that some strange blonde whose species I don't know and whose motives I can't guess is someone I should trust."

"I'm holding you responsible," she snapped, "because if you hadn't butted in, the vampire wouldn't be on the loose right now. You chose to interfere in my business."

"You brought your business into this bar, which is my business," I shot back. "Literally. Maybe you haven't noticed, but there is no bouncer around here. Part of my job is keeping this place peaceful, and I honor my debts."

"Good!" she said, as if she'd won whatever argument we were having. "Because you owe me. If your senses are as good as you say they are, you can help me track down the vampire later."

Sig polished off the coffee like it was a shot of whiskey and turned around to leave. Apparently that comment about me helping her wasn't a question.

"Hold on," I protested. "I still don't know what you are or why you're so emotionally involved in all this."

"No you don't," she agreed.

And she walked out again.

It was her loss. If she'd stuck around and bothered to earn my trust, I could have told her how I'd palmed the vampire's wallet while I had him pinned to the bar. His name, if the license wasn't a very good fake, was Steve Ellison.

Now, a reasonable person might wonder why I stole the wallet after moving to Clayburg to avoid trouble. In fact, a reasonable person might even go so far as to point out that my behavior and my stated goals were incompatible. Reasonable people can be real pains in the ass that way. All I can say is, I have never claimed to be a reasonable person. For those of you keeping score at home, I have also never claimed to be a good person, a smart person, or a particularly stable person. The truth is, I stole the wallet because the vampire's behavior was setting off all kinds of internal alarms, and old habits die hard.

I know John Charming is an unfortunate name. Believe me, I've heard them all. No, I've never been turned into a frog. No, I haven't slain many dragons lately. How could I? They've been hibernating close to the Earth's core for over a thousand years. No, I don't have any unusual shoe fetishes, glass slipper or otherwise. No, my kisses won't bring women out of any comas, though I hope they might perk them up a little.

But make no mistake: the reason there are so many stories about "Prince" Charming is that there was never one man— the Charmings were an entire family line standing between humanity and all other for generation after generation, and in the old days it was common to give any monster killer in a story royal status. That is a heavy burden, but I carried my name proudly for as long as I was able. And I am still that man. No matter what else is in my DNA, no matter what my old order says, no matter what titles have been stripped from me or how long I am forced to run and hide...I am still that man.

I think.

❧ 4 ❧

WHICH ONE OF YOU ORDERED THE STAKE?

Later that night I made the last round of drinks free so that I could close out the cash register early and actually shut the bar's doors on time for once. Sandra and Renee and our dishwasher, Greg, weren't supposed to go home before me because Dave had some fond illusion that there's honesty in numbers, but they didn't argue when I offered to close up by myself. I figured the odds of the vampire's coming back to find me after he figured out that his wallet was missing were around fifty-fifty, whereas the odds of my coworkers' telling Dave that they'd left early were roughly zero.

One of the hardest things on the nerves is to wait for a fight that may or may not happen, at least if it's a fight you're not sure you can win. I don't care who you are, how tough you are, or how many fights you've been in...unless something's seriously wrong with your brain chemistry, you're going to feel tension. Regrets and doubts and rage crawl out from under the subconscious like ants from under a hot rock. What separates a warrior from a brawler or a maniac or a doormat is how he or she handles those feelings.

Me, I've got this thing I do when my mind starts to spiral before a fight. I unfold my fingers and concentrate on them one by one until my feelings narrow into focused calm. The finger-counting is a neuro-physical trigger, a mild form of self-hypnosis that I've trained my mind to react to after decades of practice and meditation. I associate each finger with a specific phrase, and if I have time, I recite them to myself like mantras.

Pinky: I've been in this kind of situation before. Fourth finger: I've felt these feelings before. Middle finger: I've survived them every time. Index finger: Everybody dies eventually. Thumb: That includes my enemies. Then I fold my fingers back into a fist. I won't say that it eliminates fear altogether, but it steadies me.

In between wiping and racking and stacking, I rummaged around behind some bottles of truly hideous wine that Dave had let a pretty sales rep talk him into buying and removed a silver steel knife with an illegally long blade. Silver steel is an alloy with a silver quotient high enough to be effective against creatures who are vulnerable to such things, but not so high as to fundamentally weaken the metal. Its metallurgic composition is one of the many secrets of the Knights Templar, and it is one they've guarded for over five centuries.

If that sounds impressive, the truth is that modern science could figure out how to make silver steel easily; it's just that, without a belief in werewolves, there's never been a profit incentive for doing so.

Next I got the unlabeled vodka bottle full of holy water out and removed a broom from a storage closet. I snapped the bristly top off the broom, then broke the shaft into three jagged wooden stakes. I wound up using some duct tape from the same closet to anchor the stakes to the belt strap of my knife sheath.

Finally I stripped down to my T-shirt and khaki pants and sneakers. I was almost done mopping when I smelled the blood. It was a deep, thick smell, rich with bodily nutrients. The blood had come from a major artery, aortal or maybe femoral. Whoever it had come from was dead whether they were quite finished living or not.

There was a condenser unit out back where my car was parked, and it was probably what had pumped the smell of blood into the bar. The alleys behind Rigby's link several small businesses and low-rent apartment buildings. Drunks and drug deals and sexual transactions are common there. Maybe someone had wandered by while Ellison was waiting, and his hunger had been too great. Maybe he was killing potential witnesses or distractions, and he hadn't thought about the air-conditioning.

Or maybe while I was shrugging off Ellison's attempts at hypnosis, the vampire was learning about me. Maybe he knew something about knights and the geas that both binds us and protects us.

A geas is a magical oath that drives knights to fulfill a specific duty, and the Knights Templar have sworn to uphold the Pax Arcana. Basically that means that we do not harm supernatural beings unless they are on the verge of revealing themselves to mankind, but when a supernatural being is judged terminally indiscreet, we eliminate them as quietly as possible.

Steve Ellison killing people indiscriminately in an open alley behind public housing was definitely not discreet. Especially not after he'd been warned.

I'm not saying that the geas turns me into some kind of zombie with no free will; knights can be very creative about how we deal with threats to the Pax, and we can even ignore the geas, although doing this for too long or too often can result in unpleasant consequences: migraines, nightmares, hallucinations, bouts of public flatulence, an inexplicable fascination with reality television...well, you get the idea. If the situation continues to escalate, the Pax can even lead to things like waking up in the middle of a dangerous situation after sleepwalking into it, or insanity. Think Lancelot wandering around for years in the wilderness, a madman because he couldn't find the Holy Grail.

The plus side of being under a geas is that no other kind of mental magic can influence you because your mind's dance card is already filled. The geas is a jealous mistress.

I put the mop down, picked up the bottle of holy water, and walked to Dave's office, where a window faced a side alley. Throwing open the window, I was immediately hit by a wave of vampire stink. Unfortunately, it was the scent of a vampire I didn't recognize. I also smelled more blood, different blood.

Steve Ellison had hive mates after all, and they were turning the back alleys into a killing ground.

I didn't hear any movement except a distant car on Main Street, and I should have. Taking care to protect the bottle, I jumped to the ground below the window. Nothing. I closed the window. Nothing. Conditions were perfect for scanning: there were no Dumpsters or obstructions in the alley—just two old brick walls a little too close to each other and a lot of graffiti. The moon and stars were out, and the air was cold and clear and silent, but I still wasn't picking up anything.

Suddenly I heard a feeble bubbling cough from the back alleys, a death rattle from someone whose lungs weren't in one piece any longer. Fury poured through me like lava. It was only a few nights until the full moon, and they were hunting on the wolf's territory, and the geas was singing in my veins. I also had an intuition that the vampires were trying to flush me out and herd me toward the main street, that they expected me to run for safety and were prepared for it. Screw it.

I took off toward the back of the bar at a run and set off a sudden flurry of activity. Gravel was kicked up on a rooftop behind me to the east. Ahead of me and hidden by the bar, two sets of feet in the vicinity of my car were running on the ground toward the same alley opening I was headed toward. Someone on Main Street was indeed running into my alley after me. I didn't look back.

They were all moving fast. Almost as fast as I was. Vampires are stronger than werewolves, but they don't have an edge in speed, and these parasites were overconfident. They knew they had me surrounded, and I was the one running for my life.

A shadow began to emerge around the corner of the alley while I was still approaching it. I've had a lot of experience gauging the movement and speed of shadows, and I hurled the bottle of holy water underhanded at a dead run. When a tall curly-haired vampire in a black muscle shirt rounded the corner, the bottle was only inches away from his face. His supernaturally fast reflexes actually worked against him: he instinctively brought up the sawed-off shotgun he was holding to ward the bottle off, but this was a mistake. The glass shattered as he whipped the metal barrels into it, and holy water sprayed over his head, hitting his face like acid and shriveling his eyes.

The vampire's grip loosened on the shotgun as he began to keen, clawing at his steaming sockets. The sound was horrifically loud and blatantly inhuman, and it stirred up ancestral memories of a time when humans knew that they weren't the dominant species. Every human who heard that howl fell under the effect of the Pax Arcana. None of them would peer out windows overlooking the back alleys now. Squad cars would decide to stay on the main streets without knowing why. People whose needs or inclinations might have taken them through the alleys would impulsively decide to take alternate routes.

There would be no distractions now.

I had never stopped running, and I snatched the shotgun out of the keening vampire's hand and continued turning with the motion, shoulder-charging him at full speed. Just as a matter of perspective, full speed meant that we were moving so fast that I actually charged through the main body of holy water and broken glass while they were still in the air.

I caught the vampire dead center under the breastbone while he was backpedaling. Shards of glass tore into my upper right arm as they were crushed between our bodies. The vampire went flying back into the air, just in time to crash into Steve Ellison, who came tearing around the corner following on his ally's heels. If Ellison had been braced for it, the impact wouldn't have affected him, but one of his feet was off of the ground when the body hit. Ellison dropped a machete as he was torn off his feet by gravity, momentum, and surprise.

I was stumbling now, and the vampire behind me was coming up fast, so I threw myself around the corner of the alley that Steve Ellison had just emerged from. It wasn't smooth, but I tucked my head and landed on the back of my shoulder and kept rolling down the curve of my back without shooting myself, and I had a moment where there was a brick corner between the charging vampire and me. Then I had another moment because he had to slow down or overshoot the corner drastically. Momentum doesn't stop working because a vampire is faster than a human—if anything, it's worse.

I came to my feet, adjusting my grip on the sawed-off

shotgun just as a short red-haired vampire came lunging awkwardly around the corner, bracing it with his right hand in an attempt to slow his hurtling body down. The vampire tried to yank his head back before I pulled the trigger, but nobody is that fast. His head disappeared.

It wasn't a textbook decapitation, but he wasn't coming back.

A darting shadow in the corner of my eye was the only warning I had when the fourth vampire leaped at me from an adjacent roof. The tall vampire's keening and the sound of the shotgun and the rising warm air carrying scent particles upward had masked her attack. Turning my head slightly behind me while my body leaped forward, I had a brief impression of long brown hair flailing through the air and a hand taloned with long red nails coming at my eyes from above. I didn't try to brace myself but grabbed the vampire's extended wrist while still hurling myself forward, pulling her wrist as I did so.

She was still moving faster than me, but when her hurtling body overtook me from behind and above, I rolled her over my shoulder instead of being knocked off of my feet. Holding on to her right wrist, I guided her body and drove her head down into the pavement at an angle with all of my strength, all of her momentum, and our combined body weight coming down on top of it.

Her neck snapped.

This was good news. Spinal regeneration is trickier than that of mere flesh. It usually takes a while for the nerve impulses to work properly again. The female was out of it for at least five to ten minutes, and the tall one still hadn't regrown his eyes, if his screaming was any indication. The holy water had continued to eat away at his optic nerves after penetrating the soft flesh of his iris and cornea.

The problem was Ellison. Inhumanly fast, relatively unin-
jured Steve Ellison, the dumbass vampire who had started the
whole thing. He had scrambled to his feet with his inhuman
speed and picked up the machete while I was distracted and
was now bearing down on me with it. I didn't have time to
draw my knife. My only hope was to either throw myself backward or deflect the flat of the blade with a forearm or palm,
and I was in a bad position for either, feet flat and awkwardly
hunched forward. I don't know if I would have made it without losing a hand or an arm or not. I never found out because
a spear flew over my shoulder and went through the front of
Ellison's chest.

It was a beautiful, powerful throw. The metal tip of the spear
punched straight through his breastbone and out the other
side, leaving the wooden shaft of the spear bisecting what was
left of his heart. The thing that had once been named Steve
Ellison remained standing for another second with an undigni-
fied expression of surprise and protest on its face, then dropped
bonelessly.

I looked over my shoulder in the direction that the spear had
come from. At that angle, the only vantage point high enough
for that spear to have originated from was a bank building at
least a quarter of a mile away. I couldn't see anything on it, but
I'm not sure I would have even assuming there was something
to see. Unlike the eyesight of whoever had hurled that spear,
my long-distance vision isn't any better than a normal human's.

I did hear something, however. It was the voice of the blonde
from the bar, carried on a slight breeze. "I'm a Valkyrie."

∽5∽

THE NORSE WHISPERER

I had finished staking the vampires and was searching their bodies when Sig came walking down the alley. None of the vampires was carrying a wallet, though the red-haired one had a set of car keys in his back pocket and the female had a cell phone. Sig approached at a leisurely pace and plucked her spear from the bald vampire's devastated chest. That was when I noticed that the bottom end of the spear—the wooden end— had been sharpened into a stake.

There was no chance of his coming back; his heart had already evaporated.

I quickly ran through a mental Rolodex of what I knew about Valkyries, which wasn't much. The Valkyries' official title in ancient times was "Choosers of the Slain." Essentially Viking battle angels, the Valkyries would fly over fields of war on winged horses and gather the souls of brave warriors who had died. These lucky souls would be taken to Viking heaven, a huge beer hall called Valhalla where they would drink and train for a war that was going to happen between good and evil at the end of time. As I recalled, quite a few Valkyries—Brynhild being the only one whose name I could remember because of that whole opera connection—had been exiled to earth for various crimes or screwups, and they had mated with heroes and had children and died, usually tragically.

Whatever Valkyries really were, this woman was presumably claiming to be one of their descendants. Or else she was well over a thousand years old.

Sig's hair was tied up in a long braid, and she was wearing a black sweater like the ones naval commandos used to wear in World War II. She was still wearing jeans, but there was a gun holstered on her hip, and she had exchanged her shoes for black combat boots. She wasn't wearing anything that would glitter or sparkle, and a plain sword hilt protruded above her right shoulder from where the blade was resting in a back sheath. The only jewelry she was wearing at all was a dull iron collar and twin iron bracelets that showed at her wrists and probably ran about six inches beneath her sleeves. The collar was called a combat torque back when I was a knight, even though it resembled the iron collars worn by slaves more than it did Norse jewelry. The bracelets were called bracers, or in some circles vambraces. Both had been strategically designed centuries ago to protect the places where vampires instinctively bite the most, the neck and the wrists.

Sig set the butt of the spear on the ground and leaned on it like a walking stick. "That was really stupid," she said. "But I'll give you this, you almost held your own. I'm not sure I could have done as well."

I squinted at her. "But you're not sure you couldn't have either."

Sig made an either/or waggling motion with her hand.

I nodded. After that spear toss I believed it. It would have taken strength greater than mine to make that throw, and an impressive amount of skill.

Sig stared at my shoulder and frowned. It made me oddly self-conscious. Broken glass chunks embedded in my right upper arm were tearing open new wounds as aggressively regenerating flesh pushed the fragments back out. Shrapnel sucks. I once got hit with a barrel of buckshot and spent a couple of hours ejecting pellets from my hide like some kind of bizarre metal popcorn popper. It gave the phrase *sweating bullets* a whole new meaning.

Sig whirled her spear casually and pointed its metal tip at a small crimson patch on the pavement. I frowned as I realized that the patch was my blood. She looked up at me intently. "I'm going to do some magic," she said. "Old Aesir magic. But I won't if you don't trust me."

What the hell were the Aesir? I'd read about them, but I'd never been able to figure out if the Aesir were high Fae pretending to be gods among the primitives or another species altogether. Still, it wasn't the right time for a scholarly discussion. In a few hours daylight was going to completely evaporate the vampires and leave a bunch of empty clothes, some human corpses, and my DNA lying all over the place. So I stuck to the essentials.

"What's the magic do?" I asked suspiciously. Magic. Blood. Me. These are not words that I like to hear anywhere near one another.

"It's an old spell for burning blood," she explained. "Valkyries weren't really angels, you know, back in the old days. We dealt with the nearly departed, not the dearly departed."

"You were psychopomps," I said. Psychopomps are beings who help spirits pass on to the next level of existence.

She smiled in a way that seemed to signify agreement and began to talk in a slightly formal, old-fashioned manner. It suggested that she was repeating words told to her mother's mothers. "Once we were just *klok gumma*, wise women with the sight. We looked for spirits that were still bound to this earth, and if they needed to move on, we helped them."

"So what changed?" I asked in spite of myself.

"My ancestors were tired of being dominated by men and made a bargain with the Aesir who were pretending to be gods. The Aesir bred with them and produced female children who were stronger than men and had long lives and eyes that could see like eagles', and in return, we found them warriors whose spirits had left their bodies but were still linked to them."

After literally chewing on my tongue for a second to keep from asking for more details about these Aesir and why they wanted legally dead humans with a spark of life still in them, I got back to business. "So what does any of that have to do with spells for burning blood?"

"The Aesir taught my ancestors this spell in order to cauterize injuries and kill infections. It helped them stabilize and transport the critically wounded. The same Valkyrie who told me all of this taught the spell to me."

"My wounds are already healing," I pointed out with what I thought was commendable restraint.

She sighed and began speaking like a modern woman again. I think she was starting to figure out that yes, I was always this difficult. "I know that. The way it was explained to me, the Aesir used the same spell among themselves for a different reason. They don't like to leave their blood behind where enemies can gather it and use it for spells against them. If I keep chanting the spell using this patch of your blood as a focus, eventually every drop of your blood and tissue in this alley will burn up."

Still the very picture of calm, I raised the next point, which I considered critical. "But not the blood in my body?"

The look she flashed me was dry. "It wouldn't be a very

effective spell for treating the wounded or concealing evidence if it ignited blood inside the body."

I looked at the drying blood on my arm and clothes.

"Yes, that's going to hurt," she confirmed, exasperated. "But you'll heal quickly, and your blood and DNA won't be all over the alley."

"Give me just a moment," I said. My T-shirt was still soaked with sweat and holy water, so I removed it carefully with my left hand and began wiping the blood off my arms and scalp. When my arms were cleaner if not clean, I kicked off my shoes and took my wallet and keys out of my pockets and dropped them on the ground before taking off my pants.

Sig watched with a complete lack of bashfulness. I glanced at her out of the corner of my eye and couldn't tell if her expression was appreciative or impatient or amused as I rubbed the wet shirt over my body. I won't lie; I flexed as much as I could get away with without being overt about it.

"Some tough guy," she mocked. "Afraid of getting a few quickly healed burns."

"Wounds caused by fire heal slower than other wounds," I pointed out. "And that's normal fire, much less this magic crap you're talking about."

"That's true," she admitted. "By the way, I think some blood might have trailed down into your boxer shorts, there, champ."

I paused. "Are you trying to get me naked?" Somehow my voice came out more hopeful than suspicious. A dark alley with dead bodies all around wasn't exactly erotic, but survival is its own rush. Birthrates are always higher in war zones and violent neighborhoods.

She grinned. "There's a cut on your left flank."

I checked my left side. She was right. At some point there had been a bleeding graze right above the waistband of my boxers, although it had already healed. When had that happened? That wasn't even the side that had charged through the falling glass.

"The blood probably didn't trickle around your pelvic bone and into your crotch, so you don't have to worry if you're prudish," she said airily. "What's a little burning down there?"

I looked at my crotch. "Fine," I muttered, and pulled my boxers off. You don't live as long as I have and remain shy about nudity. As far as that goes, when we squires hit puberty and were at our most sexually freaked out, the knights would sometimes make us fight naked, or in pink ballerina outfits, or in bunny costumes. Their intent was to desensitize us, make us shut out our environment and focus on essentials; they didn't want us at a psychological disadvantage if we ever escaped capture after being stripped or were attacked in awkward circumstances. That's what they said, anyway. The exercises always had a kind of fraternity hazing feel to them, and some of the knights were pretty inventive when it came to dreaming up humiliating scenarios.

In any case, I didn't ask Sig to look away, and she didn't offer. There wasn't much blood to wipe away. Well, actually, there was a lot of blood; it was just rushing into that particular area from beneath my skin, not plastered over it.

Sig grinned, completely unembarrassed. "Been a while?"

"It has been," I admitted.

She held my gaze for a moment, and something charged passed between us. Then she blushed for the first time since I'd met her and looked away. Muttering, "Forget this," she touched the spear's tip to the patch of dried blood and began chanting.

The blood on the pavement began to turn brown and crumble. Apparently there were traces of blood still on my skin too small or fine to see, because I felt a growing warmth over the surface of my arm and the side of my scalp. At one point a shard of glass made its way through my shoulder at just the wrong moment and the welling blood it produced caught fire. As the Valkyrie continued to chant, the dried blood on the ground began to steam, and then it burst into flame. Nothing else ignited on my skin, but there were burning sensations that were mildly agonizing, some of them on the left side of my pelvis.

Arousal wasn't a problem any longer.

My T-shirt and pants and boxers caught fire, and several other minute fragments of flame flared up across the length of the alley, small embers smoldering on the walls. Bizarrely, the tips of the female vampire's decaying hand caught fire and created a sickening stench. Then I realized that pieces of me were on her claws.

Finally the Valkyrie stopped. "I don't think anyone is really going to comb this area over very carefully anyway," she said. "But no lab techs are going to be studying your DNA now."

"That's useful magic," I admitted. After a moment's hesitation I added awkwardly, "Thanks."

"You're welcome," she said, also a little clumsily. "You'd better find some clothes and get out of here. I'll take care of the rest."

Which was generous and all that, but what she was really saying—tactfully, in case I'd taken our brief flirting and my nakedness to heart—was that we weren't going to celebrate being alive by slipping away somewhere to have sweaty adrenaline-fueled sex. Well, that was fine. I was raised by an order of warrior monks, and while I'm not chaste, I don't believe that there's any such thing as free love either. I went through the sixties once, and once was enough. Besides, I had a lot of disturbing sights and sounds and smells and tactile sensations to forget—or at least let fade a little—before I felt human again. Well, as close to human as I get, anyway.

"If you're going to take any risks, I'll share them," I stated firmly.

"How chivalrous," she said archly, and a chill went down my spine. Chivalry was a little too closely associated with being a knight, and it was the second time that night that she'd made what could have been a veiled reference to my origins. "But if a norm shows up, I can handle it better on my own."

"How's that exactly?" I tried to sound suspicious instead of rattled.

"You mean aside from the fact that you're naked?" She removed a wallet from her back pocket and flipped it open. There was a gold badge on the inside flap.

I stepped closer and peered at it. "That's one of those bogus badges they give to those local 'friends of the police' chapters," I observed. "How much did you have to contribute?"

She crooked her lips into an almost-grin and looked a little abashed. "Most people don't bother to inspect it."

"Come on," I said. Regular medical examinations? Background checks out the ass? Psych evaluations? Spending day in, day out surrounded by trained observers in potentially dangerous situations? Who was she kidding? I had to hide among normals too.

"You're smarter than you act," she said, pocketing the wallet. "But I didn't have to contribute anything to get the ID. I really do work with the police on occasion."

"You work with cops," I repeated.

"Well, one cop mostly," she admitted. "A homicide detective. But they know me around the station. They think I'm a psychic."

I arched an eyebrow at her.

"Well, OK, I am a psychic. Kind of," she admitted. "But they think that's all I am. Even the ones who won't admit it know I'm helpful on occasion. If they find me alone at the scene of a violent crime...well, it wouldn't be the first time."

I thought about how useful someone who could see dead people would be to a homicide detective. "So why are you trying to get rid of me?" I asked. "Assuming I can find some clothes?"

Sig sighed impatiently again. I have that effect on women. "I called some friends as soon as I saw the vampires making their play. They'll be here soon, and I don't want you to see them or them to see you until I've told them more about you. There's too much potential for...misunderstanding."

At least I didn't have to worry about one of her friends being a knight. The idea of a supernatural creature having a knight on her speed dial was too ridiculous to contemplate.

"Or I could leave now, and you could just not tell them about me at all," I suggested.

"I gave you a chance to stay out of this back in the bar," she reminded me. "You didn't take it."

"So you're going to hold me to a snap decision?" I asked. "Even though I had no real information to base it on?"

She stared at me without a hint of apology or argument. "Yes."

I nodded. "Hypothetically, what's to keep me from just cutting your throat right now? That would be a way of covering my tracks."

I was expecting her to challenge me or talk trash. Instead, Sig closed her eyes and tilted her chin upward. "Go ahead."

I made a sound low in my throat. It wasn't a growl exactly, but it wasn't a sound that I could help either. Sig thought she was calling my bluff, and she was, but in wolf language she had just submitted to me.

Her eyes flew open, alarmed for the first time. I had moved closer to her, although I hadn't done it consciously. Somehow I was much more naked than I'd been a second ago.

"How do you know I won't kill you?" I managed through a mouth that was suddenly dry. She had twice dropped odd little comments that might have been hints that she knew who I was. My heart was going so fast, I could barely hear my own words over the blood pounding through my skull. God, I wanted to grab her and kiss her. The only reason I didn't was that it was a sudden animal impulse, and I was used to resisting sudden animal impulses. "You're right, but how do you know?"

Sig didn't move. She didn't seem frightened. It was more like she was fascinated. "You'll have to stick around Clayburg if you want to find out."

That snapped me out of it. It almost made me snort. It was going to be a pain setting up a new identity again, but there was no way I could stay in Clayburg now.

She sensed my change in mood.

"Go ahead, get out of here," Sig said. She also seemed to be recalling who she was and what she was about. At any rate, she was doing that pushy thing again. "And leave the vampires' possessions."

"Just like that?" I asked suspiciously.

She grinned suddenly. "Why not? You've already been debriefed."

I grimaced but didn't delay further, crouching to pull my smoldering shoes back on. There was still glass about, and no point creating new blood trails. I carefully wiped select parts of the cell phone and keys and weapons down with what was left of my jeans, noting that Steve Ellison's wallet was still in the tattered back pocket. I didn't actually have to do this; the knights had burned off my fingerprints with a mild acid long before I became a creature who regenerated, but there was no point in letting Sig know that. My lack of fingerprints was a clue in itself.

Now that Sig and I were no longer making eye contact, it felt ridiculous instead of erotic, walking around wearing nothing but sneakers and a semi. Dignity and I have never really had what you'd call a close working relationship, though. I made a detour to pick up the neck of the vodka bottle as I made my way toward my car. There was a gym bag with some clothes in it in my trunk.

Sig gave me a moment to compose myself, then walked up to join me while I was pulling on a gray T-shirt over some black sweat pants.

We stared at each other uncomfortably. It seemed like there was nothing left to say but the thing I really wanted to say, and I wasn't good at that kind of thing.

"You're fascinating," I told her. See what I mean?

She smiled, and I don't think I was imagining traces of interest and regret and a lurking what-the-hell element of challenge that she was trying to repress in the expression. That didn't change her words, though. "I'm involved with somebody else."

Of course she was. All the good Valkyries are taken.

"OK, but you maybe saved my life, and you've seen me naked," I said. "In some countries we just got married. Can I at least know what name you go by?"

"What do you mean *maybe* saved your life?" she demanded.

"Is that a no?" I asked.

She sighed. "My name is Sig."

"Like Sigrid?" I persisted. "Sigourney? Signe?"

"Like the gun." She smiled slightly and patted the sidearm in her hip holster. It was only then that I realized it was a SIG Sauer.

I thought she was carrying the whole Norse battle maiden thing a little far, but I had to admit she carried it well.

~6~

THE SCREAM TEAM

I didn't go home. I was hungry and tired and sore, but I was also paranoid and devious and used to ignoring bodily discomfort, so I parked my car behind a closed tattoo parlor and went back to the bar. A quick sprint and three jumps took me from the top of a Dumpster to a window ledge to a series of rooftops that I slid over like a shadow.

I wanted to know more about these "friends" Sig was going to discuss me with.

Unfortunately I had to stop and hide behind a parapet about three buildings farther from the bar than I'd intended. On the roof to my right, two men were climbing from a drainpipe to the top of a dance studio whose upper floor had been converted to public housing. One of them had a sniper rifle slung over his back, and the other was shouldering a nylon backpack. Both wore headsets. If they had been vampires, I would have taken them right there while I still had the element of surprise, but an errant breeze whispered that they were human. Both men were short and stocky and not ideally built for climbing, but they were also young and fit and seemed to know a little about parkour. It took me a moment to realize that they were twins.

Once on the roof of the dance studio, the sniper moved to the opposite side and positioned himself so that he was sighting down on the alley below. His partner took several foot-tall crosses with small standing platforms out of his backpack and began to set them up around himself and the other man so that the crosses formed a barricade, saying what I assume was a silent prayer before setting each one on the ground. When he was done, he removed two Desert Eagles, handguns with a whole lot of stopping power, out of his backpack. I was willing to bet that both men had special ammo. Soft-nosed high-explosive rounds or something to that effect. Rather than helping his partner sight, the second man faced in the opposite direction and guarded his back.

The sniper said something into his headset. Whatever language he was using was vaguely Germanic but had Russian inflections. Sig's voice came back in stereo from his headset and from the alley below, speaking the same language.

I was not in an ideal position. There were three sleeping kids on the roof with me, two males in their late teens or early twenties and a girl who was too young to be with them. All three were nestled together under a blanket for warmth and probably dozing with a little help from the George Dickel whiskey bottle and the cold medicine whose empty packages were all around them. A lot more cold medicine than any recommended dosage would account for. If their breathing had been any deeper, I would have felt obligated to administer CPR.

But the parapet offered me cover, and the adjacent building on the side away from the firing team was of a lower elevation. If I wanted to get out of their line of sight, all I had to do was stay low and dart around a stairwell entrance and jump over a ledge, and I could do that fast. If one of the firing team heard anything and came over to investigate, he would probably see the three kids and just think one of them had shifted in their sleep.

It was a choice between keeping a clear exit strategy or taking some risks to get a better view, and I wouldn't be able to see well anyway. Sunlight was still a promise waiting to be kept, and I don't have a wolf's night vision. I stayed where I was.

A white van with its headlights off pulled into the alley where Sig was still waiting. Three people got out, but I could see little more than their outlines. One of them was of average height and build in an overcoat, one of them was chunky and dark-skinned in some kind of tan jumpsuit, and one of them was short and maybe female beneath a bulky sweater and large round glasses.

They spoke in low voices as they walked the perimeter of the alley. A human couldn't have made out what they were saying, but I could hear them clearly.

"How many bodies are there?" This was from the brownish-haired guy with the average build, and he was definitely the cop Sig had mentioned. He had that way of talking, a brusque manner overlying an innate assumption that he was going to take control of the situation. The way he spoke was half threat and half reassurance.

"Three human, four vampires," Sig answered tersely. His attitude annoyed her, but she was used to it. "Don't use any names. Someone with really good hearing might be hanging around."

I smiled. Was she talking about vampires or me? Make what jokes you want about blondes, this one wasn't dumb.

"Why didn't you call us earlier?" the cop demanded. "We're supposed to be your partners, not your janitors."

"Back off," Sig snapped. "I didn't do this."

The cop froze.

"Who did?" he asked pointedly. "Was it..."

"No, he still hasn't recovered from...doing his thing." Sig chose her words carefully. Something about her protective manner reminded me of the way she had cautiously talked about being led to the bar by a psychic friend. If this "he" was one of the cunning folk or something, his being out of it for a while would make sense. Any kind of scrying can take a lot out of you, but peering into the future is supposed to be the most demanding kind of clairvoyance there is.

"Then who?" the cop persisted.

"Some guy I met tonight who works at this bar," Sig said. "He claims to be a half werewolf, though that might be to make him seem less dangerous."

"What is a half werewolf?" This was from the dark-skinned man in the jumpsuit. He had been rummaging around in the back of the van while the cop interrogated Sig, but now he was carrying two bulky instruments that looked like dismantled headlights.

"No clue," Sig admitted. "I've never heard of one before. He says his mother was bitten by a werewolf while she was pregnant, and she delivered him before the full moon. It might be true. He's definitely faster and stronger than a normal human."

"So he's all hurry and no furry?" the black man asked. "All bang and no fang?"

"That's what he says," Sig agreed. "But he's keeping secrets."

"I thought you said werewolves were weaker than vampires," the cop observed in that neutral way that cops have when they're interrogating a witness without being overt about it.

"He knows how to fight," Sig said.

"I guess so," the cop said, looking around.

"I'm going to bless the bodies now," the short one said. She was definitely female, her voice smooth and sweet and kind, the way a kindergarten teacher's should be and rarely is.

"We have more important things to take care of first," the cop said testily.

"No," the woman said, and her voice was soft and calm but there was real steel in it. "We don't."

The cop heard what I heard. He backed off. He didn't even tell her to hurry. "Yeah, OK."

She had already walked away. The priest, if that's what she was, bent over the nearest body and began to chant softly in Latin. "While she's doing that, I'm going to smoke what's left of these bloodsuckers," the black man said. That was when I realized what he was carrying: portable UV lamps. Battery-operated artificial sunlight. "You already took their pictures and fingerprints, right?"

"I've got their fingerprints on the weapons they used," Sig acknowledged. "But the vampires were already dissolving by the time the magic settled down enough for my cell phone camera to start working again."

"So does our big bad wolf have a name?" the cop continued quietly as if no one had interrupted him. He and Sig were conferring privately off to the side now.

"The waitress said his name was Trevor Barnes." I don't think I was imagining a certain reluctance when Sig spoke. "But his real name is John."

Every nerve end in my body jolted. How the hell did she know my first name? Psychics shouldn't be able to get a read on me for the same reason that vampires can't hypnotize me. The geas should have kept her from establishing any kind of psychic connection.

I almost didn't hear what the cop said next.

"How do we know this wolf guy isn't the one ripping out women's throats?"

"He's not," Sig said.

"How do we know?" the cop repeated.

"I know the same way I know that his name is John," Sig told him. Yeah, thanks for clearing that up, Blondie.

The cop accepted her words at face value, though. "So what happened here?"

"I came here to do a little recon on the wolf guy, and I saw the vampires attack him," Sig said. "That pile of putrid right there is one of the ones that's been raping and sucking women dry, but I don't know if this is the whole hive or not. How do you want to clean up the bodies?"

It was the first time I'd seen Sig defer to anyone, but then I realized that this was the cop's area of expertise: crime scenes. What the hell kind of monster-hunting team was this anyway? They weren't like a military unit. The snipers could have been knights—they were quiet and fit and moved like men with martial arts training—but the three down in the alley with Sig were soft. They had excess flesh and moved slowly. The cop's eyes periodically scanned his environment and his right hand stayed near his hip, but the other two hadn't even looked up yet.

So Sig had a psychic I hadn't seen yet, some kind of priest, an Eastern European sniper team, a cop, and a man with a van full of monster-disposal goodies on her speed dial? Where had she found these people? Craigslist?

I suddenly remembered that in the old stories, Valkyries existed to gather war bands together from disparate armies and regions and tribes. Could that sort of thing be instinctive? Sig had seemed interested in getting me to stay in Clayburg after she saw what I could do.

"We can't just make them disappear," the cop said. "Look at that girl's clothes. She's probably from the college. She'll be missed."

"What was she doing back here?" Sig wondered.

"That fat guy with the lip rings is Heath Cline," the cop replied. "He's a drug dealer, so we'll make this look like a deal gone bad. I don't know who the guy in the hoodie is, but he didn't get that rank just missing one shower, so if we put that machete in his hands we can hack up the bite marks and give Cline the sawed-off…"

I would have stayed to hear more, but the hairs on my neck and arms and legs all went stiff. I can always tell when ghosts and geists are around. All animals can. Oh, shut up. I think most people can sense spirits, actually, but they're conditioned to ignore or tune out any feelings that they don't have a rational explanation for, and a minute later they forget the feeling ever happened. I don't know if that's the Pax in action or human nature or both.

When I got all pimply and tingly, I froze into hyper-alertness. Something was up. Something was moving in or moving out or materializing, and the temperature dropped the way it does when disembodied presences are manifesting in an area. Sig had said she could speak to the dead. Was it possible that she could use ghosts as scouts or spies?

Or sometimes ghosts return to scenes of traumatic death, and the bodies in the alley were being set to rest by someone who seemed to know what she was doing. Maybe the priest was saying bye-bye to a ghost who wasn't quite ready to go?

Regardless, my instincts were screaming at me that something was going on, and I had no idea what it was or how to find out, so I got the hell out of there.

If I had heard screams by the time I got back to my car, I might have turned back, but I didn't.

What I heard was Sig saying, "Hey, you."

～7～

HOW TO GHOUL-PROOF
YOUR HOME

The house I was renting was on the outskirts of Clayburg, roughly ten minutes into the neighboring county. Ten minutes doesn't sound like much, but my nearest neighbors were two miles away and woods surrounded my house on three sides. This sort of isolation tends to make people from big cities anxious, but the privacy makes me feel safer. I like to hear what's coming without a lot of distracting background noise.

My abode is unremarkable-looking, an old brick farmhouse built during the 1930s and later covered with tan aluminum siding. It has two floors, one small story layered on top of the larger bottom one like a wedding cake, and a basement that was basically a root cellar when I moved in. I'd since poured concrete over the cellar's foundation and layered cinder-block walls around its sides.

I'd made other improvements too.

One of the selling points for me had been that the house had a gravel driveway. This was important because I bought a couple hundred feet of the cheapest PVC pipe I could find, then filled the sections with salt one by one and connected them until they formed a perimeter around my house. Digging under a paved driveway would have been a serious inconvenience when I made a foot-deep trench to bury the pipe in. Eventually I had an unbroken salt ring surrounding my house that couldn't be blown away by the wind or scuffed by the boot of a nosy neighbor, and salt rings are a natural barrier to certain types of supernatural menace.

All magic works symbolically to some degree, and salt is a powerful symbol, ancient and instinctively recognized on a level so subconscious that most of us aren't even aware it exists. According to folklore from the Middle Ages, salt is a symbol of purity, just like silver. This is a load of crap, although if enough people believe it for long enough, it might take on a truth of its own. What you have to remember about the Middle Ages is that after the Gregorian edicts, everyone acted as if anything related to the flesh was evil, but salt is actually a much older symbol of the body, or of having a body if you want to get technical. When everything else is gone from the human body, the last thing left is salt. When we want to preserve meat, we salt it. Salt is in the sweat we sweat and the blood we bleed. It is an intrinsic part of us, and we know this from infancy from the first time we taste our own tears. We know it even without words to express the knowing.

This is why an unbroken line of salt (circles work best because continuous cycles are a powerful symbol of life) functions as a defense against supernatural menaces that don't have physical bodies. Even a spirit that is possessing a material body will hesitate before crossing an unbroken barrier of salt, because unless it is an extremely powerful spirit that has occupied the body for a very long time, it will wind up performing an impromptu exorcism on itself.

Supernatural beings with their own material bodies, however, such as vampires, werewolves, zombies, ghouls, and so on, will cross salt barriers without a second thought, which is why I had a second layer of defense. As soon as I was alone with my new house, I began methodically removing sections of the aluminum siding, drawing crosses on the brick walls, and then replacing the siding. It's easy. All you need is a utility knife and some sealant. I repeated this process all around the house.

I have personally seen Christian, Jewish, Buddhist, Muslim, and Tibetan symbols work on undead creatures, but only when the person who had drawn them was sincere in their faith. Because I've seen this and sincerely believe that there is a higher power that a lot of people see from different perspectives, I can use just about any holy symbol and make it work as long as the religion doesn't worship pantheons or practice rituals that I personally think are evil. Crosses work best for me, though, probably because I was raised Catholic.

In any case, holy symbols work against supernatural menaces that are...well, unholy. These are mostly beings who have been summoned to a false semblance of life by death magic, or necromancy. Holy symbols represent a force that is life beyond life, something that always has been and always will be. Necromancy is an obscene parody of that force, an act that represents the ultimate lack of faith in it.

The aluminum siding covering the holy symbols on my house shortens their area of effect but doesn't negate them. If you had to see a holy symbol for it to work, vampires could just close their eyes. If you had to know the holy symbol was there and understand what it represented, then zombies could wander into a church and never care less.

This suggests, by the way, that on some level all minds and souls are linked in ways that we don't consciously understand.

If a symbol is powerful enough, sometimes we know things are there even if we don't know things are there. Lots of religions and psychologies and philosophies talk about this sort of thing. Feel free to read about some of them.

If anything does get past my outer defenses, I have a few other bells and whistles inside the house—and I mean that literally. Among some of the other defenses I've set up are actual bells and whistles, but the perimeter defenses are my main priority.

Once inside my house, I made my way straight to the Japanese sword that hangs by the living room woodstove. It isn't silver steel, but the katana is a traditionally forged Japanese sword, not some stainless steel knockoff ordered out of a catalog. My sword was blessed by its maker, who was both smith and priest, and I slung the sheathed blade over my shoulder before continuing on to the kitchen.

While it was bizarre that an out-of-control idiot like Steve Ellison had managed to scrape even three followers together, it would be a mistake to assume that we had killed his entire hive. The father I never knew had made a mistake like that. Michael Charming killed a lycanthrope thinking it was a lone wolf, and because my father was distracted with worry about an overdue pregnant wife, he was not as careful as he should have been and the werewolf's pack tracked him back to his home. Letting my dying father see that his pregnant wife had been bitten and infected with a virus that was sure to kill both her and his unborn child painfully was a conscious act of cruelty. That one lapse was the last mistake my father ever made. Well, there are some who believe that I'm the last mistake my father ever made, but you get my point.

The katana was staying within reach until the sun came up.

I keep my fridge and my pantry stocked, and the third shelf

down was crammed with homemade sandwiches. I plucked out eight from the left side, where slices of venison and Monterey Jack cheese and a light sprinkling of horseradish were tucked between split loaves of Italian onion bread. Werewolves burn calories faster than humans under normal circumstances, but when they've been exerting themselves beyond normal human limits and healing, they go through food like bipedal locusts.

After the fourth sandwich I was calm enough to locate a big bottle of spicy hot V8 juice and tilt it to my mouth. When I was done I scooped a paper plate full of fried chicken out of the fridge and made my way toward the cot I keep in the basement. I'm not particularly fond of sleeping in the basement, but it has one safety door for an entrance, no windows, and a narrow stairwell that's easy to defend.

I knew I was going to have to move again, but I was paying my current landlord under the table for "tax purposes" and trying to trace my address from Trevor Barnes's information would prove impossible. Sig's group didn't seem overtly hostile. The fact that she knew my first name freaked me out, but it's not like I don't come across things I can't explain fairly regularly. I figured I could spare one day to get out of Clayburg properly.

I hate burning up emergency identities before I've had a chance to set up any others. That's one of the ways knights get you. They force you to use up resources like safe places, false identities, and ready money faster than you can replenish them, until you're living day-to-day and hand-to-mouth, desperately reacting to whatever comes your way instead of carefully planning in advance. Despite the way I'd had to leave Alaska, I'd lived there long enough to make provisions. My time in Clayburg was a bust.

But there was nothing I could do about that. I had a deadline pressing on the back of my neck, emphasis on *dead*, and my focus was off, so I skipped the isometric exercises and the Krav Maga practice and sank down into a cross-legged Sukhasana position.

Meditation is important when you don't age normally. Post-traumatic stress disorder is caused by shutting down and putting anxiety and stress somewhere else while in crisis mode—sometimes from one intense experience and sometimes from prolonged stress over a period of years. Make that decades or centuries and you have serious problems. Last-train-to-Nutville-type problems.

The thing about sitting meditation for a guy like me is that it isn't soothing or transcendent. I don't picture myself in a temple of white light, untouchable and undistracted. Emotions come roiling up, and I just try to let them pass through me, concentrating on my breathing or moving my focus through different parts of my body. I rarely come out of it feeling peaceful though I sometimes feel drained, which can be just as good. Sometimes I meditate outside in cold air and find myself sweating. Occasionally I find realizations about things I've been worrying about sitting on my mental doorstep, with no clue how they got there. Tonight wasn't one of those times.

Finally I let myself crawl onto my cot and passed out as soon as my head hit the pillow. Despite my best efforts to defuse my subconscious, it still blew up in my dreams. There was a nightmare about the bald vampire cutting my arms off, only this time he was using my katana instead of a machete. Another dream featured a variation on the amputation theme—as I kept growing extra fur-covered limbs out of my body, a disgusted Sig kept burning them off me with her magic. Then there was one where I was in a new house starting a new life, but when I looked out the window I realized that I'd just moved into a house overlooking a river made of fiery snakes. I mentioned that I was raised Catholic, right?

My favorite was the recurring nightmare where I kept dreaming that I was finally changing into a wolf. I have this dream with increasing frequency and intensity every time a full moon comes close. This particular night I had it several times, and every single time I woke up with my heart pounding so hard that I was convinced the dream was real, that I really was in the process of changing right then and there.

It was almost a relief when the police came visiting the next morning.

~8~

BEDEVILED EGGS

There were two men arrayed behind Sig when I opened the front door. One of them was a hamster-cheeked chunky guy with freckles and an unruly patch of brown hair. He smelled like mint toothpaste and cheap deodorant and dried semen, and his sweat contained a long history of heavy meat meals. He was in his late thirties or early forties, and you could tell the guy still had some muscle beneath the fat. There was nothing likable about him on the surface—his already small eyes were narrowed and watchful, and the words "Don't Fuck with Me" were tattooed all over him in body language, but there was nothing immediately threatening in his manner either. There was a bulge beneath his jacket at the right hip that was almost certainly a holstered gun, and probably a large one at that, and he was dressed respectably enough in the kind of modest suits that working-class cops wear, a plain wedding ring on his left hand. I decided that he was the cop I'd seen in the alley.

The other man was taller than me by about four inches and shaped like an inverted bowling pin. His head, shoulders, and chest were all massive, developed to the point where his thick hips and legs looked skinny by comparison. He was in his late fifties or early sixties, the dome of his head shining out as if it were a mountain peak and his white hair the snow melting off it. I guess that would mean that the patchy white beard hanging off the crag of his chin was like frost or something. Similes aside, what was really cold about him was his eyes. They were pale blue, openly hostile, and infinitely weary. It was a strange combination. I hated him on sight.

And if he didn't have at least two weapons hidden under his shapeless gray trench coat, I was an Ankou's uncle. He smelled like a lot of things... some kind of muscle liniment, Nicorette, beef, cabbage... but the dominant smells were gun oil and wolfsbane and rage.

Unless there were other unaccounted-for people working with Sig, this was the psychic who had led her to the bar. He sure as hell wasn't a cop.

"How's it going, Sunshine?" Sig asked me cheerfully. "You look like hell."

It was nine in the morning, and she was wearing the same clothes she'd had on the night before. I was wearing an Amazing Spider-Man T-shirt and a pair of jeans I'd hurriedly pulled on over my boxers. "Bad dreams," I mumbled.

"You should have just gone without sleep like me," she informed me unsympathetically, then nodded at Chunky Cheeks before I could respond. "This is one of my contacts on the police department, Detective Ted Cahill." After the briefest of pauses, she then indicated the older man by moving her eyes sideways and tilting her head. "And this is Stanislav Dvornik, my... friend."

"Am I pleased to meet you?" I asked Cahill. I was addressing him because he was a police officer, but also because I instinctively knew that the best way to piss the older guy off would be to ignore him. Something about the way Sig had hesitated before calling Dvornik her "friend" suggested things I didn't even want to think about for a variety of reasons.

Cahill smiled mirthlessly. "No you're not, wolf-boy," he said. "Any more than I'm pleased to meet you. But I'm not here to arrest you or kill you, if that's what you mean."

Definitely the voice of the cop in the alley.

"These are some of the people I told you about last night," Sig said in answer to my expression. I'd given her a mild glare for form's sake. "The ones who helped me clean up."

"Do Valkyries need permission to come into someone's house?" I asked her.

She smiled faintly. "No. But I'm not rude either."

I raised my eyebrows at that but didn't comment directly. "I was just fixing breakfast. Are you hungry?"

Her eyes lit up and an enthusiastic smile spread over her face. It made her look like the young woman she looked like, if that makes any sense. I stared at that smile until my heart pounded on my chest as if it were trying to get my attention. "Hey, you!" my heart yelled. "Breathe, stupid! The air-conditioning in here sucks!"

"I'm starving!" she said. "These two would hardly let me eat anything at the IHOP."

"You had two plates piled high with pancakes and sausage!" Cahill protested. "The waitresses were looking at your figure and trying to decide whether to call an exorcist or a contract killer."

"Ted exaggerates," Sig informed me primly.

"Well, I made plenty," I said, turning around so that they could follow me into my house. "Even for another bottomless pit." It was true. I needed to empty my refrigerator anyway, and I wanted to stockpile as many extra calories as I could in case Steve Ellison really did have any surviving hive members.

I watched them follow me in the silvered glass mirror in the front hallway. A rapt expression came over Sig's face as the smells from the kitchen reached her. Ted was watching Sig with fond bemusement, and Dvornik was watching me watch him watch me with a look of undisguised loathing on his face. He wasn't going to look away first, and we stared at each other until I ran out of mirror.

"Those keys I took off the vampire...I guess you found his car somewhere nearby?" I asked nonchalantly as we made our way through the living room. We didn't have much to weave through. What's the point of strategically placing guns and ammunition under removable floorboards all over your house if you're going to cover them with carpeting and furniture? The only things in the room were two bookcases and a rocking chair with a quilt over it next to the woodstove.

"We did," Sig confirmed. "His name is—was—Alex Faulhaber. We checked his apartment out this morning."

Meaning they'd used one of the keys on the ring to let themselves in. I paused and looked at Sig inquiringly. Dvornik had stopped and was staring at the katana I'd placed back on the wall after the sun came up. It wasn't casual curiosity. Cahill was watching Sig and me. That wasn't casual curiosity either.

"The real find was above the apartment," Sig continued. "There's a huge attic space over the whole complex, no windows. They had turned it into a warren for human-size rats. They had cut doors in some of the partitions, nailed planks over rafters to make new floors, and cut out roof supports here and there to make headroom. We found a niche with four mattresses up there, and lots of clothes with bloodstains on them. Stanislav checked a few of the tenants, and they had puncture holes in easy-to-conceal places and their eyes weren't dilating normally."

Uh-huh. One of the signs that someone has been mentally mind-mucked by a vampire is that their pupils are slightly enlarged and don't dilate as rapidly as usual. I have no idea why. Something about the way the mental command to enter a trance state actually travels from one pair of eyes to the other, through the optic nerves and up the brain stem. The vampires had probably been feeding regularly off the tenants in the apartment building while conditioning them to ignore any unusual sounds coming through the ceiling. It would be like living above a takeout restaurant.

I resumed walking. "What about the cell phone? Did you get anywhere with that?"

There was a pause, not a long one, but noticeable. "We handed it over to a friend," Sig said. Her tone implied that she wasn't going to tell me the friend's name and that I shouldn't ask. "He's going to get back to us later."

I wondered if it was the black guy with the van or yet another someone else. It was nice that she was protecting *someone's* privacy.

"We were hoping you might be able to point us in a new direction," she added as I entered my kitchen. "We didn't really have time to talk, and if your sense of smell is as developed as you say it is, I thought that maybe you might have..."

Sig trailed off as I reached into a drawer to the side of my sink and pulled out Steve Ellison's wallet. Cahill's hand had flipped his coat aside and moved to the butt of the gun I'd spotted earlier. I flipped open the wallet to show Steve Ellison's driver's license and handed it to Sig.

She examined it wordlessly. Then Sig looked up at me, her bright blue eyes narrowing as if she were sighting a gun. "You didn't take this off of him in the alley. There's no way I missed that."

"No," I said. "You didn't."

Sig worked it out. "You lifted it off of him in the bar," she said accusingly. "You *wanted* him to come back after you when there weren't any bystanders around."

"I thought he was a lone rogue," I admitted.

She shook her head grimly. "I knew you wouldn't have just turned a heat seeker loose on the streets. It's why I went back to see what you were up to. Things just weren't adding up."

"I'm glad they didn't," I said, a little uneasily. I got that she was supposed to be some kind of psychic and that Valkyries were traditionally good judges of warriors and all that, but it still made me uncomfortable to hear her talking about me as if she knew me.

"You mind if I see that?" Cahill asked Sig, and she handed him the wallet while I went back to my meal preparations.

Breakfast was salvageable. The pound or so of fried potatoes were a bit black around the edges, but they're good that way. The sausage gravy boiling away in a big skillet had evaporated a little, but there was still plenty of it after I stirred the layer that had skimmed over on the top. The tray brimming with biscuits had a minute to go on the timer (they were two cans worth of Pillsbury home-style, not made from scratch or anything), and I'd shoveled the bacon and eggs onto platters and covered them before answering the door. The waffles were colder than I like, but I could reheat them without ruining their texture too much.

My kitchen is old-fashioned and doesn't have a counter where people can sit—hell, it doesn't have a dishwasher or a trash compacter—but the upper half of the dining table is visible from the adjoining room. Dvornik and Cahill sat where they could watch me as I got the biscuits out of the oven. I didn't take it personally.

Sig stayed up and set out some plates and coffee cups and silverware (it was real silver) while Cahill made a few pointed comments to her about werewolves apparently not having to worry about cholesterol either. I offered to make him a salad while I was carrying in the sausage gravy, and he suggested that maybe I'd like my breakfast going up my ass instead of coming out of it for a change.

It was a very uncouth comment. He and I were going to get along fine if he didn't try to kill me.

"Love what you've done to the place," Sig murmured dryly as she passed by me carrying butter and jelly from the fridge. The dining room and kitchen weren't decorated any more elaborately than the living room. No photos, no knickknacks, just basic furniture, some wind chimes in case any sudden materializing presences displaced air, and a couple of vases with flowers that were mostly an excuse for having containers of holy water lying around.

"I like to pack light," I told her, taking a jug of syrup out of the pantry.

Finally everyone was eating. Well, Sig and I were eating. Cahill was drinking coffee and watching us morosely while taking a few desultory bites of bacon. Dvornik wasn't touching anything.

"You're a good cook," Sig observed through what should have been a mouthful of fried potatoes while she slathered butter over a waffle. Her food was going down fast.

I looked at her skeptically, spearing a third piece of sausage on my fork so that it looked like a shish kebab. "You have a long life span and a huge appetite, and you're not a good cook?"

"It goes against my feminist principles," she said mock-haughtily.

"Every now and then she forgets what happened the last time and tries to cook again," Cahill told me. "You know how some people kill plants they try to take care of? She murders lasagnas and casseroles."

"This is all fine and dandy, I'm sure," Dvornik said disgustedly. His Slavic accent was thick and phlegm-filled. It was the voice of a lifelong chain-smoker who was a few years past his expiration date. "Now we're all good friends who trust each other."

He turned to Sig. It was the first time he'd taken his eyes off me since looking at my sword. "You wanted to tell him two things. Tell him so we can leave."

She stared back at him, something messy and complicated passing between them. Seeing that look, I knew for sure that they were lovers. It wasn't really a May-December thing—she probably only looked as if she were in her early twenties—but I wasn't inclined to view the two of them as a beautiful testament to love defying outside appearances either. What did I care if Dvornik was aging or sad or bitter or in love? He was an asshole.

"Yeah, Sig," I said, dividing what was left of the eggs between our plates. "Talk to me."

She turned her attention away from Dvornik and stared deeply into my eyes. This time I was ready for it, and I still felt the impact all the way to my groin. "You don't have to leave Clayburg," Sig told me.

I blinked. I admit it.

"I know you used to be a knight," she went on. "I saw your knife. I saw the way you fought... like you'd been training to go against things that were stronger than you from birth."

"Only they weren't *that* much stronger than you," Dvornik sneered. "Were they?" Words like *monster* and *hellspawn* hung there in the air, waiting for him to tack them onto the end of that sentence, but he clammed up again.

I didn't respond. I couldn't respond. This was a far deadlier secret than my quasi-werewolf status. For the past half century everyone who'd known this secret had tried to kill me, tried to turn me in for a reward, run away, or been killed. If I had known for sure that Sig had figured this much out, I never would have come home at all. I would have stolen the first old car I came across in the middle of the night and started driving.

What seemed like a long time passed. I just sat there, temporarily paralyzed, but if one of them had chosen that moment to sneeze, I would have been hurling the glass tray of hot sausage gravy toward Sig's and Dvornik's faces and elbowing Cahill in the bridge of his nose before the next second passed. Flipping my chair back, rolling, keeping in motion in case that sniper team I'd seen last night was in position in the woods around my house.

But nobody sneezed. Sig shot Dvornik a warning look. "That's right. I can't believe we've never heard any rumors about you."

Dvornik grunted. "Do you think the knights would advertise a failure of this magnitude?"

"What the hell are you people yammering about?" Cahill demanded. He looked at Sig. "I thought knights were supposed to be like supernatural cops these days. Are you saying this guy's a criminal?"

Sig sighed and began putting egg and bacon strips on a row of biscuits that she had pulled apart and laid out like open oysters. "It's not that simple, Ted," she said. "John could explain it better than I could if he would say something. A lot of what people like me know about the knights is only hearsay."

Cahill looked at me carefully then. "You all right there, Slick?"

I exhaled, a long, slow, ragged release of breath. Sometimes you look back on your life trying to pinpoint when or how something started, and sometimes you actually know you're at a turning point when it's happening. Whatever I did in the next ten seconds was either going to change me significantly or get me killed, and I wasn't ready for a decision like that. But that's life too—not being ready for it.

I had to trust Sig, at least provisionally. The only alternative was to kill her, and if I did that knowing only what I did about her, feeling the way I did, whatever soul I had really would be damned.

"Has Sig told you about the Pax Arcana?" I asked Cahill, reaching for my cup of coffee. My hand was shaking slightly, in a way that it hadn't the night before, when I'd only been worried about dying.

"That's the big 'don't ask, don't tell' magic, right?" Cahill chuckled ruefully. "She held me over a rooftop with one hand and bounced me up and down by my ankle while she explained it to me. That's what it took to make me believe it."

I smiled faintly. A supposedly impossible threat to someone's immediate survival is the quickest way to override the spell.

"She told me that the elves..." Cahill stopped and shook his head disbelievingly. Apparently he'd never heard himself say that out loud before. "She said that before the elves went back to where they came from, they made the spell to protect all the little half-elf bastards they were leaving behind."

"Call them the Fae," I advised. "Elves are just the Fae that can mate with humans, and Americans have too many weird associations with the word *elves* anyhow. These aren't toy-makers or tree-hugging hippies in white we're talking about. This is an ancient, powerful race that lived among us for thousands of years. We don't know why they came. We don't know why they left. Hell, we don't even know why they created the

Pax. It could be they're coming back someday and want there to be plenty of supernatural creatures for their armies. Or it could be they thought the whole thing was a good joke."

Cahill waved his hand dismissively to indicate that terminology wasn't way up there on his list of priorities.

"Sig said the knights are like magical bouncers or something," Cahill continued. "They aren't affected by the spell because the *Fae* made it so that no magic could mess with their heads."

"It's a little more complicated than that," I told him. "Do you know how we came up with a cure for smallpox?"

"I went to a community college so I wouldn't have to know stuff like that," Cahill said dourly.

"We injected people with cowpox," I informed him. "It was a less deadly version of the same disease, and it kept people from getting reinfected. That's where the word *vaccine* comes from. *Vacca* is Latin for cow."

He stared at me.

"I'm older than I look, and I read a lot," I said. "Get over it."

"Fine," Cahill said. "What was the point of that little nerd moment?"

"The knights are immune to magical compulsions because they're already under a similar spell called a geas that doesn't permit any other kind of mind magic to get in."

If I haven't made this clear, magical fire will burn knights, but telepaths can't see our thoughts. Magical lightning will shock us, but psychics can't predict our movements or see us in visions. Spells that actually bend light can confuse our eyes, but illusionists can't trick us by clouding our minds. Magically enhanced muscles will break our bones, but curses will slide right off us. It's why Sig's apparent ability to see me with some kind of psychic mojo was so unnerving. Was the magic of these

Aesir stronger than the Fae's? Or was what Valkyries actually did some kind of hyper-focused reading of body language and pheromones and facial tics or something? How the hell did she know my name was John?

"So what does this geas force these knights to do?" Cahill asked warily.

"It's a magically binding oath," I said. "The knights swore to not harm any supernatural beings who aren't threatening the Pax Arcana, and to eliminate any who are as quietly as possible."

Cahill fixed me with a troubled stare. His eyes really were small and beady...I'd thought maybe they just looked that way because his cheeks were so pronounced, but that wasn't the case. "So why did these knights let these Fae put them under this spell?" he demanded. "Why'd they agree to help keep monsters alive?"

It was a reasonable question. "They didn't have a choice," I told him.

"You said they swore an oath. That means they had a choice," Cahill said angrily. "What could be worse than letting things that eat us hide in plain sight?"

"The Black Death," Dvornik answered unexpectedly. His brow was lowered and he was looking at the table, chewing on his lip pensively.

Cahill gaped at him. Apparently he had heard of the Black Death.

"That's what I was taught," I confirmed. "When the Fae approached them back in the Middle Ages, the knights told them to shove it. The knights were hard-core Catholics and didn't want any part of supernatural pacts. Then the plague came along."

"It was maybe the worst plague in human history," Sig

added, just in case Cahill wasn't getting it. "In Europe, two out of every three people died."

Of course, they didn't call it the Black Death back then—we came up with that name later. Some people called it the Pestilence. Some people called it the Great Mortality. Most people who were in the middle of it called it the End of Times.

"You're all saying the Black Death was...what...some kind of big stick these Fae used to force your knights to go along with them?" Cahill asked disbelievingly.

I ignored the part about "my" knights. "When I was in the order, a lot of the older knights called the Pax Arcana the *Pox Arcana*. It's not like we enjoy having a set of instructions hardwired into our craniums. Would you?"

Cahill shook his head. "That is completely fucked up."

Just agreeing would have been inadequate, so I stayed silent. We all did, for a time. I got up and got the pot of coffee and brought it back into the dining room, touching up people's cups.

"So why are these knights after you?" Cahill asked as I poured a small amount of steaming brew into his cup. "That was what you were supposed to be telling me in the first place, right?"

"Right," I told him. "When I said that a geas was a blood oath, I meant that it wasn't just the knights who took the oath who were affected. All of their descendants were affected too. It passes down their bloodlines."

Something clever and perceptive flashed across Cahill's face before it settled into blankness again. It was like seeing shutters open and shut briefly. I realized that, far from his being dense or impatient, a lot of his attitude had been disingenuous, designed to goad me into providing further information. He really was a detective, and a big piece had suddenly fallen into place for him.

"See, the Fae don't think like us," I said. "To them a few centuries are like a few minutes: they think long-term as naturally as breathing. And a lot of magical energy is generated by faith or belief. The stronger the Pax grows over time, the more people it affects. The more people it affects, the stronger it gets."

"And?" Cahill said guardedly.

"The more successful the spell is, the more the supernatural population increases over time," I explained. "So the more people the Pax Arcana affects, the more magical events it has to conceal to maintain the status quo. Which means that more and more knights are needed every generation to clean up the increasing number of messes. The Fae set the geas up so that the knights' expanding family lines could meet that need as the need grew over time."

"That's part of the geas, isn't it?" Sig asked slowly. "The knights are compelled to raise and train their bloodlines as a way of upholding the Pax." Some things were falling into place for her too.

"The geas isn't that specific," I said. "It's more like the mental equivalent of a shock collar. But the knights are compelled to protect the Pax, and that's the only way they know how. Besides, they know their kids are going to be magically compelled to uphold the Pax too. They want to prepare their children so they'll survive. So...yeah. The knights are incredibly protective of their gene pool."

Sig snorted. "They're practically Nazis."

I shook my head. "That's a little misleading. The knights consider themselves humanity's first line of defense. They're fanatics about keeping their bloodlines pure of any supernatural influences, but that's not about ethnic issues. The only race issue they care about is whether or not you belong to the human race."

Cahill's eyes widened until they almost looked normal. "So you having werewolf blood..."

"I'm an abomination," I said simply. "They made me get a vasectomy when I was eleven on the off chance that my blood had been tainted, and that was when they were watching me every full moon, making me ingest trace amounts of silver, and electrically stimulating my muscles to see how strong my uncontrolled reflex reactions really were."

"So if you were a normal human all that time, what made you...?" Sig hesitated. "How do I put this?"

"Cry wolf?" Cahill suggested. "Do it doggy-style?"

"Become an unholy fucking perversion of nature," Dvornik supplied. Sig looked extremely pissed at this last contribution. It didn't affect me much one way or the other. I already hated the guy.

"I swallowed some swamp water and got sick when I was twenty-seven years old," I said.

"How did you..." Cahill paused. "Never mind."

"I almost died," I continued. "That was what finally made the knights who were constantly monitoring me relax a little bit. I'd made it through my developmental years, and whoever heard of a werewolf getting sick? But as far as I can figure it, that illness made something in my immune system kick in that had never had to kick in before. I started to change."

"How did they find out?" Sig asked.

"I survived an injury that I shouldn't have been able to survive," I said carefully.

"What kind of injury?" Sig persisted. "Was it on a monster hunt?"

I shook my head. "That's knight business. I'm not going to talk about that."

"So what's the big deal?" Cahill asked cautiously. "As long as you can't reproduce and you're not out there eating people... wouldn't the geas keep these knights from killing you? That's what you said, right? It keeps them from killing supernatural beings who aren't a threat?"

I shrugged. "They sincerely believe I am a threat to the Pax."

Cahill scrutinized me carefully. "Why?"

Dvornik laughed bitterly. It was clear that he didn't find the knights' attitude incomprehensible. "He exists."

Cahill was still looking at me. I shrugged again.

"I'm a monster and I know all their secrets," I said. "And I'm a walking temptation for other knights to start trying to commingle human and supernatural influences, which is dangerous. In their view I'm compromised."

Dvornik added nastily, "And I don't imagine you survived this long without killing more than a few knights along the way."

"That's true," I agreed softly, staring at him. "And that's why I have to leave Clayburg."

Sig shook her head emphatically. "No, you don't. The knights aren't as powerful as they used to be. Do you know about..." She paused and carefully didn't look at Cahill. "The big setback?"

I made an affirmative gesture. There had almost been an all-out war between knights and vampires shortly after the turn of the new millennium. If you think humans went a little crazy when 2000 rolled around, you should have seen what it was like among the supernatural communities. That conflict is why there are a lot of vampires like Steve Ellison running around without masters or hives to keep them in line now. The escalating hostilities had cost both sides dearly.

"Well, I don't know all the details, but the knights have been having similar problems with large werewolf packs in the Midwest," Sig informed me. "Plus, there was some kind of big ruckus in Alaska recently. Their numbers are down and their reputation has suffered. The Pax is breaking down and the knights are stretched thin."

I kept my face expressionless. The big ruckus in Alaska had been a massive manhunt for me.

"If we tell them that there was a renegade vampire here but that we destroyed it, I doubt they'll even send anyone personally," Sig asserted.

I didn't bother to hide my skepticism. "You're telling me that the knights will listen to you? A nonhuman?"

Sig's face contorted as if she'd bitten into something rancid. "God, no. Those assholes tolerate my existence as long as I don't break any of their rules, but they don't listen to me." Then she nodded at Dvornik. "They listen to him."

"Of course they do." My voice was so low that I was almost whispering. Dvornik and I regarded each other. If he was one of the knights' informants, one of us was going to die no matter what Sig believed. Then I remembered Sig saying that she had a friend who had visions. Dvornik was Slavic. Clayburg had a vampire problem. Sig was with Dvornik, and somehow she'd gotten into monster hunting. I'd sensed a bodiless presence the night before. All of these fragments came rushing together, and when I looked at Dvornik's brow I saw it, the slight discoloration over his left eye from where he had been born with a caul, that membrane that covers parts of some babies' faces and used to be considered a sign of psychic ability.

I leveled a finger at him. "You're a kresnik."

Something dark fluttered behind Dvornik's eyes.

"I told you he's smarter than he acts," Sig murmured, patting Dvornik's forearm.

The Fae didn't put all their eggs into one basket when they were looking for human enforcers. Back in the Middle Ages there was no way that a bunch of Europeans could have effectively policed China, or that Japanese agents could have operated discreetly in Africa. The Fae always picked small, secret societies of highly trained warriors who didn't owe political allegiance to any one king or emperor, but they diversified. In France and England they chose the Knights Templar. In Africa they chose a lost Berber tribe. In Japan they chose a bunch of warrior monks called *yamabushi*.

Kresniks are Eastern Europe's answer to the Knights Templar. After the Mongol invasion and the Knights Hospitaller scandal, Eastern Europe didn't have much use for knightly orders with private agendas, and when the Fae were looking for a small covert group to police that area, they selected Croatia's secret society of vampire slayers instead.

The kresniks' jurisdiction extended through Yugoslavia all the way to Italy, where they were called *Benandanti*.

The main difference between kresniks and knights is that kresniks are chosen on the basis of having psychic ability, not born into a family line. Their version of the geas is passed on psychically through some kind of training ceremony. This is partly why kresniks don't get hung up on working with supernatural creatures the way knights do. From the beginning the kresniks were regarded as supernatural creatures themselves, outcasts who were distrusted more than revered. They were also mostly working-class types who had a gift, not European nobles who had been raised to believe that they were superior, elite, and exclusive.

Kresniks have a long tradition of working side by side with dhampirs and cunning folk and werewolves who aren't out of control, so much so that some stories confuse kresniks with all of those things. Which probably made Dvornik's dislike of me personal rather than professional.

Anyhow, the knights respect kresniks the same way that US Special Forces respect the British SAS. Kresniks are a smaller order, but they are very effective even if they don't just hunt vampires anymore. If things were as bad as Sig said, it was just barely conceivable that the knights might listen to a kresnik out of professional courtesy.

"Why would you do this for me?" I asked Dvornik.

Sig answered for him. "I know things about people. Not everything. Not even the things I want to know the most, sometimes. But things come to me."

"How could you know things about me?" I finally asked. "The geas should keep you from getting any kind of reading off me at all."

She hesitated. "I just do."

Bullshit. She was hiding something. A big something. But every instinct I had was telling me that she didn't intend me harm.

"So what do you know?" I wasn't at all sure that I wanted to hear it.

"You're screwed up," she said. "You've been alone so long that you're on the verge of going a little crazy with it. You've been working so hard on protecting yourself against death that you're starting to protect yourself against life. You're not sure you trust your impulses because you're paranoid about being part wolf, but you're also forced to rely on your instincts because you can't trust anyone else, so you try to analyze and question and anticipate everything even though you can't. You feel guilty just about being alive because you were raised by Catholic monster hunters, but you also recognize how messed up that is and resent any kind of authority figure."

For some reason I had a sudden image of those old Charlie Brown cartoons, the ones where Lucy is offering psychiatry sessions for five cents.

Sig leaned forward. If she could have reached me, I think she would have taken my hand. "And I like you. Beneath all the anger and coping mechanisms, you're also brave. And loyal. And kind. And funny. And strong-willed. And smart. And if you don't start forming some real roots and relationships again, you're going to wither into a smaller, harder, and sadder person than you really are."

OK then.

"That...means something to me," I said slowly, and it did. What, exactly, I wasn't sure. I could have kissed her or slapped her and felt equally justified on either count. "Now shut up and let me talk to your boyfriend."

Sig looked stunned. I don't think she was used to being resisted while she was in full persuasion mode. I took advantage of her temporary silence and addressed Dvornik again.

"Why would you cover for me?" I asked him bluntly. "You don't like me."

Dvornik barked out a short spasm of a laugh. He seemed to be genuinely amused rather than making some kind of bitter, sarcastic statement. Then the amusement died out and he stared at me seriously. "If I didn't," and at this point he nodded slowly toward Sig, "she would leave me."

You know, there's honesty, and then there's too much information. We all sat there, not sure how to move forward after that last little bomb mot. Sig looked like she'd been sucker punched a second time. It was clear that she wanted to say something, but she wasn't sure what, or even which one of us she wanted to say it to. Served her right. You play with fire, you get burned. You play with intimacy, you get awkward.

Cahill cleared his throat. "You said you wanted to tell him two things," he reminded Sig, indicating me with a jut of his chin. "What was the second?"

"Oh." Sig looked as if she was having second thoughts but went on anyhow. "We could use your help going after the rest of the vampire hive today."

If she'd known me half as well as she thought she did, she would have told me that part first.

9

THE FIRST RULE OF REAL ESTATE

I hadn't lived in Clayburg long, but even I knew that once you got to the streets numbered higher than fourteen, you were in a bad part of town. The address on Steve Ellison's license was on Seventeenth Street.

There were six of us traveling in the van I'd seen the night before, an exterminator's van as it turned out. Which would have been a lot more comfortable if I hadn't had an enhanced sense of smell. Cigarette smoke and pot stink clung to the cracking black plastic of the seats, mingling with the lingering odor of pesticides and fumigants and antiseptic cleaners. And beneath all of that, the faint scent of trace molecules left behind by bodies, human and inhuman, in varying degrees of decomposition. It made it hard to pretend that I was riding in the Mystery Machine with Scooby-Doo and the gang.

The African American man the van belonged to turned out to be a guy named Chauncey Childers whose parents had obviously combined a love of alliteration with a hatred of small children. When we officially met at Dvornik's studio, Chauncey had told me that everybody called him Choo Choo for short or Choo for even shorter. He had skin the color of coffee and cream and was big-bellied and bony-assed, with lots of tiny braids coming out of his skull that were bound together by prayer beads. A long drooping mustache surrounded his goatee without ever quite touching it. Choo was somewhere in his mid-forties or early fifties, an inch or so shy of six feet, and he had a disproportionately long torso. When we were standing up, I was taller than he was, but sitting in the van he looked down at me.

Choo really was a professional exterminator. It said so on the card he showed me. The card also advertised spiritual cleansings and negative energy removal and had a Web address. When I had asked him how he had gotten involved with this group, he clapped me on the shoulder and told me that he had seen some shit exterminating old houses that I would not believe. Then he'd smiled real big and brayed a loud, slightly nervous laugh, and said, "Oh, hell, I guess you would believe it."

I was sitting shotgun while Choo drove. Sig and Dvornik were in the two bolted-down bucket seats that made a gap-toothed smile of a second row. Neither Sig nor Dvornik had said more than a few words since we'd left my house, not to each other and certainly not to anybody else. It had made it a little awkward when I was forced to rely on them for introductions. When I asked Sig where Cahill had gone, she had tersely informed me that he had a job.

At the back of the van, squatting on a large folded rubber tent amid a clutter of metal canisters, brightly colored card-board boxes, canvas bags, and sheets of plastic, were the East European twins who had turned out to be younger, smaller versions of Dvornik. Topping out at five-ten, they were dark, barrel-chested, no-necked, and silent. I was mentally referring to them as Burly and Surly. They were also Dvornik's nephews.

I had pressed a little and found out that Dvornik had a twin sister who was also a kresnik, and I briefly imagined someone who looked like Fred Flintstone in drag except with a mustache and a chain saw, but I cut that out when I found out that the sister was dead. Even though Andrej and Andro had a psychic mammy, they hadn't inherited the old psychic whammy. The brothers apparently served full-fledged kresniks as support staff. If the scar tissue under their eyes and around their knuckles was any indication, that didn't just involve fetching coffee and taking memos.

The Knights Templar also have soldiers who aren't bound by the geas, although they're called lay servants or sergeants depending on whether they serve as rear support or in a combat capacity. They're mostly people who don't come from a bloodline proper but have been orphaned or woken up from the Pax Arcana by some kind of traumatic experience.

When I'd said hello to Andrej and Andro, they'd just stared at me. Sig had looked somewhere else and explained that they didn't speak much English. I don't know any Croatian, but I'd tried saying "Guten tag," which means "Good day" in German, and "Jak sa wy robiacy," which I'm about 70 percent sure means "How are you?" in Polish.

They just kept staring at me. They were related to Dvornik all right.

Fortunately or unfortunately, Chauncey "Choo Choo" Childers didn't mind filling in the awkward silence. I wasn't really sure what to make of him. He was definitely the source of the marijuana reek, and he talked with a breezy self-assurance that I wasn't sure I trusted. There was something impersonal about his friendliness, like it was a kind of armor that he hid behind while observing the world around him dispassionately. He chatted about his interest in feng shui and made fun of his failed attempts to become a priest. Apparently he had filled out forms at various Web sites that offered to ordain you for free, but even though he was legally able to perform wedding ceremonies in most states, he still couldn't make holy water that burned undead flesh.

Choo was talking about potpourri when I tuned all the way back in. "You just put rosemary, sage, cedarwood, and fennel in a bowl," he said. "Evil spirits can't stand the smell."

"Can living people?" I asked.

He brayed that loud horselike laugh which apparently hadn't been an accident the first time. "It's just nature, man," he said. "It smells like being in the woods."

"Huhn," I grunted noncommittally. That was the sort of thing that people who haven't spent a lot of time in the woods say. Then I made the mistake of turning around and talking to Sig and Dvornik. "That apartment building you visited this morning...was it around here too?"

"It was a government assisted living complex on the other side of town," Sig answered tensely. "Why?"

"I was just wondering if all the vampires in that alley knew each other before they were turned," I said. "It might explain why they were backing Ellison instead of reining him in. The guy was reckless."

"Look who's talking," Dvornik sneered. "The cowboy who had to get his ass saved by Sig."

"I get a little impulsive this close to a full moon," I admitted.

Sig snorted, but Dvornik was undeterred. "You sound like a woman blaming her lack of control on her period."

"It's not the fear for my immortal soul, or being hunted by professional killers, or the anger-management issues that I mind so much," I said. "It's the bloating."

Choo chuckled and Sig smiled politely, but Dvornik wasn't giving up that easily. "Is that supposed to be some kind of joke?

God only knows how old you are, and you act like a teenager. You even dress like a twelve-year-old. It's pathetic."

I was actually now wearing plain white coveralls over my Spider-Man T-shirt. We were all wearing coveralls. We also had those fabric mask filters that doctors and nurses wear hanging around our necks. One thing most people don't get is that it's their breath that animals smell first because their breath is airborne. Keeping your scent from being forcibly expelled on air particles in front of you isn't that big a defense—it might add a few seconds to the amount of time it takes a vampire to sniff you—but when you're hunting a creature with preternaturally fast reflexes, seconds matter. If you wind up in a situation where you're stationary and hiding, not announcing your location by generating your own private wind makes a small difference. It was also good that we were all wearing uniforms that had been freshly washed in the same load of laundry. The overpowering detergent smells would be the same, and there's no point making it easy for a vampire you're hunting to identify how many of you there are with a nose count.

"I dress the way a twentysomething American bartender would dress," I said mildly, turning around to face them again. "If I want to dress like some grumpy-ass refugee from the old country, I'll turn to you for fashion advice."

"Come on, you two." Sig had her hand on Dvornik's forearm but was looking at me when she said this.

"Letting things slide doesn't seem to be working," I said, meeting her gaze.

"I don't care if—" Dvornik began angrily.

"Stanislav is dealing with things you've never—" Sig started to say.

Dvornik turned on her and roared, "YOU DON'T APOLOGIZE FOR ME TO THIS FREAK!"

Sig turned angrily on him. "IF HE'S A FREAK, I'M A FREAK!"

"BULLSHIT!" Dvornik barked. "Your ancestors healed fallen warriors! He turns into a filthy animal!"

Actually I didn't, but it didn't seem like the right time to bring that up.

"Oh, right," Sig said sarcastically. "That doesn't sound like irrational prejudice at all! What about Kasia? How is he any different from her?"

Dvornik's face had gone beet-red at the mention of "Kasia," whoever or whatever that was. Sig must have scored a hell of a point, because he didn't pursue it. "*You* are not the enemy," he said quietly.

"Then neither is he," Sig retorted. "Have I ever been wrong about something like that before? Ever? Give me one example. Just one."

Dvornik glared at her and worked his jaw. "He doesn't need you to protect him, and I don't need you to protect me," he said finally. "Stay out of it."

"Fine!" Sig said angrily. "To hell with both of you infants!"

"We're here," Choo announced. He turned his head as if looking out the side window and added, so quietly that no one but me could possibly have heard him. "Thank you, Jesus."

Steve Ellison's neighborhood was poor and mostly white, although a lot of the kids running around—and there were more kids outside than there would have been in a presumably safer middle-class area—were interracial. There were no women walking their retrievers here, though I did see a woman mowing her lawn with a push mower, watched by a few elderly neighbors sitting on their stoops. The houses almost all needed some routine maintenance, but the cars went to extremes: they were either flashier and more expensive than you'd see in the burbs, or they were much older. There were as many vans as SUVs, and pit bulls behind fences were more common than terriers or retrievers. Mutts, of course, are everywhere. Go team.

According to the plan, Dvornik was going to go into a meditative trance so that his spirit—technically his astral projection—could step out of his body and go check the house for hostiles. His spirit form was the presence I had sensed on the rooftops the other night.

For my part, I was going to sniff around the outside of the house for any vampire scents. If we determined that the house was teeming with undead, Choo and the nephews were going to set up a rubber tent around the house while the sun was still shining and fumigate it with a fog made of compressed holy water.

Still on edge, I exited the van. It wasn't as if my presence were helping Dvornik relax. I walked around to the rear doors and removed a plain white canvas bag from the back.

Sig got out of the van before I closed it back up and joined me wordlessly. I looked at her standing there tight-lipped and white-knuckled.

"Does this mean you really care?" I asked, perhaps unwisely.

"This means I really feel like killing something right now," she muttered, taking out her own canvas bag.

Fair enough.

Ellison's one-story house was a peeling gray porchless affair. All of the window shades were down, and every window had one. The front yard was fenced in, but there was a side door by the driveway that probably let into a kitchen. There were no cars in the driveway. I ignored both entrances and began walking around the house. Sig followed me wordlessly.

The back of the house opened up into a large common

area—at least two hundred feet by eight hundred—that formed one giant backyard for all the houses on the block. A rusting swing set from kinder times was set in the middle of the space, but no one had mowed the entire grounds, and the pathetic little playground was surrounded by shin-high grass. It would probably be waist-high by summer.

About twelve feet from the swing set was a massive pile of dirt. I indicated it to Sig.

"What?" she asked impatiently.

"Get your head out of your ass or go back to the van!" I snapped back. "I'd rather be alone than with someone who's missing things because she's pissed off."

Oddly enough, this didn't make Sig angrier. It seemed to have a calming effect on her, if anything. "What am I missing?" she asked quietly.

"Look at that dirt," I said. "It's not the same color as the rest of the dirt around it. It's pale."

She reexamined the pile more thoughtfully, then slowly turned around and looked at the plywood access panel built into the concrete foundations of Steve Ellison's house. It was the reason I'd come around to the back in the first place. Then she looked at me. "You think someone's been excavating at night?"

"Don't you?" I asked.

She nodded, relaxing a little bit. "It's pretty careless of them, though. Anywhere else in Clayburg, an ugly pile of dirt appearing from nowhere would have drawn attention from some homeowner or real estate agent worried about property values."

"Well, you know the first rule of real estate," I said.

"Location, location, location," she answered softly.

We walked toward the foundation of the house, more comfortably united in purpose now. When you're checking out a house that you suspect is a vampire lair, it's best to work from the bottom up if you have a choice. Otherwise you're likely to get grabbed by supernaturally strong hands breaking through the floor beneath your feet.

We dropped our canvas bags on the ground. Sig dug inside hers and came out with a large rectangular flashlight roughly the size of a football. This particular flashlight had a UV bulb.

I slid my right hand into my canvas bag, careful not to let everyone in the neighborhood see inside it, and grabbed the hilt of a wakizashi, a shorter version of a katana. Japanese long swords were not made for waving around in confined spaces.

My left hand carefully hovered over the wood surface of the access panel before settling down on it gently. For a moment I thought about that game where you put your palms on the top of someone else's, and they try to flip their hands over and slap the top of your hands before you can move. If a vampire hand was going to try to grab me and drag me into a dark hole, this would be the moment. I couldn't hear anything or sense any vibrations, and the only smells I was picking up were sour and old. I went ahead and removed the panel.

At first, outside air rushed past me into the opening, but then the smell of blood, shit, pus, gangrene, fear, and undead stink washed over me. I let go of the wakizashi so that it stayed in the canvas bag and rolled away from the opening, choking and gagging. Turning, I rested my back flat against the concrete wall. To anyone watching from inside the house, I would be in an invisible spot between two windows.

"What is it?" Sig asked.

"Dead bodies," I gasped, settling down on the ground. "Lots of them."

~10~

MENTAL RESERVATIONS FOR TWO

Sig swore and set her flashlight down so that it shone directly into the hole; then she removed a pocket mirror from her coveralls, snapped it open, and angled it so that she could peer into the opening from the side.

There are a lot of misconceptions around the relationship between vampires and mirrors. The most common belief is that vampires don't cast reflections, but this is a distortion of the truth.

The first mirrors were pools of water, and the next were made of polished volcanic rock, but then there was a long period of time where mirrors were made of polished metal, and the most valued of these mirrors were silver. Even after metal mirrors were replaced by glass, silver still came into play when a German chemist named Justin von Liebig created silvered glass by coating the surface of mirrors with silver nitrate. And one of the odd things about silver is that it does not reflect magical glamours. That's how the legend about vampires and mirrors got started—it's not that vampires don't show up at all; it's just that for a long time, people looking at vampires in mirrors would often see their true forms rather than the attractive forms that they were mentally broadcasting, so vampires learned to avoid mirrors altogether.

After a moment Sig came over and sat next to me. She was always pale, but now she looked deathly.

"Can you smell it too?" I asked.

She shook her head mutely, then added, "I mean, yes, a little, but that's not it."

"Then what?" I asked.

"They've turned the crawl space into a cellar at least eight feet deep," she said. "It's full of ghosts."

I absorbed this news unenthusiastically. "Can you talk to them?"

Sig shivered. "Not the severely traumatized ones. Not as such."

"OK then," I said, and inhaled deeply through my nose, trying to adjust to the stench that remained as the crawl space aired out.

"The hive isn't finished, Sig," I told her. "It's a little hard to tell with all the different odors, but I'm picking up at least three vampire smells that I've never smelled before."

"Wonderful," she said.

We sat there for a time, waiting for Dvornik to send word that it was OK to go in the house.

"I'm not going to be able to stay in Clayburg after we deal with this hive, Sig. You know that, right? It would be too dangerous for all of us."

Sig shrugged angrily, a you-can-do-what-you-want gesture. "What my friends and I do is already dangerous. You can hear and smell trouble coming. You can walk in front of us and heal from wounds that would kill anyone else. You can take out three vampires with a busted-up broomstick and a bottle of holy water. Do you hear what I'm saying?"

I did, and I disagreed. "I lived with a woman years ago. One day her car exploded."

Sig didn't seem surprised or impressed by this information.

"It's not like it was an accident either," I continued. "The knight who was after me knew that I was always careful about checking my car before I got in it. But Alison always drove when we went to visit her sister, and I didn't always check her car because I didn't ride in it very often, and I didn't really believe deep down that the knights would intentionally kill an innocent woman just to get to me."

I spat. "I thought they still had *honor*. But the geas only keeps them from taking *supernatural* life unnecessarily."

"Why weren't you in the car?" Sig wondered.

"I was going to be," I said. "Alison got a run in her stockings, and it was easier for her to run down to the drugstore and buy a new pair that matched her dress than to change her outfit."

Sig went back to her original subject. "I know you two don't like each other, but if Stanislav gives his word to keep your secret, he'll keep it."

"Why would he give it?" I countered. "Because you're emotionally blackmailing him?"

"It's not blackmail," she said angrily. "You might be an ass, but you're not evil. If he turns you in to the knights, it's for one of two reasons: he either doesn't really trust me, or he does believe me and he's so jealous he's willing to murder a basically good man. Which one of those people am I supposed to live with?"

I shook my head. "That's between you and him. But I know what it's like to have to keep a promise against your will."

She didn't have an immediate response for that, and some

of the anger seemed to drain out of her, leaving something sad and awkward behind.

We sat there a little longer. Then the hairs on my neck rose up and my back muscles tightened. I almost growled. I could feel something in the air around us, something that made the temperature drop slightly without creating any currents.

Sig didn't seem disconcerted. She was staring at the air in front of her and nodding. Then she turned to me. "Stanislav says the house is clear."

And the guy called me a freak.

"Then let's make sure there's nothing hiding in the ground," I said, rising to my feet.

One of the creepiest things about vampires in a long list of hinky is that all of them can burrow like sand crabs. This is another thing you don't see in movies or generally read about, but it's a survival trait. Digging burrows is a way to escape sunlight in a pinch, and that's not even considering how many vampires wake up to their new existence buried eight to ten feet beneath the earth. Some claim that vampires don't need to breathe, but that's just silly...stolen blood doesn't do them any good if their lungs and hearts aren't moving to pump it through their veins. They just don't have to breathe as much or as often. Fortunately vampires generally prefer to roam in cities where concrete infrastructures render their ability to burrow mostly moot.

Mostly.

Sig fished two flares out of the canvas bag, lit them, and tossed them into the crawl space. I got that creeped-out feeling again...as if invisible fingers were playing my spine like a xylophone. It was the presence of the ghosts Sig had mentioned.

There was a ladder at the back of the basement, and it led to a hole that had been torn into the ceiling and covered with plywood from the floor above.

I turned to Sig. "Something isn't right here."

Sig uttered something I won't repeat. Let's just say it involved my grandmother and a highly inappropriate act of animal cruelty and leave it at that.

"Listen," I said, indicating the plywood. "It's like you said about the pile of dirt...these vampires are sloppy. So how have they survived this long without being discovered? Because I'm telling you right now, there are a lot of bodies buried in that dirt floor."

Sig brushed this observation off. "Worry about that later. Are there any vampires hiding in the dirt?"

I grimaced. She was right, but the feeling that I was missing something wouldn't go away. I just hoped that whatever I wasn't seeing didn't wind up biting me on the ass. Or the neck. Or anywhere, really.

Then I caught the scent, woven in with the other smells like a small bright-red thread in some hideous dark tapestry. Blood breath. Something had expelled carbon dioxide into that cold room full of dead air recently. Something waiting beneath the surface of the cool ground. I waited a while longer and smelled it again, but I didn't catch any breaths with different signatures.

"There's nothing in there," I said finally, nodding my head in a big emphatic yes and holding up one finger.

Sig reached into the canvas bag and removed a CD player. "Then do you mind if I put on some music? I still have to look this place over, and it's creeping me out."

"Go ahead," I told her, not that she really needed my permission.

Sig flicked a switch, and some kind of death metal music with a heavy bass and a lot of shrieking emerged. I found myself hoping that Sig had just bought it to frighten away predators.

Then a high-pitched squeal drove into my eardrums at a frequency too high for a normal human's hearing. Somebody in Sig's group was messing around with LRADs (long-range acoustic devices) and gearing them toward a vampire's audio range. Sig didn't seem to notice the sound that was making me clench my teeth at all. I didn't protest, though. I could handle having my hearing become a painful disadvantage if it meant that any vampires around had to deal with the same distraction.

Lastly Sig removed a sword from her canvas bag, sliding it carefully so that her body was shielding it from the sight of the outside world. It was a custom-made blade with a weighted tip that made it look like a Roman spatha, except that it was longer and edged on both sides as well as pointed.

With a sudden flick of the wrist Sig sent her blade into the crawl space, where it anchored tip-first in the dirt floor. That was one advantage to having a weighted tip that had never occurred to me. Then she dropped onto her rear end in front of the opening before I could stop her, stuck her feet through it, and grabbed the edge of the frame with her hands. Her upper body strength pulled Sig through the opening as if she were being shot through a torpedo tube.

Sig landed on her feet roughly seven feet in front of me, and the sword was in her hands even as a vampire erupted from the dirt floor. The vampire was female and dressed in a sleeveless black T-shirt and panties, and it was flailing its long black hair and hands in every direction, spraying dirt all about. Fortunately the vampire was facing the opening that I was watching through, not Sig. It tried to whirl and grab her legs, but Sig lopped its left forearm off at the elbow. The vampire shrieked and leaped completely out of its hole, sending a blinding spray of dirt up into the air that forced Sig backward.

As soon as the vampire turned its back to me, I dove into the crawl space. I caught my fall on my fists with my sword in my hand and pointed outward, away from my body. Rolling forward onto my back and then to my feet, I came up in a boxing stance with the wakizashi held in a reverse grip in front of me. A right hand came flying at me, and I batted it aside—but there was no vampire attached to it.

I watched as Sig delivered the kind of high front kick that martial arts schools teach but that you should never actually do, the ones that are way too easy to grab—provided the opponent has hands to begin with. Sig's foot caught the vampire square on its chest, and it literally flew eight feet across the room and smashed into the cement wall, causing cracks and clouds of dust. The vampire somehow stayed on its feet as it bounced off the wall, waving its handless stumps around and screaming mindlessly before Sig took its head off with a two-handed swing of her sword.

How did that Lewis Carroll poem about the Jabberwock go? Something about a vorpal sword going snicker-snack.

A shadow flickered across the floor, and I looked up to see one of Dvornik's nephews peering into the opening with a machine pistol in his hand. For some reason the pistol was trained on me. I made a turning-down gesture with my hand, and he obligingly turned the music off. Sig was leaning on her sword at this point, and she said something to him in Croatian that made him lower his pistol. After another long moment he left.

I didn't say anything or move for a time. Fights stir up a lot more than adrenaline and dust, and it's best to let someone who's just been in one have whatever space they need. Sig kept her hand on the hilt of her sword and continued to lean on it, pressing the tip into the ground. Her eyes eventually lost their hyperfocused quality, and her breathing became normal again.

After a while she looked up at me. "The ghosts are still here. We'll have to give them a proper burial."

"This vampire didn't kill them," I offered. "It's newly turned. Look at it. It's still human-looking."

Vampires don't turn everyone they bite into vampires. Creating a new undead is an intentional act that takes time and planning, not a side effect or an impulsive accident. I don't know all the steps involved in a vampire's creation, but I know that it takes multiple bites over an extended period—some legends say three bites over three days, but legends say three times about almost everything. The act also requires an exchange of blood—the victim has to drink the vampire's life fluids as well as donating their own—and the victim has to be buried for days—again, most legends say three. I don't know why the burial aspect is important except that we're talking about magic here, and putting things in the earth has obvious symbolic significance. You bury things when they're dead. You also plant things in the ground to make them come to life.

If I was right, the vampire Sig had just killed had come out of the ground for the very first time today.

Sig nodded tiredly. "I recognize her. I spent a lot of time talking to prostitutes when I was trying to figure out why the ghosts of butchered women were wandering around town. She said her name was Vicki."

I thought about that. "Why would a vampire want to turn someone like that?"

Sig shrugged. "She was still attractive in a way. Bad teeth. Great body. Maybe one of the vampires knew her from its previous life."

We stayed quiet for a while.

"You go ahead and check the house out," Sig said finally. "I'm going to see if I can learn anything from these ghosts."

I peered at her closely. It was hard to read her expression with the light of the flares casting shadows over her face. "I thought you couldn't talk to them."

She hesitated. "I want you to picture something for me, OK?"

"Sure," I agreed.

"Imagine an open doorway. It's dark beyond that door and you can't see what's on the other side, but you can see a hand clutching on to the door frame where someone is trying not to get pulled all the way in."

"OK," I said.

"A ghost is like that hand," Sig asserted. "It's not the whole person. It's just a very small part of them that won't let go. And the worse the death, the less effectively a ghost communicates. Some of them can't even think, much less speak. The worst of them are just residual echoes."

"And these died badly," I said. It might have been the most obvious statement I'd ever made.

Sig winced. "I can still examine them. Maybe identify who they were later." Her face hardened then. "And put their killers down if that will help lay them to rest."

No wonder she had bags under her eyes. Something occurred to me. "Can Dvornik see ghosts too? When he's... you know..." I made a butterfly out of my hands and pretended that it was flapping out of my chest and taking off over my head.

"Yes," she said.

I nodded slowly. That would make for one hell of a bond.

"You did the right thing," I said.

"The woman I met was a lost soul even before she was undead, but..." Sig trailed off and didn't finish whatever she'd started to say. Probably that it was harder to destroy a vampire when you'd personalized them, even just a little bit...even when you disliked the person they'd been. Instead, she said simply: "We live in a very ugly world."

It was hard a point to argue with, standing in the middle of an improvised burial mound, lit by the hellish red light of road flares and surrounded by dismembered body parts. I tried anyhow. "We live in a world that has very ugly things in it. And you just put one of them down."

"I did," Sig agreed. Her voice didn't contain any noticeable enthusiasm and her expression was unknowable, but she was looking at me steadily.

"Damn straight," I said, stepping up and slapping her shoulder lightly. "Now stop trying to seduce me and soldier up."

It took a moment for that to register. "What?" she said.

"Don't think I don't see what you're doing," I said. "You know tomorrow night's a full moon..."

"Are you still going on about the full moon tomorrow night?" she interrupted, a bit more animated now. "News flash: you don't turn into a wolf. Quit whining already."

"We live in a very ugly world," I said in a falsetto voice, batting my eyelashes.

She laughed reluctantly, then punched me in the upper arm. It wasn't all that light a punch. "Get out of here," she said.

"Do you need to get out of this hole for a while?" I asked her seriously.

She shook her head. "No, I don't want to have to come back. I just want to get this over with. I'm not some princess who needs rescuing. You go do what you need to do in the house."

So I did.

~11~

BLOOD, BATH, AND BEYOND

Choo joined me as I made my way toward the front of the house. He was carrying a metal spray gun attached to two plastic tanks on his back by a hose.

"Where are the sunshine twins?" I asked.

Choo grinned. "They're guarding Dvornik's body while his spirit tries to come all the way back home. That's standard operating procedure. It's not like we can talk with each other anyway."

I frowned doubtfully. "Who's going to talk to them if Dvornik dies? Are they good at charades?"

Choo looked amused. "Why? You planning on killing him?"

"I wouldn't call it a plan," I said. "A really vivid fantasy maybe."

"Don't let the way Sig talks to Dvornik give you the wrong idea," he advised. "The man's been killing people like you for a long time."

"I was born before World War Two, Chauncey," I said softly, the formal use of his first name deliberate. "I've been killing people like him for a long time."

He looked at me, then looked away.

The front door had an old-fashioned mail flap. I crouched in front of it and opened the flap, taking a deep whiff of the house. I caught traces of disinfectant and fear sweat and vampire stink and blood and loosened bowels, and underlying those were fainter traces of chewing tobacco and spilled beer and solo sex. The air inside was so stale that I could tell it had been at least a few days since a door or window had been opened. Whatever this house was, it wasn't where Steve Ellison had been holing up lately.

"By the way," I said to Choo, standing and looking over my shoulder as I fiddled with the lock. It was a cheap lock, and I didn't bother with the tension picks I'd brought along, just used my laminated Clayburg public library card. "The number of new vampires I've smelled is now up to four."

"Yeah?" Choo said tensely. "Dvornik said there aren't any vampires in there."

I popped the door open. "I didn't say they were in here now. Just that they were in here at some point."

"Give me a second," Choo said. "Just in case." From his bag he removed a metal cylinder about the length of a standard-size flashlight and three or four times as wide. It was white with bright red Japanese letters crisscrossing it. The top of the cylinder had a folding tab that Choo pulled out and then up.

"It's a refillable steam canister," he explained, tossing the object into the house and shutting the door. "This one is full of compressed holy water. We'll be able to walk through it no problem, but for any vampires, it ought to be like getting caught in an acid cloud."

After a few seconds I could hear a hissing sound emerging from beyond the door. "Nice," I commented, and meant it. "Will it fill the whole house?"

"No," he said shortly, removing another cylinder from the bag. "One of these will fill up an area about the size of a living room. Give this one two minutes to stop spewing and another minute to let the steam settle after that."

I nodded. "How did you meet Sig?" I asked.

"We got a mutual friend," Choo said. "And I'll die before I tell you that person's name because you're some kind of freaky-ass half-monster thing and I don't know you from nothing, so don't ask."

Actually, he stopped after "We got a mutual friend." The rest was said too, but it was communicated nonverbally.

We didn't fill up the rest of the three minutes with a lot of talk.

It wasn't like a London fog when we opened the door. The air was a little damp, but visibility was normal. The living room was decorated with a big Confederate flag and pictures of NASCAR events mixed in among photos where everyone had a beer or a cigarette in their hand and was trying to look excited. A rectangular metal box with a glass front had been hung on the wall, but instead of a fire extinguisher there was a can of beer in it, the words "In case of emergency, break glass" painted on the outside.

I pulled my wakizashi from the canvas bag slowly.

Choo pulled a sawed-off shotgun out of his bag. I smelled salt. The Catholic Church doesn't just bless holy water—it also makes a sacramental out of salt, though not as commonly. You can pack shotgun shells with blessed salt the same way some people pack them with rock salt, and the resulting ammo will hit vampires like a blast of acid.

Choo repeated his trick with three more steam canisters as we swept through the house, removing wall panels and examining interior spaces, checking for any inexplicable presences. He unscrewed the air vents and peered around in them using mirrors on extendable rods while I checked out the fridge and washer and dryer. The washer and dryer were both full; the refrigerator wasn't. Making our way to the bedrooms, we found the other side of the homemade plywood trapdoor that I'd seen in the basement. It was in the central hallway and poorly concealed by a rug. We slid the plywood aside but didn't say anything as Sig looked up at us, illuminated by red flare light. She appeared sinister and otherworldly and preoccupied.

"I know you're not a plumber, but...do you have stuff in that bag for getting into pipes?" I asked Choo quietly.

He gave me a dubious look. "What you got in mind?"

"Check out the bathroom," I said, and left it at that. The smell of Clorox coming from there was so strong that it felt like my nose hairs were shriveling.

Choo grunted unhappily but obliged, and I went back to check out the main bedroom more thoroughly. There was a personal computer in there, and I wanted to see what I could see.

I had been tooling around Steve Ellison's browser and Internet options for about ten minutes when Sig came up the ladder. "Sig," Choo called from the bathroom. "Get in here."

Choo, good old friendly nonjudgmental Choo, had found something in the bathroom I had pointed him toward and then waited for someone else to come in rather than call me over. Maybe I shouldn't have made that comment about killing people. I've never been good at small talk.

When I joined them Choo was crouched in the bathtub. He had removed the drain cover, and half a dozen clotted clumps of hair and flesh were on a towel laid out on the floor beside him. The water collected around the drain was red.

"Do you see that hole?" he was saying to Sig, nodding upward.

She looked. From over her shoulder I could see a hole where something big had been screwed into the ceiling. Sig's shoulders hunched and her head went back down. "That explains the marks on their ankles," she said quietly.

Choo didn't hear her. He held up one of the stiff tendrils of hair and dried blood. "I'm thinking they hung people over the bathtub from the ceiling by a hook and bled them out like they were butchering hogs," he said grimly.

Sig looked at me. "Did you tell him about the bodies?"

I shook my head. Maybe Choo wasn't the only one who had to brush up on teamwork skills.

She turned to Choo. "When the vampires were done, they buried the bodies under the house."

"I didn't see any blood stored in the refrigerator," I told her. "I haven't seen any other kinds of refrigeration units or coolers around here either."

Choo interjected. "Is that wrong?" He was watching the dawning comprehension on Sig's face warily.

"Vampires don't need to feed every night, and they don't need to drain a human when they do it either," Sig explained. "It's more like putting oil in a car than it is a human being eating their normal amount of food in blood. If John is right about the amount of bodies under this house, the vampires have been taking a lot more blood than they needed just to survive. So where is it?"

Choo swore angrily. It was the only indication I'd seen that any of this was getting to him. "This isn't their base, is it?"

"This used to be Steve Ellison's house," Sig said grimly. "But I think he was one of the vampires sleeping in the attic space above Faulhaber's apartment complex. The vampires were just using this place as a...what? Butcher shop?"

"That fits with what I found too," I told them. "Come here for a second."

Sig and Choo followed me back to the bedroom, where I sat down and showed them what I'd found on the computer. "I haven't been doing anything fancy here," I said. "Just seeing what comes up in the search history. I've only gotten to *B*."

"Somebody likes their porn," Choo commented, reading down the list of phrases with references to babes, bikinis, and bimbos.

"Skip to the word *blood*," I said quietly.

They did. It was quite a search query list. Blood bags. Blood banks. Blood coagulants. Blood clotting. Blood diseases. Blood donors. Blood draining. Blood regeneration. Blood restoration rates. Blood storage. Blood transfusion. Blood transport. Blood types. And farther down, after lots of references involving bodies and boobs, there were also references to bottling wine and butchering.

"This is worse than we figured," I said. "One of the vampires we haven't met yet spent a lot of time at this computer. I'm pretty sure it was a female—it wore a lot of perfume, anyway. And it was much smarter than Steve Ellison."

"I've been wondering about that ever since you mentioned it," Sig said. "Smarts, I mean. If there are as many bodies under this house as you say there are, this hive has been active a lot longer than two weeks."

Oops. I could have told her that. I'd known this operation was at least a few months old the moment I'd opened the crawl space and gotten hit by that blast of decay and decomposition.

"And they weren't just abducting locals either," Sig continued. "They must have been taking people from other towns and cities and bringing them here. Clayburg just isn't big enough for this kind of body traffic to go unnoticed."

"But you did notice it," Choo pointed out.

"Yes, and very quickly after locals started disappearing too," Sig said impatiently. "That's my point. For some reason, this hive's hunting pattern changed."

"I think I know why," I said. "I've smelled four new vampire scents, and they haven't been in this house in a while."

Sig raised her eyebrows. "As in a couple of weeks?"

I met her gaze levelly. "Something like that."

"OK, what are you two talking about?" Choo demanded. "Don't go looking all significant at each other. This is my first vampire hunt."

"We're thinking that the original hive split into two different groups a couple of weeks ago," Sig informed him. "That's why there were only four mattresses in the den above Faulhaber's place. That's why their hunting pattern changed."

"Something's been off about this from the start," I added. "I couldn't figure out how a moron like Steve Ellison lasted long enough to form a hive. But if he broke off from a larger hive where a smarter vampire was helping him survive, it makes more sense."

"Or maybe the smarter vampire broke off from Steve," Sig said. "Maybe he turned her, and she started struggling for power as soon as she realized how limited he was."

"Maybe," I said. "It would explain all the weird discrepancies."

Choo sighed theatrically.

"Like turning the crawl space under the house into a private cemetery," I elaborated. "That was smart. Dumping the dirt outside in the public common area? That was lazy and stupid."

Choo didn't look convinced.

Sig pitched in. "Pretend you're a smart vampire for a second, Choo. You've been draining bodies in your bathtub, and you want to build a trapdoor to the basement below so that you won't have to carry the bodies outside when you're done with them."

"OK," said Choo.

"How would you do it?" Sig asked him. "Think about it."

"I guess I'd cut a hole in one of the closet floors in one of the bedrooms," he said slowly.

"Right," I said. "Some out-of-the-way place where people wouldn't walk much and you could cover it up with shoes or dirty clothes or something."

Sig vaulted off the bed and marched into the hallway, pointing at the hole in the floor. "Look at this, Choo! Some moron didn't even use a saw. He just punched a hole in the floor right outside the bathroom because he was too lazy to do any work or carry the bodies any further than he had to!"

Sig walked around the hole, demonstrating how hard it was to get around to the bathroom or the far bedroom now. "They had this big awkward ugly hole that everybody had to step around, and they didn't even conceal it very well. They put plywood over it because they either didn't know how to build a trapdoor or they were too lazy."

"You're saying the smart one would have done a better job," Choo said.

"That's right," I agreed. "A smart vampire was coming up with bright ideas. A dumbass vampire took advantage of those ideas but kept screwing them up because it was too lazy or too stupid to do them right."

"So why didn't the smart vampire kick his ass or kill him?" Choo said.

"Because the smart vampire wasn't in charge," Sig speculated. "It could make suggestions, but it must have been weaker than the dumb vampires, either physically or socially."

"This isn't usually how hives work," I said for Choo's benefit.

"Usually an older, more experienced, smarter vampire is in charge. No new vampires are made without the boss's permission, and when a new vampire gets turned, the hive explains the realities of how to survive to it. Sometimes vampires will break off and become loners, but lone vampires who can't adapt or control themselves wind up getting hunted. Idiots don't last."

"But sometimes the checks and balances get thrown out of whack," Sig added. "Like when the knights raid a hive and kill the older, more experienced vampires. You might have a few survivors who are newbies and don't know the ropes running around, left to their own devices with no clear leader."

"Or a vampire might crawl out of the ground, and there's no one there to supervise because the vampire who made it was killed," I said. "Like the one we found today. That vampire might try to start a hive of its own with no real idea how to go about it. It might turn some dumbass friends from its former life, and they might start doing dumbass things."

"Sounds like you're both getting too much from not much to me," Choo grumbled.

"Want to bet?" Sig challenged. "Loser pays for pizza."

Choo made a *pssshhht* sound. "The way you eat?"

Sig grinned briefly, then refocused. "So if we're right, there was a power struggle, and Ellison either killed the smart vampire and its friends in the hive, or the smart vampire figured out that Ellison was going to get them all destroyed sooner or later and ran away with a couple of vampires that it convinced to go along."

"Right," I said. "Which is why Ellison started screwing up and hunting easy prey locally as soon as he was making decisions on his own again. The vampire who had been acting as his safety brake was gone."

Choo leveled an index finger at me. "What you mean is, you killed the dumbass vampires who were making sloppy mistakes, and now there might be a smart one on the loose who's going to be a lot harder to catch."

"You're welcome," I said sourly.

A grin flashed across his face, bitter, brief, and unrepentant.

"It makes sense that the smart vampire was a woman." Sig's voice was reflective.

Choo snorted.

"Is that some kind of sexist statement?" I asked her.

Sig scowled at us. "Any vampire is strong enough to do its own digging, but this one let the dumb males do a bad job of it instead. I'll bet we're looking at a vampire who got in the habit of letting men do the physical work in its previous life. Maybe she was used to hanging around men who were bigger and dumber than she was and letting them think they were in charge."

"I still think you're being sexist," Choo said teasingly. "You're not a sexist pig. You're a sexist Sig."

I smiled slightly.

Sig turned on Choo and got up in his face a little, poking his chest with her index finger. "Tell me this, Mr. Exterminator. Do you know why people who know what they're talking about call vampire groups *hives*?"

"I just figured it was because they were dangerous to kick over," he said warily. From the way he was rubbing his chest, that index finger had left a bruise.

Sig shook her head. "It's because the biggest and most powerful groups are almost always ruled by queens."

Choo's mouth opened before he realized that he didn't have anything to say.

"Either way," I said, tapping the screen in front of me. "I don't like where this smart vampire's mind was going."

Sig came up closer and put her hand on my shoulder as she leaned down to look at the computer screen again. Her breath was warm on the side of my face and smelled like peppermint. "What do you see?"

I shifted in my seat awkwardly and pointed at some of the terms on the query list. "Blood transfusion? Blood restoration rate? Why would you have to worry about transfusions or how often somebody can donate blood if you're just going to kill them and drain their carcass?"

Sig's hand tightened on my shoulder. It wasn't painful, but I could tell that she really was stronger than I was. Vampire strong.

"Aw hell," Choo whispered, seeing it. Maybe exterminators are used to thinking in terms of parasites.

The vampire was thinking of keeping people alive as a constant food source. This has been done before, obviously, but usually vampires with more experience use their glamours to seduce people into becoming walking blood banks for them willingly, often with a promise of eventual immortality. The vampires get someone to pay their bills and guard them during the day this way as well, and there's much less risk of discovery involved. Plus, it's one of the options for gathering blood that is tolerated by knights. It sucks (literally) for whoever gets chosen to play Renfield to the vampire's Dracula, but the Pax isn't about enforcing morality; it's about ensuring discretion. And let's face it, humans willingly subjugate themselves to others all the time: to pimps, parents, drugs, abusive partners, asshole employers, deadbeat lovers, children, peer groups, etc.

Either way, based on what we'd seen, I suspected that this hive was thinking more in terms of taking and keeping prisoners. They had all the transfusion equipment they needed built into their gums; they wouldn't be investigating other means of blood withdrawal and storage unless they were interested in setting up their own personal blood bank.

"This smart female vampire we're talking about," I mused. "If she exists, she's a nasty piece of work even as vampires go."

Choo snorted a no-kidding-genius kind of a snort.

"I'm just saying," I said. "Anybody smart enough to come up with this operation is smart enough to figure out easier ways to feed. When you get right down to it, all a vampire has to do is take a little blood from a hard-to-spot place and hypnotize someone into forgetting it ever happened. There's no need to do all this when they've got Craigslist and online dating services."

"That's true," Sig agreed. "Vampires are narcissists and sociopaths. Even the smartest ones usually use their brains to figure out the route of most pleasure with least effort."

"This one either has a lot of hostility," I said, "or has ambitions we don't know about. Why does she need so much blood?"

Sig snapped out her cell phone and hit a button on her speed dial. "Stanislav!" Sig said, straightening up and taking her hand off my shoulder. "We need you."

My sharper-than-average ears heard him ask if she was in trouble, and the van door was already opening in the background.

"No," said Sig impatiently. "We have a computer that needs coaxing."

He hung up.

"Click on that e-mail site," she said, turning back to me and pointing at an icon in the top window.

I obliged. "It could be Steve Ellison's e-mail service," I reminded her.

"That's why we need Stanislav," she informed me. "Sometimes he can tap into the psychic impressions left behind by a person, and his hands will automatically type the same pass-words and names that the person did when they were sitting in the same place on the same computer. Sometimes he can type out entire e-mails."

I made an appreciative grunt. "What about that tech guy you gave the cell phone to..."

I trailed off as Dvornik stormed into the house. I stood up and made room for him at the computer, and somehow he still managed to shove past and shoulder-check me as he came into the room and sat down. It was a weak shoulder check, though. His face was haggard and pale as he looked at the screen truculently.

"What do you..." He paused and coughed a feeble cough that turned into a violent series of hacking ones, his shoulders shaking. The guy really did not look well. "What do you need now?"

"We need some of your magic," Sig informed him, kneading his shoulders. His spine eased under her touch, and his attitude seemed to thaw slightly. "Can you get into that e-mail account, or have you spread yourself too thin already?"

Dvornik eyed me balefully, clearly wishing that Sig hadn't asked him that question in front of me. If Sig honestly didn't want him to overtax himself, she clearly didn't understand male psychology.

Dvornik grunted, then slowly, hesitantly, put his fingers over the keyboard without touching any of the keys. We all stayed quiet. I could hear his breath go shallow and even, then his heartbeat. His body took on the pose of a master pianist poised over his instrument. Suddenly his fingers plunged down onto the keyboard, pulled by some magnetic current. His back arched, sharp cracks popping from his spine as if he were a log on a fire. A gargle escaped from him and he bit down on his tongue so violently that blood leaked from both corners of his mouth. His head thrashed back and forth and his shoulders hunched and unhunched.

From the way Sig and Choo were cursing, this wasn't standard operating procedure. Finally Stanislav's eyes rolled up in their sockets and he collapsed.

Sig yelled his name and dropped down to her knees on the floor next to him.

I hate show-offs.

~12~

ALL THE LONELY PEOPLE

I was back behind the bar at Rigby's at ten o clock that night. I was planning on ditching my Trevor Barnes identity soon, but the slight possibility that vampires might come check out the place where their former hive mates had died had kept me from quitting right away. It was Friday, which meant that Dave insisted on tending bar with me although it wasn't that much busier than a Thursday. I think he just wanted to have somewhere to go on the opening night of the weekend, and someone to go there with. Dave was a sixty-eight-year-old widower, a bland-faced man with a midsize potbelly. He had gray hair and a gray life, and I think the main reason he bought a bar when he retired was that he wanted to be colorful. That sounds harsh, and I'm not trying to be mean. I like Dave.

There were five guys and three young ladies at the round table—the only circular table in the place—who were getting a little rowdy. It was nothing mean-spirited; in the absence of a live band and in the presence of a jukebox that played country-western songs, they had decided to make their own entertainment. Basically, they were just having an animated conversation, and every time someone said something toast-worthy, one person would repeat it, shouting it out, and then they would all laugh and shout whatever it was and clap and drink. So far they were being amusing and livening up the joint; in another three or four rounds we'd see.

This time it was Ted Cahill who walked into the bar and all up in my business. He was alone, and he seemed a little bemused as he looked around, probably wondering if he'd wandered into a Cracker Barrel by mistake. He still had on the same jacket he'd worn that morning. It looked kind of stupid with the collared pink fabric shirt and dungarees, but it did the same barely adequate job of hiding his gun.

I indicated the spot at the bar where Sig had sat the night before. Cahill nodded and made his way over there.

"That guy's a friend of mine," I told Dave. "Is it OK if I talk to him for a minute?"

Dave surveyed the crowd doubtfully. I only call it a crowd to be polite, by the way. Dave, though, was an optimist. To him, the bar was half full.

"He's a cop," I said. "They hang around pubs a lot. If he likes it here, maybe he'll bring some friends along next time."

I was pushing Dave's buttons for all I was worth—hell, I'd even remembered to call the place a pub. "Sure," he said, magnanimous in retreat. "Talking to the customers is part of your job."

"You hear that?" Tracy said to me. Tracy was a honey blonde who was sitting at the bar and celebrating being fired from a manager's position at Dollar Mart. She had nice eyes and full breasts that hadn't started to sag and full hips that had started to thicken. Her skin was unwrinkled but looked like it might crack from excess makeup and time spent in a tanning booth.

"Come back soon," Tracy called after me as I moved down the bar.

Cahill greeted me warmly. "I get my drinks free, right?"

"Huh," I said. "I guess you really are a cop."

"One of Clayburg's finest," he agreed, settling on the stool with practiced ease. "Give me a draft."

I obliged, and he watched skeptically as I drew him a beer. He seemed to have a hard time believing that I really was a bartender. I didn't take it personally. I had the same problem myself. I watched as he took a sip.

"Shouldn't you be polishing something?" he demanded.

"I am," I said. "My manners. That's why I haven't told you where to put that free drink yet, you pushy bastard."

He laughed and removed a wad of folded-up papers from inside his jacket and tossed them onto the bar in front of me. "Go ahead," Cahill said. "It's the juvie file of that other vampire who was using Ellison's computer. Parth couldn't get a real name off her e-mail registration, but I got a print that wasn't Steve Ellison's off the computer keyboard and came up with this."

Parth was an Indian name. Was this "Parth" Sig's mysterious tech guy or a cop that Cahill worked with?

I unfolded the photocopied papers slowly. A picture of a young girl with pronounced cheekbones, frizzy brown hair, and dead eyes was in the top left corner of the first one.

"Your mystery vampire is a seventeen-year-old high school dropout," Cahill said quietly. "Her name is Anne Marie Padgett. She went missing in Tennessee a year ago."

I was scanning the pages. "Not for the first time, apparently."

Cahill snorted. "No. Her biological mother's a drug addict serving time for another year and a half, and her biological father is anybody's guess. Anne Marie was taken away from Mom when she was eight. Since then she's spent as much time in the juvenile detention system as she has in foster care."

"So how hard are people looking for her?" I asked.

"Fairly hard, actually," Cahill said with a small smile. "Ever since her last foster family was found in pieces all over their home six months ago."

I absorbed that information thoughtfully while noticing that Anne Marie's IQ was listed on the second page. It was genius-level.

"Our smart vampire," I said.

"Probably," Cahill agreed.

If she was turned when she was small and physically weak, it would explain why she might have a hard time controlling a bunch of macho morons, too.

"VIAGRA!" yelled the group at the round table, and they all applauded and drank.

I refolded the papers and shoved them into my jeans pocket. "By the way, do you think you could get some more police types to come by this place?"

"Not a chance," Cahill informed me matter-of-factly. "There's a bar up the street owned by an ex-cop."

Sorry, Dave. Cahill didn't say anything else for a while, just sat there with both elbows propped up on the edge of the bar and periodically drank his beer. In the background some country singer tried to convince a woman that she just needed a little whiskey to get a little frisky.

"That chick with big breasts wants you," Cahill said suddenly, staring at Tracy. "She keeps looking at you and giving me the stink-eye."

"She's got a hole in her life," I said. "And she's decided it's penis-shaped."

"So?" Cahill said, returning his attention to me. "You saving yourself for somebody else?"

I shot him a look. Now we were getting to it. "Just say whatever you have to say about Sig and get it over with," I advised.

"All right," Cahill replied. "I want you to take Sig away from Dvornik."

I stared at him.

"I watched you two this morning," he said. "And I think you've got a shot. She likes you, and it's obvious you like her. Plus, you got all that stuff in common."

I kept staring.

"Like, you're both freaks who still think you're human," Cahill amplified. "And you won't grow old on each other."

Staring was working out really well for me.

"AUSTRALIA!" roared the round table happily.

"Come on, are you telling me you haven't thought about it?" Cahill prodded.

"Are you serious?" I finally asked cautiously.

"NO, I'M NOT SERIOUS YOU FUCKING MORON!" Cahill yelled, slamming his empty beer glass down on the bar for emphasis before lowering his voice again. "Sure, you're all lean and muscly and square-jawed and shit, and you're funny under all that attitude. But Sig's not the kind of woman who's going to have a fling with a drifter."

"Ah..." I began.

"No, you're worse than a drifter, you're some kind of fugitive!" Cahill went on. "What do you want to do, ask her to go on the run with you? Even if she said yes, which is doubtful, what kind of life would that be for her? And how would you keep a low profile with a six-foot-tall blonde timber truck running loose in china shops everywhere you went?"

"Uhm," I said, nodding at Dave to let him know it was OK.

"And even if that weren't true," Cahill went on, "how would you two get away from Dvornik? The guy's a psychic, you jack wagon!"

When I finally started to say something, Cahill held his

right palm up to cut me off. "Yeah, I know, you're some kind of tough guy. You can kill vampires when you have to. So what? Dvornik isn't a killer, he's a murderer. I've been around a lot of sociopaths and trust me, any conscience that guy had burned out a long time ago. Sig and this geas thing you guys keep talking about are the only things keeping that asshole halfway human. And don't give me any bullshit about how that's ironic either. I don't care."

Cahill looked at me then.

"The..." I started to say.

"Yeah, I know," he interrupted tiredly. "She and Dvornik aren't going to last much longer, anybody can see that, but Sig hasn't admitted it yet. She's stubborn and loyal and she's invested a lot of time in that piece of shit."

"But if he..." I began.

"She can't see it," Cahill declared promptly. "She's tried so hard and spent so much time making excuses for him that she can't see what he really is anymore. Trust me, when their relationship finally falls apart, he is not going to take it well, and a guy in your situation is not going to want to be around for him to blame."

"Maybe..." I said.

Cahill cut me off. "What, you're going to kill him? If you did that, Sig would never forgive you, and you'd have a bunch of psychic vampire hunters with scary accents and long last names with no vowels coming after your ass... and that's in addition to all those knight guys."

Cahill sadly looked down at his beer, which had become empty at some point during his... what? Rant? Lecture?

"I'm really glad we had this conversation," I said dryly, taking the glass away and refilling it.

"THE G-SPOT!" yelled the peanut gallery at the round table. That was my signal to get involved. Dave shot me a questioning glance, so I nodded and told Cahill I'd be back and circled around the bar.

"It's about time," Tracy said as I walked toward her. "Might as well sit down and have a drink while you're on this side." She patted the stool next to hers invitingly.

I stopped for a moment. "You're hot," I told her. "But I'm hung up on somebody else at the moment. Sorry."

I didn't look back to see her reaction, but I could hear her swearing under her breath all the way over to the round table.

"I have a party game for you," I told the big kid with the goatee and the football jersey. I say *kid*, but he was as old as I looked. I had him and his friends pegged for people who had graduated from Stillwaters University but were still hanging around Clayburg, holding down whatever marginal jobs they'd gotten to see them through college. They probably had a sense that they should be getting on with their lives but were ignoring it for as long as they could. The leader's eyes were fogged over with drink, but they held a shrewd glint. He seemed like the sort of person who didn't mean any real harm but preferred chaos to boredom or introspection. He would push limits just to see if he could, further than he should be able to most of the time because he was smart and charismatic and ballsy, and every now and then he would push things too far and blame someone else when the shit hit the fan.

I could tell that I'd picked the right one to talk to because the entire table quieted down to listen.

The alpha male failed to see any sign of fear or nervousness or hesitation or bullshit on me or in me, and he didn't know what that meant, but he knew that he didn't trust it. That's one of the qualities of a natural leader: good threat-awareness. He held up his palms placatingly. "It's all right, man. We're not causing trouble."

"Neither am I," I said. "I want you all to have a good time

and keep spending money. That's why I want to play a game. It's called 'Identify the Off-Duty Cop.'"

That made him pause. He actually looked around the bar, stopped when he saw Cahill, and stared at him for a long moment. "The guy you've been talking to," he said.

"That's the owner's brother," I lied. "It's just something to keep in mind."

He raised his glass. "TO THE POLICE!" he toasted.

His table laughed and raised their glasses and shouted, "TO THE POLICE!"

I winked at him and walked back across the bar. The leader had saved face, but he was smart enough to keep his table from crossing the line now.

Tracy didn't say anything as I went by.

"Sorry about that," I told Cahill.

"You outed me," he noted.

"I did," I agreed.

Cahill glanced over at Tracy and caught her sneering at us before she looked away.

"How much you want to bet that I can swoop in and tap that in another drink or two now that you've broken her poor drunk heart?" he asked.

"That is a wedding ring you're wearing, right?" I asked him. "You didn't just put it on because you wanted to wear something pretty?"

"My wife and I have a misunderstanding," he said.

It was a mildly amusing line, and I liked him less for it.

Cahill drained his glass and pushed it toward me. I obligingly drew him another draft and set it in front of him. "That's your last one," I told him. "You were hanging around Sig this morning, so you might be a target."

"I know the drill," he said testily. "That's why I'm here."

I looked at him. "I thought you were here to talk about Sig."

He waggled his hand back and forth. "You can talk about smart vampires all you want; there's a chance some of those things will come after you again tonight, and Sig won't be here to back you up this time. I wanted to check on you."

"OK," I said.

"Because, you know, Sig's busy," Cahill added.

"OK," I said.

Cahill spelled it out. "Having makeup sex with Dvornik."

I didn't say that was OK. I also didn't ask him if he'd ever seen a real vampire before, or make any pointed comments about what he expected to do if any heat seekers did show up. I contented myself with an observation. "If any do show up, I'll have a lot more than a bottle of holy water and a knife this time." It was the truth. I'd spent two hours driving up and back to a storage unit a few towns over just so I could drop some stuff from my house off and pick my custom-made guitar case up; in fact, the guitar case was only ten feet away from me, leaning against the west wall. It had a guitar in it and everything. If it had a false bottom and weighed about fifty pounds more than it should, that was my business.

"So what do you think?" Cahill pushed. "About what I was saying about Sig."

"About her having makeup sex with Dvornik?" I asked.

He made a waving-away gesture. "You know what I'm asking."

"I think I've known Sig for twenty-four hours," I said. "And it doesn't take that long to know she's something special, but it's still just twenty-four hours. I also think I'm leaving this town about ten hot seconds after the last vampire is staked, for reasons you already know."

Cahill sighed and took a deep pull on his last beer.

"And I think you're the one in love with her," I said.

Cahill laughed softly. It wasn't a happy sound. "That's why you should listen to me. I know what I'm talking about."

I didn't say anything.

"I thought she was just another nutjob the first time she showed up at my desk talking about being a psychic," Cahill said reminiscently. "I probably would have blown her off if she wasn't gorgeous, but I figured if she was crazy, I might have a chance of getting a blowjob. By the time I figured out she was for real and off-limits, it was too late to run away."

"That's kind of how our world works," I said.

"The truth is," Cahill said, not giving any indication of having heard me, "my wife is probably cheating on me, and I don't blame her or care. I'm just waiting for her to leave me so I won't have to pay as much alimony. I spend every day thinking about a beautiful woman who's not even a woman, and if she was, she'd be way out of my league. And being Sig's friend isn't enough, but it's something."

I wondered how long he'd been waiting to tell this to someone. Cahill's expression was unguarded for a moment, and his eyes were wistful. "She and Dvornik probably establish a connection with the local police force every time they move into a new town. With her looks and her whole I-can-see-dead-people thing, it's probably always a male homicide detective too. It doesn't matter."

"You're still not getting another free drink," I said.

He laughed again.

I poured him a cup of coffee and added, "You should be telling this stuff to your wife."

"Fuck you," he said with no discernible emotion.

"OK," I acknowledged.

"This is good coffee," Cahill said when I came around to check on him a little later. "Is it a special blend or something?"

"No," I said. "You just have to clean your coffeemaker every once in a while and use trial and error. It's not that hard to learn how much coffee from a particular brand goes right with the specific coffeemaker you're using. For the one here, I have a big spoon that I use because I couldn't get the proportions right with the small plastic scoop that came with the can."

"You're weird," Cahill commented. "You know that?"

"Coffee is one of the few constants in my life," I explained. "No matter where I go, no matter how crappy a day I'm having, no matter what kind of mood I'm in, coffee is always there to make me feel a little better."

"You really are a lonely son of a bitch, aren't you?" Cahill observed.

I grimaced. "I live like a Nazi war criminal or a serial killer... like I have something to be ashamed of."

"Do you?" Cahill asked.

"I was raised to believe that werewolves are demon-infected, and I am one," I said. "I know I don't change into a wolf, but come on. I can smell that you had pork and corn and broccoli for dinner a couple of hours ago. If you shot me in the heart with a lead bullet, I'd live."

I leaned forward and looked him in the eye and snarled. "This is the first time in almost twelve years that I've been able to be myself. And I have to leave and go back to hiding who I am and watching everything I say as soon as this vampire thing is over."

Cahill tilted back slightly. "See, that's what I'm talking about. One second you're sounding like a metrosexual talking about coffee preparation, the next you look like you're going to rip my heart out and eat it."

I backed off. "You asked."

He nodded. "You said this was the first time in twelve years. Who were you with twelve years ago?"

I thought about not telling him, but to hell with it. "I lived with a woman who knew everything."

Cahill looked at me steadily. "How did it end?"

I had already told Sig. I didn't feel like going into it again. "Badly," I said tightly. "Let's just leave it at that."

He ignored this advice. "But you..."

"When I tell you to leave something alone this close to a full moon," I growled, "you leave it alone." The tips of my fingers itched, and they wanted to be on his throat. If I'd had sharp canines, they would have been showing.

Cahill held his palms up. "OK," he said, meaning the opposite but willing to postpone the conversation.

We didn't talk about anything significant after that. After a slightly awkward silence, Cahill asked a few questions about what Dvornik had looked like while we hauled his unconscious body out of the vampire lair and back to his studio, about how Sig had reacted, about when and where we were all supposed to get together again. I asked him a few questions about how Clayburg looked from a cop's point of view, and he got me to tell him a few things about the Knights Templar that didn't violate any oaths on my part.

An hour later he left with Tracy.

I watched them leave and thought that Cahill was right: I really ought to be polishing something.

~13~

GEAS, THAT'S TOO BAD

Sig was waiting for me when I got off work, sitting shotgun in a Nissan Versa parked outside the ass end of Rigby's. The driver was the short stocky woman who had said the blessing and sprinkled holy water in the alley. April nights are chilly in the Blue Ridge, but this woman was dressed for winter, wearing thick blue mittens and a puffed-up pink parka and a green beanie with thick earflaps. What little I could see of her face was obscured by a thick pair of round mirrored glasses, so all I could really tell was that she had healthy pink cheekbones and a strong jaw.

They both stepped out of the car to greet me. It was at this point that I saw the plain but huge silver cross—at least nine inches long—hanging from the driver's neck, draped outside her parka.

"It's three thirty in the morning," I growled. "I'm nocturnal. What's your excuse?"

"I don't need an excuse," Sig snapped back, adding a few words that you can't say on network television. She obviously wasn't in a great mood either. "My *reason* for being here is that a certain pain in the ass needs to get a cell phone."

Not only can cell phones be tracked and listened in on, but black arts can do things with cell phones using sympathetic magic that scare the bejeezus out of me. "Cell phones annoy me," I said. "And speaking of annoying me, why are you here again?"

Sig opened her mouth to say something, but her friend stepped around the hood of her car and got between us, holding out her right mitten. "I'm Molly Newman," she said. "I've heard a lot about you."

I stared rudely at her hand for a moment. The reason we hold up our right palms to wave hello is that this is how people used to signify that they weren't holding a knife in their fighting hand (this is also one of the reasons lefties were considered sneaky and untrustworthy). We clasp right hands on the same principle, and I don't do it as lightly as normal citizens. Bad mood or not, though, the awareness of being an asshat was starting to creep in around the edges of my perception. I took her hand grudgingly. "Then you know I'm John," I said. "Your existence has been kept secret from me."

"Oh for God's sake," Sig exploded. "What is your problem?"

"I want you, and it pisses me off," I said. "Because your friend Cahill just reminded me that I'm not allowed to have things like relationships that might actually mean something in my life."

Well, maybe I didn't use those exact words. Maybe what I actually said was, "Forget it. I told you, it's a full moon tomorrow night."

"Well, get over your pre-moon syndrome," Sig retorted. "We've got more important things to worry about."

I felt the geas yank at me like a fishing hook—one that was attached to the chakra behind my navel. It was a sharp, experimental tug that subsided quickly. Apparently I was being given more line.

"What's happened?" I asked cautiously.

Molly cleared her throat. "Maybe we could talk about this in my car?"

"That depends. Where are you going?" This was just a formality on my part. If they had intended to sell me out to the Knights Templar, I was already standing in the ideal ambush site. It was about twenty-four hours too late to play it smart.

"We're taking you to meet another member of our little coffee klatch," Sig informed me, still not asking. I was beginning to realize that the pushy thing was a permanent part of her personality. "Our tech guy. He wants to meet you."

In other words, there had been a disturbing new development. Let me explain something about my geas. I have a little bit more leeway than most knights with regard to the magical pact that my ancestors entered into. For one thing, the geas was designed to protect supernatural creatures who aren't a threat to the Pax, and I'm one of those creatures... most of the time. For another, being a quasi-werewolf comes with its own powerful drives, and these sometimes pull in the opposite direction of the demands of my blood oath. These conflicting influences can cause a certain amount of insomnia, but they also give me a little more wiggle room in the free will department.

Before Sig told me that there had been a new development, I probably could have sneaked out of Clayburg with no consequences other than a mild headache. Now that there were hints that I'd be leaving a more serious problem behind though, I had to determine its nature or risk dealing with nightmares, migraines, and the kind of withdrawal symptoms that an addict goes through while detoxing. The geas does not give up easily.

Once, the geas actually made me blind. It lasted for two

weeks, and it was the only thing that kept me from going on a suicide run and hunting down and killing every knight I could find after Alison died.

"Sure," I said. "Can I put my guitar case in your trunk?"

I could.

Molly's car was untidy, but not in a public-health-violation kind of way. The backseat was covered with a salmon-colored bed sheet that smelled like dog, and there were a few empty plastic Diet Dr Pepper bottles in the back floor. A tower of CD cases was crammed precariously in the crack between the two front seats, and only the fact that they were jammed so tightly together kept the whole structure from collapsing.

As soon as Molly started the car engine, Harry Connick Jr. came on the CD player singing some song about Santa Claus. I ignored him.

"Pre-moon syndrome?" I said to Sig's shoulder. "PMS? Really?"

She smirked at me in the rearview mirror. "You don't like it?"

"That depends," I said. "Are you going to buy me chocolate and kiss my ass for the next couple of days?"

"You really are in a charming mood tonight," she observed. Was I imagining the droll emphasis on the *charming*?

"Sig," Molly chided, a certain note of impatience entering her voice as she turned onto Main Street. "Tell him."

"Tell me what?" I asked.

Sig told me. "Stanislav had a vision when he tried to tap into the psychic impression the female vampire left behind. He says we have to kill her now. He says she's bad news."

"Well duh."

"No," she said emphatically, turning in the seat to catch my eye. "Really bad news. The kind that only gets worse."

"Worse than what we saw today?" I asked skeptically.

"Same kind of bad but on a bigger scale," Sig amplified.

"You should try holding your spear when you say things like that," I noted. "Maybe wear a winged helmet and a fur cape too, stand on a mountain peak with a lightning-filled sky as a background. Molly, do you have any opera CDs in that—"

"Stanislav says our smart, newly turned vampire is a teenage girl named Anne Marie who likes shedding blood more than she likes drinking it," Sig interrupted impatiently. "He says that he's never gotten a reading as powerful as the one she left behind. He says that he had a vision of her being a black oak, burrowing down in time and spreading her roots beneath the years. The longer she lives, the deeper her evil will spread, and the harder she'll be to root out."

Mariah Carey came on the CD player, singing that song about how all she wanted for Christmas was you.

"OK, I know I've been a little rude," I said to Molly. "And I apologize. I really do. You seem like a good person, and you haven't done anything to me...you just caught me off guard on a bad night. But I really need to know...what's with the Christmas music? And the parka? And the beanie?"

"I'm celebrating Christmas," she told me.

"It's April," I pointed out, just in case this was necessary.

"Vampires scare me," she said reasonably. "And Christmas makes me happy."

"Oh," I said lamely. "OK."

We rode in silence for a time after that, or at least we didn't talk while Molly's homemade CD continued to play random pseudo-carols. A lot of the music blurred by, but I remember that Blues Traveler did a Christmas song at some point. So did Jonny Lang.

We were past the 81 southbound exit ramp and headed toward the higher elevations outside town when I finally spoke up over the "skating" song from the Charlie Brown Christmas special. "How sure a thing is Dvornik's vision?"

"He doesn't see the future very often," Sig said matter-of-factly. "Which is good because it takes a lot out of him. You saw that for yourself. Especially when a vision comes to him out of nowhere like today. But when he does get a precognitive flash, he's dead-on."

"And how did you get involved in all this?" I asked Molly. "Or is that too personal?"

"I used to be an Episcopal priest," Molly said. Sig turned slightly and smiled at whatever my expression looked like. "A few years ago Chauncey came to me asking me questions about exorcisms. He'd been hired to exterminate some family property that he was convinced was haunted."

"Why did he come to you?" I asked. "I thought the Episcopal Church was pretty lightweight in the exorcism department."

"There's kind of a don't ask, don't tell policy," she admitted. "They don't train priests for it in the seminaries, or have specially appointed priests like the Anglican and Catholic churches. The Book of Occasional Services refers to exorcism rites but doesn't talk about them specifically."

I nodded. I'd heard stories about a book that passed over the Atlantic when the Episcopalians and the Anglicans split... a book with a limited distribution, to which only bishops are allowed access. It's supposed to have a major rite of exorcism in it.

"But Molly went with Choo and checked the house out anyway," Sig said. Her voice was both rueful and affectionate.

"I had seen this show about an Episcopal priest named Andrew Calder who was very vocal about performing exorcisms," Molly explained. Her voice was detached, not defensive. "I wasn't sure what I believed, and it made me curious.

And all priests know a minor rite of exorcism. It's part of the baptism ceremony. And honestly, deep down I thought I was helping an emotionally troubled man, not walking into something truly supernatural."

"But you were," I said.

"But I was," Molly agreed cheerfully. "And I haven't been entirely right in the head since, if you want to know the truth."

Sig was quick to rush to Molly's defense. "When Molly holds a holy symbol, it packs a punch like nothing I've ever seen. I saw her knock a draugr back like it had been hit by a bus. Literally. She broke its neck just by holding a cross up. She can still make holy water by blessing it too."

They saw a draugr? I let that one go.

"But you're not an ordained priest anymore?" I asked. I was thinking of Choo and how he'd been complaining about being ordained in two or three different made-up religions and still unable to make holy water.

"I'm not a practicing priest," Molly said. "And your next question *is* too personal."

"OK," I said.

We went back to letting the music make all the noise for another five minutes or so. This time it was Molly who started speaking. "I had a nervous breakdown," she said. "I still performed my duties as a priest, but I felt like too much of a fake after that."

Sig patted Molly's arm and turned back to glare at me as if I were interrogating her friend ruthlessly. "Remember how I told you most ghosts aren't all the way in our world? She and Choo ran into an evil spirit. A fully sentient one."

I winced. Intelligent geists are the worst. They have a way of getting inside your head—well, not mine, because of the geas, but you know what I mean—and using your fears and insecurities like a piñata.

Molly ignored both of us. "When I first became a priest, it was really me up there in front of the congregation," she continued. "I kept a lot of thoughts and emotions to myself...I mean, of course I did...everybody has a secret self...but I was comfortable with it. But after I broke down, there was this gap between the me standing up there telling people how to live their life and the real me, and it made me feel terrible. I never stopped believing in God, but somehow that made needing Paxil worse. I was preaching about faith, and I couldn't trust God enough to sleep at night."

"You're being too hard on yourself," I said.

"That's what I tell her," Sig agreed.

"I'm OK," Molly said. "It was just time to express my faith in a different way."

"So you became a monster hunter to deal with your fear?" I asked.

"It's the only kind of therapy that works," Molly said. "Don't ask me why."

"I get it," I said. And I did. For a certain type of person, running toward the things that scare them is the only thing that gives them any sense of control. Anything else feels like living helplessly in fear. Molly looked and sounded like a soft-voiced meek little thing, but she was her own kind of warrior.

"'Take arms against a sea of troubles,'" I quoted, "'and by opposing end them.'"

"Exactly!" Molly smiled, pleased. "I like *Hamlet* too."

"Of course, that doesn't change the fact that it's spring, and I'm listening to Gwen Stefani singing 'Oi to the World,'" I noted.

"Hey," Molly protested mildly, turning up the volume. "This is No Doubt."

The road became narrow, winding, and dark as we threaded our way up a mountain that probably had a name like Lookout or Hightop. Every now and then I would get a glimpse of Clayburg's lights through breaks in the trees. Finally we pulled up to a walled gate that looked as out of place in that part of the Blue Ridge as a Bentley at a stock car race. The gates swung open as soon as Molly pulled up to them.

The road we were leaving was gravel and barely large enough for two cars to pass side by side, but the driveway was paved smooth and wide enough for three cars to fit comfortably. Fountains abounded on the estate to either side of us, set off by marble statues and sculpted topiary and bright lights.

"This is the home of a hacker?" I asked uneasily.

"I never said he was a hacker," Sig said. "Parth is a software mogul."

"And he lives in the mountains?" I asked. "And handles your tech for free?"

"Money doesn't mean anything to Parth," Molly said affectionately, despite the obvious displays of wealth on every side of us.

Sig was more cynical. "Parth helps us because he's an information addict, and one of the things he's researching is the supernatural. He learns as much from the questions we bring him as we do from his answers."

The house itself was as huge as I'd expected based on the front gate—it was a mansion, really—but the drive up had led me to expect something classical in design, something Greek or Gothic or Florentine. This sprawling monstrosity was distinctly modern. It wasn't so much one building as a compound, and the sections didn't blend geometrically. Separate wings might be blocky or towerlike or triangular, all of them connected by sections that were big enough to be residential dwellings in their own right. The only thing the different areas had in common was that all the roofs were covered with solar panels and wind turbines and small satellite dishes. It was god-awful ugly.

"What's with the dome?" I wondered. "Is that a gym or something?"

"An observatory," Molly corrected as she pulled up and parked. I shut up and followed.

The front door was opened by a pretty young Indian woman in a white bikini top and a sarong. She was round-faced and round-hipped, with long hair that wasn't bound in any way. Despite the hour, she seemed alert and friendly.

"Hey, Kimi," Sig said. "This is John."

I managed not to wince. I was going to have to remember to tell her not to toss my real name around anymore. At least she hadn't added "Charming."

"Parth is eager to meet you," Kimi told me, smiling without showing any teeth.

I just nodded.

The inside of the house was sweltering, the humid air filled with a thick cloying smell from some kind of incense. Sig and Molly had begun taking off their jackets before they even stepped inside, and they draped them on a rather ornate coat rack whose top looked like an octopus uncurling its tentacles. I left my jean jacket on. The knife sheathed at my side was plainly visible, but I wasn't comfortable enough to let Kimi see the Ruger Blackhawk holstered at the small of my back.

"Parth likes to keep his house hot," Molly told me. "He says it reminds him of home." Divested of her outer layers, she was short, compact, apple-cheeked, and cute. Her short hair was chestnut-brown.

"He keeps the whole place this warm?" I asked. "His heating bill must be massive in the winter."

Kimi smiled at me. "Parth doesn't stay here in the winter."

We were led down a long, large hallway whose walls were made of thick glass. Behind the walls were massive tanks full of salt water and various species of iridescent fish that I suspected were exotic. Marine biology isn't my thing.

The hallway led to a pentagonal room that seemed to serve as both large greeting room and hub: a circular area in the middle was full of bamboo furniture with brightly colored silk cushions and covers—couches, chairs, tables—and the room was surrounded by four large arched hallway openings. Small rounded pillows designed for sitting meditations were strewn out over the floor in a rough circle, and there was a gong in the middle of the room. Kimi led us east down a curving hall where several doors on either side were separated by large paintings. Their common theme seemed to be optical illusion.

At irregular intervals we would pass rooms with open doorways. One room was covered with brightly colored stamps. One room was filled with expensive-looking urns, and a crematory furnace was in the far corner. One room was filled with plastic action figures in their original packaging. One room had walls that were covered with paintings from floor to ceiling. One room was filled with busts and sculptures. Another was filled with long white cardboard boxes, and comic books in plastic sleeves covered the walls.

"The stamp room is one of my favorites," Molly confided.

"Parth likes to collect pretty things, doesn't he?" I said neutrally.

Despite the size of the house, there didn't seem to be a second floor; the hallway's ceiling was at least thirty to forty feet high for no reason that I could see. I was starting to feel like I was in a James Bond movie, except instead of Dr. No the villain was Dr. Seuss.

Spaced at regular intervals were small tables that held incense candles and lava lamps. I stopped to stare at one of the lamps.

"Parth loves lava lamps," Kimi said, smiling. "He says they're a metaphor for life."

"Does Parth take a very large hit off a hookah when he says things like that?" I wondered. My jacket was plastered to my body by sweat, and the incense was irritating my nasal passages. It occurred to me that incense could be used to mask more than the smell of marijuana.

"Shhh," Kimi admonished. "He'll hear you."

I looked around and down the long stretch of hall. I didn't see or smell or hear anyone except for somebody who was making a lot of splashing sounds about two hundred feet away. Something was definitely not quite right in Whoville. I almost asked if I could go back to the car and get my guitar case out of Molly's trunk.

Finally we came to the large three-tiered room the swimming sounds were coming from. On the lowest level was a swimming pool, but instead of having your standard boxy edges, the pool was an artificial lagoon sloping gradually into the second layer of the room, which was like a cove except that the stone-paved floor gradually flattened out and had drains in it. There were a lot of lounge chairs and small round tables in this area.

The east end of the cove had a layer of stairs that led up into an area that looked like a war room. There were nine large-screen televisions on different walls, and at least five large glass-topped tables whose edges looked like some kind of space-age black plastic and whose surfaces glowed and cast light on the ceiling. I looked at those a little more carefully. The plastic-encased legs were sunk into small recessions *in* the floor rather than *on* the floor, and I was pretty sure the glass surfaces of the tables were computer displays. The scattered light revealed small holes and seamed lines in the edges of the plastic table frames, power outlets and places where you could put flash drives and slots that probably slid out so that disks could be inserted. I'd be willing to bet that the tables transmitted to printers somewhere too.

Each table had several chairs around it. Some kind of high-tech conference tables. Or perhaps teleconference tables.

I could smell that the swimming pool on the lowest level, unlike the aquariums, was full of fresh water. A tall, thin, bald man of Indian origin and indeterminate age was swimming in it. He wasn't doing any kind of stroke that I recognized, but he was gliding through the water effortlessly. When we walked into the cove area, Kimi led us to the edge of the water, where a pile of white towels was stacked next to a cotton bathrobe. Parth disappeared under the water, then reappeared in front of us and began walking up the slope toward us so smoothly that it almost seemed like the water wasn't holding him back at all.

He was wearing a small tight blue bathing suit, his body lean and sinewy. He moved with fluid precision, watching me with dark eyes. "Molly, Sig," he said genially, bending down to pick up a towel. "Lovely to see you as always."

"You too," Sig said with an exaggerated eyebrow lift as he briskly rubbed himself dry with a towel.

He laughed and turned toward me. His face was narrow and bony, his eyes intense. I was watching carefully while his mouth moved, but I couldn't see his tongue. "And you must be the strange and wonderful hybrid Sig has told me about," he said.

"That's pretty ironic," I said. He was close enough now that I had his scent despite the incense, and I chose my words carefully. "Coming from a naga."

"I don't think so," he said, and from the pool behind him a twelve-foot wave gathered up and came crashing toward me.

∾14∾

COMING UP SNAKE EYES

A word about knightly training might be appropriate here. Being mere humans, knights have slower reflexes than most of the creatures they hunt. Because of this, brief pauses are a luxury that knights simply can't afford, and a lot of their training focuses on eliminating hesitation. Occasionally this leads to mistakes, but knights believe that it's better to err on the side of decapitation. When you need them, those unwasted moments are pearls beyond price.

Factor in that my reflexes are actually much faster than those of the knights who trained me to compensate for slower reflexes in the first place, and maybe it will explain why I caught Parth off guard even though he attacked me. I didn't stand there stunned by the impossibility of the wave that he brought crashing down on me, nor did I instinctively go limp and let it carry me back with its greater weight. I was already leaning forward as soon as the water level rose dramatically. By the time the wave surged to intercept me, I was turning my body into as thin and straight a line as possible and hurling myself like a spear toward Parth's knees, forced to aim low so that I could slice through the approaching wave beneath its breaking point.

Parth was as surprised as a cat who finds itself being attacked headlong by a mouse that it thought entrapped. Startled, he tried to step farther back into the wave that wasn't having any visible effect on him, but I grabbed his ankle as my hands broke through the back of the wave, then hung on and yanked his heel upward hard as the rest of my body was snatched back and dragged away from him again. Parth fell straight back and cracked his head hard on the floor, and the wave abruptly dispersed around me, collapsing in on itself as if a giant water balloon had just been burst.

We both began to scramble. I was still holding on to Parth's foot, and I yanked him back to the ground at the same time that I pulled myself to my knees. He lashed out at my hand with his other foot, but by that point I was on my feet and dragging him by his ankle as fast as I could while he vainly clawed at the wet stone with his hands, managing to cover twelve feet in this awkward fashion. Sig was walking beside us yelling something, but I was focusing on keeping Parth too disoriented to concentrate while getting him as far away from the water as possible.

Finally he twisted and pulled himself toward me, bending his knees and arching his back. I was bent over slightly, and his hands managed to reach the sides of my jacket and cling on with grim strength as he pulled himself closer to me. I didn't try to fight or grapple; instead, I let go of his leg and dropped down onto my butt, grabbing his arms while he held on to my jacket. Continuing with the motion, I managed to curl my legs in close to my body and plant my feet in his stomach while I rolled onto my back. Parth released my jacket in an attempt to avoid getting pulled over the top of me, but it was too late. At the apex of my roll, I went back on to my shoulders and straightened my legs, literally catapulting him through the air with greater-than-human strength and sending him over and off me, bouncing toward the stairs at the other side of the room. When we scrambled to our feet, I was between him and his artificial lagoon.

Sig was suddenly beside me, sticking an arm out across my chest as I lunged forward. It felt like a steel beam. I stopped, still watching Parth as he regained his equilibrium. Bronze scales began to emerge from under his skin and overlap, forming a type of epidermal chain mail. His pupils expanded until his eyes were solid black orbs, and his jaws elongated. His limbs and torso telescoped until he was at least seven feet tall, and I knew that if he opened his mouth, fangs longer and narrower than any vampire's would be revealed at each corner.

It actually could have been worse. Naga combat forms can be pretty freakish. I once met a naga who could turn his arms into long thick snapping snakes. I've seen illustrations of nagas who had the upper torsos of men and whose lower halves were long giant snake bodies ending in barbed tails.

For her part, Sig didn't seem impressed. "Don't kill him, John," she said angrily as she glared at Parth. "The idiot is just playing some kind of game with you."

"Maybe," I said, my voice shaking with adrenaline and rage. There are all kinds of conflicting stories about nagas—sometimes they're good, sometimes they're evil, sometimes they eat humans, sometimes they're ascetics who stick to seafood—but there are at least four points on which most stories agree: (1) Nagas live near water. (2) Nagas have forked tongues no matter what form they're using. (3) Nagas are avaricious collectors of knowledge and treasure. (4) It is never, ever a good idea to piss a naga off. The best-case scenario is that they'll just use their water-shifting abilities to cause drought or floods in your region. The worst-case scenario is...well...I was looking at it.

"Or maybe," I snarled, "he knows how much I'd be worth to the Knights Templar now that you've been telling my story to everyone you know."

"I only told people I trust. Parth isn't like that," Sig said, but her voice lacked 100 percent conviction. Molly was nowhere to be seen.

"Then get him to stop," I said grimly. "Or get out of my way."

"PARTH!" Sig barked angrily. "Cut it out!"

In answer, fog suddenly coalesced around us, so thick that I couldn't see six inches in front of my face, and I was under Sig's arm and running toward Parth before she could do more than grab the tail end of my wet jean jacket. She was left holding the entire jacket, cursing.

Parth tried to lose himself in his homemade cloud cover, first darting left, then up the stairs behind him to the next level, but I followed with my ears and nose. He was backpedaling and I was running forward, so I was close enough to see him as a silhouette within seconds, and by that time the silver steel knife was in my hand.

Suddenly the mist between our faces parted as if invisible hands had pulled open a set of window drapes. I found myself staring straight into his eyes, and for the briefest of moments I felt that itch I get behind my forehead when supernatural creatures try to dominate me mentally. I swished my knife past his nose to disrupt his concentration, careful not to actually nick him. Nagas have poisonous blood, and if I was going to risk getting some on me it wouldn't be for a slice. "Last chance to stop this," I growled.

In answer, the fog closed between our faces again, and fat

beads of water began to condense and gather on my face and crawl toward my nose and mouth.

I feinted, and he tried to trap my wrist as if it were holding a knife, but all that did was tell me that he couldn't see through the fog he'd summoned any better than I could.

My knife wasn't in my knife hand any more. I homed in on his throat and thrust the knife toward his carotid artery with my left hand instead.

Here's a little tip: when facing a humanoid being who regenerates rapidly—and nagas are at the top of that particular pyramid, regrowing entire lost limbs in less than a minute—go for the carotid artery and keep hacking or choking. You won't kill them, but all you have to do is interrupt the blood's flow to the brain long enough for them to pass out. Regeneration might repair damage, but it doesn't make you wake up from a nap any faster than anybody else.

By this point, incidentally, the fog was thinning as rivulets of water condensed and streamed over my face and poured down my nose and throat, putting pressure on my tracheal passage to open as they gathered and began to reassemble into a living tendril. I had maybe another second or two before I started drowning standing up.

The bad news was that Parth blocked my knife thrust. The good news was that he did it by crossing his scaly forearms and catching my wrist in the V they formed, pushing the V upward so that my knife thrust went straight up and I was pulled slightly to the side. He was hoping to use his superior height and strength to pull me up off my feet, but he wasn't used to dealing with someone as fast as he was.

The natural inclination in this situation was to grasp the knife tighter, but I'd been broken of that habit by a knight who wielded a bamboo pole the way a nun uses a ruler. This particular instructor used to call the instinct to clutch a weapon while your hand was being immobilized the *monkey trap*. In India, hunters who want to trap monkeys will hollow out coconuts and leave a hole just big enough for a monkey's hand to fit through. Then they'll put some sweet rice in the coconut. The monkey will reach into the coconut and grab the sweet rice, making its fist too big to get back out of the hole, trapping itself. It never occurs to the monkey to let go of the rice...their brains just aren't wired that way.

I abandoned the knife immediately, letting go so that my fist became a flat palm that slipped through the vise Parth was trying to make with his wrists. His hands, which were pulling upward, were suddenly and unexpectedly encountering no resistance and shot up over his head, leaving his torso completely unguarded and his feet flat on the ground. I went with the motion as I surged downward onto my back foot, tilting my torso down toward the ground as I shot a side kick up into Parth's midriff before he could bring his hands down or jump back. I tried to drive my heel up all the way through his stomach. Kicking his scaly skin was like kicking Kevlar, but he was lifted off of the ground and sent backward into the air, smashing into one of his high-tech glass tables at the same time that my gag reflex started.

Parth's body went straight through the glowing tabletop and into the plastic frame on the far side, smashing through it. I don't know what kind of circuitry was running through that glass and that frame, but there was a bright ozone-burning flash, and then the lights went out as Parth and I collapsed simultaneously. The difference was that I was still conscious, even if I was convulsively vomiting what felt like a couple of gallons of water through my mouth and nose. Parth was inert.

Electricity, by the by, is another good bet against creatures who regenerate quickly. It may not keep their flesh from regrowing like a continuous flame will but a large-enough jolt will mess with their brain activity and cause their systems to shut down.

A lot of knights carry illegally amped-up Tasers and cattle prods for this reason. I'd had to leave one behind in Alaska myself.

"PARTH!" Kimi screamed, rushing forward as the last of the fog thinned into transparent wisps and a backup generator kicked in and caused the room lights to come back on. She didn't seem to care that Parth's prostrate form was still in his hybrid snake mode, and would have rushed to him if Sig hadn't stopped her. At least the ruins of the table frame weren't sparking.

I dragged my own waterlogged carcass off my knees and rose, coughing, to my feet. Sig walked around the wreckage of the table, inspecting the fragments carefully for sparks. Then she hauled Parth's body away from the remains of the table with one hand, grabbing him by the wrist and unceremoniously slinging his body across the room as if it were a bag of flour. I realized that I was holding the knife again, having somehow grabbed it unconsciously even while I was throwing up. I pointed it away from her as she walked around to me.

"Are you all right?" she asked, half patting, half thumping me between the shoulder blades.

"Is *he* all right?" Kimi demanded hysterically, rushing to Parth's side and slapping his cheeks.

"Parth will wake up soon if you stop mauling him, Kimi," Sig said unsympathetically. "It would take a wood chipper to take him out."

"But he's not breathing," she fretted, and something in her voice made me think of all those Asian subcultures and communities that still believe that they are the descendants of nagas and humans. Nagaland, a small province in the northeast section of India, is the most obvious example.

I splut—and yes, I just made that word up—another coffee cup's worth of water out of my nose and mouth and gasped, "Nagas have a low heart rate." I wasn't sure why I was trying to reassure her. I had a feeling that Parth could have dissected me on the dining room table and Kimi would have been put out with me for bleeding on the tablecloth. After another breath I added, "They're cold-blooded."

Both of those statements were true, but when I implied that Parth was breathing and that Kimi just couldn't tell, I was lying. I don't hear heartbeats, but I *can* hear them. What I mean is, most of the time I unconsciously shut heartbeats out the same way people who live near airports stop hearing airplanes. If I didn't, I'd go crazy. Edgar Allan Poe's "The Tell-Tale Heart" kind of crazy. But when I consciously focus—which I was doing at that particular moment—I can hear heartbeats, and Parth was legally dead.

On the other hand, I was also confident that his body would be coming back online soon, and I was too busy coughing water out of my windpipe to explain why. As far as I know, the only thing that will truly kill a naga is completely burning it down to ash or dissolving it in acid or severing the connection between its brain and its body through decapitation. And even then I'd burn or dissolve the head just to be safe. If anything could survive decapitation, a naga could, and I've never tested that limit.

At this point Molly came walking back into the room carrying an elephant gun that was almost as long as she was tall. "Here," Molly said, handing the enormous double-barreled rifle to Sig. "I think this thing would snap my spine if I tried to fire it."

"Parth keeps this monster loaded?" Sig asked dubiously, taking the massive rifle by the stock with one hand.

"All the weapons in his weapons room are loaded," Molly said serenely, producing a World War II Mauser C96 that had been slung carelessly over her shoulder. "I've always liked this one. It looks like a *Star Wars* blaster."

I've used Mausers before; they were the guns of choice among knights in the first half of the twentieth century, at least until the .357 Magnum came along—but glancing at the exotic-looking long-barreled semiautomatic, I had to admit that Molly had a point. She also had the gun on safety. I reached over to the left side of the hammer and gently changed the setting. She had probably gotten confused by the selector switch next to the trigger guard.

And yeah, it probably would have been a better idea to leave the gun on safety and not say anything, but Molly had just tried to come through for me. I have my faults, but letting an ally walk around thinking she has a weapon that works when it doesn't isn't one of them.

"That gun can fire more rounds a minute than its barrel can handle," I told her. "So fire short bursts if you actually have to use that thing. But don't fire it around Parth unless you're a good distance away or you figure death is better than being taken alive."

"Why not?" Molly asked, her wise, childish eyes serene and big behind her glasses.

"Naga blood is poisonous," I explained. "Splattering bits of Parth all over the place would be a quick death for you and Kimi."

"What about you and Sig?" Molly asked.

I glanced over at Sig. "I don't know."

This wasn't entirely true. The one time I got naga blood on me, I wiped it off with a wet rag figuring that I'd be fine since it hadn't landed on any open wounds. I was able to function for several hours before spending the next day burning up in a delirium of sweating, vomiting, and cramping. OK, fine, I lost control of my bowels too. Satisfied?

"So those guns are useless," Kimi said eagerly.

I shrugged. "They're a last resort."

Molly accepted my statement without acknowledging it one way or another. Instead, she turned to Kimi. "Do you know why Parth attacked John?"

"Parth is your friend," Kimi said tearfully, which I took to mean no. She went on: "Why are you taking this stranger's side? Maybe Parth recognized him from somewhere and was trying to save you."

"Every time we've ever come here, Parth was waiting for us in the greeting room with refreshments ready," Sig said tiredly. "But tonight he made sure he was surrounded by water."

Sig continued to tick points off with her tone rather than her fingers. "He was in the one room where he could toss that water around and not cause a lot of property damage. And he was almost naked so he could shape-shift quickly. Face it, Kimi, Parth planned this in advance, which means he had plenty of time to warn me. He didn't tell me what he was doing because he knew I wouldn't go along with it."

Kimi didn't say anything.

I glanced at Sig with a certain amount of respect. She had worked that out fast. I decided to let her take the lead in handling Parth when he woke up. I was the one he had attacked, but Sig was the one whose trust he had betrayed. She was also the one holding the big-ass gun.

And the truth is, I was curious. I wanted to see what she would do.

A second later Sig looked at me pensively and said, "Let's take him to the crematory."

～15～

THE LESSON OF THE LAVA LAMP

Apparently being legally dead takes a while to come back from, even for a naga. Parth's heart started beating again, but he stayed unconscious while I dragged his inert scaly form to the urn room by the ankles, and I wasn't particularly gentle. Kimi wasn't particularly quiet either. He also stayed under while Sig fetched an eight-foot boar spear from one room and Molly fetched some chains and manacles from another.

"What kind of collection did those manacles come from?" I wondered.

Molly blushed and refused to answer.

It's hard to bind shape-shifters, but Parth's wrists and ankles weren't all that much smaller in his human form than in his half-snake one, and I fastened the manacles so tightly that they ought to at least slow him down. His flesh was so oily and malleable, though, that I doubted any physical restraints would hold him long. I also knotted the chains around his chest and throat in such a way that he couldn't stretch or burst them without centering all the pressure on his windpipe. When I was done we placed him on the sliding tray of the crematory oven.

Thankfully I'd had to use a fully automated furnace that was run with a PC once before, in Alaska, and it didn't take me long to figure out how to manually operate this one through the user interface. That might also have had something to do with the fact that this time I wasn't in a funeral home that I'd broken into with a windigo's body wrapped in plastic. I went ahead and turned Parth's furnace on.

Next I took my Swiss Army knife out of my jean jacket and extended the four-inch blade. Then I peeled my jacket and shirt off and wrapped my right hand in the wet shirt before draping the rest over Parth's face so a damp layer of fabric was between my hand and possible blood spray. Clenching the casing of the knife through the fabric, I positioned the tip of the blade over Parth's ear canal.

"What are you..." Kimi started to protest, but her words ended in a scream as I drove the blade into Parth's left ear.

Parth still didn't wake up, but his heartbeat picked up and his body convulsed.

"John?" Molly said questioningly.

"Relax, he's fine. It's an old knight's trick for regenerators with psychic abilities," I explained, careful not to let any blood drip onto me as I pulled the shirt away and tossed it aside. The red knife handle remained jutting out of Parth's ear. "His brain is already resealing and rerouting connections around the blade. In a few minutes his speech and memory will be unimpaired, but he won't be able to concentrate enough to move water around or hypnotize any of you for a while."

With psychic creatures who can't regenerate, knights will sometimes drive steel tacks into their skulls to disrupt their focus, but I decided to keep that information to myself.

"Is that really necessary?" Sig asked carefully.

"Yes," I said.

Sig nodded and changed the subject. "You seem pretty familiar with nagas."

"I met one once before when I spent a few years in India," I said.

"Sightseeing?" she asked lightly.

"You could call it that," I said. "I did visit the Taj Mahal."

Sig nodded again, then looked over to where Kimi was edging closer to the Mauser dangling loosely at Molly's side. "Don't," she said firmly.

Molly and Kimi both started and jumped away from each other.

"Sig, what are you planning?" Kimi asked fearfully.

Sig debated whether to answer for a long moment. "I'm going to try to avoid killing Parth," she said at last. "The best thing you can do is believe that I'm trying to save him and let me concentrate."

"If you don't want to kill him, just don't," Kimi said in a rising whimper. "This is insane."

Sig shook her head sadly. "If you really want to be a part of Parth's world, Kimi, you're going to have to start learning the rules. Unfortunately, I don't have time to explain them to you right now, so I'm telling you as your friend: keep your mouth closed and listen. Please."

"But how do I . . ."

"Shut the hell up, Kimi," Sig said, not unkindly. "If you say one more word, I'm going to knock you out." This was presented as a simple statement of fact, with neither reluctance nor eagerness.

Kimi shut the hell up.

We waited awhile longer. Parth's eyes still didn't flutter. His breathing didn't change. His heart rate stayed consistent. The heat began to build and become slightly uncomfortable as the furnace came to life with loud violent clanking noises, but no one suggested turning it off.

I started peeling off my jeans, which were starting to feel like they were trying to suck the skin off my legs.

"Ummm...John?" Sig kept her voice level as I kicked my way out of the clinging fabric.

"Relax," I said, draping my jeans over the furnace door, where they would dry faster. "I'm keeping my boxers on this time."

"This time?" Molly wondered.

Sig blushed slightly.

"She used magic to get me naked the first time we met," I informed Molly.

"I was just trying to get change for a twenty," Sig responded gamely. "I didn't realize he worked at that kind of a bar."

Molly looked me over. "Maybe you should have."

This time I was the one who got a little uncomfortable. Sig bit her lower lip and looked at Parth.

We waited a little longer.

"You know, it's weird," I said to Sig conversationally. "I saw a naga get knocked out once before. He was in human form, and he stayed in human form just like Parth here is staying in combat form."

"You saw another naga get knocked out?" Sig asked skeptically. "Or you knocked him out?"

"Uhm," I said.

Here's another little safety tip. It doesn't matter if a creature regenerates or not; if a brain gets sloshed violently enough and smacks against the skull hard enough, the sloshee is getting knocked out. Of course, it's harder to achieve that effect against beings who have stronger neck muscles and less sensitive nervous systems.

"Maybe that's why Parth attacked him!" Kimi said triumphantly. "He must…"

Whatever else Kimi was going to say was cut off by the short, efficient punch that snapped her head back and sent her toppling backward. Molly managed to catch Kimi's falling body, although she dropped the Mauser in the process.

Sig didn't shake her hand or wince, which meant that her bones were probably harder than a normal human's. Her fist had connected with Kimi's jaw. "Why is that weird?"

"Well, there are all kinds of Hindu and Buddhist stories about nagas," I said, "and none of them really agree on what a naga's true form is. In some stories they're humanoids who can change into snakes, and in others they're giant water serpents who can turn into humans, and sometimes they're half-and-half critters like Parth is right now who can go either way. No naga will give you a straight answer on the subject, but you'd think they'd change into their true form when they got knocked out. Most shape-shifters do."

"I know what Parth would say if he were awake." Molly didn't look up from her efforts to make Kimi's unconscious body look comfortable on the floor.

"Probably something like 'Ow, ow, ow!'" I offered.

"He would say that your assumption is based on an illusion," Molly informed me with an odd primness. "Parth would say that there is no one true form."

Ah yes, the lesson of the lava lamp. I managed not to make any sarcastic comments out loud.

"Parth and Molly have talked a lot about religion," Sig explained.

"Parth is awake," I said.

He went ahead and opened his eyes then. It took him a moment to take in his surroundings and situation.

"You have some explaining to do," Sig announced.

"What issss in my ear?" Parth said irritably, and it was bizarre hearing everyday words from that inhumanly sibilant voice. Apparently Parth realized this because his scales began to recede back into his skin and the black of his eyes started shrinking back down into normal-size pupils. His jaws commenced retracting back into his skull as if he were some kind of biological PEZ dispenser. Then he convulsed and gave out a strangled cry, and poisonous blood began to pour out of his punctured ear around the bright-red pocketknife handle that was still sticking out of the side of his head like a slot machine lever.

Sig stroked his now-human-looking forehead absentmindedly, her voice mild. "Better keep the party tricks to a minimum, Parth."

"What happened?" Parth gasped as soon as he could talk again. "Did he...was I...he did!" He looked at me and his face lit up with a radiant joy. It was a bizarre sight under the circumstances.

Parth made to raise his neck to get a better look at me and Sig palmed the forehead she'd been stroking and pinned him back down onto the sliding tray. "Nuh-uh."

"Sig, please," Parth said, as if telling her to give him a break rather than asking permission.

Sig reached out and grabbed the chains that had slackened around Parth's neck. I wanted to tell her to watch out for his blood, but I didn't. "You had a chance to be reasonable," she said. "If you try to get loose before we come to terms, this truce is over. I'm going to take that spear over there and stab you through the top of your skull and stir your brains around a little. Then I'm going to shut you in the furnace."

"This isn't..." Parth choked.

"John here doesn't trust easily," Sig interrupted. "But he trusted me when he came here tonight. Do you understand, Parth?"

"I . . ." he began, and Sig cut him off by pulling the chain tight again.

"I promised to hold his trust and keep it safe," she said. "I vouched for you, and you attacked him. I asked you to stop, as my friend, and you kept attacking him. Do you have any idea how that makes me feel?"

For the first time Parth began to look embarrassed. "You don't understand . . ."

"Explain it to me." Her tone was implacable. "And make it good. You offered me your hospitality."

He finally took her seriously. I've mentioned that there are rules that are literally older than mankind, treated with utter life-and-death seriousness by some races that were old when dinosaurs were walking on this planet. People like me don't have to obey those rules, but taking them lightly is a fool's game. If word gets around among some species that you don't honor their value systems, you lose all kinds of respect and rights of mutual conduct. And the codes governing hospitality are particularly inflexible. In expecting Sig to ignore his breach of etiquette, Parth had both disrespected her and tried to take advantage of their friendship. He had, in effect, assumed that she was either too powerless or too passive or too ignorant to take serious offense. By formally invoking the rules, Sig was letting Parth know that court was now in session. Oddly enough, it didn't frighten him. It pissed him off.

"I had to test him!" Parth said impatiently. "If he is what you say he is, he's unique! The knights' geas will not allow any outside supernatural force to dominate their consciousness, and lycanthropy completely takes over the mind at least once a month!"

Sig's spine stiffened slightly. She practically had the words OH! MAYBE THAT'S WHY HE DOESN'T CHANGE INTO A WOLF! appear over her head in neon.

"Do you honestly think that no knight has ever been bitten by a werewolf or a vampire over the centuries?" Parth continued. "They don't transform, they die! They commit suicide, or their minds shut down, or the geas causes such physical strain fighting the transformation that their hearts rupture!"

We were all silent.

"Do you understand now?" Parth yanked his chin in my direction. "He could be the vector point of a new evolutionary bypass! The first member of an entirely new species combining the mental defenses of a knight with the physical advantages of a lycanthrope! Who knows what's in his sperm!"

"Hey," I protested mildly.

His eyes went distant and dreamy. "Did you see how fast he was? How he tracked me? The way he threw off my attempt to enthrall him?"

I'd never heard anyone describe getting their ass handed to them quite so rapturously.

Parth's eyes focused again and he stared at me fervently. "You are beautiful, sir. Truly beautiful!"

"Uhm?" I said.

Sig was amused. I'm not sure how I knew that; neither her expression nor her body language changed. But she was amused.

And then she wasn't. "It stops here, Parth," she said, her voice becoming a cold and desolate thing. "That's my price for letting you live. You don't tell anyone else about John, and you don't ask him any questions about how he came to be, or try to take DNA samples from him, or anything else."

"What harm would that do?" he protested indignantly.

I laughed, except it wasn't really a laugh. "You planning on starting your own little eugenics program, Parth?"

Sig grunted agreement. What would trying to make more people like me even entail? Kidnapping women who had knight blood in their veins? Impregnating them against their will? Holding them captive? Forcing their hands into a cage with a werewolf in it when they were near term? Performing a caesarean on them before the next full moon? It would be a death sentence for the mothers even if their geas didn't fight the transformation. Only the strongest survive the first were-wolf change, and a woman who had just had surgery to remove her child unnaturally from her womb wouldn't stand a chance. And who knew what percentage of the infants would survive even if the circumstances of my birth were re-created exactly? I was either a miracle, a long shot, an aberration, or a fluke, depending on how someone looked at it.

"You don't understand," Parth protested. "I don't want knowledge because I want to...do anything with it." He said that last part as if the very idea were vulgar.

Uh-huh. There's a story in the Mahabharata about how nagas became immortal. Basically they were out to steal the secret of the elixir of life from the gods, and through a series of circumstances that would demand way too much background context if I went into detail, they blackmailed a minor deity into bringing it to them. This birdlike being, Garuda, brought them the elixir just as he'd promised, but he hadn't promised to give it to them once he did. Some of the elixir spilled in the resulting struggle, and one naga was so obsessed that he got on the ground and began feverishly licking the grass, managing to get a few drops of elixir but cutting his tongue in the process. According to the story, that's how birds and snakes became enemies, and that's why nagas have forked tongues no matter what shape they appear in.

It's probably not a literal story. It's probably a teaching tale. And the moral it teaches is: don't trust nagas when they're obsessed with getting something.

"I want your oath," Sig repeated.

"An oath made under duress is not binding," he forced out. "Everyone knows that."

I almost admired his tenacity.

"Humans know that," she corrected. "I want your oath. Provided that satisfies John."

"It doesn't," I said. "But I'm willing to trust your judgment." The truth was, Parth was the only one I could see keeping Kimi quiet without killing her, and I wasn't willing to go there. Yet.

"I appreciate that," Sig said tonelessly.

"I can't think with this pain in my—" Parth started to say, and Sig pulled the chains around his throat tight.

"I'm going to shut you in the furnace now," she told Parth. Behind Sig, I saw Molly's mouth open as if to protest, then shut again.

Sig released the chain. Somehow her voice carried over Parth's gasping. "Last chance, Parth. I'm not kidding."

She wasn't. Or if she was, she was the best bluffer I'd ever seen.

He laid his head back against the tray. "I promise—" he began.

"Swear by Vasuki," I interrupted. "Manasa too, and Apam Napat while you're at it. In Hindi."

Even under those circumstances, Parth gave me a startled look.

I speak pretty serviceable Hindi, but my language skills weren't up to saying, "Yeah, that's right, bitch," without losing the context in translation. I still gave it a good try.

∼16∼

OH

It was some time before we finally got our act together enough to actually have the conversation we'd come for in the first place. The atmosphere wasn't genial, but once freed and cleaned up and having reassured Kimi with a lot of stroking and petting, Parth seemed to take Sig's admonition about having violated the rules of hospitality to heart. He pointedly inquired after our needs at regular intervals, though his manner couldn't be described as warm while he did so.

We were sitting in the room full of Papasan chairs and meditation cushions. Kimi was serving tea, which I smelled very carefully before sipping. Parth was drinking something that smelled like hot frog. I was wearing a bathrobe while my jacket and jeans and socks and underwear rotated in a dryer somewhere. The shirt with poison blood on it had gone into the furnace. I still had the Ruger and the knife holstered to my body, though.

Sig was the only person who seemed completely relaxed, smearing caviar on an unbroken graham cracker sheet. "You didn't just lure us over here for this dumbass stunt, did you,

Parth? I mean, you do actually have some information that can help us track down this Anne Marie Padgett, right?"

A number of responses flickered behind his dark eyes, but he finally looked at me ruefully, shook his head, and uttered a dry bitter laugh. "Oh yes."

The *oh* worried me. People don't say *oh* like that unless the crap has gotten truly deep in a way that nobody has anticipated.

"OK," I said. "Why are you smiling like that?"

"Because I know what kinds of things Anne Marie has been doing online besides researching blood-related topics," Parth said. "And you aren't going to like them."

Sig indulged him. "What?"

"She's been sending e-mails to the Netherkind," Parth announced, patting a stack of printouts on a small table next to him. It was a fairly impressive pile.

If this was supposed to be a big dramatic moment, I wasn't feeling it. "I've never heard of any monsters called the Netherkind," I admitted. This was a somewhat difficult confession to make.

"I have," Molly said chirpily.

Sig smiled faintly. "They're not real monsters, John. They're one of those movements for vampire wannabes. If you'd spent any time in big cities recently, you probably would have seen some of their hangouts."

"Oh," I said. "Like those people who say they have human bodies reincarnated with the souls of vampires or something like that?"

"Like them," Sig affirmed. "But the Netherkind have taken it to the point of religion. They believe that if they try to live their lives by vampire values, vampires will come along and make them immortal."

"What the hell are vampire values?" I demanded. "Besides an oxymoron."

Sig rolled her eyes. "The usual clichés."

"Avoiding sunlight?" I guessed. "Dressing in black? Drinking blood?"

"Yes." Sig sighed. "Those. Promiscuity, S and M, anarchy, and bad taste in music too."

Parth picked up the conversation smoothly. "As of two weeks ago, Anne Marie was negotiating with several of them."

"Negotiating for what?" Sig asked suspiciously.

"With what?" I asked, equally suspiciously.

"She was offering to transform some of them into real vampires for money and allegiance," Parth said with a certain malicious glee. "Lots of money by her standards. Ten thousand dollars."

I leaned forward and pulled an e-mail out of the stack at random, then sat back in my chair staring at it. It was the first tangible proof that our smart vampire was really out there, that Anne Marie Padgett had become a thing of terror and need. Beneath the to and from signifiers and the date, the e-mail read:

Dylan.

Every rebirth requires two things: faith and sacrifice. You have crawled through this life mocked and afraid, and the only thing that has kept you going is a sense that somewhere, somehow, a greater destiny was calling you. The one great truth is that this world is cruel and ugly, and only strength can make it beautiful. Deep inside you know this. The world has told you that wanting power is something to be ashamed of, but you know in your soul that being a lamb will not lead to salvation. Your destiny is to be a tiger. I will have you, Dylan. You will serve me, and I will set you free. We will not walk on water. We will dance on the bodies of your enemies and drink their blood.

The e-mail wasn't signed, and Anne Marie had deleted whatever messages had preceded it. Presumably the prior dialogues were in Parth's stack.

"They all have the same pseudo-religious imagery and anger." Parth still seemed to be enjoying himself. "They all appeal to a need to belong. For desperate souls with no sense of irony or awareness of cliché, it's a potent mix."

"I suppose these Netherkind would be more inclined to believe her than your average citizen," I said reluctantly. Some of them would be posers or goths trying to get laid, of course, but the fanatical and the emotionally disturbed and the artistic have always been less susceptible to the influence of the Pax.

"As I said, they were in the middle of negotiations," Parth said. "Protestations, conflicting claims about who the real vampire was, demands of proof. Some of it was quite amusing."

"And this stopped a few weeks ago?" Sig asked.

Parth agreed that it had.

Sig looked at me. "She created a new e-mail address when she left the computer in Steve Ellison's house behind. I'm thinking Steve Ellison is the one who made her into a vampire, and Anne Marie was trailing along in his group until she realized he was an idiot and began to make plans of her own."

"But you have the e-mail addresses of the people she was talking to," I said to Parth. "You can hack into those people's accounts. Find their names. Find out what new e-mail tag she's using to contact them. Get their cell phone numbers and addresses."

He sipped from the frog broth. "I have and I am. This Anne Marie seems to require that her recruits go off the grid as part of their ... contract. At least eight of the people she was in contact with have not used their cell phones or Internet services for weeks. I tracked the location of a few of her recruits' cell phones and discovered that they are traveling interstate all over this country in different directions, often stopping at warehouses and truck stops."

I rubbed my eyes tiredly. I had been getting a lot of exercise and stress and not much sleep. "You're saying she's using burner phones and getting rid of her followers' cell phones by hiding them on trucks or buses?"

Parth agreed. "And continually abandoning e-mail addresses and creating new accounts as well. Whatever her ultimate goal, this young woman obviously expects to be hunted at some point. You should find that ominous."

"But she's still just an adolescent," I nudged. "And you're how many years old?"

He gave me a hooded stare. "You understand that I have only been searching for twenty-four hours and have other interests."

"Will you keep looking?" Sig asked gently.

Parth didn't answer again for some time, and we let him mull that one over. I almost regretted stabbing a knife into his ear. Or I wanted to do it again. I wasn't sure which.

"I suppose I will," he said eventually. "Even without Stanislav's warning, I don't like how events are shaping up around this girl. When you've been around as long as I have, you learn that big wheels turn on small axles."

He looked at me significantly as he said this. Or perhaps I should say *sssssignificantly*. I ignored the implication.

"What was the other thing?" I reminded him. "You said she was doing *things* online. Things plural."

"I went into her system commands," Parth acknowledged. "She's been printing off every article about the making of Vietnamese tunnel networks that she can find."

Oh.

~17~

PSYCHOPOMP AND CIRCUMSTANCE

It had been the second long night in a row, and I was a little surprised when Sig got out of Molly's car at Rigby's.

"I need a cup of coffee," she said, though the bar was obviously closed.

"And Molly doesn't?" I wondered, looking through the driver's window. Molly waved a mitten at me tentatively.

"We need to talk," Sig admitted. "I've been waiting for the right time, but I don't think there's going to be a better one."

I didn't accept this information happily, but I didn't say anything either. I'd been waiting for some kind of ax to fall ever since Sig first used my real name. My movements were a little stiff as I let us into Rigby's . . . and not from physical soreness. We stayed silent while I let myself behind the bar and made some coffee. My movements became more and more rapid as the numbness wore off, until I was yanking cherry danishes out of the mini-fridge angrily and clattering the plates around.

By the time I slid a steaming mug over the surface of the bar, my stare was pissed off and challenging. "What?" I demanded.

Sig didn't respond to my attitude. She sipped her coffee slowly, cradling the cup with both hands as if it were a bird's egg. "Alison wants you to calm down," she said matter-of-factly.

It took a moment for that to kick me in the gut. When I could speak, my voice was strained. "You're talking about my dead fiancée?"

Sig didn't look up from her coffee. "I'm talking *to* your dead fiancée."

If I hadn't had my elbows braced on the bar, I think my legs would have collapsed from under me.

"I saw her standing behind you the first time I walked into this bar," Sig continued quietly. "She followed me out while I was trying to chase down that vampire you let go and begged me not to hurt you and told me that you were a good man. She's been talking to me off and on about you ever since."

My fingers scrabbled over the bar like a blind man's. When my hand found what it was looking for, it clutched the ceramic coffee mug as if it were a lifeline. I didn't bother to drink. I had met Alison in Pennsylvania. She had been sweet and giving and funny and smart and vulnerable. She had also been a little self-centered, and sentimental, and moody, and had terrible taste in music. She loved sex and making food and curling up under covers and I don't know what the hell I'm trying to say. I can't make it fit into words. I loved her. Loved her desperately and selfishly when I had no right to do so.

Alison hadn't belonged in my world, but I'd been so lonely for so long that I'd lied to myself, told myself that I could leave my world behind and live in hers. And my world had found us. No wonder Sig hadn't been surprised when I told her Alison had died.

Except...

"I can sense ghosts," I said. "I can't see them like you can, but I can sense them."

"You've probably been living with this one so long you don't even notice anymore," Sig said, way too matter-of-factly for somebody who was talking about my dead fiancée.

"So you've been catching her up on her favorite soap operas? Letting her know how the Steelers are doing? That kind of thing?" I forced the lame-ass joke out of my mouth, but the words were hollow. I couldn't feel anything except dread.

"Of all the dead, the ghosts who are kept here by love are the most articulate," Sig told me sadly. "But I told you before, they only talk about the thing that's keeping them here, and they don't really listen."

"This is bullshit," I said, but I knew it wasn't. This was how Sig had known my name. This was how Sig had gotten so much insight and information despite my geas. She hadn't gotten inside my skull. Someone who knew me had gotten into hers.

Sig had said that she was a pyschopomp. A speaker for the dead.

"You used to make fun of Alison because she ate sandwiches with nothing but mayonnaise on them," Sig informed me. "She says she made you watch a show called *Gilmore Girls* with her over and over. She says you were her Luke, whatever that means."

I tilted my head up and stared at the ceiling, as if that could keep tears from building up in them. "Stop," I gasped.

"What I'm about to tell you is all her, OK?" Sig said. "Alison says you owe her for the way she died."

I nodded without taking my eyes off the ceiling.

"She says there's only one thing you can do to make it up to her. She says if you really love her, you'll do it."

"What?" I demanded hoarsely. What could I possibly do? Kill myself? Kill every knight on the face of the planet? I couldn't do those things. I'd already tried.

"Stop trying to be perfect," Sig said.

That floored me. I did look at Sig then. "Perfect?" I said incredulously. "Is she insane? God, I know I'm not perfect. I'm nowhere close."

"So stop trying," Sig said, and now she was looking at me too. "You've been trying to be someone who could have kept Alison from being killed. You never relax, you never give yourself a break, and you don't trust anyone or anything. You don't let anyone get close to you. You won't admit it, but you're still trying to make amends. And you can't. She's dead, John. Let her die."

I didn't argue. My tongue felt like it was three sizes too thick. Tears were trickling down my cheeks, but I didn't wipe them away.

Sig ran a palm over her face. I realized that she was crying too. "She loves you, John. You love her too. You don't ever have to apologize for that. Everyone dies."

Sig got up a little unsteadily and began to walk out of the bar. Then she stopped, took a deep breath, and turned around again. She walked toward me like someone in a trance. "This is her too, OK?"

She grabbed me by the collar of my shirt and pulled me across the bar into a kiss. At first I didn't respond, but then my lips softened into hers and I was kissing Alison again. Sig was taller than Alison, but her lips kissed my top lip instead of my fuller bottom lip the same way that Alison's had, a gentle pressure. Sig's hands found the exact spot in the small of my back and rubbed it the way that Alison's had. When Sig breathed my name, her voice said it the way Alison had. And then I was putting my arms around Alison and pulling and lifting her across the bar so that her ass was on the counter and she was lying back into my arms.

And then Alison left. I swear to God, I felt her pass from Sig through me. Alison left me there kissing Sig with a trace of mischievous affection. It was Sig kissing me back hungrily, and it was Sig's hands sliding under the back of my shirt while I lost myself in the warmth of her mouth, and...

Sig broke out of the kiss gasping, and it felt like she had ripped my soul in half. I stepped back and put a palm on the bar to steady myself while Sig scrambled to her feet.

I couldn't say anything. It felt like I would never say anything again. This time when Sig walked out of the bar, her gait was unsteady. But she didn't stop.

Something was wrong. Something was missing. After a panicked moment I realized that it was Alison. A weight that had no name had lifted, and I wept like a child. Hot scalding tears poured down my face while I choked on feelings that were too big to articulate. I was sad, but it felt like the sadness was pouring out of me instead of poisoning me. It felt like I had been sleeping in the dark, not knowing I was in a coffin until someone pried the lid off. It hurt, but it was good, the way love is supposed to be.

~18~

YOU'RE NO GENTLEMAN'S CLUB

It was odd, but when I got home I slept like a dragon. It was a healing, dreamless slumber despite the emotional roller coasters and the approaching full moon. When my alarm woke me five hours later, it didn't feel like I was waking up from sleep; it felt like I was crawling out of a shell. Every sensation seemed new and intense and highly significant. So this was the taste of my coffee. This was the slight discomfort in the small of my back from the rocking chair. This was the feel of a cotton shirt being pulled over bare skin.

When Molly called to tell me that Parth had found an active cell phone mentioned in one of Anne Marie's e-mails, I absorbed the news with a sense of detached resignation. I didn't want to see any horrible things, or be scared, or get angry, or kill anything, but who does? Whatever else had changed, I still wasn't going to let people I was starting to care about walk into a potentially dangerous situation without me.

I felt ridiculously awkward and self-conscious when Sig and her crew came to pick me up in Choo's van. I had experienced something profound, and it seemed to me as if they were seeing me for the first time. But habits began reasserting themselves, and I could feel my old life...my old shields and attitudes wrapping around me like armor as I climbed into the van. It was comforting in a way, and a bit frightening. I didn't dislike that person, exactly, but I didn't want to be him anymore, and I didn't know how to be anyone else.

This time I was sitting in one of the bucket seats next to Sig. Dvornik was still recovering from his recent mojo no-no, and Molly had claimed the shotgun seat. Andrej had stayed behind to watch Stanislav, but Andro was in the back.

"You're alone," Sig said softly.

"I know," I said. "Thank you."

Sig examined me carefully. "Are you sure you're ready for this?"

"No," I said. "But you're not going without me."

Sig went from protective concern to mild irritation in the two seconds it took me to buckle in. "We got along fine without you before you came along, you know. It's not like you're the center of our universe."

I had a feeling Sig hadn't slept particularly well after our séance/make-out session.

"Can I at least be Uranus?" I wondered, drawing out the pronunciation *your anus*.

Sig's face froze, then she looked away, trying to hide a smile while muffled immature sounds came from the front of the van. She shook her head the way people do when they don't know what else to do. "Idiot."

The location Parth had given us turned out to be a strip club about forty minutes away in a place called Between. Between, as its name suggested, was a town or county vaguely located in one of those long flat stretches found so frequently in North Carolina. We passed a few wooden houses, an unnamed convenience store with one gas pump, a barbecue place whose owner's name was painted on its white walls in big red letters, and an old building that either sold antiques or considered itself one. At some point we also passed Between.

"Go easy on me now, I've never been to this place before," Choo grumbled as he turned around. He had a portable GPS locator on his dashboard, but it had told us to go through a creek.

"We should have brought Ted along," Sig observed. "I'll bet he's been to every strip club in a two-hour radius."

"In one capacity or another," Molly agreed.

"Where is Cahill?" I asked, not really giving a shit.

"He's looking into Anne Marie's background some more. His partner isn't the mentally flexible type," Sig said. "And Ted can't get us out of jail if he's in one."

"Maybe the next person we recruit for our little monster-hunting club ought to be a lawyer," Molly suggested.

"Ha!" Sig had polished off a paper cup of coffee the size of a small vase and still seemed a little tired and grumpy. "I'd rather recruit a monster and start a lawyer-hunting club."

Choo agreed so enthusiastically that I wondered if he was divorced. I didn't ask.

Instead, we talked about places with strange names for a while. I had been to Nowhere, Oklahoma, before, and Choo talked about a town near Danville called Tight Squeeze. Molly said that she had always liked a place called Conception, and Sig swore that there was a Butts, Georgia. I wondered if a name like that made it harder or easier for the board of tourism, and we spent some time coming up with bumper stickers. "I love Butts" and "Drop on by and look at our Butts" and "Come into Butts."

"You realize that if we die today, this will be the last conversation I ever have," Molly pointed out.

"You're right," Choo said. "Let's talk about basketball."

Sig gazed at the back of Molly's seat fondly. "Let's just not die."

We found the strip club at the end of a dirt road surrounded by distant trees and a lot of land that looked like it ought to be growing something. It was a one-story building, but it was a very tall, large, and long story, and I doubted that it ended well. The club had a gravel parking lot surrounded by football stadium lights, and there was a domed storage building about a quarter of a mile away, but those were the only signs of civilization that I could see. The place had thick concrete walls and was apparently closed during the day. Large steel slat shutters had been rolled down to cover the windows from inside. There were no neon signs, although the canopy-covered walkway leading to the front doors did say MIDNIGHT ESCAPE at the top.

We stopped well before we got to the parking lot, and Choo put in a Buddhist meditation CD and turned the volume on low. I had given him the CD as an alternative to the high sonics that he was experimenting with, and he had accepted it enthusiastically once I explained its properties.

It's an unfortunate complication, but audio recordings of Christian prayers and rites don't have any impact on undead beings. There are complex doctrinal reasons for this, but it really boils down to belief. Most Christians believe that the power of prayer comes from establishing an active, living connection with God. Ask most Christians if an evil man could use a tape recording of a holy man to banish evil spirits, and for most the instinctive, primal response will be *no!* In fact, this is where the Holy Spirit comes into play in the Christian religion. The Bible itself says that the devil can quote Scripture—it is the presence of the Holy Spirit that makes the word of God true and alive. And a recording is a soulless thing. Don't get me wrong, someone listening to the recording with humility and honesty and reverence might get something out of it, but vampires aren't that kind of audience.

With Buddhist recordings, however, there is a kind of theological loophole for sound-based holy weapons.

Buddhists believe that the sounds of their chants are sacred in themselves, whether you believe in them or know what they mean or not. If a serial killer repeats Buddhist chants while dismembering an innocent victim with a hacksaw, Buddhists believe that the serial killer's soul will be marginally improved on some level even if the chants aren't affecting his or her actions in a material, tangible way at that very moment. The chants can't be desecrated, and they aren't contingent upon intent.

I'm intellectually OK with this idea, but I don't really believe it, any more than I believe that eating beef is bad for my karma. Fortunately I don't have to believe it, because all over the globe thousands of Buddhists are reciting the actual chants at any given moment. That—I don't know, call it *psychic resonance*— drives into a vampire's ears like carpentry nails. The effect won't kill vampires, but it will cause pain and distraction and lack of focus, and cover up a lot of background noise.

Short version: if you don't want vampires overhearing you, play Buddhist meditation CDs.

Taoist incense works the same way on a vampire's sense of smell, by the way, but I didn't have any on hand, and it's important to not just order sacred incense off the Internet. Taoists believe that the smoke of ceremonial incense is imbued with the holiness of the temple that a priest blessed the incense in, but they also believe that the yin energy of incense that is improperly dedicated will attract hungry spirits.

"Friendly-looking place," Choo commented, gazing at the club.

"There are a lot of cars parked here for a place that doesn't open until after eight," Sig observed. There were ten vehicles of varying quality, sports cars and sedans and beat-up pickup trucks and a tan panel van with dark-tinted windows.

"It's the crows I don't like," I murmured, staring at the lights where dozens of the black birds were hunched.

Molly looked over her seat at me inquiringly.

"Carrion birds," I explained.

"How much business could a place like this do?" Molly wondered.

"We're not in a big city, we're in the Bible Belt," I said. "There's a certain kind of strip club customer that likes out-of-the-way anonymous places. And certain kinds of strip clubs that don't like to do lots of public advertising."

"You can call me Ms. Jackson if you're nasty," Choo said for no apparent reason.

"I'll bet lots of lonely single men come here by themselves and don't use their real names or tell anyone where they're going," Sig reflected.

"And that storage building over there would be a great place to hide vehicles or bodies if things got out of hand," I agreed. "For a vampire, this place would make one hell of a Venus fly-trap. Call it a Venus guy trap."

"So how do we want to do this thing?" Choo asked impatiently.

He was asking Sig, so I stayed quiet even though the wolf didn't like sitting in a metal box. It wasn't the right time to be stationary or cut off from the air currents that would warn me of approaching enemies. But groups can't have more than one leader in a dangerous situation, and Sig knew these people and what they could handle a lot better than I did, so I waited.

"We have a couple of hours of sunlight left," Sig mused. "Let John and me do our things while we scout around."

Nobody had a problem with that.

There were no visible security cameras, and all the windows in the strip club were covered, so I walked around freely. We were definitely in the middle of vampire central. The parking lot held over half a dozen different vampire scents, though I didn't smell Anne Marie or her perfume anywhere. The panel van was empty.

With the all-too-familiar scents came a rush of adrenaline and anger that washed away the last of my reluctance, the wolf recognizing its ancestral enemy. There was a reason the parking lot wasn't concrete. People had died here, and when they had, the vampires had just dumped more gravel to cover the bloodstains. There were probably bags of the stuff in that storage silo along with God knew what else.

I dug my hand deep into one of the patches where the smell of death was particularly strong and came up with a handful of gravel. One of the small rocks had an edge that was stained red.

The world shouldn't be like this.

When we reconvened in the van I spoke grimly and tersely. "I smell eight vampires. Seven males and one female. But I don't smell Anne Marie."

"The head vampire is named Ivan," Sig added. "But he's not Russian, he's French."

More ghost gossip?

"Wait," Molly said. "We know Anne Marie is the head of her group, but she's not in charge here? And John can't smell her? Why is her phone here?"

"We don't know it is her phone," Choo pointed out. "All we know is Anne Marie gave a number to some vampire wannabe in an e-mail, and the phone that number belongs to is here."

"That's not all we know. Parth says that the same phone was used to call Steve Ellison a few times a couple of months ago," Sig corrected.

"But we're pretty sure Anne Marie didn't desert Ellison's group until two weeks ago." I wasn't really confused, I was evaluating the information. "If they communicated by phone, why would it only have been a few times in a specific period with a phone that's still active? And why wouldn't Anne Marie have ditched that phone like she did all the others?"

"Maybe this Ivan also broke off from Steve Ellison's group, but he did it earlier?" Molly asked. "Maybe he sort of inspired Anne Marie?"

"No, Ivan has been a hive master for a long time," Sig said with certainty. "There are ghosts around that have been here for years."

"Do you know anything else about this Ivan that might be useful?" I asked her directly. Never mind how she knew it.

"He's arrogant," Sig said. "And old. He likes people to know who he is before he kills them. He likes people to take that with them when they die."

"He's got himself a credit record and legal ID and all that mess too," Choo said thoughtfully. "Or the human running all this is his bitch. You don't just go and get yourself a liquor license."

Sig was looking at me. "This is like Ellison's house all over again. Things just don't add up."

"Maybe this Ivan's a middleman," Molly speculated. "Maybe he's like a vampire broker, or Anne Marie's mentor."

Vampires don't have mentors. They have masters. There is no in-between, not even in Between.

"Why don't we ask him?" Sig wondered.

So we did.

We didn't try to hide what we were. Sig, Molly, and I went up to the front doors, and Sig and I both had swords slung over our shoulders in back sheaths, and firearms at our sides. Molly was wearing an overcoat over the cross draped over her chest, but if she was as powerful as Sig said, vampires would have trouble even sighting a gun on her from a distance. She was carrying Sig's spear like a walking stick in one hand and a gym bag full of stakes and holy water in the other.

Andro moved to the side of the door holding a riot shotgun with the bow of a crossbow mounted on the barrel, the pull lever anchored on the shotgun stock. It was a nice weapon, if a little unwieldy-looking. The right kind of ammo could cover a wide range and slow a fast-moving vampire down. The wooden bolt fired from the crossbow mount would finish the vampire off.

Choo drove away in the van. He didn't like it, but his specialty was killing things from a healthy distance, and if we wanted answers from vampires, we were going to have to get in close. In that regard Choo's absence was a greater threat than his presence would have been. As long as someone else knew that we were in there, the vampires would be far less likely to act without talking first.

The double doors of the strip club were wooden. Since I healed the fastest and had the best sense of smell and the least developed sense of self-preservation, I knocked on one of them from the side.

A thin but taut man with long brown hair and a sketchy beard cracked the left of the double doors open immediately. The Buddhist CD chants must have made the vampire hive sit up and take notice. He was human and dressed like a carny, but he was clean, and his Ozzy Osbourne T-shirt and jeans had been washed recently before being pulled on over a Kevlar vest. He was also wearing aftershave, and it smelled expensive.

There was a human hiding on either side of the doors, presumably armed. Both of them were women. They were all scared and covered in vampire stink.

"We need to talk to your owner," I told him.

"You mean the club's owner," the man challenged.

I gave him a flat stare. "I know what I said."

These people had knowingly helped monsters treat other humans like livestock, and I could tell from the way his pupils had adjusted to the daylight coming through the door that he wasn't hypnotized. I didn't particularly want to kill him, but I also didn't want to let him live.

"Opening hours start at eight." The man made to close the door and I stopped it with a foot.

"Vampires, vampires, vampires," I said. "Now do you want us to wait out here in the sunlight or inside where Ivan can come at us if he wants to?"

The man hesitated.

"We're not waiting until sundown," I informed him. "You close this door and we'll leave, but you won't know who we are or when we're coming back. You think Ivan is going to be happy about that?"

It had been a while since the door greeter had made a decision by himself. "Come in."

I heard the people hidden on the sides moving to cover us, and I saw the tip of a double-barreled shotgun on the left moving around the edge of the door. Again, knights are trained to react to threats without hesitation, and it was the day of a full moon, and I reached out and pushed the tip of the shotgun away immediately. This might have been a mistake, since the odds of their weapons' having silver ammunition were very low and they probably just wanted to cover us, but I never thought it out that far.

These people weren't trained. The brunette who was holding the shotgun panicked and discharged both barrels as soon as the shotgun began to move. This caused a problem because the door greeter was stepping back and drawing a 9 millimeter ArmaLite from behind. The brunette wound up blowing a chunk of his right shoulder and lower throat away.

I yanked my would-be assailant forward by the shotgun barrel I was still holding and stepped behind her as I entered the club fast, ducking while I pulled my Ruger with my free hand. The woman on the opposite side of the doorway fired a rifle point-blank into her moving partner's head while trying to track me. I fired as soon as the collapsing body cleared my field of fire and shot the other woman in the face while she was still frozen by the realization of what she had just done.

Neither of the women was wearing Kevlar. In fact, neither of them was wearing much of anything at all, just a tank top and some kind of leather garment that covered the crotch and not much else.

Sig busted the right door open with her shoulder like a line-backer and swiveled her SIG Sauer around the swinging edge, then saw three dead bodies and stopped. She gave me an eye-brow that said *Really?*

I shrugged.

Holstering her namesake, Sig called out to the depths of the strip club, "Sorry about that."

Her voice lacked complete sincerity.

I stamped on the floor. It was solid concrete. At least we didn't have to worry about anything coming up through it at us.

The lobby itself was fancier than the outside of the building suggested, with lots of black velvet carpeting that probably made bloodstains harder to identify. A crystal chandelier hung from the ceiling, and there were paintings on the walls instead of posters, and wood paneling all around us. A long counter at the back of the lobby had two large thick doors on either side of it, both closed. To the left and right of us, open doorways led to an old-fashioned smoking room and a billiards room respectively.

Sig continued addressing the air in a normal tone of voice. "I don't know how good you are at distinguishing gunshots, but your minions fired first. They tried to take us captive, and we won't allow that, but I apologize for the mess. We came here because we have information you need to know, not to start a war."

There was no response.

"Fine, we'll wait while you work up your courage," Sig taunted. "But we're leaving before the sun goes down. And tomorrow I'll come back with explosives."

Molly shot Sig a questioning look, but I understood what she was doing. Far better to make vampires come to us than to search through narrow doorways and dark rooms while they waited to ambush us from carefully prepared hiding places.

"Want to play some pool?" I asked Sig, nodding at the billiards room. It would get us out of the direct line of fire from the doors at the back of the lobby.

She shrugged. "Why not?"

So we walked into the billiards room and set up a pool table. Molly remained silent, and Sig gestured her toward a far wall. Andro went over to a minibar in the southeast corner of the room and positioned himself behind it. He never took his hands off his...what should I call it? Rifle-bow? Cross-rifle? Sig and I took pool cues off the wall and racked the balls on the table nearest the doorway.

We weren't as nonchalant as we were acting. I still had flecks of the door greeter's blood all over me, and the billiard balls smacking against one another were making Molly's pulse jump. But our adrenaline was still up and our priorities were still narrowed and Sig had said that this Ivan was vain. We were making him look weak and foolish in front of his hive.

What I hadn't considered was how similar a pool cue was to a spear, or how keen Sig's eyesight was. False modesty aside, I'm a very good pool player, but Sig was in the process of methodically kicking my ass all over the table when I heard the doors at the end of the lobby open. Eight vampires came stalking into the billiards room.

Ivan was maybe five foot six, and at first glance he looked more human than most old vampires manage. His skin looked like it was in the beginning stages of a bad sunburn, but that was because he was wearing makeup to cover a complexion the color of fish belly. His black hair was an expensive toupee, and I only knew that because I could smell the glue. He was wearing a light-blue silk suit over a black T-shirt, and I could tell that he wasn't wearing a bulletproof vest. He was one of the few vampires in the room who weren't. Most of Ivan's followers were wearing Kevlar vests over bare pale concave chests, and jeans, sweat pants, or shorts.

Ivan had lost honor and face, and his going without a vest was a declaration of courage and power. Native American warriors would have called what he was doing counting coup. The only other vampire not wearing a vest was the lone female, one who was recently enough turned that her complexion was still an unbroken deep black despite a lack of any recent exposure to sunlight.

The human females hadn't worn Kevlar either. Sig had said that Ivan was old, and it's weird the way sexism can play out even among supernaturals. Ivan probably resented that the most powerful vampire leaders tend to be female. Maybe his being a strip club owner wasn't just a strategy for luring blood donors; maybe he had issues with women.

In any case, Ivan's hive was flowing into the room around him like water around a rock. Except for Ivan, all the vampires were armed, some with handguns, some with butcher knives, one with a fire ax and one with a pump-action shotgun.

Someone growled a low rumbling sound that was both a warning and an expression of outraged disgust. Oh wait, that was me.

We all stared at one another.

"What do you have to tell me that's worth the lives of three of my followers?" Ivan demanded, except it really came out "Whut dew yew hayuv ta tayell meuh thauht's wuth thuh lah-ves of threeuh of mah followuhs?"

Ivan's accent was pure Louisiana. So he was probably a refu-gee or survivor of the New Orleans conflict between knights and vampires.

"Ah pay hayulth insurance for those humans," Ivan contin-ued. "Do yew have any ideuh whut a rectal pain it's goin' ta be coverin' theuh deaths up?"

Sig straightened up at the long end of the table and leaned on her pool cue. "A vampire named Anne Marie Padgett is causing trouble and leaving your phone number behind. We thought you'd like to know."

Ivan's eyes narrowed. "Who the fuck is Anne Marie Padgett?"

If he was lying, he was doing a good job of it.

"Foxy face. Frizzy brownish-red hair," Sig said. "Seventeen and slender. Small yellow teeth, not bad but she never went to a dentist. Used to belong to Steve Ellison's hive."

"Wears cheap perfume that smells like a peach barfed on a lilac," I added. It was a detail that would stand out to another being with a sensitive sense of smell.

The only light that would ever dawn on Ivan was in his eyes. "That little bitch wuz one a' Ellison's blood cows. Ah told Ellison he'd be bettuh off breakin' her neck raht then an' theah. Ah almos' did it mahself."

He meant that Anne Marie used to be one of Ellison's human minions.

"Why?" Sig asked.

"Because she wuz a lot lahk yew," Ivan said. "No respect foah propah boundah-ries. You see humans lahk that sometahms. The only thin' they want to do moah than die is kill. They get a sniff of whut a vampah is, and tuh them, it's the bes' of both worlds. They get ta die an' kill at thuh same tahm. That girl would have fucked anythin', killed anythin', eaten, sniffed, or shit anythin' ta be one a' us. The little bitch wuz a starvin' dog, an' Ellison treated her lahk a tame puppy."

"Ellison didn't listen to you," Sig said grimly.

"Maybe not about her." Ivan clenched his teeth in a smile that made his fangs draw drops of black blood from his own lips. "Ah tol' that mo-rahn he either had ta join me or stay out a' Nohuth Carolinah, an' he stayed out."

"He's dead," Sig said with no ceremony. "Not undead. Disco dead. I take it you gave Ellison your phone number while he was thinking your warning over?"

This was a little too close to being interrogated for Ivan's liking. He still had face to save, and anger was eating away at him like acid. Ivan moved closer to Sig and showed her his fangs. "I think it's mah tuhn ta ask thuh questions. For stahtahs, whut are yew? And whah does yoah boyfrien' ovuh theah smell like a dawg?"

"What I am is my business," Sig said calmly. "And he's not my boyfriend."

I'd like to think it was the shock of learning that I wasn't

Sig's boyfriend that silenced Ivan for a moment, but it was probably her impertinence.

I tried to use the pause to good advantage. "Anne Marie is a vampire now. She laid a false trail here knowing that if anyone tried to track her by e-mail, they'd come right to your door."

"Oh, ah understan' that." Ivan's voice dropped several octaves. Apparently he liked to speak softly while being a big prick. "Ah intend tuh have a discussion with that little tramp, nevuh yew feuh."

"She's trying to get her enemies to eliminate each other," Sig added. "She wants one of us to kill the other."

"Oh, ah know that too," Ivan said. "Which is the onlah reason ah'm considerin' lettin' yew leave heuh alahve. Aftuh yew give me one of yoah humans, of course."

"Not happening," Sig assured him, holding an open hand out toward Molly. Sig might have been commenting on an oddly shaped cloud. Molly stepped forward and placed the spear in her palm.

"Yew killed three of mah humans," Ivan said reasonably. "Ah only want one of yoahs as a gestuh of respect."

"Go suck yourself." Sig's voice was flat and calm, but it was the quiet of sky before thunder.

Ivan looked at me. "Whut about yew? Yew strahk me as a lone wolf. Is this bitch's pride wuhth dyin' fo?"

"Yes," I said.

The room went silent at that.

"People know we're here," Sig observed. She sounded bored.

"Ah'm sure that boy hidin' behin' the bah will tell me all about 'em," Ivan assured her. "If ah ask him."

I never saw the signal. One of the vampires who had drifted to my right started to raise a handgun. My sliding step turned into a lunge and my katana was in my hand and cutting his arm off at the elbow before he finished the motion, the tip of the blade continuing down to slice open the straps binding the Kevlar vest beneath his armpit. I shouldn't have tried to get fancy. I was using the katana one-handed because I wanted to hold on to the pool cue, and I could already tell from the sound the blade was making through the air that the strike was effective but not flawless without the guiding hand. The motion took my blade farther down, and though I was faster than my target, he was still fast enough that his right hip knocked my blade even farther down while he was stumbling backward, and then his backpedaling brought his right foot down on the flat tip of the blade. The hilt flew out of my hands.

I should have brought the shorter wakizashi.

Chaos erupted, but I couldn't track all of it. In my peripheral vision I could see another vampire jumping over the pool table, about to land behind me. The pool cue was still in my left hand, and I shifted my weight onto my back foot and whirled the heavy end like a bo staff, sweeping it behind his feet in midair so that he landed heavily on his back. The shotgun he was holding discharged into the ceiling.

A vampire's nervous system can handle a lot of trauma, and the one whose arm I had amputated wasn't going into shock; he was turning and bending down so that he could use his remaining hand to pick up the handgun he had dropped. I flowed back to my forward foot and whirled the pool stick so that both my hands were on it when I rammed the narrow tip of it through the opening in his vest, underneath his breast-bone and up into his heart.

The vampire froze, and I broke the top of the stick off over his rib cage. I flicked my eyes around and saw that Sig had impaled the vampire I had floored, driving the tip of her spear beneath the Kevlar vest at his collar and punching it straight down through bone and heart.

A bullet from somewhere tore through my flank and glanced off a left rib while I was turning, but I didn't have time to register it because Ivan was flipping the pool table over at me. I dove into a sideways slide that took me under the table, its edge taking off a piece of my scalp. At the slide's termination I rammed my knee behind Ivan's as my weight settled onto my right hip. I don't know if you've ever been caught by a blow directly behind your knee joint, but when just the right place is hit, a four-year-old can make your leg buckle.

Ivan hit the floor on his back, and I was already surging to my knees and bringing the jagged end of the broken pool cue up while he was trying to find purchase for leverage. I drove the impromptu stake up through his heart before he could bring his hands back up or scissor his legs around me to stop me. A severed head flew over us, dripping black blood over Ivan's face while he ended.

The head was presumably Sig's work. I didn't have time to verify that she had unsheathed her sword, though, because the female vampire was bearing down on me with the fire ax. I released the pool cue and twisted under the haft of the ax, grabbed it with both hands, and used her downward momentum to roll her body weight over my shoulder. The upturned leg of the pool table was right there behind me, so I drove her body onto it as I flipped her to the ground. The leg broke through her back and erupted upward through her chest like some horrible birth.

I glanced over and saw Sig swinging her sword two-handed into the side of a six-chamber revolver that a vampire was trying to line up on her, and there must have been something special about her sword, because abnormal strength alone couldn't account for the way it actually broke the gun apart in his hand and exploded at least one of its bullets. Sig kicked one of the vampire's feet out from under him while he was distracted by the loss of several fingertips, and she kept going with the motion, whirling into a full turn that brought her sword back around through his neck before he could regain his balance.

The vampire beneath me released the haft of the ax as she shuddered out into infinity, and I took the weapon with me to a vampire who was lying on the floor next to a dropped knife. His brain was trying to reroute nervous signals around the crossbow bolt jutting out of his forehead. My cracked rib complained, but I was ready for the pain and swung the ax, taking the vampire's head off at the neck.

Across the room another vampire was pinned flat against the wall by the sheer force of whatever was emanating from Molly's cross. He was still holding a gun, but his hand was flat against the wall, head turned to the side, his mouth actually peeled backward so that his left fangs were bared. He looked like he was on one of those cylindrical amusement park rides that spin people around so fast that they're pinned to the walls by momentum. The vampire couldn't even raise his hand to stop me when I swung the ax a second time.

And then it was over.

∽19∾

STRIP SEARCH

I never did find out exactly how old Ivan was, but the safe in his private room was as old-fashioned a monster as he was. It had inch-thick steel walls and a rotary combination lock, which was fortunate because I didn't have the equipment for black hat hacking or auto-dialing. The lock's wheels were serrated with false tumbler notches, though, and it was still a bear to crack.

It didn't help that Sig kept talking at random intervals. Molly was blessing the humans we'd killed, and Andro was off somewhere talking to Stanislav on his cell phone.

"So Anne Marie started out in Ellison's hive as a human blood bag," Sig reflected. "I guess now we know why she didn't have much control over the hive at first."

I took my ear off the safe. "You get that she was more dangerous than Ellison even before she became undead, right? She probably didn't hang around any longer than it took to win over a few of his followers once she finally manipulated him into turning her into a vampire."

"Oh, I get that," Sig assured me. "She knew someone was going to come for Ellison eventually, and she left Ivan's number on an e-mail just on the off chance that someone got a hold of Ellison's computer and hacked into her e-mail account."

Sig had worked her blood-burning magic on her own spilled blood as well as mine this time, and we had both brought spare clothes along. Sig was wearing a red shirt with long sleeves, and I was in jeans and a gray cotton shirt.

"She used Ivan like a trip wire," I said. "And she didn't much care who got hurt in the explosion. Either we'd eliminate a future rival, or Ivan would take care of any hunters on her trail. And we'll probably have a few days after we put the CLOSED sign up, but as soon as word about this strip club gets on the news, she'll know we're after her for sure."

"What kind of seventeen-year-old thinks that way?" Sig asked, flipping through the books on Ivan's bookcase. They all looked like the kind of books people buy as decorations instead of reading material. We hadn't found any other vampires or captive humans when we searched the rest of the strip club, but Sig refused to sit on any of Ivan's furniture.

"A technologically savvy seventeen-year-old who grew up knowing the world was out to get her," I said.

Sig was obscurely offended. "We're only out to get her because of the choices she's been making."

"Yeah, well, being a genius doesn't guarantee self-awareness," I commented. "Now be quiet."

Sig gave me the finger.

I thought I had figured out which numbers were part of the key and was playing around with different combinations when Sig started talking again. "This girl is moving us all around like checkers on a checkerboard. We need to stop jumping where this Anne Marie wants us to jump."

"What we need to do is to stop her before she crowns herself," I suggested.

Instead of groaning at the checkers reference, Sig looked up sharply. "You really think this girl could become a queen?"

"I think this girl was a monster long before she became a vampire," I said. "And yeah, I think she could become the kind of evil queen people will tell stories about a thousand years from now. She's already using the Internet more effectively than any magic mirror."

"She's building tunnels like the ones she's been researching, isn't she?" It wasn't really a question. "We're going to have to go in some dark underground place to find her."

"Probably," I said.

Sig sighed. "Parth is looking into the tunnel-network thing. We should all get together and compare notes tonight."

"The whole scream team?" I asked.

She rolled her eyes at the nickname. "Yes. Would you like to come?"

"Do I need to learn a secret handshake?" I asked.

"No," she said. "But you will have to pay dues."

"I'm working on that," I said.

Sig became silent again, which was just as well. I popped the safe open.

"I thought you were just showing off," Sig admitted. "I'm pretty sure I saw an episode of *MythBusters* that said you can't do what you just did."

"I have enhanced senses," I explained. "And it's an old safe."

"Stanislav could have opened this safe, but he would have gotten the combination from reading the psychic impressions." There was something awkward about the way Sig added the comment. Like she was reminding me that Stanislav existed, but her heart really wasn't in it.

"Mmmnnnn," I grunted. I was carefully sifting through the safe in case Ivan had left any booby traps in it. The lower shelf held a lot of false IDs and accompanying documentation. They were good quality. The only way I knew they were cover identities was that some of the same faces had different names. The top shelf held a load of bearer bonds that I handed over to Sig.

Some of the IDs must have been made for Ivan's lieutenants. One of them was for someone named Jeff Holiday who was close enough to my height and weight that I could probably work something out. Jeff's birth date indicated that this was an identity that Ivan was cultivating for a few years down the road. Jeff had a Social Security card, a driver's license, and two credit cards that looked to have been used to start a credit history, if the bills beneath them were any indication.

Maybe Virginia wasn't such a bust in terms of setting up a new identity after all.

"There must be two million dollars in bearer bonds here," Sig said.

"How do you usually split stuff like this up with your group?" I asked absently while I was going over Jeff Holiday's papers. "Do you split it eight ways every time, or do the people who actually do the work on a particular hunt get a larger percentage?"

Sig hesitated.

"What?" I said.

"It's never come up before," Sig explained awkwardly.

"Oh," I said. "I've been on the run so long, ransacking places like this is second nature to me."

"Andro and Andrej usually do the cleanup," Sig admitted.

The comment hung in the air like a freeloader who won't leave a funeral reception.

"OK," I said. "Well, I'm planning on taking a ninth of the split."

"Fine," Sig said angrily.

"OK," I repeated.

"I'm not a thief." Sig had moved closer to me, her fists clenched.

I stood up and faced her. "I'm leaving the bonds with you, Sig. I haven't counted them. Does that sound like I don't trust you?"

"But you think Stanislav has been cheating my friends," Sig gritted out.

This time I was the one who moved closer to her. Our faces were inches apart. "I'm not the one you're angry at. I haven't forgotten what you did for me this morning. I will never forget what you did for me this morning. But I am not your whipping boy."

And I walked around her and started to head toward nowhere in particular.

"John," Sig called after me.

I stopped and looked back. "What?"

"I wish you could have had more time," she said.

I didn't ask her to explain. "Thanks."

~20~

GETTING A LITTLE CHILI IN HERE

Quitting my job at Rigby's hadn't been hard. I'd told Dave that someone close to me had just died, and it hadn't been a lie.

The war council at Sig and Dvornik's place was at eight o'clock, but the wolf wouldn't just let me go straight there. Normally I can pretend that there isn't a human side and a wolf side—it's crowded enough having a me side and a geas side—but the closer it got to midnight, the more difficult it became to ignore my copilot. The human was feeling tentative and distracted, and the wolf was stronger and more focused than it had ever been.

Which is why I found myself parking at a point some two miles away from Sig and Dvornik's home and walking around my destination in wide, slowly shrinking circles. I knew that I was doing this because it's the way that a lone wolf compensates for the lack of a surrounding pack, but I couldn't stop myself: instincts that were a part of me but were not my own were pulling at me in some kind of psychological undertow. And here's the part I found really unsettling—somehow the wolf instincts were incorporating knowledge that came from the human part of my consciousness. I was scoping out likely elevation points for snipers and looking for out-of-place vehicles.

This is why I hate days when there's going to be a full moon. The wolf is almost strong enough to tear down the cage...and I'm the cage.

I finally made it to Sig and Dvornik's loft about twenty minutes late. They lived on the second floor of a large downtown stone building that had been converted into a sculpting studio. The building had been a bank once, and it was obvious that whatever problems Sig and Dvornik were having, money wasn't one of them.

At first I had assumed that the sculpting studio was just a great cover for Dvornik's monster-hunting activities: Dvornik could make his own hours, and whenever he needed funding his kresnik society could finance him by paying whatever sum he needed for some crap piece of sculpture he tossed together. There would be a perfectly legitimate paper trail for the IRS and everything. With the ex-bank as a headquarters, he even had bulletproof windows and a large vault for locking away questionable discoveries.

The large windows of the front lobby were filled with statues, though, and I had no doubt that they really were Dvornik's. Almost all of them portrayed supernatural creatures in the act of committing various depredations. In one piece a Boo Hag was skinning one of her victims, her emaciated arms still managing to suggest an unnatural sinewy strength. In another an adaro was standing up on his finned feet and scaled legs, preparing to hurl one of the small poisonous sea urchins that they use like throwing stars, his serrated teeth snarling over the stringy rubbery tendrils coming out of his chin. What, you really think that all boat disappearances are caused by pirates and storms?

The centerpiece of the window display was a vampire sucking on the fingers of a dismembered human hand as if nibbling from a bunch of grapes. The sculptures were disturbing, but they possessed an odd, dark beauty. The bastard had real talent.

I wondered if Dvornik made a sculpture every time he killed something. Was this his version of putting stuffed heads on a wall? Or was this what Dvornik did with bad dreams?

A fire escape on the side of the building led straight to the loft, and I set off several motion sensor lights as I made my way up. They had UV bulbs in them, which made me smile. I couldn't hear a thing through the wall on the first floor. The soundproofing must have been exceptional. About ten stairs up I did hear a voice coming from a back alley. It sounded like Dvornik's nephew, Andrej; he was talking—presumably on a cell phone—to a jealous lover. He was explaining in a thick Eastern European accent and perfect English (the sneaky bastard) that he wasn't seeing anyone else, that his job just demanded strange work hours.

As soon as I got to the top of the fire escape, Sig opened the door. She was clean and watchful, wearing a tight blue Minnesota Vikings T-shirt. Her hair was unbraided and smelled like strawberries, and the shirt barely brushed against her black sweat pants, exposing flashes of firm stomach and navel.

"You're late," she said briskly. Which was her way of saying that she didn't want to talk about anything that had happened earlier.

"I know," I said. "I've been struggling with myself."

"Who won?" Sig demanded, unimpressed.

I ignored this and offered her the thick cylinder of sausage I was carrying. "Here."

She eyed the sausage doubtfully. "Is that thing Freudian?"

I smiled. "It's cervelat. Good stuff, and Swiss. Flowers would have been awkward, and I've never seen you drink alcohol, so I didn't know if wine would be appropriate."

She hesitated. "It wouldn't have been. But you know, there's this thing called cheese."

This observation flustered me more than it should have. "Of course there is, it's just...oh hell."

"John?" She sounded concerned. My heart was beating as if I were being attacked and I was blushing like a twelve-year-old. I wanted to turn around and run. "What's wrong?"

"It's the wolf," I babbled. "I just realized...It's a full moon. I mean, I didn't just realize that it's a full moon, but the wolf...it never even occurred to me what I was doing."

"What are you doing?" Sig asked curiously.

"Wolves like meat," I observed inanely. "Nothing else even occurred to me because of the full moon."

That's not why I was acting like an idiot. The giving of meat is highly significant to wolves. I had just realized that the wolf was acting out a mating ritual.

"It's OK; it's not that big of a deal." Sig laughed a little nervously. I wasn't the only one who was flustered. She struggled for a moment before flushing and awkwardly adding, "Thank you."

"Sure."

She looked at me a little sadly then. "You know Stanislav won't eat this."

The top of my skull exploded from the pressure of all the comments that were struggling to escape through my mouth. Well, OK, no it didn't. But I thought it might for a second or two there. "Will you?" I asked.

A twitch tugged at the corner of her mouth. "Are you seriously asking me if I'll eat your sausage?"

I tried not to smile and failed. The grin came out big, but I managed to tone it down to something wry. "You helped me today. I'm asking if you will accept my gift, which I am offering in good faith."

She kept looking at me. I stared back. Her eyes were large and clear, and I couldn't get to the bottom of them. "Yes," she said.

Sig turned around abruptly and led me into the loft. The second floor was a series of small and large rooms that had once been offices and conference areas. I'm sure they were decorated with all kinds of distinct furnishings and personal touches, but I didn't notice them.

Almost everyone in Sig's ragtag band of would-be heroes was seated at a dining table in one of the larger rooms. Not *around* the dining table, mind you—everybody was on the side that put their backs to the wall so that they could view some kind of smart screen on the other side of the room. A diagram of a series of underground tunnels was illustrated there.

Dvornik was seated on the far left, looking like he should have been on a fishing vessel in a thick red flannel shirt and what looked like wool pants. Next to him was an empty seat, presumably Sig's, with an open laptop on the table in front of it. Next were Cahill and Choo, both of whom looked like they were ready to play basketball at the Y, while Parth was wearing a white business suit with no shirt. One of the side effects of being an immortal is that for the older ones, the fashions of various decades tend to blend together. Molly was on the far right, still loaded down with cross-shaped jewelry and wearing a red sweater with reindeer on it.

It was an odd-looking crew. Sig seemed to be the only common link binding us all together.

Choo was smoking a cigar and greeted me with a discreet

wave of the fingers of his right hand. Cahill nodded and smirked an all-purpose smirk. Molly pulled out the chair next to her at the far end of her table as an invitation to sit down. Everyone else ignored me, including Sig, who walked back out of the room again, taking my gift with her. I sat down next to Molly.

"You're late," Molly told me.

"PMS," I said. "What are Dvornik's nephews doing?"

I hadn't lowered my voice, and Dvornik answered. "Andrej and Andro are busy documenting and disposing of the bodies we found at Ellison's house."

"They're downstairs," I said.

Dvornik stared at me. "I keep a vat of acid in my sculpting studio."

Well, I asked.

There was a tray of crackers and cheese and apple slices on the table, and two pitchers of water and tea respectively. On the table in front of my seat was a manila folder, a yellow legal pad, a mechanical pencil, and a picture of Anne Marie Padgett, whose angular face was glowering at me over a column of statistics about her age, weight, hair color, and distinguishing tattoos. I looked over and saw that Molly also had a picture of Anne Marie in front of her. She had drawn a little Adolf Hitler mustache on it.

I glanced through the manila folder. There was a thick sheaf of bearer bonds in it, at least two hundred thousand dollars' worth. Everyone else at the table had a folder too.

"Hey, John. We were just talking about making you the human sacrif— I mean...point man of this little expedition," Cahill announced. "Assuming that these vampires are actually making tunnels and that we can find them."

"I'm the logical choice," I agreed unenthusiastically.

"Good," Cahill said. "Dvornik says he and his nephews can spot trip wires and pits pretty well, but we figured you probably know how to do that stuff too if all this knight talk isn't a load of bullshit, and you heal fast and have sharper senses."

"Also, no one will care if you die," Dvornik added. It didn't sound like he was joking.

Molly patted my forearm. "I will," she said cheerfully.

Choo cleared his throat. "That sense of smell of yours is the big thing," he said uncomfortably.

Sig came back into the room carrying two plates of cut sausage wedges. I hoped she wasn't sending me a message. "Did I miss something?"

"We've all agreed that I smell better than your boyfriend and his nephews," I said, and Molly pinched me.

Sig opened her mouth to say something, but Parth jumped in. "John has agreed to be your scout," he said smoothly. "Now we need to figure out how to minimize the risk to him as much as possible."

"Cahill had a point," I said. "How likely is it that there will even be tunnels? I mean, I know vampires can dig like nobody's business, and I think this Anne Marie is going to try, but it's not that simple."

I know a little about tunnels. Not a lot, but I've hunted things that burrow before. Gesturing at the drawing on the screen, I continued. "You can't just start something like that in your backyard, not unless you excrete some kind of building material or adhesive. You need a low water table and soil that packs well and dries hard."

Choo cleared his throat again. "We're living in a place called *Clay*burg. You ever wonder how this city got that name?"

As a matter of fact, I had not.

Somewhere during all of that, Sig had put the sausage plates on the tray and seated herself behind the laptop. But Parth simply spoke and the picture on the screen scrolled through several other pictures and stopped on a map of Clayburg and its outlying counties. A large area between some mountains and a forest preserve was circled in black.

Parth cleared his throat to get everyone's attention, and I wondered why he wasn't the one set up to give this presentation in the first place. It was his material, after all, and the tech was reacting to his voice commands. He had a far better setup at his house. Then I looked at Dvornik sitting on the far side of the table with his arms crossed and his chin lowered as if he were about to ram his head into something. It occurred to me that I might not be the only supernatural being that Dvornik barely tolerated because of Sig.

And here I thought kresniks were supposed to be more tolerant and open-minded about working with monsters. Well, not all Irish people are poetic, not all Italians are good cooks, and not all Asians are hardworking. Maybe Dvornik was one of those people who justifies being an asshole under the guise of stubborn independence, or maybe kresniks had recently adopted some policy that supernatural beings are acceptable company only if they have blonde hair, blue eyes, and a nice rack. God knows how you would word that in a solemn oath or a secret kresnik ceremony. It was probably one of those unspoken rules.

"What's with that area that's all lit up?" I prodded.

"I've been tracing the positions of the cell phones that Anne Marie has been placing on buses and trucks," Parth replied. "I have a computer program that has been backtracking them by accessing the truck and bus routes and triangulating a common point of origin and blah blah blah some technical terms."

Look, I'm not cell phone–savvy, okay? Basically, I got from what Parth said that Anne Marie's tactic would have worked with a single cell phone, but ditching twelve cell phones in the same fashion had given Parth enough information to estimate the general locale where the phones were converging before being abandoned from different locations.

Cahill massaged his temples with both hands. "So basically this is what we've got: according to John, he can smell that there are at least four unaccounted-for vampires running around. According to Dvornik, they're being led by someone who is big trouble waiting to happen. We have computer evidence that someone has been researching how to transfer blood from a living body and store it. We found actual drained corpses. We also know someone is researching how to build underground tunnel networks. And e-mails and phone records indicate that someone has been promising to turn hard-core vampire fans into the real thing for a ten-thousand-dollar fee and servitude." He looked up. "Am I missing anything?"

"Most creatures who are extremely old and powerful are slow to adapt to new ways," Parth said softly, and there was a hint of self-satisfaction in his tone. He clearly viewed himself as exempt from such folly. "And most vampire rulers are very old and powerful. It is why the species as a whole has been slow to take advantage of new technologies. But this Ann Marie creature is very adaptable. I find the way that she is utilizing network skills frankly terrifying. She is tapping into a potentially limitless supply of recruits."

"The ten-thousand-dollar price tag is actually kind of inspired too," Molly said. "It'll help her weed out the posers from real fanatics and get her hands on some seed money at the same time."

Sig piped up. "I'll tell you something we're missing. There's no way these vampires want to live in a dirty hole in the ground. They like soft, dry, warm places with electric lights and cable television just like we do. That's not what this is about."

"So what is it about, Sig?" Cahill asked. His voice was a caress. I don't think he noticed.

"She's building an out-of-the-way place to hide all the humans that she wants to abduct and keep alive as a constant source of blood," Sig said. "This place isn't a home. It's going to be a dairy farm except with humans instead of cows and blood instead of milk. The vampires will probably work there in rotation."

"But why?" Molly asked.

"One of the biggest problems vampires have is that they can't gather in large numbers without becoming noticeable," I said. "It's why the knights knew what they were doing in New Orleans around the turn of the century. Too many predators hunting in the same hunting ground is going to draw attention sooner or later, Pax or no Pax. But this underground fast-food restaurant that Ann Marie is working on would make it a lot easier for large groups of vampires to meet and feed without logistics problems."

"So basically, she's found a way to recruit hundreds of potential fanatical followers," Cahill summarized. "And she's making preparations so that she'll be able to discreetly feed large numbers of vampires gathered in one place without having them all out hunting at once. It sounds like our Little Miss Teen Scream has big plans."

"How big an area we talking about here?" Choo asked, indicating the diagram on the wall. His voice sounded faintly strained.

Parth considered. "The search radius will be slightly less than a hundred miles."

Cahill made a pained sound that suggested he'd been on more than one hunt for a missing person in a wilderness area. "That's the radius," he repeated.

"But John here will be able to smell them out, right?" Choo asked hopefully.

I nodded. "Eventually. It would be nice if we could narrow the target area down, though."

"Well, if we do," Choo said, "I still have that fogger that makes clouds out of holy water. We ought to be able to gas these things like gophers in their holes."

Everyone in the room perked up at that. After a moment, though, I saw the drawback. "It probably won't work," I said reluctantly.

"Why not?" Choo demanded.

"He's right, Childers," Dvornik said tiredly.

"Why not?" Choo repeated.

Dvornik got up and turned to Parth. "Put that drawing of a tunnel network back up." It wasn't a request.

For a moment Parth looked like he was going to demand that Dvornik say please. Curiosity or maturity or both won out, though, and he pulled the picture up.

Dvornik walked up and pointed to several different tunnel points as he talked. "It wouldn't matter if your mist was slightly lighter or heavier than air," he said. "See how some tunnels go straight up and some drop straight down? The Viet Cong designed them that way to impede gas attacks. If the vampires are really sticking to the diagrams, somewhere on this level there will be a waterproof, airtight trapdoor leading to another level with its own ventilation shafts for an independent air supply. An escape shaft too."

He looked at Sig. It was an ambiguous look. It might have been saying, *See? The old dog still knows a few tricks.* Or it might have been saying, *The herd bull is still a stud.* Or maybe it said, *If I look unhappy all the time, no one will know when I have gas.*

"Well, yes, but their leader is a teenager," Molly said argumentatively, and the jut of her chin and the uncharacteristic quarrelsomeness in her tone told me that she didn't much like Dvornik. "A modern teenager who's been a vampire for less than a year. Maybe she is some kind of genius, but do you really think they'll have the patience or the experience to do that good of a job on their first try?" She turned to me. "What do you think, John?"

I appreciated the gesture and all, but I was still feeling a little tentative and raw and didn't really want to get in the middle of it, so I passed the attention back to Dvornik. "Ask the Amazing Kreskin. He's the one who says he can see the future."

"It's kresnik," Choo said irritably. "Not Kreskin." Sometimes I forget how old I am. I thought about explaining that Kreskin was a famous stage psychic whose name was an anagram of *kresnik*, but let it drop.

Then Dvornik scowled at me, and I found it hard to keep my mouth shut after all.

"Molly makes a good point, though," I said. "The other thing to consider is whether or not we want to go in these tunnels at all."

"I was thinking that too," Cahill admitted. "Why not just find the tunnel entrance and wait outside with a sniper rifle? Or a crossbow, or whatever you use to take a vampire down? Just taking the girl out is the priority, right? We can take the rest of them anytime, any way we want."

"A high-enough-caliber rifle and the right ammo would do it," I assured him. "But getting a clear shot at a vampire from a distance is kind of iffy. Trying to get a clear shot from up close is even worse."

"It's possible if you fire from far enough away and keep your emotions out of it," Dvornik said, as if correcting me. Then he addressed Cahill and admitted, "But it is always chancy. They're limited telepaths and have phenomenal hearing and scenting ability as well. They can sense when someone's looking at them, especially with hostile intent. And if we didn't kill her with the first shot... catching a supernaturally fast being with a lot of woods to run through at night is always problematic."

Dvornik glared at me then. "Isn't it?"

I just stared at him. Did he know about Alaska? Had he been asking around? How much had Sig told him?

"Maybe we should just call these knights you all keep talking about," Choo drawled. "This is starting to sound a lot more dangerous than anything else we've done."

"We've talked about that," Sig said, flashing me a half-guilty look. "But the nearest chapter of knights are Crusaders."

My entire torso puckered.

"And that's bad?" Cahill demanded. "I thought all the knights were crusaders. We're talking about the Knights Templar here, right?"

One side effect of the Pax Arcana is that over the centuries, many sects and chapters and schisms have formed within the Templars. This is because the knights are human and the geas prohibits anyone from quitting being a knight. Even I, who am generally considered an outcast and traitor and abomination and all-around sign of the apocalypse, find myself still trying to fulfill the order's mission statement to the best of my ability.

On a practical level, this means that knights can no longer settle policy disputes and personal issues the old-fashioned way.

Knights can't leave the Templars to start their own orders, for example, or kill one another, or betray specific chapters to kings who are greedy to refinance their next war, and so on. The geas won't let knights do so because weakening the order as a whole would directly endanger the Pax.

Human nature is human nature, though, and so there have been political factions and doctrinal disputes and personality clashes, and the order has been forced to accommodate a broader spectrum of opposing viewpoints than it otherwise would, often ungracefully. It's a lot like being a Jew, except instead of being rooted in ethnicity, the knights' bond is rooted in...geasnicity? Geasiprocity? Geasiness? Anyway, there are agnostic knights, atheist knights, religious knights, old-school knights, technology-loving knights, knights who believe the order should study magic, knights who believe that no magic should ever be studied, and so on. There are even some individuals with knight blood in their veins who believe that the order's goal should be to go among supernatural creatures and make peace instead of keep the peace. These radicals are called *bug huggers* and tend to be marginalized and mocked relentlessly. And of all these splinter groups, the most religious and conservative is the Crusaders.

"In this context *Crusader* is a slang term," Parth explained, enunciating precisely. "They are the most fanatical of knights."

Choo looked at me. "Is that right?"

"It's been a while," I said. "I don't exactly get the company newsletter anymore. But I think the Crusaders' basic belief set still goes something like this: they believe the knights never should have agreed to the Pax Arcana. They think the order should have let humanity be destroyed by the Black Death and let the faithful go to heaven."

"Well, maybe that does sound a little hard-core," Molly admitted.

"Now they believe the Pax is a penance," I continued. "And one that God will deliver his most devout knights from if they do their duty faithfully. On that day, God's wrath will descend upon the monstrous filth like me that infest this world and true knights will be a flaming sword in his hand, amen."

"Amen," Dvornik said, not quite under his breath.

Sig shot Dvornik a look that should have turned him into a pile of salt.

"Don't mean they can't do the job better than we can," Choo argued. "Sounds like they're highly motivated, anyway."

"Let me put it this way, Choo," Sig said angrily, displacing some of whatever she was feeling about Dvornik. "New Orleans used to be the home of the biggest vampire hive in the United States. The Templars told them they were becoming too visible, and the hive told the knights to bugger off."

"Someone's been watching BBC again," Molly commented.

Sig ignored her. "It became an all-out war, Choo, and the vampires were actively seeking out people with political power and military training and turning them into vampires to strengthen their cause. They were forming alliances with other hives. So the Crusaders stepped in. When there was a huge storm in New Orleans, they used it as a cover to end the war by blowing up the levee."

Choo's face turned stony. "You're talking about Katrina."

"Completely immersing a vampire in running water will destroy it just like sunlight will," I informed him. A lot of people have forgotten that little nugget of lore, but it's true. It's because water is a symbol of life, and moving water is a symbol of change. Plus, immersion in water is a symbol of both birth and baptism, all of which are things of which vampires are the antithesis.

Sig's voice stayed low and even. "Some of the most powerful vampires in the United States had gathered in New Orleans to formally commit their hives to a war with the knights. And they all died as their bodies were covered in running water. They couldn't even leave their hiding holes because of the sunlight. And all the Crusaders had to do was kill a few thousand innocent civilians to do it."

"You're saying these knights caused the flood in New Orleans," Choo repeated, his voice rising a little.

"I think what she's saying," Cahill said, patting Choo's arm, "is that we don't want to call these guys."

"Not unless it's a last resort." Sig's voice didn't bear any trace of uncertainty. "They might decide that the best way to smoke the vampires out would be to burn down the whole forest preserve."

"Fine," Cahill said. "Let's make calling the knights in door number three. So far it sounds like trapping Anne Marie in her own tunnels is the best idea."

"Why can't we just do that?" Molly asked. "Trap her in the tunnels and wait for her, I mean. She'd have to come out eventually."

"Did you ever read *Fantastic Mr. Fox* by Roald Dahl?" I asked her.

"I love that story!" Molly said excitedly. Then her expression fell. "Oh."

"Vampires dig about as well as the foxes in that book," I said. "Remember what happened when the farmers tried to trap them underground? If we pen Anne Marie up in a tunnel, we're going to have to go in after her before she and her hive can dig a new escape route anyway."

"Maybe it won't be that bad," Sig said. "Like you said, these aren't tunnel experts. Americans usually picture tunnels as these big mining shafts."

Dvornik took over again and stalked back to the drawing. "The Vietnamese made their entry tunnels small," he said, as if Sig were disputing that point. "They wanted intruders to have to crawl through them one at a time. If these tunnels are made correctly, we won't have room to swing swords, and we won't be able to fire shotguns or automatic weapons without hitting the person in front of us or becoming deaf. It will have to be silenced handguns and stakes. I don't have any UV bulbs made for miners' hats either, and they'd interfere with our night-vision goggles if I did."

"Do you want some of this, John?" Molly asked as she slapped a wedge of cheese between two crackers. She said it so soon on the heels of Dvornik's remark that it implied she wasn't listening to him.

"Just the meat," I said warily, taking a chunk of sausage off the plate. "I'm not really feeling like an herbivore tonight." Some thought was trying to form in my mind.

"Hold on," Sig said, and got up and left the room again.

"Sig's right," Cahill said. "These aren't Vietnamese peasants. These are modern American-citizen vampires who probably spent most of their pre-vampire lives on a couch with a remote. I'm picturing some big-assed version of a tunnel from a movie about coal miners. They're not going to want to crawl around every time they go in and out. They're going to want to walk."

"Wait," I said, holding a palm up. "There might be a relatively risk-free way of doing this after all. I just thought of something."

It was a measure of the underlying tension in the room that no one made any sarcastic comments. I kept my palm up until everyone was listening, then turned toward Parth. "Parth here is a hydrokinetic."

"Hey, no need to get personal," Cahill said. Nobody laughed.

"He can control water," I elaborated, just in case Cahill wasn't kidding. "He can move it around with his mind. If Choo makes a mist out of holy water, Parth here can move it up and down tunnels in front of us no matter how they're made."

The others did not seem excited by this revelation.

Somewhere in the building I could hear Sig rummaging around in a refrigerator.

I continued. "He's cold-blooded too, so the vampires won't be able to see him in complete..."

"I won't be going into the tunnels," Parth interrupted. "I don't take an active role in these things."

I stared at him. "Excuse me?"

"I will not knowingly end the existence of another being," Parth said calmly.

No one else seemed surprised by this information.

"You're telling me you're a pacifist," I said slowly.

"I didn't attack you, John," he said carefully. "I was testing you."

I gave him my best skeptical look, which, if you haven't caught on by now, is pretty damn skeptical. I disbelieved what he was saying so hard that I probably created an alternate universe where it wasn't true.

If he'd had the skin tone for it, I think Parth would have flushed. "I have a temper," he admitted. "My species is predisposed toward violent behavior. It is why I do not participate in it directly."

"Don't let her youth fool you," I said. "I've hunted a lot of monsters in my day, Parth, and I'm telling you, this girl is dangerous."

Somewhere Sig was turning on a microwave.

"That's the way it always starts," Parth said. "You say you

will not commit violence, and then someone asks what you would do if you saw an old woman getting mugged."

"What if you did?" I challenged.

"And then," Parth continued, "someone says it's not enough to react. We need to do something to prevent old women from getting mugged..."

"You're not going to change his mind, John," Molly said gently.

I glanced at her. She wasn't being judgmental. "I'm just having a hard time making the distinction," I said to Parth. "You'll help us, knowing we're planning on destroying these things, but you won't do it yourself because of a moral stance?"

"Perhaps I am being hypocritical," he acknowledged. "But I am an alcoholic, and violence is my wine."

That sounded like he was quoting a scripture or something. This had all the earmarks of turning into one of those philosophical discussions that take three hours to go nowhere and piss everybody off. "I...OK," I said.

Choo cleared his throat. "That was a good idea, though. Anybody else thinking outside the box?"

We brainstormed a bit more, kicking a few thoughts around: planting crosses in the ground every twenty feet, using magnesium flares to mess up their infra-vision, carrying riot shields with crosses drawn on them by Molly, and so on. We were still going over possibilities when Sig came back into the room carrying a large steaming bowl on the palm of her unprotected right hand. She thunked the bowl down onto the table and spatters of meat flew everywhere.

"That's got to be the worst Martha Stewart impression I've ever seen," I told her.

"You said you wanted meat, and I've got a ton of leftover chili that I've been trying to get rid of." Sig shot Cahill a dirty look. "Some people around here like to make fun of my cooking."

I glanced sideways. It was more a futile attempt to move my nose out of the path of the smells that were assaulting it than anything else, but Parth thought it was a cry for help.

"I don't eat beef," he said with a trace of smugness. "Or beans."

"It's true. I've never seen Parth eat anything except frog legs and caviar and snails," Molly chimed in helpfully. "And I'm a vegetarian."

And I'd thought Molly was on my side.

"Come on, try it," Sig urged.

"Yeah, John," Cahill agreed with a certain malicious glee. "Try it."

I was searching for some excuse to decline when the wolf took over again. Before I realized what was happening, my hand was grabbing the spoon and sticking it into the chili; it sank into the surface as if into deep mud, and then the surrounding chili oozed back into the suckhole the spoon had temporarily created, tugging at it. I looked at Sig.

Apparently Sig thought that this was normal chili behavior. She looked back at me expectantly.

I watched, dismayed, as my hand troweled a spoonful of the sludge out of the bowl and forced it toward my face. I could smell it coming, but I had to open my mouth or smear hot chili all over my chin. The entire table had gone quiet, transfixed with horror. Whoa. Rancid, ripe, spicy, sour flavors assaulted my mouth. "Oh my Gah," I gasped, still holding chili in the cradle of my lower jaw. "Now I know wheh bah beans go when 'ey die!"

Cahill cracked up. Molly turned away, but not before a small smile began to tug at the corners of her lips. Sig stared at me, her expression stony.

"That chili was fine when I made it," she said ominously.

I forced the chili down just to make it go away. It blazed a trail all the way down my esophagus. "What decade was that? This stuff would gag an Er Gui!"

In hindsight, perhaps I could have been more tactful.

"Fine!" Sig snapped, and reached down to take the bowl back.

My left hand swatted hers away. I growled. It was a low, animal growl from the depths of my chest.

Sig stepped back. She didn't look angry, just concerned. Not the kind of concern you'd show for a friend . . . the kind of concern you'd show if you weren't sure a dog had rabies or not. I knew that at least three hands in the room were suddenly resting on the butts of large handguns.

"I'm not trying to start a fight," I managed, my face burning in the dim light. "You don't snatch food away from a wolf."

"You don't even like the chili," Sig observed cautiously.

"I hate the chili," I mumbled, pulling the large bowl closer to me and digging another spoonful out. At least it gave me somewhere to put my eyes. "But I appreciate the gesture."

A strange expression came over Sig's face. It was impossible to tell whether she was touched or insulted. I could feel Parth's gaze on me as well, and I didn't have to glance over at him to know that he was looking at me with that "Ah, if only I had you under a microscope, my lovely" expression.

Molly patted my arm. "It's a full moon, Sig," she said quietly. "He keeps telling us that."

The tension in the room went down a notch at that, until Dvornik chimed in from across the room with a voice that was like a silk cloth draped over a chain saw. "It thinks you're bringing him meat because you're asking to be his mate. It will eat whatever you feed it."

"I'm. Not. An. It," I ground out, still forcing my eyes to stay on the chili as I dug out another spoonful. "And I do not."

"I'm not talking about you," Dvornik said dismissively.

And this was the guy who was going to be watching my back in a dark tunnel?

∿21∿

NEVER GET CAUGHT WITH YOUR PANTS DOWN ON A FULL MOON

There's a certain kind of person who, when anything bad happens to you and you express unhappiness, they just give you a look and explain how they have it worse.

And it's not like they don't have a point, these people. Hell, I'll admit it, sometimes I am one of these people. But somehow, I never feel like looking at them and saying, "Gee, you're right; thanks for restoring my sense of perspective, wise friend!" I just want to tell them to shove it up their ass.

I mention this because, technically, I don't really lose control during a full moon.

Again, I have no desire to eat humans, although there are some I want to kill. I never wake up the next day with no memory of what I did the night before. I don't go through the agony of physical transformation. So compared to what full werewolves go through, my lunar jaunts are trips to Club Med, and that's not even mentioning all the benefits that I get from my condition, to the point that I practically have superpowers. It could be a lot worse, and I do realize this.

I mean, yeah, I lost everything I ever worked for or cared about or believed in because of my condition, and I can't ever just relax and enjoy life because the great-grandchildren of people I grew up idolizing are trying to hunt me down and kill me, and a woman I loved was killed because of me, and I sometimes feel this other thing scratching away at my consciousness, and I can't tell if it's trying to get in or trying to get out, which is a little unsettling, and according to the little voices that were beaten into me from an early age by strict Catholic monster hunters, I'm damned and going to hell, which can be a bit hard on my self-esteem to put it mildly. But it could be worse. So, yeah, I'm lucky, OK? I'm blessed. And by the way, shove it up your ass.

I was the first to leave Sig and Dvornik's studio, because it was getting late, and I have a rule: I don't hang around people on the night of a full moon. Any people. Ever. And I was barely out of their house before I started getting urges to go back and talk to Dvornik some more. And by talking, I mean taking him by the throat and shaking him around with increasing forcefulness until either he submitted or his neck snapped.

This wasn't insanity. This was clarity. Sig and I really would be much happier if we just brushed away all the meaningless social clutter clinging to us like so many spiderwebs and followed our instincts. More specifically, tore our clothes off and had sex next to Dvornik's dead body. This solution seemed so obvious and simple to me that I couldn't believe I'd been struggling over it.

But I had my rule. This wasn't my first full moon, not by a long shot. I had spent years in India refining meditation techniques specifically in hopes of dealing with my condition, and part of me remembered the rule and seized it as if my mind were a fist that refused to let go. Avoid all humans.

Following this rule is complicated by the fact that it's almost impossible to stay inside a house on a full moon. I can't concentrate on any one thing: I want to eat, or fight, or have sex, or... hell, I don't know what I want, but I want it so badly that it feels like I'm going to explode out of my skin. So on this particular night, I did what I often do on full moons. I ran.

The woods behind my house lead to several patches of forest that don't disappear completely for hundreds of miles, and I ran west as far and fast as I could. I ran and ran and ran and ran, silently flickering through the forest like heat lightning, stopping only to drink thirstily out of creeks that I normally wouldn't touch. Stones and thorns tore into my skin—no matter how tightly I lace them, somehow I always lose my shoes at some point, but don't grow pads to protect the bottoms of my feet. But it was a full moon, and I barely noticed the pain while my body recovered from the damage almost instantly. My skin was hot and the wind was the only thing that felt good on it. Lactic acids were washed away as fast as they could build up in my muscles, and my red blood cells were multiplying so fast that my oxygen intake remained undiminished. I was tireless, directionless, running in a fever dream of running, swerving to avoid any far-off sound or smell that seemed remotely human—not because I was afraid, but because somewhere in the center of my consciousness there was a part of me that was still reciting the rule I would not break, over and over like a mantra.

Avoid all humans. Avoid all humans. Avoid all humans.

And then I smelled the vampire.

It was like getting hit with a dose of smelling salts: for a second my human psyche snapped back into full awareness with a disorienting lurch.

Somehow, without being aware of it consciously, I had been

running over the target area outside Clayburg that Parth had identified as likely vampire territory. How the hell had that happened? Had the wolf somehow taken the memory of the maps on the screen and applied my human knowledge of cartography because it wanted to hunt? Or had my subconscious brought me here while I was distracted dealing with the wolf? Was this some aspect of the geas at work?

Reaching for my silver steel knife, I got my second shock: I was completely naked. When had that happened? Again?

I was in the middle of a large clear stretch of flat land on the edge of a forest, surrounded by waist-high grass and assorted weeds and thornbushes. Crouching low, I swayed from side to side, sniffing the air to determine the direction from which the smell was freshest. Then the wind shifted, and I began to pick up other vampire scents. Lots of them, from every direction, including the one I had just come from. There were large gaps in the circle if I was any judge, but I was still surrounded. No way that had happened by accident. They must have heard me running by from a distance at some point and formed a wide net in case I came back.

And that's when I got my third and worst shock. I felt the wolf become as alarmed and surprised as I was. Baring fangs that I didn't have, I tried to flex nonexistent claws. I had no pack. I was alone and vastly outnumbered in enemy territory and had no pack.

Up until that point my entire experience with the wolf had consisted of me trying to control its aggressive impulses. I hadn't really believed that the wolf could feel fear; it wasn't a welcome discovery.

Something came whistling through the air from the direction of the first vampire I'd smelled. I leaped aside, and a heavy object crashed into the ground next to me. I growled. It was a large metal scoop: someone with great strength had ripped the wheels off a wheelbarrow and tossed the top half.

Wolf instincts and knight training merged in that instant—both were telling me to do the exact same thing at the exact same moment, and something fell into place that had never really meshed before. When psychologists talk about merging multiple personalities into one persona that can use the memories and strengths of both, they call it *integration*. This felt something like that. For a moment at least, two opposing viewpoints were fused together by a need to survive that was stronger than either of them.

I ran toward the vampire who had thrown the wheelbarrow. When you're trying to break out of a circle of enemies, don't try to avoid contact unless you're completely powerless against them. If you aim for a point between two enemies, you'll just find yourself being closed in on from two sides that each only have half as far to travel. The knight knew that his best bet was to aim for the closest vampire and go through it before its neighbors could arrive. The wolf knew that it had been attacked.

The vampire didn't come to meet me. He just kept yelling slightly different variations of the same words. "OVER HERE! IT'S OVER HERE! GET OVER HERE! HERE!"

All vampires are predatory by instinct, but predators prey on the weak, and this particular vampire had not been brave in its human existence. It knew that I wasn't human, and it knew that a lot of vampires in Clayburg had been disappearing recently. This knowledge was evident in the tension of its voice.

At the speed I was going, the vampire came into sight within seconds, although I didn't orient on him until he threw a rock the size of a milk pail at me. The hunk of stone was dark and flying at over a hundred miles an hour, and it actually scraped my shoulder as it went by. I adjusted my angle to meet him.

The vampire was at the edge of the woods and, turning to a tree behind him, he tore a low jutting branch off from the trunk with a loud crack. He was an average-size male, a little shorter than me and a little stockier. There was a pile of reddish clay on the ground some thirty feet in front of him; it had probably fallen out of the wheelbarrow top he had thrown. I slowed down just enough to scoop a large lump of the clay off the pile but kept running. The vampire broke the top half off the branch he was holding until it was a manageable club, probably figuring that he only had to slow me down for a few seconds or so before help arrived.

In a move similar to the one that I had used with the bottle of holy water in the alley, I hurled the lump of red clay directly at his face as I closed in, running. He had infra-vision, but the clay was cold, and in the dark all he could see was that something ___ ng at his head. He smacked the hunk of soil ___ keshift bat he was holding, but the clay burst ___ ed fragments of dirt into his face. His eyes ___ ey blinked, momentarily impaired.

___ vampire made two mistakes, both of them ___ was that he swung the tree branch blindly to ___ y himself a few moments to clear his vision. ___ sitant opponent this might have worked, but I charged in as soon as the branch went past and found him wide open.

His second mistake was that he was backpedaling, again in an instinctive attempt to buy himself a few more instants. It's counterintuitive, but when you're blind you should charge forward, get in as close to your opponent as you can, grapple, and not let go. It's true you won't be able to see what he's doing, but at least you'll be able to feel your way to tying his body up or striking back instead of just waiting helplessly to get hit by some unseen enemy darting in and out of your reach.

In this particular case backpedaling was an even worse move, because the vampire was stronger than I was, even under a full moon, and he wasn't using any of that strength to keep me from knocking him back. He was actually traveling in the direction I wanted him to go. I charged underneath his arms and into his body, lifting him up and bull-rushing him backward like a tackling dummy into the broken fragment of branch that he had foolishly left behind him. He was immediately impaled, the branch entering his back and exiting his chest.

A quick swerve to the left and I was bounding past the tree, leaving the vampire spasming out his last twitches as he dangled helplessly above the ground. There were sounds of pursuit behind me, voices and the sharp cracks of snapping wood and the hiss of whipping leaves, but I was in my territory now. It didn't matter if they had unnaturally sharp senses of smell. It didn't matter if they were as fast as I was. For the first time in a long time, there wasn't even a part of me that was ambivalent about my own survival. I wasn't being tugged in several different directions at once by training and instincts and geas-driven compulsions and guilt. I wanted to live, and the knowledge filled me with a fierce and exultant joy until I felt like flame in a world made of paper. I wanted to live.

I howled my defiance to the sky and ran.

~22~

THE TRUCK STOPS HERE

So I finally found a section of the New River," I said. "And I jumped into it and thrashed my way toward the middle and then pretended to drown when the vampires came out of the woods and followed me to the bank. I knew there was no way they were going to jump in after me in deep running water."

"And the vampires bought that?" Molly asked incredulously.

"I waited until the cold began to lower my body temperature," I said. "Then I stopped moving and sank down for a few minutes before swimming off underwater. The sound of the current covered me, and I found a protruding rock to come up behind."

"Vampires see in infrared," Sig informed Molly when she saw her blank expression. "He's saying the vampires saw his heat outline sink into the water, stop moving, and gradually fade out. That would be pretty convincing. Especially if these vampires are as inexperienced as we think they are."

"So your core temperature got that low, and you were underwater for minutes?" Molly still seemed skeptical.

"My blood is more oxygenated than a normal human's,

especially when I've been exerting myself for hours," I explained. "I can hold my breath for a long time."

"The vampires weren't the only ones who thought you were dead," Sig observed as she cut her double order of French toast into dainty little bite-size portions. "I'm going to shove a cell phone so far up your ass that you're going to burp ringtones."

I smiled. Sig could be in a bad mood if she wanted. The full moon was over, and I was free. Energized. Light. "I spent most of the night running around naked and then slept for eighteen hours in a cave. I couldn't have called you much earlier even if I'd had a cell phone."

"Why is it that every time I see you, you're either taking off all your clothes or telling some story about taking off all your clothes?" Molly asked.

"Seriously," Sig said. "Should we warn the waitress?"

"I think I can restrain myself until after dessert," I said.

The three of us were at a truck stop about thirty miles outside of Clayburg. I had called Sig from there after finally locating my sweats and my knife. The place was OK. The waitresses were older women with wedding rings who looked like they'd had hard lives but didn't take it personally. The food was simple and abundant, with lots of gravy and cheese and fried meat and your choice of canned and reheated vegetables. There wasn't a lot in the way of frills. Every section was a smoking section, and the view of a jumped-up convenience store area at the entrance wasn't emotionally uplifting, but the floors and tables were clean, the coffee was strong, and there were small plastic bottles of hand sanitizer on every table along with the usual condiments. What more do you want at four thirty in the morning?

"So this nest you stumbled into," Sig said. "Can you show Stanislav how to get there?"

"Him in particular?" I asked.

Sig idly stuck her index finger in her cup of steaming-hot coffee and stirred it. I couldn't decide if this was mildly erotic or mildly disgusting. "It's no secret that Stanislav and I are having problems. But this thing where you two are acting like thirteen-year-old boys is really annoying."

"He started it," I said.

She failed to see the humor. "Stanislav can check the area while he's out of his body," Sig reminded me. "He can locate the tunnels, map out their layout, and tell us how many vampires are waiting there with virtually no risk."

That made sense, unfortunately.

"I can show him the area on a map," I said.

"Good. Let's all meet up at Choo's house this afternoon." Sig returned her attention to her food. "We'll get our act together and then raid them in a day or so at dawn."

"Your whole group?" I asked.

"Since we're talking about acting like adults," Molly chimed in, "how about you and Sig let us normal humans make our own decisions about what is and isn't too dangerous?"

Sig looked slightly uncomfortable. "Molly and Ted and Choo and I already had this conversation."

"I'll be there," I said. I had misgivings, but the vampires were too numerous, the environment was too defensible, and the stakes were too high. I needed the backup.

Besides, I wasn't really going in as part of a team. I was going in to set off trip wires and draw fire. Back when I was a squire, my confanonier (a knight who's half drill sergeant and half nanny) had a name for anyone who made too much noise when they moved: he called them *Polish land mine detectors*. This was shortly after World War II, when people still believed the old Nazi propaganda about the Polish army attacking tanks with horses and swords, and England and America were being flooded with more Polish immigrants than their economies could comfortably handle. Polack jokes were everywhere.

When one of the more ballsy squires asked what a Polish land mine detector was, our confanonier put his hands over his ears so he wouldn't hear any explosions and began stomping on the ground as hard as he could.

Obviously I'm way too horrified at the ethnic stereotyping to find that amusing now, but at the time we all laughed.

Now it occurred to me, more than half a century later, Dvornik was Slavic, and I was his land mine detector. They say you should be careful what you wish for. If you survive long enough, you learn that you should be careful what you laugh at.

"I went by your house," Sig said. "When you disappeared."

"Went by it or went in it?" I asked.

Sig paused. She had just crammed about ten of her dainty morsels of French toast into her mouth and didn't want to speak while chewing. I suppose good table manners are important when you're female and bench-press small cars and eat enough food to choke a python. You don't want people getting the wrong idea. In an alarmingly short time she answered my question obliquely. "You've moved a lot of stuff out in the last two days."

"The important stuff," I said.

"So you're still determined to disappear?" she challenged.

I smiled again. "We need to talk about that."

Molly stood up and scooted her chair back from the table. "And I have this sudden urge to buy some magazines and sit in the bathroom for half an hour or so."

Sig shot Molly a dirty look, confirming my suspicion that she'd brought Molly along as a chaperone of sorts. "Then maybe you should eat more fiber."

"I want to make it easier for John to hit on you," Molly explained.

"First of all, everyone needs to stop talking about John and me in front of John and me," Sig said irritably. "This isn't high school. We haven't done anything, we're not going to do anything, and it wouldn't be any of your business if we did. And second of all, even if it were your business, you've known him less than two days!"

"That's one way of looking at it," Molly agreed. "Another way of looking at it is that I've known Stanislav for more than a year."

And then Molly was gone.

"Wipe that idiot smile off your face," Sig warned, turning back to face me. "Or I'm going to throw this plate at you."

"You mean that spotless plate that used to be full of French toast?" I teased. "My God, where did the syrup go?"

"Bite me," Sig said.

"Actually, that's kind of what I wanted to talk to you about."

She gave me a look that wondered just how many bones she was going to have to break.

"The werewolf thing," I explained. "Something happened last night."

"I know," she said testily. "You warned the vampires that we're still out there looking for them. Nice job by the way."

That one got through my good mood a little. "It's not like I planned it." I kept my voice even. "And if this Anne Marie is as smart as we think she is, her intelligence will actually work against her here. Even if she doesn't think I'm dead, she'll figure out that if I were a monster in control of my actions, I would have taken weapons along. Or if I were a wolf controlling a man's body, I wouldn't remember any of it after the full moon anyhow. Either way she would be covered. I'm pretty sure she'll decide that I was some kind of crazy non-wolf non-man freak of nature."

"I suppose a smart person would decide that," Sig said dryly.

"Which brings me back to my point." I was still grimly holding on to my temper. "I've always thought that when people turned into werewolves, something was taking them over. Something outside of them, like a kind of demon rabies."

"You don't believe that now?" she asked, curious in spite of her bad mood.

"I know I'm not 100 percent USDA-approved werewolf, but this weird thing has been happening the last couple of days," I said. "There's been this overlap."

"Overlap," Sig repeated.

"Last night, when I was in danger, the parts that I've been thinking of as my wolf brain and my knight brain had the same idea at the same time, and it was as if something fused together."

"Fused together," Sig echoed. She was going to have to stop that soon.

"Wolves always know where they are," I said. "But they can't read maps. Men can read maps, but they don't always know where they are."

"Yes," Sig said condescendingly. "That's why we invented maps in the first place."

I held my hands out as if framing a photo shot. "Last night I visualized a map of the area I was in like a man. And I knew exactly where I was on that map. Men can't do that without landmarks. Wolves can't do that. But I could. The man part of me was taking what the wolf knew and visualizing it or translating it into map knowledge somehow. Or vice versa."

"You said this has been happening for days," Sig observed, leaning back in her chair.

"At that strip club, the wolf started the fight but the knight was using cover and lines of fire. When I was late to your house, it was because I was circling it like a wolf would, but I was checking for things a wolf wouldn't have any knowledge of. Rental cars and out-of-state plates and sniper vantage points, things like that."

"So why aren't you freaking out?" Sig asked, reaching over and switching her empty plate with Molly's, which was half full of pancakes. "Isn't this the sort of thing you've always been afraid of?"

I looked at Molly's plate.

"That's what the traitor gets," Sig said. "Why aren't you worried about the big bad wolf becoming more powerful?"

She made air quotes around the word *wolf.*

Like there's an easy way to say that becoming a werewolf is so alien and intense that the human mind completely goes into emergency mode and shuts that part of itself out as if it were a different personality. That the only reason I'd even gotten a glimpse of this was that my geas acted as a set of brakes that kept the experience from being too overwhelming. I settled for "I've realized that it's still my soul, Sig. It's still just me in there."

I stopped and we waited while a waitress cleared our plates and refilled our coffee. Sig asked for some hot chocolate and a hot fudge sundae and a hot fudge cake for her friend. I asked for another country-fried steak and managed to keep my clothes on.

"I still don't understand why you're so excited," Sig told me as soon as the waitress was gone.

"I'm excited because this means my soul isn't being eaten up by some supernatural cancer," I said, my voice going a little shaky with emotion. "This means I'm not a coward for not finding a way to commit suicide years ago, geas or no geas."

"John," Sig said for no apparent reason.

"All those years being hunted like some kind of monster," I said. "And deep down, I've always thought I deserved it."

Sig's hand reached across the table and took mine. I don't think she was aware of it at first. We stayed like that for a while, and then the energy passing between us stopped being comforting and started becoming something else. She took her hand away.

"I'm not damned," I said quietly.

"I could have told you that, dummy," she said, looking away.

"How? Your sight doesn't work on me, does it?" I said. "Because of the geas. The stuff you knew that you couldn't know... it was all Alison talking to you. And she's gone now."

She looked at me warily. "I don't need a third eye to see some things."

"And your sight doesn't work on Stanislav either, does it?" I went on. "Because of his geas."

"Why do you care?" she asked.

"Because you're still with Stanislav," I said. "And the guy's an asshat."

Two bright red spots appeared on her cheekbones. "I am with Stanislav. And you need to respect that. Especially since you're leaving anyway."

"I'm coming back, Sig," I said.

I think she'd been half expecting me to ask her to go with me. In any case, my words surprised her. She blinked.

"You were right," I said. "This fugitive life is wearing me down. I've been getting more and more sloppy and self-destructive and bitter."

"You've been running from more than just the knights, John," she said quietly.

I nodded. "I know, or I would have admitted all this a long time ago. I have to square things with the knights somehow."

"How?" she demanded.

"I have no idea," I admitted. "But when this vampire thing is over, I'm going to find a way. And then I'm coming back here. If you and Stanislav are posing for Christmas cards and knitting pot holders when I do, I'll deal with it. Hell, I know you don't have to choose me even if you two do break up. But I'm coming back. I want to court you."

She started to protest, then faltered as a number of incompatible emotions warred across her face. Anger. Pleasure. Confusion. Guilt. Amusement. "I...court me? How old are you, John?"

I ignored that question out of habit. "I know we just met, but I like you, Sig. I think you like me."

"Look, I know you can smell..." She hesitated and blushed. "I know the female body produces...lubricants...when it's aroused..."

"It sounds so romantic when you put it that way," I said.

"I'm just saying, I admit I find you physically attractive," she said angrily. "But you shouldn't take that for more than what it is. You had a lot of pent-up feelings about Alison, and I helped you release some of them. It's easy to get confused when you've had that kind of a powerful emotional experience after keeping feelings repressed for a long time."

"I know what emotional displacement is," I said. "I was attracted to you before I even knew about Alison. I was attracted to you in spite of her, not because of her. And you know it. That whole connection doesn't turn me on...it freaks me out. And I'm attracted to you anyway."

Sig shook her head. "I don't like what's going on with Stanislav and me, but I know I need to talk about it with him before I talk about it to anyone else. I owe him that much. And I'm not going to talk about it with him in the middle of a vampire hunt. We all need to focus on surviving, not relationship drama."

"I'm not trying to get you in a bathroom stall for a quickie," I told her. "And I'm not asking you to make a decision about anything right now. I'm just telling you my intentions. I'm either going to get to a place where I can have a real life, or I'm going to get myself killed trying. But if I survive, I'm going to find you again and try to figure out if this thing I'm feeling is real."

"You probably won't survive," Sig said under her breath.

"It doesn't matter," I said, staring at her. She was beautiful, and I didn't care if she saw me thinking it. "I'm not going to deal with the knights for you. You're just the reason I realized that I need to do it."

This just made her angrier for some reason. Female isn't my native language; I'd probably messed something up in translation. "Do you want to know how Stanislav and I met?" she asked, looking at me squarely.

"No," I said with complete truthfulness.

Sig ignored me. "A lot of supernaturals go a little crazy with extra-long lives. I think it must be hard, watching people you care about die generation after generation. A lot of them either have massive survivor's guilt and start hating themselves, or they start to lose the ability to empathize with humans."

"Or the desire," I said. I had a little experience with that myself. I'd spent a lot of time living out of sheer stubbornness.

Sig nodded. "I don't even know how long my mother lived, but I think it was hundreds and hundreds of years. She wasn't handling it well by the time I came along. Having me was a form of suicide."

"Excuse me?" I said.

"In a lot of the old myths, Valkyries start aging if they

lose their virginity," Sig explained. "But that's not really how it works. Valkyries can only have one child, and it's always a girl. Once the Valkryie has a child, she starts aging. It was the Aesir's method of population control. They didn't want their creation getting out of hand and outnumbering them one day. They wanted servants, not competition."

"So all those stories about Valkyries getting cast out of Valhalla and losing their immortality and mating with men..." I began.

"They got the facts right but the cause and effect backwards," Sig interrupted. "Valkyries didn't mate because they'd lost their immortality. They lost their immortality because they mated."

"Waitress," I said.

Sig looked confused for a moment, then realized that the waitress was approaching from behind her. The woman set Sig's chocolate orgy out in front of her and deposited my steak on the table.

"Y'all must work out," the waitress observed a little sourly. She apparently did not.

"I'm going to throw this up later," Sig said expressionlessly.

"I have a tapeworm," I said cheerfully.

The waitress left, and I made a mental note not to order any more food. Sig didn't touch her plate. "I've heard that people who try to commit suicide regret it at the last second. People who have had guns misfire when they tried to shoot themselves, or didn't know the safety was on? They say that none of them just try again. They say that as soon as their fingers pulled the trigger, as soon as they thought it was too late, they changed their minds at the last second. The same with people who freakishly survive jumps from high places."

"I don't know if that's true or not," I said.

"Me either," Sig acknowledged. "It's kind of sad to think about, though. All those people jumping off buildings spending their last seconds wishing they could fly. All those people drowning themselves, trying to make it back up to the surface as soon as the water hits their lungs and finding they've gone too far down."

"You're saying your mom regretted having you," I said.

"I think she regretted it two seconds after she found out she'd gotten pregnant," Sig said.

"Did she resent you?" I asked.

Sig picked up a fork and began digging into her hot fudge cake. She ate mechanically and didn't answer for a while. Then she said, "My mom went through all kinds of bizarre stages. She tried to be the perfect housewife. She tried to become this ultraconservative Southern Baptist. She ran off and went on drunk binges. She tried to act like I was the most precious thing in her life. She acted like I was some kind of demon spawn. She didn't have a center. She was totally self-involved and terrified and grasping for any kind of comfort the whole time I knew her, which wasn't long."

Sig finished her cake and let out a long breath, as if she were deflating. "The thing I can't forgive her for, though, is that my mom didn't tell me what I was. She never told me she'd been a Valkyrie, or even what a Valkyrie was. She always acted like my gifts were some kind of demon curse and made a big deal about hiding them. I thought she hated me because I was a freak, but now I think she hated me because she envied me."

"Is that why you're so into the Norse thing now?" I asked.

"You mean am I overcompensating?" Sig laughed bitterly. "Probably. I had all kinds of crazy ideas growing up. I thought I was like Joan of Arc while Mom was going through her Christian phase. Then when I was thirteen years old Dave Hagan showed me this comic book called *The X-Men*, and I thought I was a mutant. Then that whole missing-time craze came along, and I decided that I was a star child…that my mother had been abducted and impregnated by aliens or something. She'd been dead from alcohol poisoning and God knows what else for a couple of years by that time."

I noticed that she wasn't talking about her father at all, and whatever was between her and Stanislav, I had a feeling there had to be daddy issues involved. I didn't press, though. The truth is, love is everyone's inconsistency. It makes all of us stupid. The dumbest and weakest things I've ever done all involved trying to make my life fit around someone I wanted, or trying to make someone I wanted be someone they weren't.

"Anyway, I was always trying to find some purpose for my life, you know?" Sig went on. "Some reason that I could see monsters and dead people and toss football players around like pillows. All adolescents want to do is belong, and I wasn't even human."

"You don't have to be a human to be human," I said, then winced. It sounded like an odd bumper sticker.

Fortunately Sig wasn't really listening to me. "And I was angry. Really angry. I went through a phase where I just drifted around, listening to shitty music, partying too much, fighting too much, leaving burned bridges behind me everywhere I went while I was looking for any kind of money or trouble I could find. I wasn't real mature, and I didn't have the best role models growing up."

"A phase," I commented.

She smiled lopsidedly. "A decade. The nineties kind of went by in a blur."

"And that's why you don't drink now?" I asked.

She looked at me for a long moment, some story she didn't want to tell passing behind her eyes. "No."

"OK," I said.

"I did something I'm not proud of," she sort of elaborated. "It doesn't matter what. Use your imagination and you probably won't be far off."

"OK," I said.

Sig's tone had become a shade defiant, as if I were arguing with her. "I don't know if I'm an addict or not, but I swore I'd never drink again, and I haven't."

"What's all this got to do with Stanislav?" I asked quietly.

"He's the one who told me what I was," Sig said. "I thought he was a ghost the first time I saw him. I'm at this rave in a cellar in New York, right? This was before I quit drinking. And Stanislav shows up and starts talking to me, only no one else can see him. He's telling me that this party I'm in the middle of is actually a vampire trap. That all the guests are like me, drifters and addicts and kids straight off the bus who won't be missed. It's how this particular vampire hive liked to party. I don't know what they wanted with me. It's not like they could drink my blood."

"They're territorial," I speculated. "The stationary ones don't like other supernaturals wandering onto their hunting ground. And you're beautiful, and some of them like to polish off blood gorges with a bit of rape. But you know that."

"I know that," Sig agreed darkly. "So Stanislav tells me that the place is about to be raided by some very badass people… some of your knights as a matter of fact, but I didn't know that then. He told me that I very much didn't want to be around when these scary individuals showed up."

"So Stanislav was doing that walking-outside-his-body

thing." I know, that was obvious. I was just talking to keep her talking.

She agreed. "Stanislav's spirit form led me down this passageway to a storage closet and told me to break through the west wall. It was thin, and there was a tunnel on the other side. The music at the rave was really loud—probably to cover up screams…but I could still hear explosions and gunfire starting behind me while I was leaving."

"I'm surprised the knights didn't track you down," I observed. "If you were still half impaired."

"This woman named Kasia came and found me in the tunnel," Sig said. "She was Stanislav's first partner."

"You mentioned her in the van," I said. "She was some kind of supernatural too, wasn't she?"

"The bitch was inhuman all right," Sig agreed tightly. "Kresniks aren't like knights. They don't mind working with other supernaturals."

"They're smaller in number," I commented. "They have to be more flexible. What I don't get is how Stanislav knew you were a Valkyrie."

"He'd been tracking me and watching me for months trying to figure out what I was," Sig admitted. "I never noticed."

"And when he figured it out, he approached you and told you?" I asked.

Sig shook her head. "He didn't just tell me, he took me to another Valkyrie he'd found."

"The one who taught you that spell with the blood," I noted.

Sig ignored this. "Stanislav trained me. He gave me a purpose. He gave me something I could hold on to."

I kept silent, but my mind was busy filling in blanks. Sig obviously hadn't liked this Kasia, and if she and Stanislav's first partner had been rivals, it would have made Stanislav more attractive. And the father Sig wouldn't talk about was some kind of powerful emotional button. And Stanislav had been her mentor. And he could see dead people, the gift or curse that had been making Sig feel alone her entire life.

Sig stood up so abruptly that I almost jumped out of my own chair by reflex. "Would you mind riding with Molly? I have to go clear my head."

"I don't mind," I said. I would have said more, but she was already walking out of the truck stop. Was I right to give her the space she seemed to need right then? Should I have tried to follow her out? Grabbed her by the arm or tried to kiss her? Forced a fight? If so, I had been alone too many decades, become too used to guarding my own privacy, too used to not getting pulled into other people's personal orbits. It's not the kind of ingrained behavior pattern you change overnight, epiphanies or no epiphanies. I just watched her leave.

∽23∾

THREE'S A CROWD

Drop me off here," I told Molly.

She blinked owlishly but slowed her car to a halt. Even at six in the morning the road leading up to my house is too narrow and curvy for a car to stop just anywhere, and we were on the last straight stretch before my long winding gravel driveway.

"Who do you think is waiting for you?" she asked.

"Nobody," I said. "But if I thought they were waiting for me, it wouldn't be much of an ambush, now would it?"

"Thank you," Molly said gravely.

"For what?" I hadn't been much company since chasing Sig off.

Molly smiled shyly. "For making me feel mentally healthy."

I opened the door. "You're welcome."

"Wait," she called as I climbed out. "You're not going to just leave us because things didn't go well with Sig, are you?"

"I'll be at Choo's later," I promised.

"Then be careful," she said. "I don't like the look in your eye."

"Don't worry about me, Molly," I told her. "Worry about anybody dumb enough to mess with me right now."

She started to say something else but I shut the door.

*   *   *

Slipping into the woods was like shedding a skin that didn't really belong to me. The sun hadn't come up yet, and there weren't a lot of leaves on the ground in April, and nowhere near as many briars and vines as at the height of summer. I moved through the darkness like smoke.

I really wasn't expecting trouble, but it was possible that the vampires had tracked my scent trail all the way back to my house, and it was possible that my recent activities had attracted the attention of a knight, and it was possible that... wait.

I smelled pine.

There weren't any pine trees around my house. Some oak, hickory, and maple trees, a couple of other kinds of evergreens, but no pine trees. Not within a few miles. Keep in mind that I live in a world of scents as much as the average citizen lives in the world that he or she sees. I was no more likely to be mistaken about a strange scent than a suburbanite was to be mistaken about a lawn ornament that didn't belong in their yard.

And pine-scented sprays are popular among hunters who want to mask their smell.

I had a few weapons stashed in the woods around my property—mostly because I had bitterly regretted not having them in Alaska—and the closest weapon to me was a Beretta M9 hidden in a tree about two hundred yards away. It didn't have a silencer, which would have been nice, but at least it was in my hands when I located the source of the pine stink: two men who were aiming Barrett M82A1s at my house. These are military-grade sniper rifles that have been used successfully against light armored vehicles. Forget silver bullets—causing a supernatural being's head to explode like a grapefruit counts as decapitation.

The two men were about three hundred feet apart, lying on

the ground beneath dirt-covered tarps and wearing camouflage and green ski masks and fingerless gloves. I recognized them by their identical builds even before I got a faint whiff of their real scents. Andrej and Andro. Dvornik's nephews. Had Sig called Dvornik after leaving the truck stop? What exactly had she told him?

I could see my house from where I was watching Andrej and Andro. Dvornik's car—a green Crown Vic—was parked in my driveway next to mine. My front door was open. Dvornik was announcing his presence and challenging me to come in after him. Maybe he had expected me to go straight into the house after pulling into my driveway. If he had hunted werewolves, he would know how strong the instinct to protect territory is, how fast and hot the rage at trespassers can run.

Which is why I waited. The full moon was over, and I don't care how fast you are, how quietly you move, or how well you make use of cover; the most important quality in being stealthy is patience. Dvornik's nephews were within sight of each other, and in woods that quiet and with the equipment I had, there was no way I could take them both out silently unless I was willing to kill at least one of them, and I wasn't ready to go that far. It takes seven to thirteen seconds to choke someone out under perfect circumstances, and hitting someone hard enough to make them pass out makes noise.

So I waited some more. I was willing to wait all day until the bastards started packing up to go to Choo's that afternoon if I had to.

My moment came somewhere between one and a half and two hours later, when Andrej got up to stretch and take a piss. He moved upwind of my house and went far enough away that the smell of his urine wouldn't mark his location immediately, which was sensible. It also made it possible for me to take out his brother by moving silently behind him and using the butt of the M9 like a blackjack.

There were several trees that I was able to keep between us as Andrej returned to his camp. He didn't sense me until there were fewer than six feet separating us, and as fast as I am, six feet is too close.

Andrej never got off a shot. I tore the rifle out of his hands and slammed its butt into his jaw in the same motion.

That still left me with one essential question. Dvornik's nephews might have been a hit squad, but it was equally possible that they were just there as a safety precaution. It's not as if Dvornik hadn't made it manifestly clear that he didn't trust me. The question was, had he come here to talk to me or kill me?

I decided to ask him.

∾24∾

WOLF'S BANE

One of the perks of hunting supernatural creatures is that monster hunters have access to salves, powders, and compounds made from those creatures, and some of these have unusual properties. I smelled something I'd never smelled before the moment I stepped onto my porch, and I never did find out for sure exactly what magical drug Dvornik was on. In retrospect, though, I'd be willing to bet that it was camahueto horn.

The camahueto is an extremely rare animal in Chile, and its horn can be ground up into a drug that's like PCP, steroids, Viagra, and crack all rolled up into one. Humans are capable of some amazing feats under stress—those stories about mothers pulling cars off their children one-handed or PCP users snapping handcuffs as if they were made of aluminum foil aren't urban legends—and camahueto horn takes a normal human straight to that place where they're mainlining adrenaline, insulin, and testosterone. It can make a man as strong as a vampire for brief periods, though it also makes controlling aggressive and sexual impulses difficult, and the person taking camahueto horn often comes off the drug with muscles that have been torn to shreds.

One of the big debates among knights in the middle of the twentieth century was whether or not pairs of camahuetos should be captured and bred like alpacas for their horns. A faction of knights calling themselves the Swords of Solomon believed that using magic to fight magic is only sensible. The traditionalist factions worried that this would violate the terms of the Pax, while the Crusaders thought it would compromise the knights and their insistence on remaining free of supernatural taint. The bug huggers were divided: some looked at the proposal as harvesting the camahueto for their ingredients while others saw it as a way to save an endangered species.

I don't know how that whole thing shook out. I was forced to leave the knights while the debate was still raging. I also don't know where kresniks came down on the whole issue. But Dvornik was using some kind of drug. Whatever I was smelling was combined with his sweat... it was literally coming out of his skin.

The other thing I smelled as soon as I got near my house was wolfsbane.

Everybody knows about silver bullets, but most cultures have forgotten that wolfsbane is one of the few natural toxins that will actually kill werewolves. It's not easy introducing enough of the stuff into a werewolf's bloodstream to do this, because a werewolf will smell it from a mile off, and a slash from a knife dipped in the stuff will just make a werewolf mildly nauseated and feverish—but it can be done.

Some people say that wolfsbane works on werewolves because it was one of the ingredients in whatever magic ritual created werewolves in the first place, and therefore they have no immunity to it. Others say it's because hunters used to dip their arrows in wolfsbane while hunting wolves, and over the centuries this took on some kind of symbolic/supernatural significance all on its own, the way magic does sometimes. I didn't really care which was true at the moment.

Dvornik was in my house and packing werewolf poison.

His face stayed expressionless when I walked into my dining room. There was a survey map of Clayburg spread out on the table before him, and the bastard was sipping coffee from one of my mugs. The coffee was laced with the stuff I'd never smelled before, something acrid and pungent. Whatever it was, he was sweating heavily and didn't look good.

There were all kinds of ruses I could have used. I could have tried to sneak up on him. I could have pretended to walk into the house not knowing that he had posted his nephews outside. But I was sick of mind games. I threw his nephews' sniper rifles on the dining room table with a loud clatter. "Next?" I said, as if I were at a deli counter waiting to give out the next order. And today's special was kicked ass.

In answer Dvornik stood up and kicked my dining room table upward and toward me. It was not a small table—it was made of real oak and could seat at least ten people, but it went flying as if it were a TV dinner tray. That was the second indication that whatever was in Dvornik's coffee wasn't a sugar substitute.

My reflexes kicked in the moment the table went airborne. I dove sideways into the living room while the table was crashing into the wall and breaking the window over my porch. Dvornik thought I was pinned beneath the table and began emptying his pistol—a .357 Magnum—into the tabletop, puncturing it with softball-size holes. I could see this clearly through the room's entrance when I rolled back to my feet, although Dvornik was hidden from view.

I didn't pause but charged toward the dining room wall in the rough direction of where Dvornik was standing on the other side of it. The wall was basically held together by a few slats of very old wood, some plaster, and some wallpaper. I burst through it like a stripper popping out of a birthday cake.

Surprise.

Things got very frantic very fast. I got ahold of two pressure points around the radius bone of his wrist and Dvornik lost the gun, but somehow he managed to tilt and throw me off him with his artificially enhanced strength. The outer walls were a lot harder than the interior walls, but I still dislocated more than a few bricks and my right shoulder when I smashed into the side of the house. Dvornik pulled a strange-looking knife that was the source of the wolfsbane smell and tried to pivot and corner me against the wall. Limiting my range of movement was smart. Whatever Dvornik was on was giving him an edge in strength, but I was faster. Fortunately for me he had pulled his knife from the side of his body that wasn't facing me, and that gave me an extra moment to bounce off the wall and smash the heel of my left palm directly over his heart as he turned toward me.

A strange expression came over Dvornik's face. He slowed and swiped the knife feebly at me, and I took advantage of his weakness to block his knife hand at the wrist with my left forearm, then leaned in with all of my weight and hit him in the same spot above his heart again with my left elbow.

This wasn't arbitrary on my part. The guy was old and mainlining some kind of major stimulant, supernatural or not. Which is why I wasn't surprised when the knife dropped from numb fingers and Dvornik tottered backward clutching his chest, his lips already turning blue.

He dropped to his knees, then fell backward.

I watched Dvornik twitch and gasp and seriously considered just letting him die while his feet kicked. I'd just gone to all that effort to kill him—it seemed a shame to waste it. I definitely wasn't going to give him CPR: there was no way the wolf was exposing its throat to an enemy, dying or not. Finally I sighed and rammed my right shoulder against the wall, popping it back into place. Then I picked up the knife and the gun Dvornik had dropped and went through the kitchen doorway toward the bathroom on the first floor.

My medical bag is one of the last things I pack when I leave a house, for obvious reasons, and my first aid kit is a little more thorough than your average collection of Band-Aids, gauze, and antibiotic cream. Rummaging through the airdrop bag under my sink, I found the hypodermic of adrenaline. I sniffed just to make sure it wasn't the one full of mandrake root extract—which is effective against people who are possessed by a walk-in spirit—and went back to the dining room.

Dvornik hadn't moved. At all.

After *Pulp Fiction* came out, there were a lot of movies where actors stabbed someone in the heart with a hypodermic full of adrenaline, and the actors always gritted their teeth and winced, and audiences always groaned and ooh'd in sympathy. I didn't wince when I stabbed Dvornik.

The truth is, I kind of enjoyed it.

~25~

WELL, THERE GOES THAT SECURITY DEPOSIT

Dvornik's knife was strange-looking. I had plenty of time to notice because when a man Dvornik's age pulls himself back from that undiscovered country, he does so slowly. This was the second time I had legally killed one of Sig's allies, and I wasn't sure if this was something to be proud or ashamed of, so I studied the knife.

There was a seam running up the middle of the blade and a button in the cylindrical handle. I'd never actually held one before, but I was pretty sure it was a WASP Knife. WASP Knives were originally designed for divers and hold a small canister of compressed carbon dioxide in the handle. When you press the button, the knife injects carbon dioxide into the target. This can freeze an area of tissue the size of a basketball, or force someone's internal organs to move around in ways they weren't meant to move around if you stab the right body cavity.

The knives were issued to Navy SEALs for a while, but were eventually phased out as little more than an expensive gimmick. A knife is a lot more than a stabbing weapon if you know what you're doing, and it was felt that the WASP Knife's design actually limited effective fighting techniques. Besides, what can a turbo injection system in a knife really do that a severed artery can't do better, faster, quieter, and cheaper?

But given the wolfsbane smell...I didn't think the canister in Stanislav's knife held compressed carbon dioxide. He'd either converted the knife to inject liquid, or he'd figured out a way to vaporize and pressurize wolfsbane.

Well, it was mine now. I'd figure it out later.

Eventually my table was upright again, and so was Dvornik. I placed the survey map over the holes he'd blown in my table to make it look more domestic. I even got him a new coffee cup and filled it with water.

In his ham-size hand, the mug looked like one of those tiny plastic toy cups that little kids play with. The hand didn't tremble, but Dvornik was moving stiffly and slowly.

He coughed a weak cough. "We should have a real drink for this conversation."

"I don't have any alcohol," I said.

"Self-control issues?" He was pretty sardonic for a guy who had just gone grave shopping.

"You're still alive," I pointed out. "That ought to count for something."

"It might," he said, absentmindedly rubbing his chest. "But you and I both know why you brought me back from the brink."

I rolled that one over a little. He wasn't talking about the geas. I gave him a slight nod to let him know that I got it and agreed. "Sig."

"Sig," he agreed as if answering a toast. Maybe he was.

"So why are you in my house?" I asked him. "And why were your nephews in my woods?"

"You need to stop sniffing around my woman," Dvornik told me. His voice came from the depths of his overdeveloped chest, and there was a tautness to it.

"That's difficult," I admitted. "I really like her, and I really don't like you. And you're not my neighbor, and she's not your wife."

"She and I have been together longer than most legally married couples," he noted with the matter-of-fact tone of a man signing death warrants. "Far longer than any relationship you've ever managed to scrape together, I suspect."

Alison had been killed by a man a lot like Dvornik, but I let that one go.

"So how come you never popped the question?" I wondered. "Or if you did, how come she never said yes? Is Sig your dirty little secret? Are you afraid the kresniks will take away your secret decoder ring?"

He built a smile around his teeth. "Don't think today means shit. I won't stop trying until I get you, and I know how to keep someone alive while I do damage to them. And that's just normal humans who don't regenerate the way you do. If you touch Sig, I'll have fun with you for weeks. Your mind will disintegrate before I'm done with you. You'll be nothing but an armless, legless, eyeless stump, shitting and pissing and screaming and whimpering from a mouth with no tongue or teeth."

I stared at him. His pulse hadn't fluttered even slightly.

"I've seen what's left of living beings who have had that sort of thing done to them," I said carefully, looking at him. His eyes were bright and unwavering. A madman's eyes, or a saint's. "That's one of the reasons I didn't kill myself when I found out that I'd been infected by a werewolf."

"The other reason being that you were a coward?" he asked politely. "Selfish? Weak? Evil?"

"The thing was," I continued as if he hadn't spoken, "I knew that no matter what anybody said, I could never be as big a monster as a lot of the people who claim to be human."

He made that expression with his teeth again. "If you're going to start quoting Nietzsche, you're wasting your time. Pretty words won't change what you are."

"Sig says I'm not evil," I pointed out. "And she says she's never wrong about that kind of thing."

"I don't care if sunbeams come out of your ass and an angel chorus tells me to leave you alone," he said bluntly. "Touch Sig, and I'll take you apart with a carving knife."

I leaned forward slightly and showed him my own teeth. "Threaten me one more time, assbreath. You already used your *Get Out of Dead Free* card."

Neither of us said anything for a while after that. Finally Dvornik broke the moment by leaning back and crossing his arms. I let him.

"Are my nephews alive?" It had taken him a while to ask, and he didn't seem particularly concerned.

"They're fine," I said. "They're probably having some circulation issues right about now, but that's their problem."

Dvornik shrugged his massive shoulders, then tilted his head sideways and cracked his thick neck. It sounded like an iron bar breaking. "There's an issue here that's bigger than both of us," he said regretfully.

"I haven't forgotten Anne Marie," I assured him. "Have you? Because I didn't need to hear about your big dream vision to know that she is one dangerous bitch."

"I haven't forgotten," he snarled. "I wasn't entirely sure my own geas would let me attack you until I saw my nephews' rifles. But I haven't forgiven either."

"I'll tell you what I told Sig," I said. "I'm leaving Clayburg after this, and I'm not coming back until I've come to terms with the Knights Templar."

To his credit he didn't laugh. His eyes went kind of fuzzy and condescending for a moment, though.

"By the way, Sig shot me down," I added.

Dvornik cleared his throat. "That's what she told me too. She sounded upset."

He looked down at his left hand, which was curling and uncurling, fist, palm, fist, palm, as if his hand were a heartbeat. "I didn't like the way she sounded."

"She doesn't seem like the cheating kind," I said. "And if she leaves you, that's her right."

"You Americans love to tell other people how life works," he grunted. "And you're nothing but loud, spoiled children. You walked ass-backward into a rich country, and you think it makes you wise. It just makes you fat."

I shrugged. "You can try to make this about me or my country if you want. But I notice we're not having this conversation in your wrecked dining room."

"You're the one trying to seduce another man's woman," he growled.

"I told her how I felt. She rejected me," I reminded him. "I took it. She told you she was staying with you, and you flew off the handle."

Stanislav drained the water in a huge gulp and slammed the cup down as if he'd just done a shot. I remembered Sig doing the same thing in Rigby's. They'd been together a long time. "You don't believe she loves me."

There are a lot of variations and gradations of love. But no, I didn't believe Sig loved him. And neither did he.

"I believe she has the right to choose whoever she wants," I said. "And I don't think she's going to choose either one of us, ultimately. She probably shouldn't. And that hurts."

"It hurts," he mocked. "You've known her a few days. You have no idea what it's like to give your life to someone, to grow old while she stays young and watch her get farther and farther away while she's still right next to you. To see strangers staring at you with loathing and disgust, unable to figure out what your beautiful lover could possibly see in you, thinking you must be rich."

"So you're going to kill anybody she might choose over you," I said. "And make them die badly. That's your idea of being the opposite of a spoiled child."

"That is my idea of protecting what is mine," he corrected.

"How many young men have mysteriously disappeared from Sig's life over the years?" I wondered. "How many of them have wound up in hospital beds or unmarked graves? She must attract a lot of attention, and you didn't just get this way overnight. I can't be the first guy you've ever been jealous of."

He went quiet and still. He knew what a werewolf's senses were capable of, but he had also trained to beat lie detectors.

"At least one, right? More than that?" I asked.

He still didn't say anything. His pulse didn't flutter.

"She doesn't know, does she?" I shook my head. "Or she doesn't really want to know."

"You don't know either. And somehow I don't feel like enlightening you." Stanislav leaned forward. "Stop trying to make trouble or I promise you this. A day will come when I will remind you of this moment."

"Tell you what," I said slowly. "If Sig ever says she's willing to give me a chance, I'll track you down and kill you before I sleep with her."

This time his smile was real. Feral and cruel, but real. "Who could ask for more?" he said softly.

For a moment we understood each other perfectly. It was the closest to a truce that we were ever going to come.

"Sig says that you know where the vampire tunnels are," Dvornik said abruptly, carefully taking a pen out of his pocket and setting it on the map in front of him. "She says you can pinpoint the location on a map."

"That's true," I said.

He knocked the pen toward me with a violent flick of his middle finger, sending it upward and off the table. I snagged it out of the air.

Dvornik shoved the map toward me and snarled, "Prove it."

∾26∾

BOYS AND THEIR TOYS

Choo's basement was a concrete room half again as large as the house above it, with thick metal poles spaced eight feet apart to help support the weight of the upper level. There were no rugs or pictures or tattered sofas or old TV sets because these weren't things you'd find in an army surplus store.

The left half of the basement was a series of aisles formed by crates, duffel bags, boxes, and footlockers. What was at least a two-year supply of MREs (meals ready to eat) was stacked against the west wall almost to the ceiling, and I spotted three flamethrower units and seven grenades laid out on a plaid blanket like a picnic in hell. The smell of cordite and grease was strong in the air, and umbrella stands full of machetes were strategically spread out over the room.

The right half of the room was a small-scale machinist's shop full of industrial drill presses, band saws, sanders, vises, acetylene torches, and a big-ass smelting furnace.

At half an hour early, I was the first one there. It was a little awkward initially. Choo offered me a beer, which I declined, and he didn't have any cute little sandwiches or polite conversation on hand. It didn't take long, though, for us to start talking about weapons.

"These are the guns we'll be using." Choo indicated ten handguns laid out side by side on a long aluminum folding table covered by a blue cloth. Each one had four magazines and a suppressor spread out beneath it. "These are Glock 31s, .357 SIGs. The magazines hold ten rounds. Hollow points."

I nodded. Hollow points got their name from having a small pit hollowed out of the center of a bullet tip. Notches are made at the opening of the pit, which causes the tips of the bullets to fold back like a banana peel when they hit the target, instead of being compressed inward. This increases the size of the hole the bullet makes as it spreads into lead petals like a blossoming flower while tearing through a person. It also slows the bullet down once it's past the skin, making it less likely that the bullet will exit cleanly through the body.

I picked up one of the Glock magazines and ran my fingers over the small holes in its side (these are called *witness holes* and allow gun owners to visually confirm their bullet count). Then I smelled my fingers just to verify where the smell I'd picked up was coming from.

"Verbena," I said. "Nice."

Verbena is an herb that is the floral version of holy water. According to legend it was the herb they packed in Christ's wounds after he was stabbed with a spear—which may or may not be true. Verbena was considered a holy herb long before Christ came around—Greeks and Romans used to brush their altars off with it—and the medieval church might have made up that cross story because it liked to try putting new Christian spins on old pagan traditions that refused to die out. That's how Yuletide became Christ-mass and then Christmas, after all.

Either way, it's possible to soak bullets in a distillation of verbena the same way Italian mobsters used to soak their bullets in garlic, but you want to take some precautions to make sure the bullets don't become sticky and more likely to jam. Spray some PAM in with the water while the verbena is boiling, disassemble your gun, polish everything with a product called Gun Scrubber, and don't buy cheap bulk federal ammo.

The resulting bullets still won't kill a vampire, but the vampire's body won't push the bullets out because the tissue right next to them won't heal. Instead, the entry wounds will seal behind the bullets, and the vampire will be left with these hunks of metal burning like a bitch inside it. You can disable a vampire with the bullets if you shatter a knee or an elbow, and if you lodge one of these bullets in a vampire's heart or brain, it will cause the vampire's system to shut down. It will be unconscious until the bullet is removed or the potency of the verbena fades or its organs evolve a way to work around the wounded area, all of which can take anywhere from hours to days.

"I never even heard of verbena until Dvornik told me about it," Choo confessed.

"Most people haven't," I said. "A lot of vampire lore never made it to the big screen. I saw an episode of some TV show about vampires that called it vervain."

Choo walked down the table and pointed out six steam canisters like the ones he had used at Steve Ellison's house. "Thanks to Molly, these are full of compressed holy water again."

I whistled appreciatively. "Will open tunnels make those things more or less effective?" I asked.

"I'm thinking they'll fill up about twenty feet worth of tunnel with steam before punking out," Choo said. "Throw one in front of a vampire and you'll buy yourself a little time. Throw one behind a vampire, and you should drive it toward you."

"Good," I said.

Choo grunted. "Better you than me."

"Got anything else?" I asked.

He showed me eight WASP Knives full of vaporized and compressed holy water and seemed a little hurt by my tight-lipped reaction.

"Anything else?" I repeated.

He scratched his head. "Got some magnesium flares, some riot shields and body armor with crosses painted on them in glow-in-the-dark paint, some wooden escrima sticks with sharpened points, stuff like that. Got a sonic emitter that I can't use because it'll hurt you more than the vampires, and those meditation tapes you gave me work better anyway. We can't use anything with too big of a bang down there either, or we might bring the tunnel down."

"Here's the thing I don't get, Choo." I gestured at the stuff all around us. "How did you become like that Q guy in the James Bond movies for Sig and Dvornik? This place looks like an ATF raid waiting to happen."

Choo's smile was a wince that was trying to be polite. "I used to be a supply sergeant in the army. I still have some old connections."

"That's not what I'm asking," I said.

He fiddled with some wooden daggers that were carved in the shape of Philippine throwing knives and basically useless to him—vampire reflexes are way too fast for anything thrown by a normal human to be effective against them. "After a few years in the army, all I wanted was to be my own boss." He looked at me to make sure I was keeping up. "Exterminating houses seemed like a good way to make decent money when I got out. A lot less trouble and risk than starting a restaurant and less training than you'd need to be an electrician or a plumber, or at least I thought so at the time."

"Makes sense," I said neutrally.

"So anyways, I'd been exterminating for a year abouts when I got this job. Some couple was trying to sell a house that had been vacant for a couple of years, and they wanted me to get rid of anything strange in it. That's how they put it . . . anything strange."

"Uh-oh," I said.

He snorted. "Now you got to understand, vermin have never much bothered me. It's not because I grew up in the projects either, if that's what you're thinking."

"I know you grew up around here," I said.

"You can smell that too?" he demanded.

I tapped my right ear. "I'm good with accents."

He grimaced and went on with his story, if that's what it was. "The one pest that does kind of get to me, though, is ants. My momma used to love to talk about Africa when I was a kid. She was always reading me African children's stories about Anansi and the Masai and about all the different kinds of animals and shit. She was a real good storyteller."

I laughed. "She told you about killer ants, didn't she?"

Choo gave me a grin that was both affectionate and cha-grined, but it was aimed at his mother, not me. "Oh yeah. She called them *hordes*. Man-eating ant hordes. In Africa millions and millions of them will come boiling out of the ground all at once and nobody knows why. They'll march together for miles and miles eating everything in their path, so thick on the ground and trees you can't see anything else. And Momma would describe how these stampeding elephants and zebras and giraffes and such would get trapped between the river and these ants and how the ants would strip them down to their bones in seconds."

"Nice," I said.

"I don't know how old I was... three maybe, or four." Choo held up his thumb and index finger. "But when I was an itty-bitty, I used to stomp on any ant I could see. I guess I figured I was keeping them from building up."

I wondered if that was why he'd been drawn to the idea of being an exterminator. It's weird, the seeds that get planted in our youth without our ever realizing it at the time.

"And one day, my friend and I found this mound of dirt and there were some ants on it. Red ants. Big red ants. I'd never seen an anthill before, and nobody had ever explained them to me. So I stomped on the ants."

Choo laughed ruefully. "Next thing I know, I've got ants crawling all up my shoes and legs. I couldn't move. I just stood there looking at them, watching them crawl all over and up me, and I really thought I'd kicked open some door to some ant horde. Then they started biting me, and I wasn't paralyzed no more.

"Ants were stinging and my friend was screaming at me, and I'm running my ass off slapping at myself while I run, but I wasn't going to stop and take off my pants for nothing. It wasn't because I was embarrassed either. I knew I had to get as far away from that hole in the ground as I could. By the time I made it home I was about half crazy and covered with ant bites."

"That would do it," I agreed.

Choo stopped to make sure I was still with him. "So I go to this house to spray it, and the place has already got this bad feeling. You ever walk into a house and just felt something bad about it? Like you just know serious things have been happening there?"

He laughed before I had a chance to respond. "Forgot who I was talking to. Well, this house is putting off the strongest bad vibe I ever felt in my life. It's empty, but it don't feel like it's empty, you feel me? I just know I'm being watched. I know it."

Choo rubbed his eyes. "So I finally go down to the basement? And you know what I see?"

Ants, obviously, but he needed to say it. "What?" I asked.

"I see at least a couple thousand ants on the wall," Choo told me. "And they're spelling the words *GO AWAY.*"

"It wasn't a coincidence—the fact that it was ants, I mean." I remembered what Sig and Molly had told me. "Whatever was in that house, it was one of those geists that can get inside your head." My geas protects me from that kind of mind-messing, but from what I hear, the beings that can peel back your psyche like a fruit and take a bite out of it are the worst of the worst. Maybe the ants were a hallucination, or maybe the geist could summon and direct organisms with low intelligence.

Choo laughed. "I used to watch these clips of black comedians talking about how there was a reason movies about haunted houses always had white people in them. I think Richard Pryor was the first one—he said that if a black man ever walked into a house and heard a demon voice say, 'Get out!' he'd say, 'OK,' and that would be the end of the movie."

"What did you do?" I asked.

"I couldn't move. It was like standing on that anthill all over again," Choo said. "Knowing I'd kicked over something a lot bigger than I ever wanted to. I just stood there and stared until the ants started to move toward me."

Choo cackled. "Then I moved. I ran like hell until I got back to my van, and then I drove like hell."

"But that wasn't the end of the movie," I said.

"Naw, it wasn't," Choo said, shaking his head. "I went back. To this day I couldn't tell you why."

"Is that when you got in touch with Molly?" I asked.

He nodded. "I wish I hadn't. That thing...whatever it was...it used to be a little girl who got abused. And then it became a grown-up who did its own abusing. And then it killed its own children when the eldest got too old to control and then it committed suicide."

"It showed you all that?" I said.

Choo abruptly left and went upstairs. I waited. When he came down again he was holding a beer. He picked up right where he'd left off as if nothing had happened, staring stonily at the empty air in front of him without looking at me. "It didn't show me all that. It made me live all that. I felt things that I would never feel...but they were my feelings because I was the one feeling them and that's the thing I can't get past."

He took a long pull on the bottle of Heineken. His hand was shaking. "That dead bitch violated me. She wore me like a suit. There just isn't no other way to put it."

I didn't have anything to say.

"Do you know how Molly finally got rid of it?" he asked finally.

"No," I said.

"She said she forgave it, whatever that means." Choo seemed angry and bemused at the same time. "Can you believe that shit? That thing put Molly in therapy, and she says she forgave it to death."

I started to say something, hesitated, then decided to hell with it. There was a part of me that wanted to express some of the emotions still roiling around from my own recent experience in this area, and he had a right to know. "Not all exorcisms are acts of aggression. You know, 'Begone evil spirit, I compel you!' and that kind of thing. Some of them are acts of kindness."

Choo's head tilted down and his mouth tightened. He wasn't buying it.

Well, I wasn't selling it either. He could take my words any way he wanted. "See, sentient geists are rare. The reason that most of their psyche is intact is that the messed-up part of them that is anchoring them to this earth was the major part of their personality. Their lives were completely screwed up and miserable, and they're angry and lashing out like wounded animals. It doesn't matter how forcefully you say the words, or fan the holy smoke, or scatter the ashes from the sacred fire, or dance the dance of your ancestors or whatever the hell you're doing; most rites and ceremonies are about connecting that lost spirit directly to a higher power that it should have been joining in the first place. It's like you're plugging something into a light socket. You wouldn't be able to survive tapping into the light socket either, so you have to use tools and steps to insulate yourself. Except instead of electricity, we're talking about a source of pure unconditional love."

"And that destroys it?" Choo asked.

"I don't know," I said. "Destroys it. Heals it. Absorbs it. Releases it. How would I know? It makes the spirit go away."

"So what happened to Molly?"

"Sounds to me like instead of opening the door and stepping aside, Molly tried to be the source of unconditional love," I said. "If they were linked, and that thing was making her feel what it felt, and she turned that around and made it feel what she was feeling somehow...and she was forgiving it...yeah, that might have made it pack its bags."

"Why is Molly all fucked up then?" Choo demanded angrily. "If all she did was give that thing a hug?"

"Because humans aren't a source of pure unconditional love," I said. "Even the best of us. We just aren't."

"Hell, some of us aren't human at all," Choo muttered.

I let that comment hang there for a moment, and then Choo held up his palms and apologized. "Sorry. Remembering that stuff got to me is all. I feel bad about Molly."

"What about you?" I asked.

He looked at me and his gaze was hot, some dark emotion burning behind it like a coal. "I didn't forgive that thing, if that's what you're asking."

"No, I mean, how have you been dealing with what it did to you?"

He gave me a look that could have been ashamed or defiant or amused and pulled a plastic bag full of marijuana buds out of his pocket. "The black man's Paxil."

I shook my head.

"What?" he demanded.

"I'm trying to figure out if I'm allowed to call you a racist," I said.

"No," he informed me.

"Good to know," I said.

∾27∾

BLOW MY MINE

At some point in the 1950s the good city of Clayburg stopped using a particular network of utility tunnels. Maybe the city upgraded the way it heated homes or ran wire or diverted water, or made some sort of technological shift so profound that it was cheaper to abandon millions of dollars' worth of infrastructure than to just build new tunnels. Or maybe it wasn't really necessary, but some congressman got money to start over in order to provide new jobs for his district. If Choo knew the answer, I never asked him. I just assumed that he had discovered the abandoned tunnels in the course of his job as an exterminator, and that's still the most likely explanation.

What I do know is that we spent two days using one of Clayburg's old utility tunnels to practice moving underground as a team. Well, maybe *team* is too strong a word for what we were. Sig wasn't talking to me except in monosyllables, and she made Dvornik look talkative.

Making matters even more awkward, I had told Dvornik that I wasn't helping him hide things from people who I trusted a hell of a lot more than him even if that wasn't saying much, and he had reluctantly told Sig's war band the truth about his nephews—that the twins who only spoke Croatian in fact spoke flawless English. Molly and Cahill and Choo were still processing the fact that the Dvornik family—and Sig—had been pulling one over on them from the beginning.

Part of me had wanted to move in on the vampire hive immediately, but the wait served two purposes. It gave us a chance to figure out how to work together in tunnels, and it gave Anne Marie and her group time to settle down and believe that I really was some dead and random occurrence after spotting me in their backyard.

The particular tunnel we were using today was big enough to walk through at a slight crouch, and the pipes and ducts running along the sides of the corrugated steel walls hadn't been maintained in a long time. The concrete floor was covered with at least six inches of compacted mud and rat droppings and trash, formed over years of flooding that had carried silt and debris and rust slush through the tunnel and then abandoned them there.

Andrej had spent several hours booby-trapping the tunnel and then hidden in it. Our designated task was to hunt him down and use the paint guns we were carrying to shoot him with head or heart shots.

I was in the lead of our line. As the scout, I was to find and disable any traps and tell the rest of the team what was what, who was where, and how many of them there were. I would also be the first to engage.

Behind me was Sig. This was partly because she and Molly were the only ones I would trust behind me, but fortunately that never became an issue. Sig was holding a large steel shield in front of her as she moved along. It wasn't a classic shield that they had gotten from a museum or a historical reenactment society—the shield was a two-and-a-half-foot-long monster whose bottom tapered into a triangular point. Choo had made it out of a steel door that he had salvaged and/or illegally removed from the husk of a decommissioned navy battleship. Fabric straps would have busted, so he'd had to weld steel rings on the inside that Sig could slip her arm through. No normal person could have carried the shield on one arm, even for three-foot intervals. I could have, but I would have gotten tired fast.

The front of the shield displayed a glowing cross that Molly had painted on it in luminous paint, so that any vampire charging it in a narrow tunnel would come to a dead stop (no pun intended) about ten feet away.

If I was the offensive probe, Sig was the first line of defense.

Third in line was Andro, supposedly the best sniper we had. When I identified a threat, his job was to provide fire support from behind or around or over the cover that Sig would be providing. He was using a Barret .50 caliber rifle now because he had to be reasonably mobile.

Next was Cahill, who was supposed to be pretty quick and accurate with a pistol. He'd had both training and experience in raiding hostile environments—usually apartments and trailers and the occasional meth lab, he'd told me—and Sig had assured me that he had a cool head and steady nerves in stressful circumstances. I never did get the full details on how she knew this.

And last in our insertion team was Choo, who was functioning in a support capacity. He was armed, but he was also carrying extra supplies we might need and had some basic first aid training.

Molly's job would be to move behind us, covering the tunnel conduit that we cleared with holy symbols so that we would have a place to retreat where the vampires couldn't go, and so that no vampires could dig their way behind us from other nearby tunnels.

On the actual raid Dvornik was going to do his out-of-body thing and identify how many vampires we were dealing with and where they were before I went down the tunnel, and this would presumably take him out of the action for a while. He and Andrej would be our reserve force.

We were using night-vision gear that projected a small light from a headband so that the goggles below it could amplify that light and use it to scan the environment beyond. The biggest drawbacks to the goggles were that they identified where we were in the dark, they had limited range, they had no peripheral vision to speak of, and any sudden bursts of light would be doubly blinding, but at least we were able to function.

I sprayed a strand of glow-in-the-dark Silly String into the air and watched as the liquid hardened into a plastic thread, arcing downward before splitting in half on some invisible obstacle. Son of a bitch. I was about fifteen feet away from an exit point, and this was the eighth trip wire I'd found.

"Rupt," I said, and Sig halted behind me. We had figured out that among us Sig, Andro, and I spoke about ten different languages fairly fluently, but English was the only one we all had in common. Andro knew Latin as well as I did, though, and Sig was familiar with a lot of the roots—her middle school had emphasized them as a way of building vocabulary or something. Anyhow, Sig remembered her Latin roots the same way that a lot of adults still remember their state capitals.

Sig rested the steel shield on the ground and lay down behind it.

Holstering the Silly String, I removed a can of glow-in-the-dark spray paint. I sprayed the area where the Silly String had parted, continuing to spray as an almost microscopically thin wire appeared in the air as if by magic, glowing ghostlike before me. Surely the vampires wouldn't have this kind of high-grade monofilament? There was enough room to crawl under the wire, but that wasn't really an option with a mine planted somewhere in the vicinity.

Unlike with the other trip wires, with this one I was catching a faint whiff of actual TNT. TNT doesn't mean dynamite sticks, by the way; it stands for trinitrotoluene, and it's a common ingredient in land mines and improvised explosive devices. Even before Alison died I had made it a point to be familiar with the smells of most explosives. Most poisons too, for that matter. It's one of the prices I pay for being so popular.

I scooched up a little closer and examined the trip wire. It disappeared into a hole in the side of the rusty corrugated wall and went downward, where it was undoubtedly buried in the silt and attached to the trigger of a land mine. Presumably the land mine was an empty shell and the explosive I was smelling was a lingering chemical trace, but I wouldn't put it past Andrej to put something painful in place. He was still sore—in both senses of the word—from where I'd taken him out of play in the woods the previous morning.

Was this realistically something I would actually have to deal with in the vampire tunnels? I mean, pits and Punji sticks sure, but land mines? Anne Marie was supposed to be smart, and putting untested explosives where they could bring down untested tunnels would not be smart. On the other hand, you never can tell what amateurs are going to do, and land mines are frighteningly easy to make. I could do it myself with a plastic food container, some wire, four checkers, a pushpin, some explosive propellant, and one or two other items that I could get from a grocery store but won't mention because I don't want kids trying this at home.

There are only two practical ways to disable your basic homemade land mine. The safest way is to detonate the mine remotely from a distance. The more dangerous option is to try to disable the trigger. Assuming the trip wire is actually wrapped around the trigger, this would entail uncovering the land mine without touching the wire and moving the mine in the direction that the trip wire is coming from, creating enough slack to cut the trip wire safely or enough distance to crawl by the mine.

Even if I wanted to try to disarm the mine, though, I wouldn't in real life, so I moved back. I crouched behind Sig and her shield and laid the can of Silly String on my thigh so that she could silently hand me a steam canister that Choo had provided for practice purposes. I didn't say anything to Sig or to Andro, who was lying on the ground behind me in a classic sniper sprawl. If Andrej had really been a vampire, he would have had enhanced hearing.

This is why all knights learn to sign and read lips. Kresniks learn sign language too, but I had found, to my frustration, that Dvornik and his nephews knew a European variant that I didn't have time to master. To paraphrase Steve Martin, it's as if those Europeans have a different word for everything.

I pulled the ring tab on the steam canister and lobbed it overhead toward the fire door. The canister filled the concrete room up with a cloud made out of holy water, and I heard Andrej come running down the tunnel ahead of the cloud, firing his paintball gun as he ran. I had to grin. Andrej was stuck between staying in a cloud that was supposed to be like acid to him, or running down the tunnel and triggering the traps that he himself had set.

That's what you get for trying to ambush someone with enhanced senses.

Andro had rolled slightly to the right of Sig's shield and was returning fire, so I moved slightly to the left. I held my gun in my left hand and fired blindly around the shield a few times before peering out, estimating the location of his center of mass from the sound of his footsteps.

I needn't have bothered. I had hit Andrej in his left thigh and twice in his stomach, but he only had human reflexes and Andro had marked the center of his brother's forehead with a paintball. This actually pissed me off a little bit. In the real tunnels the vampires would be moving too fast for that kind of fancy shooting. Firing down the middle zone was the best way to slow them down for a proper shot. Whether the shots went high or low, anything that forced vampires off their feet would be a good thing.

I had mentioned this before. After every practice we sat together and went over in detail what we had learned, then talked about how we could improve our chances, and then started the whole process over again. But Andro and Andrej were still showing off, and Sig would hardly talk to me at all.

They didn't seem to care that the actual raid wouldn't be as easy. I thought about that as I reached for some beef jerky from my canvas belt. Then again, maybe Sig had the right idea. As much as getting the cold shoulder from her sucked, maybe it was less distracting than getting all hormonal and dewy-eyed and drama-prone. Maybe the last thing Sig and I should do was talk before the vampire thing was done.

~28~

SIG AND I TALK BEFORE THE VAMPIRE THING IS DONE

It was the last evening before the actual raid. Molly started taking orders for takeout Chinese food, and I announced that I was going to go to the health food store to get some supplies of my own. It was roughly twelve hours until we climbed down into a nest of heat seekers, and I knew that Sig's group wasn't going to let me disappear on my own without a chaperone. I didn't even resent this, not really. It was true that everyone else got to come and go to take care of their personal lives, but I didn't have a personal life, and I was the unknown quantity in the group. Still, I was more than a little surprised when the person who volunteered to go along with me was Sig.

She was still not speaking to me when she opened the passenger door and silently climbed into my car.

"You know, you kind of give me mixed signals," I said. My newfound peace with myself hadn't exactly evaporated; I still felt more comfortable in my own skin than I'd felt in a long time. My conscience was clear, my eyes were bright, and I knew in my heart of hearts that Allah smiled upon me for mine was the sword of righteousness. By the same token, I had opened up to a woman who had then spent the next few days acting like she never wanted to talk to me again, been threatened by her homicidal lover, and was probably going to die the next day.

"I know," Sig said. "I just don't like the idea of going down that hole tomorrow with this thing hanging over you and me like..." She stopped and struggled for a good simile.

"Like an open airplane storage locker?" I offered.

She smiled a tight smile. "I was trying to think of the name of that sword that used to hang over a king's head. Was it the sword of Pericles?"

I just looked at her. Did she really want to talk about a sword?

"Come on, I know you know it," she prodded. "I saw all those books when I was in your house the other day."

"It was the sword of Damocles," I said.

"Right," she agreed. "Anyway, I like the 'open airplane storage compartment' thing better. It means there's a journey with lots of baggage."

"And things being balanced precariously," I added.

"And a lack of closure," she said.

"OK," I admitted. "I could start bullshitting about frequent-flier miles or something, but I can't really think of any more good ones."

"So shut up and drive," she told me.

I shut up and drove.

"Why are we going to a health food store anyway?" she asked me after a while. "Choo has plenty of verbena. He grows it in a patch of woods near his house."

"I have a feeling that's not the only plant he grows there," I griped.

She waved that aside. "He won't be smoked up tomorrow."

I made a noncommittal noise.

"So why are we going to the health food store?" Sig repeated.

"To get my secret weapon," I said. "Most people don't know this, but vampires can't stand tofu."

"Why should they be any different?" Sig agreed. When I didn't respond, she gave me a sideways look. "But seriously. Talk to me."

"I tried that," I pointed out.

"So what, you only dump a lot of emotional stuff on someone when they're not ready for it? Stop being such a diva." Sig's tone was impatient. "I didn't ask you to talk to me then. I'm asking now."

OK, fine.

"I'm not used to spending this much time in a group," I admitted. "I was kind of hoping to clear my head and get some high-protein energy bars for tomorrow. I'm probably going to need to heal a lot if I survive at all. I'm not sure why you're going along."

Sig took her time answering, which was all right with me. Right then I preferred silence to small talk. "I've been thinking about what you told me," Sig finally said. "About how I'm not the reason you need to come to terms with the knights, but that I am the reason you realized that you have to."

"That's true," I acknowledged.

Sig blew out a puff of breath. "I need to break up with Stanislav."

I played it cool and continued to drive steadily even though internally I was stomping on the accelerator and running through red lights at intersections and pressing down hard on my horn. "Yes, you do," I agreed.

"I feel like I've been cheating on him," Sig said unhappily. "With you."

I didn't deny it. "Good."

"Good?" she challenged. "It's good that I'm a cheater?"

"You haven't cheated," I said. "But it's good that you feel that way. It means I haven't been imagining us having something."

"Don't go getting cocky," she warned dourly. "I'm not in the mood."

I smiled, but only slightly. "Look, Sig, it's obvious you and Stanislav have had problems for a long time now."

She bit her lip. "I want to wait until after the raid is over to tell him. We need Stanislav, and we need him holding it together. If any of us are going to die, I don't want it to be because of this."

I didn't say anything.

"And I wasn't going to tell you anything until I talked to him first," Sig continued, not looking at me. "But I don't want to wait until after the raid tomorrow to talk to you. In case we...you know. I don't want one of us to die with you thinking I...hate you. So if I'm doing something wrong here, I'm doing the best I can."

"I get that," I said, and I did. When you're half convinced it's the last night of your life, bottled-up feelings have a way of getting out. If Sig had been Catholic, she'd have gone to confession.

It wasn't the ideal moment to have to deal with parallel parking, but suddenly we were at the health food store, and life doesn't have any respect for dramatic pauses.

"I'm not doing this because of you, though," Sig said while I began the back-and-forth process of wedging the car between a pickup truck and a jeep. Suddenly there were all kinds of sharp, pointy emotions in her tone. "You're just the reason I realized that I need to do it."

"I can live with that," I said.

"And I want you to know I like you too." Sig admitted this as if it were a character flaw.

I didn't tell her that I could live with that. I wasn't entirely certain that I could, literally. It probably also wasn't the right time to tell her that I'd promised to kill Stanislav before I slept with her. "Good," I said simply.

"Good?" she demanded.

"Look, I'm not great at relationship stuff, Sig." I finally parked the car. "Do you want me to tell you how I feel so you can tell me to back off until you talk to Stanislav, or do you want me to give you space so you can keep your head on straight?"

She smiled faintly at that. "Yes."

I snorted.

"It's important to me to do the right thing," Sig continued.

"Sure," I said. "Because you grew up feeling blamed for things you had no control over, by people who were supposed to be taking care of you. You knew that there was some secret reason your protectors were keeping you at a distance, but you didn't know what it was. Instead of giving you unconditional love, they gave you a code and a roof and just enough encouragement to keep you from becoming a complete asshole, but you wanted more. You wanted to prove to yourself that the world was wrong, that God was wrong, that whatever mysterious fucking power in the universe was making you feel guilty all the time was wrong, that you would be a good person given half a chance. And you worked hard for that chance, you're still working for that chance, but you don't really believe deep down that anyone else is ever really going to give you a fair shot."

Sig absorbed that. "Wow. Repress much?"

I laughed a little shakily. "Shut up."

Sig did not, in fact, shut up. "Is that why we seem to get each other? We both grew up not human and not knowing it? Or is this some weird aftereffect of me seeing you through Alison's eyes?"

"I was born in 1937, Sig," I told her. "And I still don't know why some people get each other and some people don't."

"I just know I can't be the only thing Stanislav cares about anymore," Sig said with a lack of inflection that seemed more exhausted than emotionless. "It's too much work. His life is too sad."

I just nodded.

"He's too angry," she added. "I can make it better, but I can't make it good."

"It's not your job," I said.

Sig looked away. When she spoke, her voice was quiet. "I feel disloyal. We've survived so much and saved each other so many times. You'd think him aging would make it harder to stay with him. The truth is, it makes it harder to leave him because everyone thinks that's the reason. It's like wanting to break up with someone who just got diagnosed with cancer or crippled. I feel sorry for him."

I didn't. I had a feeling that Stanislav had been playing that card against her for a long time.

"I find myself thinking, why not just wait it out?" she continued. "Any of us might die at any time, and he only has a few decades left at best. I could have centuries. Isn't that messed up?"

"He's messed up, Sig," I told her. "You just don't want to admit how messed up."

"John." That was it, just my name. A warning, and one I ignored.

"He threatened to kill me slowly and painfully, Sig," I informed her. "I'm talking really sick torture-porn kind of stuff too. And he wasn't kidding. He as much as admitted that he's gotten rid of men who were hanging around you before."

She didn't want to hear it. "He was trying to frighten you. Stanislav is a hunter, John. You should understand that better than anyone."

"Yeah, I hunt monsters," I countered. "That's why I know one when I see one."

"Stanislav isn't a monster," Sig said tightly. "He's just messed up like the rest of us."

"You're not afraid of hurting him," I said. "You just don't want to feel responsible for what he might do."

She was getting angry now. "Stop telling me what I feel."

I almost said, "I forgot; telling other people what they feel is your job." But I stopped myself. Why was I doing this?

"OK," I said instead.

That wasn't what Sig had been expecting. After a moment she backed away from whatever emotional precipice she'd been about to jump off. "I said that I'm going to deal with him, and I will. I'm just not looking forward to telling him."

I pictured Stanislav's hand when he'd been in my house, the way it had opened, closed, opened, closed. "He already knows."

Sig shook her head. "That just makes it harder."

I knew what she meant. Sometimes there are conversations that have been going on for years, unspoken, full of repressed emotions that have built up like an explosive charge. All it takes to set them off is for someone to verbalize them.

"I'm going to tell him after the raid tomorrow," she said.

My instinct was that she should find the son of a bitch right then and force the issue into the open, but my instinct was also to stab him immediately afterward, multiple times. I still had no idea how I was going to broach that topic with Sig. She didn't drink wine, and even if she did, I didn't know if red or white was appropriate for telling a woman that you want to kill her former lover. Do they have greeting cards for that sort of thing?

"After you leave," she added.

Something suddenly made sense. She thought she could handle Stanislav, but she was worried about me. Worried about what Stanislav might do to me, or what I might do to him.

"You're trying to protect me," I said stupidly.

She looked at me oddly. "Of course I am, you idiot."

"I'm not used to that," I confessed.

She reached out and squeezed my hand.

I leaned over until our eyes were only a few inches apart. "Let me explain something to you."

And I kissed her. I don't remember much about that kiss. I had just meant it to be a short one, but I think it lasted ten minutes and temporarily melted my brain. Somehow our lips never separated while our bodies shifted and groped and merged awkwardly over the emergency brake between the front seats. At some point Sig pulled away and gasped and said, "We can't do this."

"OK." I pulled my hands out from beneath the back of her shirt, but when I tried to pull my face away from hers she grabbed me behind the neck with both hands and pulled me into another kiss.

I wasn't the only one who had been lonely for a long time.

"We have to stop," Sig said the next time she came up for air. By this point she was pressing me against the driver's side of the car, one hand against the window and the other beneath my shirt, palm over my heart. I had her long hair twined in my right hand and was caressing the seat of her pants with my left.

"OK," I said, and kissed her again. I'm not sure where we would have finally wound up if a police car hadn't stopped alongside us in the middle of the street. One of Sig's hands was slipping into the back of my jeans, and I had the right side of her shirt bunched up in my hand. Even with my enhanced hearing, it still took a nightstick rapping on my window to snap us out of it.

Sig and I separated in a series of awkward lurches and bumps. The officer on the passenger's side of the police car smirked and mimed rolling down a window. He was a plump guy with a crew cut and mustache, in his late twenties or early thirties, and he kept the nightstick dangling lazily outside his window.

Once I had obediently rolled down my window, he peered across me and said, "Sig? Is that you?"

"Hi, Brock." Sig's voice was resigned as she adjusted her shirt. I had forgotten that Sig had been hanging around Clayburg's police station under the guise of being a psychic.

"What happened to your old man?" I don't think I was imagining a cruel emphasis on *old man* in Brock's voice.

"We just broke up," Sig said tersely.

Brock sneered and looked over at his partner. "Well, I guess it didn't take a psychic to see that one coming." When he turned, I could see the edges of a green tattoo sticking out of his collar. It looked like twining snakes.

"Apparently not," Sig said, her voice tight. "You're holding up traffic, Brock."

He laughed. "You're the one stopping traffic, darlin'. Families shop at this health food store."

I pulled the keys out of the ignition. "Sorry about that, Officer."

He winked, then laughed and motioned lazily to his partner to drive on. "See you later, Sig."

A few cars followed him and went by as he drove away. I looked over at Sig. Her arms were crossed over her chest and her face was closed up tight. Shopping hours were over.

"Well, I guess you made your point," Sig said. She seemed a little short of breath. "Don't do that again."

I studied her. "Ever?"

There was something in her solemn, steady gaze that made my skin tingle. "I've wanted you ever since I saw you in that stupid bar."

"I wanted you from the start too," I assured her.

"Yes, but I'm good at judging people." Her tone was arch. "You just thought I had nice boobs."

"Well, in my own defense..." I started, and I never finished the smart-ass flirty comment that I was about to make because Sig put her index finger on my lips. It was probably just as well.

"I need to break up with Stanislav," she said.

I unlocked my car door. "Yes, you do."

∾29∾

ONE CRAZY KNIGHT

I didn't smell the knight right away.

This was partly because Sig and I were surrounded by our own intense emotional field. I could blather on about my training and heightened senses and paranoia some more, but the truth is, there was this thing between Sig and me that seemed new and immense and fragile, and neither one of us knew what the hell we were doing, and I wasn't really focusing on anything outside a three-foot radius of her.

Sig wasn't saying anything. I reached my hand out and held it palm open next to hers, and after a moment's hesitation she took my hand and squeezed it. I felt absurdly happy.

We were a couple of badass monster killers all right. Maybe on the way back to Choo's she'd let me buy her an ice cream cone.

In regard to the knight I didn't smell right away, it is also true that when you have a highly developed sense of smell, stepping into a health food co-op is the olfactory equivalent of a laser light show. While a lot of the merchandise is still prepackaged and franchised, many co-ops grind or pound their own herbs on the premises, and plastic bins full of different kinds of nuts and spices are opened and closed constantly. Incense candles sit on shelves next to homemade soaps and potpourri, and all over the store handcrafted pottery holds various offerings from the local back-to-the-land types: anything from fresh-baked bread to organic produce to floral arrangements that supposedly recharge your chi.

In fact, if I were going to ambush someone like me, a health food co-op would be a great place to do it.

Finding the energy bars wasn't hard. There was a whole display of them in front of the first aisle, bars that were mostly protein held together by chocolate and peanut butter and fructose syrup if the packages were at all accurate, a few that were trail mix held together by syrup or honey. Sig and I paused in front of the display, and it was a good thing that we did.

When I check anything out, I inhale deeply through my nose. It's instinctive, the same way squinting and focusing the eyes is instinctive for a normal person. And I smelled frankincense and myrrh.

There was a Crusader roughly ten to thirty feet away to the north. If you're wondering how the smell of frankincense and myrrh told me that a member of the most fanatically religious sect within the Knights Templar was around, allow me to explain.

When a small group within a larger group feels like it is special and elite, it inevitably starts coming up with ways to assert its individual identity. Usually this is done with specific garments, like the Scots and their kilts, or tattoos like those worn by triad gang members, or weird haircuts or jewelry or uniforms. One of the ways that Crusaders assert their uniqueness within a larger order of knights the Crusaders think are soft and hell-bound is to wear a cologne whose base is frankincense and myrrh—the gifts that the wise men brought to the baby Jesus. Frankincense and myrrh are valuable for the same reason that most knights avoid them—because they have very distinct and powerful odors. Pragmatic knights like my old confanonier think the Crusaders are wack jobs. What kind of idiots would associate themselves with a signature scent and then broadcast it to every supernatural creature with a sensitive nose, for no tactical advantage?

Well, as it turns out, fanatically religious idiots. Although, to be fair, Crusaders want monsters to attack them: it releases them from the restraints of the geas.

The one good piece of news was this: the Crusader wouldn't have been wearing that particular cologne while specifically looking for me. Generally inviting attack is one thing— alerting a specific target so that he has a better chance of getting away is something else entirely. The most likely explanation for the Crusader's presence was that while Steve Ellison had been running around pulling God only knows how many stupid vampire tricks, he had sent up a red flag somewhere, and this Crusader had been sent to Clayburg to look around.

Avoiding any sudden movements, I tried to use my hearing to get a better fix on the bastard. He definitely wasn't the person in aisle three. That individual stepped too heavily and breathed too hard. The Crusader was somewhere in the next two aisles, then, and staying still. Probably aisle four, the one that would have been my next stop. The herb section.

Releasing Sig's hand, I grabbed a double handful of energy bars and turned around and walked back toward the cash register by the entrance, not rushing it. When he's not being distracted by six-foot blondes, a knight's situational awareness tends to be pretty high. If my footsteps became too hesitant or forceful, there was a chance the Crusader might hear them and pick up on their irregularity. Ditto if Sig and I spoke and our voices were forced or strained. Fortunately Sig was still wrapped up in her own thoughts and just followed me without saying anything.

I paid for the bars, watching the area behind me in the reflection of the front store window. Nobody emerged from the aisles except for a young girl with more tattoos and jewelry than actual clothes.

Sig and I left the store.

When there's more than one of them, Crusaders generally divide themselves into groups of three, five, ten, or twelve: the Christian holy numbers. If their mission requires really high numbers, they group themselves in multiples thereof. I tried to be subtle about scanning the outside of the store, but Sig finally came out of her cocoon and noticed something odd about my behavior.

"What's wrong?" She kept her voice low and didn't look around.

I spotted the knight's vehicle across the street, a Dodge Charger with North Carolina license plates. There were other parking spaces closer to the health food store, but the car was parked next to the intersection so that no other cars could pull in front of it. The co-op was on a corner, and the knight would have been able to check out the adjacent street before exiting the car. It was the spot I would have taken if it had been available.

"There's a knight in the co-op," I said, walking toward my own car while committing the knight's license plate to memory.

"Nobody said anything to Stanis—" Sig began, and then stopped. The thought that had just hit her like a ton of bricks was the realization that Stanislav might not have told her if any knights had contacted him. In fact, what if Stanislav had contacted...

"The guy I just smelled is a Crusader," I told her. "He wouldn't trust some foreign kresnik who's shacking up with a monster. He might check up on Stanislav, but he won't check in with him."

I opened Sig's car door first. A trained killer who has sworn to eradicate you lurking in the vicinity is no reason to forget your manners. Or maybe it is if the way Sig was eyeing me was any indication. By the time I circled the front of my car and climbed in, she was holding a gun—one of the Glocks that Choo had showed me instead of her SIG Sauer—beneath the dashboard.

"How do you want to handle this?" she asked.

Sig was ready to risk pissing off what amounted to a large organization of professional assassins if I asked her to, just like that.

"Wow, you are really stupid," I said.

She looked at me, followed my eyes, which were staring at the gun in her hand, and suddenly grinned.

"I just want to see him," I said, removing my own gun. "He's not looking for me in particular or I wouldn't have smelled him. He's just poking around."

Sig did not seem reassured. "Will he recognize you if he sees you?"

"The last time a knight saw me I had shoulder-length blond hair and a full beard, and it's dark and this is a pretty well-concealed spot," I said. "The car parked in front of us smells like the guy who was working the cash register."

"It's not that well concealed," she argued while I cracked my window open so I could listen to the store entrance better. "Won't he wonder why we're staying in the car?"

"No," I said, and kissed her.

After a moment Sig mumbled against my mouth, "If you're

making all of this up just so you can make out with me some more, I'm going to shoot you."

"I'm not," I assured her, and caught her tongue between my lips.

Eventually she pulled her lips a slight distance from mine and observed, "You're not acting like someone being hunted."

"I'm listening for him," I assured her. "And smelling."

"Still," she said.

"I don't want to bring other knights down on us by making him disappear," I said, caressing her cheek. "But if he identifies me, I'll take him out. I will not let you wind up on the knight's things-to-kill list because of me."

"If he identifies you," Sig corrected, "*I'll* take him out. No geas will make me suffer for it later."

I kissed her again. It was made only a little awkward by the fact that we were both still holding guns below dashboard level.

The second time the store entrance opened, I spotted the knight with my peripheral vision. He wasn't difficult to identify as he walked toward his car. Anywhere from his late forties to his early sixties, he was a broad-shouldered man with gray hair razored down to stubble. His movements seemed restless within his carefully conventional middle-aged-male clothes: a blue jacket, light-blue collared shirt, and gray slacks.

He was a veteran who was being given recon assignments because he had beat the odds and made it to middle age, I decided. A man who was finally slowing down and fighting it day by day, losing the battle by a few seconds here, a blood pressure point there, maybe a pound or two where none had ever existed before. He probably sucked at being an officer or an administrator.

Sig stilled while her face was partially turned toward the store. I turned her face back to mine with my palm and saw that her eyes were unfocused. She was doing that soul-gaze thing again. It really wasn't just psychic. She must have been picking up on body language cues, maybe even picking up pheromones through the window without realizing that she was doing it. Whatever she was doing, it involved some kind of hyper-focus.

"That's what you've been running from for decades?" she whispered when she unfroze.

"Yes."

This time when she kissed me she wasn't playing around.

"He's leaving," she said later as if I couldn't hear his car receding. "He didn't even notice us."

"He noticed us," I assured her, and leaned past her to adjust the side-view mirror on her side of the car. I could have just asked her to do it, but that wouldn't have involved as much rubbing.

"What are you doing?" Sig put her fingers on my chin and smiled wryly. "He's gone."

"He might circle back," I said, adjusting the rearview mirror so that Sig would be able to see over her shoulder while facing me.

She was still smiling, and I clasped her straightened fingers in my hand. "I am completely serious," I told her gravely. "He saw two people who might be staking him out staying in their car and kissing. He probably doesn't think we're really up to anything, but it won't cost him anything to circle around the block and see if we're still here making out after we think he's gone, either. That's how knights' minds work."

"You and your whole order are nuttier than a Christmas fruitcake, you know that?" she said.

"Kiss me anyway?" Somehow that came out sounding more vulnerable than I'd meant it to.

Sig stared at me searchingly, then with a what-the-hell shrug went back to work.

The next two minutes were a pleasant haze. Then the head-lights shone through the back of the rear window.

"You have got to be kidding me," Sig murmured against my mouth.

"It's him," I said. "I recognize the engine."

He drove past us without slowing down, reassured by the fact that we hadn't tried to follow him.

"My God," Sig whispered.

"Come to think of it, he might come back again in half an hour," I murmured.

Sig laughed shakily and kissed me again, then put her palm on my shoulder and pushed me away so that she could look at me. "You were actually right all along. You've got to leave Clayburg."

"I will," I said. And then: "Why did you say *actually* like that?"

She smiled but refused to be distracted. "I know you won't leave before the raid, but after that you leave. And I break up with Stanislav. And then you get in touch with me and let me know you're alive or I will come after you and kill you."

"I've already made arrangements to drop this car off at a chop shop and get another one there." I could say that truthfully without agreeing to leave right away. I didn't trust Stanislav or her objectivity in regard to him.

We'd blow up that bridge when we came to it.

～30～

EAT, DRINK, AND BE WARY

Choo let us through the front door and we found Sig's entire war band (well, except for Andro—he was on tunnel-watching duty) waiting for us in his living room. Dvornik and Parth and Cahill were sitting on a wraparound couch with a space left open next to Dvornik, and Molly was sitting all the way back in a reclining chair. In the center of the room was a long coffee table loaded down with those generic white Chinese takeout boxes with red dragons and flowers on them, and everybody was eating off plates on bamboo trays except for Molly, who had both a beagle puppy and a plate of food vying for attention in her lap.

The beagle puppy pressed itself against her and made a low sound that was half whimper and half growl as soon as it got a whiff of me.

Andrej did a human version of the same thing.

He straightened up from where he was leaning over the coffee table and scowled at me as I moved around Choo. "Have a nice ride, lover boy?"

Sig was between us literally before I could speak. Her sudden proximity caused Andrej to step back and her greater height forced him to look up at her. This bothered him.

"You are one wrong word away from hitting the floor," she told him.

I wondered if this was how all women would act if they were physically stronger than men, or if there was some sort of essential Signess at work.

"He doesn't need you to protect him." Andrej's voice was defiant, but there was something about it that sounded childish.

"She's not protecting it," Dvornik said tiredly from the couch. "She's protecting you, Andrej. The creature is at least twice as fast as you, three times as strong, and it's been fighting longer than you've been alive. And you're standing there taunting it as if to prove that you're not afraid, which makes us all think the opposite."

Andrej started to protest and Dvornik overrode him, giving me a dead-eyed look as he did so. "You know how to take down a werewolf, Andrej, and it's not by mouthing off at it from three feet away."

"Yeah, have backup with sniper rifles," I retorted. Then I put my hand over my mouth as if chagrined by having said something awkward.

I was jerking Andrej's chain a little, but Sig wanted to keep her decision to break up with Dvornik to herself for another day, and I didn't agree with that, but it was her decision and I was mainly just backing her play. If I suddenly started acting mature and conciliatory, Dvornik would know something significant had changed.

"Don't listen to its mouth." Stanislav still wasn't taking his eyes off of me. They were as dark and unfathomable and predatory as an insect's. "It's trying to lure you into thinking of it as a human."

"Would you all just chill?" Sig turned and addressed the room. "John is leaving Clayburg as soon as the vampire raid is over tomorrow. He doesn't want to talk about it, and our lives depend on how well we work together, so everybody grow up. You know... common cause? Greater good? The enemy of my enemy is my friend? Any of this ring a bell?"

"Great speech, Coach." Cahill didn't look up from his plate.

I looked at Stanislav and held my arms open. "What about it, Stan? Want to hug it out?"

"I don't know if I can drop you or not," Sig told me through clenched teeth. "But we're about to find out."

"Fine," I grumbled. Sig was a great actress. It was almost as if she were really irritated with me.

Then I had a thought that chilled my blood. What if Sig really was a great actress? What if she had no intention of breaking up with Stanislav? What if she was only saying whatever she had to say and doing whatever she had to do to keep me motivated until her group didn't need me as cannon fodder any longer?

Grabbing a bamboo tray just to give myself something to do, I began heaping Chinese food onto two paper plates until there were two indiscriminate mounds on my tray. I had been on the run too long. There was no point worrying about whether Sig was faking it or not. I was going on the raid regardless of how I felt about her, and it wasn't like I was going to emotionally protect myself at this point. If she was playing me, then it was going to be the emotional equivalent of a huge sucking chest wound no matter what I did. But if she was real, and I really believed that she was, then getting paranoid could mess everything up.

Of course, feelings really don't care whether or not they have a point. That's what makes them feelings, not, you know, conclusions or strategies. Now I felt shaky, like I'd just taken a hit. Look, I'm good at a lot of things, OK? It's just that being in love isn't one of them.

Wait...I was in love? That was crazy. I hadn't known her long enough.

Choo had pulled a piano bench out from under the piano that was against the wall next to the entry to the kitchen, and he was sitting on it. There was nowhere else to sit except a rocking chair next to the wraparound couch, and I wasn't going near that thing. Instead, I sank down onto the floor between Molly's recliner and Choo, adopting a cross-legged position and setting the bamboo tray across my knees.

Molly's puppy made a whimpering question of a growl again. "This is Lewis," Molly said.

I stared at the puppy and growled. After a second it crawled over her lap toward me on its belly while Molly frantically maneuvered her plate out of its way. I let Lewis lick my hand cautiously.

"Hey," Molly said, watching Lewis grovel. "Did you just break my dog?"

"I let it submit," I said. "It's the only way it's going to feel safe. It'll be OK after a while. Puppies are adaptable."

"Well," Molly said. "I guess I'm still glad you came over to sit at the unpopular kids' table."

"How could anybody dislike you?" I asked, forking some sweet-and-spicy chicken off my plate. "You're a bundle of sunbeams."

"I'm a mean mother-hmmnhmmnh man of God," she informed me. "Except that I'm a woman, of course."

"You just quoted something, didn't you?" I asked.

"Yes, I did," Molly agreed. She seemed calm, but her heart was beating fast. *"From Dusk Till Dawn*. It's a vampire movie with George Clooney."

"Is it too late to get a different priest?" Choo wondered. "Like maybe one who quotes *the Bible*?"

"I watched horror movies all last night," Molly confessed while she stroked Lewis's back. "In a weird way, they help me relax."

"That's kind of the opposite of listening to Christmas music, isn't it?" I wondered.

"It's like alternating hot and cold compresses on a sore muscle," Molly explained. "I alternate scary and happy things on my sore mind."

"Makes sense," I agreed.

"The hell." Choo shook his head despairingly. "Maybe letting you two meet each other wasn't all that good an idea."

"Too late." Molly smiled at me.

Another bad thought occurred to me then, and for a second I got uneasy.

Molly reached over and patted my shoulder. "It's OK, sweetie. I'm a lesbian."

"That's it. I definitely want myself a new priest," Choo said.

"Episcopalians will let anybody in," Molly agreed. "It's all the drinking that goes on at our conferences. Half the time when our bishops are raising their hands to vote, they think they're ordering another scotch."

I looked at her suspiciously. "You blessed the holy water *before* you started this conversation, right?"

"You have to bless holy water?" Molly asked innocently.

Choo started to laugh and leveled a thick index finger at her. "Don't. Even. Joke."

From the lack of conversation, it seemed like things were much less fun over on Sig's side of the room. Just chewing sounds, and Parth occasionally talking about aboriginal tribal tattoos, and monosyllabic responses. I didn't look over, but I knew where Sig was at every second.

Break up with him, I urged silently. She could tell Stanislav, and we could take him out and sedate him until the raid was over if she didn't want to hurt him. What was all this really about anyway? One last monster hunt for old times' sake? Respect? Guilt? I was starting to figure out that loyalty was one of Sig's primary motivators, but I doubted Stanislav would be loyal to Sig if he thought she had betrayed him, and he would view her not loving him as a betrayal.

Working as part of a team again was...different. It felt good, sort of, in some ways, but it had been a long time since I wasn't making all the decisions for myself by myself.

I looked over at the piano Choo was sitting in front of. He was finished with his food, so I nodded at it. "That piano. Can you carry a tune?"

Choo was morally outraged. "Carry a tune?!? Bitch, I can perform CPR on a tune if I have to."

Just as a side note, calling a male werewolf a bitch isn't really all that good an idea. In fact, it's a really quick way to get your throat torn out. I'm not as sensitive about that sort of thing as full werewolves who are part of a pack, though, so I let it go.

"How about some music?" I asked him. "Might as well make this a party." I left out the part about this maybe being the last night of our lives, but from the look that rippled over his face like some kind of emotional earthquake tremor, Choo heard it anyhow.

He took the bamboo tray he'd been balancing on top of the piano and went into the kitchen. I heard a trash can open, then a cabinet open, then a clink of glasses and ice. When he came back he was carrying a small glass of amber liquid.

"Just one," he assured me, seeing my look.

"What is that?" Molly asked.

"Kentucky bourbon," I said.

Choo stared at me.

"I've got the nose, remember?" I told him. "And I've been a bartender."

"Ooh, I want one!" Molly said, and extricated herself from the recliner by handing her puppy over to me. Lewis whined and licked my chin. It would take a long time for him to nip me playfully.

Choo swiveled around and lifted the cover off the piano keys and let his fingers ripple over them experimentally. He played a few snatches of something classical. I can't tell Vivaldi from Bach, but it sounded OK.

Molly came back in and sat down with a glass of bourbon in her hand, and Cahill got up, no doubt to investigate the fountain of alcohol that had mysteriously started bubbling up in Choo's kitchen. I kept the puppy.

"Your real name is Chauncey," I said to Choo. "You play classical music. You grew up around here."

He flashed a quick grin at me. "My mama used to teach at the university here. Now she teaches in Chicago. She put a lot of pressure on me to go to college, so naturally I went into the army right out of high school."

"How did she take that?" I asked.

"She replaced me with twins," Choo said. "I got two half sisters who are nineteen years younger than me, if you can believe that shit, and I expect they'll both be in school for the rest of their life. Mama doesn't like me to be around them much. Afraid they might get disappointment poisoning."

Choo didn't want to talk about his mother anymore and

launched into something classical and stirring that I didn't know. He was good. He was really good.

I didn't look at Sig, but I knew the music was making things a little better. Maybe if the vampires didn't kill us all tomorrow, and Stanislav or his nephews didn't contact the knights, or hadn't contacted them already, and didn't try to shoot me in the back as soon as my usefulness was ended, and the knights didn't show up as a result of their own investigations...

Damn. That was a lot of maybes.

～31～

CHARGE OF THE NIGHT BRIGADE

The first thing that went wrong was that Dvornik didn't come out of his trance. He was breathing shallowly and rapidly, and he seemed unable to stay awake for more than four seconds. Sig assured me that shaking him awake was a bad idea; she was crouched behind Dvornik, who was sitting in the passenger seat next to Choo. Sig, Andro, and I were all in the back of Choo's van. He had unbolted and removed the backseat but left a frame to which we could anchor our climbing harnesses. We were in the middle of the clearing where the tunnel entrance was supposed to be, far from the eyes of man, and ready to jump out of the van and start rappelling.

"He's been pushing himself too hard lately." Sig had her fingers on the pulse in Dvornik's throat. She looked guilty and stricken. "His body can't take as much strain as it used to, and he's been under a lot of physical and emotional stress."

I remained silent while Andro glared at me. We knew how many vampires there should be—eleven—and a rough map of the tunnels that Dvornik had drawn two days ago, but it would have been nice to have had some verification from our psychic scout on the day of the actual raid.

Oh yeah, and I was worried about Dvornik too. I was worried he might come out of it.

"Should we postpone for another day?" Choo asked quietly from behind the wheel.

Sig and Andro and I all answered at once. "No."

Ahead of us, the Crown Vic that Molly and Cahill were riding in with Andrej pulled to a halt, and Choo began maneuvering so that he could back the van next to it.

There wasn't really any point in trying to take the vampires by surprise. With their enhanced hearing they would detect the vibrations of our feet or whatever vehicle we approached in. The truth was, we weren't mounting a raid so much as a siege with a twelve-hour time limit. Our biggest tactical advantage was the sun over our heads. We might not be able to sneak up on the vampires, but as long as it was daylight we had a safe place to pull back to if things went sour. Plus, we didn't have to worry about them swarming up out of the ground like angry wasps and overwhelming us while we set up a base of attack.

Or that was what we thought, anyway. Vampires stay out of the sun because it affects them psychologically as well as physically. If their skin were just extra-sensitive, they could bundle up or wear tons of sun block. No, vampires have an instinctive fear of the sun that goes all the way down into their bone marrow. It's as if they're naughty children, and the sun is God's eye.

Which is why I knew something was wrong as soon as I climbed out of the back of the van. I've hunted things that burrow before and recognized the sounds I was hearing even if I couldn't see what was causing them—the scuffles, the scrabbles, the crumbling and sifting of dislodged earth showering down a straight surface to a bottom far below. Somebody was climbing up a tunnel. No . . . not somebody . . . some bodies.

It didn't make sense, and I had no clue what was going on, but sun or no sun, rules or no rules, I knew that letting normal humans get within ten feet of vampires was a bad idea. Firearms are ineffective against vampires at close range, at least if you don't have shotguns or faster-than-human reflexes. Cahill was still behind the wheel of the Crown Vic, but Molly and Andrej had already gotten out of the car and were starting to walk around.

I couldn't see the tunnel entrance. Choo had followed Dvornik's car in, but according to Dvornik the hole was covered with a mud-smeared tent whose corners had been slit. The canvas had been spread out like a lopsided pressed flower, and grass and brush had been rubber-cemented to its surface so that it resembled the surrounding landscape. The former front entrance of the tent was facedown and next to the edge of the tunnel it was covering so that a door could be made by unzipping the canvas. But if I couldn't see the entrance, I could smell chemical preservatives and glue and had a rough sense of where the sounds were coming from. I yelled "PERI!" which was our word for incoming danger while I grabbed the katana I'd placed against the wall of the van.

I almost hadn't brought the katana. Two-foot-long curving razors aren't really useful for rappelling or fighting in enclosed spaces—but I hadn't been sure what was going to happen today, so I'd brought both my swords along. Now I unsheathed the katana in a fast but unhurried motion—because you never rush the unsheathing of a katana, even when you're doing it fast—cutting the rappelling cord that I had already run through my harness before turning on my left foot and running toward the sounds that had just pissed in my porridge.

Sig and her crew probably thought I'd gone insane, but I'd only taken a few steps when the earth twenty feet in front of me seemed to get pulled down a drain. It simply disappeared like a napkin being pulled through a ring and was replaced by a gaping hole twelve feet around. Vampires began appearing at the rim of the exposed tunnel...one...two...three...four...they were covered from head to toe in black. Black ski masks, black sunglasses, black sweat shirts, black pants, black gloves. I'd never seen anything like it. I've seen individual vampires brave daylight for brief stretches at a time, bundled up and scurrying from one point of cover to another, but they had been caught outside and were running *from* the sun, not *into* it. And I'd never seen a group of vampires in the sun en masse.

What the hell kind of a hold did this Anne Marie have over them?

I aimed myself at the first one to come leaping over the rim, a vampire whose bound carried him some ten feet beyond the edge of the tunnel. I charged him in a running hasso-no-kamae stance, the sword held vertically toward my right, the guard at cheek level. He landed and stumbled forward, and I made a hidari kesa cut to his left where his hand was clawing for the gun holstered at his side, reaching my top speed by pushing myself forward in time with the stroke. He realized the danger and tried to bring his arm up to block at the last moment, but my blade moved from his left shoulder toward his right hip, cutting into the base of his neck. In ancient times this would have been the place where his armor was exposed.

I veered past him and his head fell off. Unfortunately I was now moving too fast to avoid the hole, and there was no way I was going to be able to stop in time to avoid throwing myself over the edge. Three vampires were jumping over the rim now, all in different directions. Rather than try to slow down, I maintained speed and shifted my sword to one hand, hurtling myself over the pit with my arms spread wide, aiming toward the vampire on the north side because he wasn't facing me.

I folded my arms and brought my katana toward my left shoulder as I landed, still running forward. The vampire ahead of me heard me and started to pivot. If he had kept running away from me he might have had time to react, but when he stopped moving forward...I didn't. And I was moving fast. I closed with him before he was completely turned around and launched a one-handed strike that was half katsugi waza and half wild-ass tennis backhand swing.

Despite what they show in movies, kenjutsu really isn't designed for running battles. His head came off, but my blade angled and lodged in the bone of his upflung upper arm on the opposite side, and I stumbled on the uneven ground and had to let go of my katana or risk cutting myself. I rolled and came back up on my feet, but now I was the one hearing someone else landing behind me and coming on fast.

I ducked and pivoted, sweeping my left foot behind me.

A bullet tore past my skull so close that I could feel the disturbance in the air, and my heel hooked behind the front foot of a vampire who was charging me with a cheap-ass .38 Special in his right hand. I had caught his foot in midair, and it doesn't matter how strong you are, if someone catches your foot off the ground, they can push it whatever way they want and there's not a damn thing you can do about it because you have nothing to push against to give yourself leverage.

I yanked the vampire's front foot out from under him, but his momentum kept the bottom half of his body sliding forward even while the top half of his body slammed into the ground hard. His legs wound up cutting my own feet out from under me as if he were sliding into a base, and I fell on top of him. His gun fell on the ground next to him, but I didn't have time to try for it.

Weaponless and grappling on the ground with a sharp-toothed someone who was stronger than I and could go without breathing for long periods of time was not a position I wanted to be in. His hands went for my throat and I tucked my chin in and darted my hands toward his collar. His thumbs were digging around my windpipe and his fingers were getting ready to crack bone and crush cartilage when I ripped the black shirt he was wearing down to his navel. Sunlight hit his exposed chest and sizzled into his flesh, releasing stench and steam. He screamed and let go of my throat and frantically reached for his shirt to pull the fragments back together. Freed, I threw my upper torso backward and brought my feet up toward his head; now we were both on the ground with me lying on top of him in the opposite direction, his feet beneath my head and my feet over his face. I managed to wrap my legs behind his head, locking my feet behind his neck while my right hand went for my Glock.

The vampire tried to wrap his right arm around my legs while his left hand pulled and held his shirt in place. He was pressing my right calf into the space where his mouth was behind his mask: I could feel his fangs tearing through the mask and into my flesh when I pivoted my hips and broke his neck. His limbs dropped like a de-stringed puppet's. I scrambled to my feet, my Glock in my hand as I surveyed the rest of my team.

It was the first time I'd really thought of them as my team.

The situation seemed to be under control. The Crown Vic was barely five feet away from the edge of the tunnel and there was a piece of black fabric hanging off the grille. As soon as

Cahill had realized what was going on, he must have hit the accelerator and rammed into another vampire that had just jumped out of the pit, knocking the heat seeker back down.

Sig was dangling an impaled vampire off her spear as if holding up a fishing rod, waiting for its body to reach the point of no return. And Molly... Molly was wearing a white cassock whose front bore a cross made of hand-sewn sequins, and she was advancing on another vampire who stood between her and the tunnel. The vampire was struggling to lift his weapon, a Browning of some kind though I couldn't see it well enough to identify the model, and it was as if he were struggling against a hurricane. As Molly advanced, the vampire took first one, then another step backward, and I have no doubt he would have been forced back over the tunnel edge if his head hadn't exploded. But it did. Andro had brought his .50 caliber rifle into play.

That made... at least six vampires in on the attack.

Six vampires who weren't afraid of the sun... or, if they were afraid, capable of overcoming that fear. That was insane.

And then it occurred to me that maybe it was. Insane, that is. Mentally unstable types don't usually become vampires, because vampires are generally pretty selective about whom they let in their club. Vampires are all about survival, hunger, and competition. None of these are incentives for creating other vampires who can't control their impulses. Morons like Steve Ellison are the exception, not the rule, and he is a case in point.

But if Anne Marie was intentionally finding emotionally unstable fanatics who were already so borderline suicidal and easily led that they could be turned into kamikaze vampires willing to walk around in the sunlight as long as they wore layers... and this sort of anti-instinctive behavior could be learned and culturally reinforced...humanity would lose its first and best defense against the undead.

I was picking up my katana to finish the vampire I'd paralyzed when I heard him gurgle the words: "Take...back...the light."

It sounded like a prayer. If so, it was the first one I'd ever heard a vampire make. I took back his light.

～32～

GETTING THE SHAFT

We were blasting Buddhist chants from two speakers in the back of Choo's van, and Andrej and Andro were watching the pit with their rifles trained downward while the rest of us gathered around the back of the van. Actually I was reanchoring the nylon cord I'd severed. Everyone else was gathering around me, and it was making me a little uncomfortable. I wanted to keep a clear firing zone around me.

"Those vampires were waiting for us to come close to the hole!" Cahill's fingers were white around the butt of his gun, and I noticed that he wasn't taking his eyes off Andrej and Andro. He jerked a thumb in my direction. "If wolf-boy here hadn't tumbled onto them, we'd be dead right now."

"But John was here," Sig said tonelessly. "And now they've blown their big surprise and lost half their number."

Her face was expressionless, but for a moment there was a gleam in her eye as she looked at me that might have been possessive or sexual. I had to look away before I found myself returning it. My adrenaline was still running high.

"Yeah, but how did they know?" Cahill demanded. If he'd

noticed anything unusual between Sig and me, he was ignoring it. "Are you telling me that six of them dress like that and stand around at the bottom of that shaft every day, twelve hours a day, just waiting?"

"No," Sig admitted. "But vampires move fast, and I don't know how far away they can pick up on a van's vibrations underground, do you? Maybe what just happened is some kind of drill they've been working on. John killed one of them a few nights ago. Maybe they're still paranoid."

There was a subtext here. Cahill was wondering if we might have a traitor in the group, and Sig was reluctant to open that discussion because she was starting to realize that nobody liked Dvornik except his nephews, and she was still inclined to protect him out of guilt and loyalty and habit. Dvornik, by the way, was still zonked out in the back of the van.

"Do you think the snake alerted them?" Andrej called from the edge of the pit.

It took me a moment to realize that he was talking about Parth.

We all chewed that over for a minute. Parth was the only one who knew about the raid who wasn't there. We had humiliated him in his own home, and he wanted to get my body on a lab table pretty badly. It was also possible that he might not have any more emotional investment in humans than in vampires.

"There's something else," I said reluctantly. By this point I was rethreading the nylon cord through the rappelling devices hooked to my climbing harness. "A vampire died here recently."

Cahill squinted. I think. With his beady little eyes it was hard to tell. "No shit, Sherlock."

"No," I said. "I mean, another vampire died here before this morning. Sometime in the last two days or so. I smelled it when I was walking around the pit."

"You're sure about this?" Cahill demanded.

"When a vampire decomposes, it's kind of like coffee being boiled all the way down to the bottom of the pot," I answered. "It leaves a very powerful stench behind. So yeah, I'm sure."

Sig looked troubled. Maybe she was thinking about the knight we'd seen. I know I was. "What killed it?"

"My nose works well," I said testily. "It's not a crystal ball."

"Maybe Anne Marie killed one of her followers," Sig said slowly. "It had to have taken a lot of convincing to train them to go out in the sun like that. Maybe she's taking control of her new hive with her claws out."

"Maybe," I said.

"Or maybe Parth came here to talk to them," Cahill said. "And Mr. Pacifist had to rip a sentry's head off before they took him seriously."

Molly looked like she wanted to object, but she didn't say anything. She hadn't said much of anything all morning.

"Stanislav said there were only eleven vampires down there," Sig thought out loud. "And we just killed six of them."

"Damn straight," Choo said.

I didn't see much point in talking any longer. Like Cahill, I was troubled by the ambush we'd almost walked into, but there was no way we were going to turn around now because of a few questions with no definite answers. We'd had a lot of those when we started—hell, that's why we were here in the first place. I had been worried about Dvornik and his nephews before the ambush, and if Parth had tipped the vampires off... well... the element of surprise had never been a big part of our plans anyhow. Nothing had changed.

Sig seemed to have reached a similar conclusion. "Let's do this." At her words the energy in the air shifted discernibly from angry and panicked to frightened but determined. I felt a surge of something...fondness? Admiration? Sig had the knack for being the spine of a group. I, myself, do not.

I started feeding my line downward into the pit. The line ran through two rappelling devices locked to my harness by carabiners, one at my back and one by my side. I probably didn't need the backup 'biner for a fifty-foot drop, but I'd always worn one when Australian rappelling in the past. Friction and tension and weight can warp metal fast.

Australian rappelling, by the way, is a slang term for rappelling facedown. It got its name from the fact that the only people who do this are military commandos and insane rock climbers, and an unusually high percentage of the latter happen to be Australian. The advantage of rappelling facedown is that you can fire a weapon downward as you approach a target. The disadvantages are that the physical and psychological strains are greater, and relatively minor things like stopping and landing become more complicated.

My rope hit the bottom of the shaft, and I gave Choo a nod. He pulled the tab on a steam canister and tossed it down the tunnel mouth.

I looked at Sig while I waited to hear the steam canister start hissing. Have you ever tried to use your eyes to tell someone that you want them, that because of them you're going to do the best you can to survive but that you're willing to die if that's the cost of putting yourself between them and anything that means them harm? That you don't care if they're playing you, or if what you have is really love, or if the two of you have a shot at lasting, that the very fact that they exist has made you come back to life in some way that's terrifying and exhilarating? A few seconds isn't long enough, especially when the person you're looking at is staring back as if she wants to pull you inside her and crush the two of you into one being. We were already wearing our air filter masks, and when I pulled my night-vision goggles down over my eyes, it felt like I was cutting myself off from her.

Then everything started happening too fast.

The steam canister started hissing before it hit the bottom of the shaft.

Sig tossed her shield and spear down into the pit.

Something down below let out a startled curse and began making scrabbling sounds, as if hands and feet were both on the ground.

I realized that I really, truly did not want to go down into that vampire nest.

Drawing my Glock, I ran along the cord toward the tunnel mouth and threw myself headfirst down into the hole.

My Glock was pointing at the darkness like a spear tip while I plunged straight down, controlling my descent with my brake hand. Static rope has only 2 percent stretch, and I halted my descent just above the area where the shaft opened up into another tunnel, the entrance at least eight feet high. Whatever had been moving had stopped, maybe because the steam from Choo's canister was already dispersing.

From here I could see where the heat seeker Cahill had knocked back into the tunnel opening had landed. The vampire had broken through a Punji pit at the bottom of the shaft, smashing through the thin mud-covered reed mat and impaling itself on the multiple sharp wooden stakes below. One of them had gone through its heart.

I fired my Glock into the mud below.

At this signal Choo dropped the flash grenade. That was what we'd agreed on.

A steam canister to make them back off.

A pistol shot to make them focus their eyes forward.

A flash grenade to blind them.

Infra-vision doesn't keep you from being blinded by sources of heat and light. If anything it makes you more easily blinded, although vampires and werewolves also recover more quickly. Fast healing applies to retinas too.

I closed my eyes, and as soon as the flash grenade made the insides of my eyelids go orange, I lowered myself another four feet. I was dangling upside down, my shoulders now beneath the top corner of the entrance and my Glock pointed down the tunnel. Well, actually, it was pointed up the tunnel. The vampires had made the connecting tunnel into a twenty-foot upward slope roughly as steep as a children's slide. At the top it leveled out into another tunnel that I couldn't see. Dvornik's map hadn't indicated the elevation change.

The good news was that this tunnel was eight feet tall by eight feet wide; the vampires had built for comfort rather than to limit their firing zone and increase the tunnels' defensibility. Cahill had guessed correctly: these were amateurs, and amateurs build big.

The bad news was that there was a vampire waiting at the top of the tunnel slope, only visible from the shoulders up. He was lying on the flat surface at the top where the tunnel leveled off, his rifle in front of him, preparing to fire down on me. Fortunately he had been blinded by the flash grenade and his hearing was being messed with by the Buddhist chants echoing from up above, but he knew that something was coming and he fired at the exact moment my head peeked out past the top of the tunnel. The shot plowed into the ceiling of the tunnel a good six feet ahead and two feet to the left of me in a shower of mud. Flecks of it got on my left goggle. The next shot followed immediately and slammed into the floor of the shaft beneath me.

He was a brown-haired lanky son of a bitch in a dark T-shirt and none of that mattered because the rifle he was aiming was obscuring part of his face, and I needed a good head shot. I was upside down and aiming one-handed while my feet braced to keep me from swaying, but I saw his rifle rise a few centimeters and to hell with it, I began firing.

One of my shots must have panicked him because he tried to move backward by pushing himself off the ground using his Winchester as a lever. He would have been better off letting go of the rifle and using his hands and elbows to shove himself backward flat on the ground. My next shot clipped him on the side of his skull but the bullet either grazed him or bounced off or lodged in bone or missed his brain. The shot after that hit the lower half of his face as he continued to push himself up. Another shot took him in the forehead, and he twitched and dropped back down. The two shots after that missed entirely because I was still raising my gun trying to anticipate the rising motion he was no longer completing.

"Cas!" I shouted, and covered the sloping tunnel while Sig dropped down, maneuvering herself onto the solid ground around the stake pit. Then she picked her shield and spear up off the ground and advanced to the tunnel entrance, where she covered me while I lowered myself and worked free of my harness. A few feet above the ground I grabbed hold of the nylon cord and pulled myself upward to create a little slack, then flipped to my feet with smooth ninja-like efficiency.

Or maybe I hit the ground between the pit and the tunnel on my shoulder because my foot caught in the cord when I tried to roll, and then I spent a few seconds flopping around like a fish who'd somehow managed to get a hook caught in its spine.

I forget which.

Removing a can of Silly String from my canvas belt, I started up the slope. I sprayed strands of plastic left and right and high and low, but I didn't find any trip wires or see any obvious irregularities in ground surface. The slope was actually helpful because it made it easier to keep my nose close to the ground. At one point I smelled wood and dead skin cells in a much more intense concentration than anywhere else, and I veered to the left, spraying a big circle around the area.

When I made it to where the vampire sentry was lying prone, his body was still twitching as his brain tried to reestablish neural connections. I peeked over the edge and got a massive whiff of ammonia.

I pulled the sentry's body down onto the slope with me, then checked him for ammunition. There were half a dozen old-fashioned silvertip bullets in his jeans pockets. *Silver* just refers to the color of the bullet tips, by the way—the nose points are actually aluminum. I rolled the vampire's body down toward Sig but kept the rifle, a .338 Winchester. While I was reloading the Winchester I heard heavy wet rending impact sounds behind me as Sig decapitated the vampire by slamming the edge of her shield down on his neck. She was strong and the shield was heavy and roughly triangular, but the narrow base didn't have a sharp edge, so she had to repeat the motion.

Still lying flat, I inched up and peered over the edge of the slope again, scoping out the next tunnel connection while holding the Winchester. This tunnel seemed to be level and headed straight west. At least that was consistent with the diagram Dvornik had drawn us. The tunnel traveled something like forty yards before bending south. About halfway down that length, I noticed something odd. The center of the tunnel had been reinforced with a series of wooden beams in much greater concentration than anywhere else I had seen yet. Had that section of tunnel collapsed a few times while they were digging?

In the middle of that area was something that looked like an unusually large speed bump made of mud. According to Dvornik there was supposed to be a sentry with a rifle using that barrier as a shield to hide behind, but maybe that was the vampire Sig had just ended. Maybe he'd heard the commotion and left his post.

I couldn't hear anyone else within twenty yards, though I did hear sounds of movement echoing from farther down the tunnel, around its next bend. Vampires are capable of complete stillness, though, and the wooden beams around the small mound bothered me. Could someone be flat against the wall behind them? Were the beams there because there was some kind of trap that affected the stability of the tunnel?

My job at this point was to give the rest of the team time to establish a...well...not a beachhead...a tunnelhead, I suppose. Choo needed to get our heavy weapons down here, and Molly needed to sanctify our perimeter.

I didn't like the fact that I wasn't repulsing any more attacks. Dvornik had said that the vampires didn't have an escape tunnel finished, so what the hell were they doing? Why was I hearing clinking sounds from farther down the tunnel system, like chains? Anne Marie had built this place to hold human prisoners—were the vampires making a wall of human shields to rush down the tunnel? Or were the chains for us?

"What the hell is that smell?" Sig asked as she moved up the slope beside me. Bringing herself up to her knees, she raised the shield over her head and straightened briefly before hammering the shield's bottom into the ground at the edge of the slope. Once the shield was firmly anchored, she slid her arm from the metal grip and placed herself behind it.

"It's cat urine," I said grimly. Cat urine is often used as a masking scent. It not only has a powerful stink that covers other smells but also an ammonia base that breaks down the molecules of the other smells and gradually destroys them. "They were prepared for someone with a sensitive nose."

"They did see you in the woods," Sig said pensively.

"Yeah," I agreed without really agreeing. Shouldering the Winchester, I sighted on the mound and took a shot at the top of it. Mud and a spray of gravel from newly busted rock flew outward from it, leaving a small hole behind. The hole should have been bigger. That mound was concrete covered with mud.

"What are you doing?" Sig asked. "We could use that mound for cover later."

"If it's got explosives in it, I'd rather find out from here," I said tautly, adjusting my aim slightly. It was the first time I'd ever used a .338 Winchester. Even though I'm stronger than a normal human, the rifle still had a kick. My ears were ringing from the sound of the report within the tunnel too.

"Explosives?" Andro crawled up on Sig's other side and began to set his rifle up on the right side of her shield.

"See how many of those beams there are?" I asked, and fired again. I hit the section of mound right next to my earlier shot, and this time, after the initial burst, a larger portion of the mound collapsed into the gap I'd already created. "Why so many there and nowhere else? And what are they trying to keep me from smelling? We already know there are vampires."

I loaded two more shells into the Winchester.

"St—my uncle saw a marksman hiding behind that thing two days ago," Andro argued. "They wouldn't use packed explosives as cover! Especially not underground."

"You're probably right," I said and fired another round dead into the mound's center. There was a loud crack and a shower of dried mud and a cloud of dust. Maybe there was a land mine in the area between me and the mound instead of inside it, and the mound was there to protect a sentry lying behind it.

When there was no explosion, I handed the rifle to Sig. "Cover me."

"That's not...." she started to say.

"That's my job," Andro interjected. He was acting angry, but his heart didn't seem to be in it.

"I like to have backups for my backups," I told him. "It's a character flaw."

I removed my can of Silly String and sprayed it into the air. It didn't hit any trip wires. "I want to get a closer whiff."

"You need to follow your orders." Now Andro's anger seemed real.

Instead, I took a steam canister off Andro's belt and threw it ten feet down the tunnel without pulling the tab. After an initial startled movement, he didn't protest.

"This tunnel is a turkey shoot," I said. "If this is what it looks like, you two can hold this area without me. And if this isn't what it looks like, we need to find out right now."

I started crawling down the tunnel, Glock in one hand, Silly String in the other, keeping my nose close to the ground and my eyes on the mound while I pulled myself on my elbows. Nobody tried to talk me out of it or grabbed my ankle. The Silly String only had a range of about ten feet, so I had to stop, drop the can, and toss the unused steam canister ahead of me again. If I got in trouble I planned to shoot it to provide cover.

The movement I'd been hearing down the tunnel, around the bend at the end, gradually...stopped. No chains. I crawled another ten feet, occasionally lifting my head up so that I could see above the mound ahead of me. It was while doing this that

I caught my first whiff of something besides cat urine, and it momentarily froze me. It was just the faintest lingering trace of a smell, almost the ghost of a smell really, but it was a very distinctive odor.

I smelled silver azide. If there had been silver azide in the mound, I would have caused it to blow up when I shot it, but I must have stirred things up enough to kick up some lingering scent molecules and send them airborne.

Silver azide is basically a solid, explosive form of silver nitrate. It is extremely volatile and can be set off by impact or ultraviolet rays. A few chemical agents can make it into a more stable paste, a few packaging tricks can make handling it safer, but the modern industrialized world has never bothered to really explore them.

The problem with killing werewolves with conventional explosives is that you have to use a lot of them to really be certain. With silver azide you don't have to commit over-kill, because if a were-being is in close proximity, any damage caused by the initial blast won't heal. Silver azide would be the weapon I would use if I wanted to kill a were-being with a small explosion that wouldn't bring a tunnel down.

But you can't learn to use silver azide off the Internet.

There was no way silver azide had been weaponized down here without instruction from a monster hunter. A knight... or a kresnik.

I dropped the Silly String and unobtrusively pulled the tab on the steam canister. Acting like I was about to throw it forward, I waited until the steam began to emerge and threw the canister backward instead, rolling to the side and to my feet as I did so. It was the only protection from Andro's .50 caliber that I was going to get, but his rifle didn't fire.

Then I was running through the emerging steam cloud and back toward the ridge, bringing my Glock up in case Andro was aiming his rifle at me. There was an impossibly loud noise. My eardrums ruptured. My skin was blown off my back.

That's all. I don't even remember those last things, really. It's just the impression I get when I close my eyes and try to remember, and it makes me wince.

~33~

IF YOU BATTLE MONSTERS

You know, you kind of give me mixed signals."

"I know. I just don't like the idea of going down that hole tomorrow with this thing hanging over you and me like..."

"Like an open airplane storage locker?"

I tried to smile and my lips felt like they were stuck together. I pulled on them with my jaw muscles and it made my face hurt, which made my head hurt, which made my neck hurt, which made pain trail all the way down my spine. It was like I was caught in a sadistic children's song.

"I was trying to think of the name of that sword that used to hang over a king's head. Was it the sword of Pericles? . . . Come on, I know you know it. I saw all those books when I was in your house the other day."

Was I in a hospital? I couldn't remember the last time I'd been in a hospital. My nose was full of sharp acidic and antiseptic smells. Clay, laminate, and chemicals, lots of chemicals.

"It was the sword of Damocles."

"Right, Anyway, I like the 'open airplane storage compartment' thing better. It means there's a journey with lots of baggage."

"And things being balanced precariously."

My eyelids felt heavy. They wanted to stay closed, and my mouth was dry. That was me and Sig talking, but I wasn't talking. We'd already had this conversation.

My eyes opened.

Everything was white. The walls were white, the lights above me were bright, and there were three pale sculptures around me. I focused on them and realized that all of the statues were of Sig.

"And a lack of closure."

"OK. I could start bullshitting about frequent-flier miles or something, but I can't really think of any more good ones."

"So shut up and drive."

It didn't feel like I was in heaven. For one thing I was stripped down to my boxer shorts and lying on a cold metal table. A very hard metal table, and I was bound to it by heavy chains and manacles that bit into my flesh. My arms were bent above my head and my ankles were pulled shoulder-length apart.

For another thing I was smelling Dvornik now. He was breathing behind me, heavily, blowing traces of himself and scotch all over the room.

My brain finally started taking the sensory data and making connections. The voices were a recording. I was in Dvornik's sculpting studio. Suddenly the voice recording stopped and the sound of a stool on wheels clattering over a floor filled the room. Then Dvornik was sitting above me and next to me, toward my right. He was wearing pale blue hospital scrubs that looked bizarrely frail on his overdeveloped upper torso, like wrapping paper on a bulldog. His eyes were full of pain and malice and he looked like he hadn't slept in three years. The little hair he had on top of his forehead peak was going in several different directions, and the expression his mouth was making was somewhere between a smile and a snarl and a gasp of agony.

"I've been trying to decide if you are incredibly lucky or incredibly unfortunate," he mused. "I had decided to kill you quickly, just to be safe. You were supposed to be past the mound when the bomb went off. Instead of channeling the backblast into you and protecting the others, the barrier protected you."

I heard the words, but I didn't really understand them at the time.

"You bugged Sig's purse," I said, except it came out "You buh huh pur."

"Yes, I did," Dvornik agreed, stroking my forehead with a proprietary tenderness that was more terrifying than a punch or a slap would have been. "But you can do better than that. You're so good at coming up with smart things to say."

"Where's Sig?" I croaked.

"I thought about cutting off your arms and legs while you were asleep." He held up a small acetylene torch and thoughtfully examined the blue flame that emerged from it. "I thought, what could be more horrible than that? You wake up, you open your eyes, and then you realize that you are completely helpless. Nothing but stumps."

Dvornik leaned forward slightly and made sure that I could see his face. "But I want to see your eyes when I start removing your limbs," he whispered. "And I want to see your eyes as you grow them back."

"Where's Sig?" I repeated, or tried. My throat was so dry I could barely make a sound. Dvornik frowned in incomprehension.

"A moment." He set the torch on the floor and scooted his stool out of my line of sight. A moment later he returned with a bottle of scotch and poured a large quantity of it over my mouth. I choked and blew some of it back before going into a coughing fit.

"I told you," Dvornik said. "Some conversations require a drink."

"Sig," I gasped.

He slapped me then, hard. His hand was covered with blood when he brought it back up, but I couldn't tell if it was from my nose or my mouth. Everything stung and was numb at the same time. "STOP SAYING HER NAME!"

"What did you do to her?" I rasped, and blood leaked into my mouth.

"I left the faithless whore the same way I FOUND HER! Shot up full of drugs and a plaything for vampires!" he barked.

Sig.

You hear about the mind's eye. You never hear about the mind's throat. Mine was starting to scream. Scream and scream and scream, and it wasn't getting hoarse.

"How did you do it?" I asked, as if I weren't having a hard time focusing. "How did you get around your geas? Were you making that stuff about Anne Marie up? The stuff about her growing to become truly dangerous if we didn't stop her?"

Dvornik made a sound like a drain unclogging. "No. I didn't make that up. Andro killed that vampire bitch two nights ago, right when she was returning to her hole at sunrise."

I must have looked confused.

"We have a trick," he explained. "I stand right next to the vampire in my spirit body. They can sense something there but they can't see it, and it distracts them enough that my nephews can line them up in a sniper scope without setting off their internal alarms. Andro blew Anne Marie's head off from over seven thousand feet away."

There was something wrong about that. I tried to think.

"That was a good shot," Dvornik said, like a man conceding something. "Andro was a good shot. The vampires were much more ready to listen after that."

"You made a deal with vampires?" I showed my bloody teeth. "Stanislav Dvornik. Vampire friend."

He smiled a lifeless, mirthless smile. "I've had to deal with a lot of vampires in my day. Do you know how to make vampires do what you want them to do? Make them think you're serving them."

"By killing one of them?" I growled.

"But I didn't kill their leader." Dvornik pointed at me. "You did."

I couldn't think of anything to say to that.

"You have never understood how powerful a psychic I am," Dvornik continued. "When the vampires made an escape tunnel for the next night, I was waiting for them on the other side."

"They should have killed you," I said fervently.

"I told them I knew who had killed their leader." Dvornik pointed at me again. "Then I told them a story about a werewolf with a knight's training who went around killing vampires to make himself feel less like a monster himself. They recognized your description from the night you ran by their tunnel and killed their hive mate."

Dvornik suddenly grabbed my throat and squeezed.

"I told them that you'd stolen my woman," Dvornik whispered. "That you thought I was too weak and old to do anything about it. I begged them to let me do things for them. I offered to warn them when you were coming again. I made them a trap that would destroy werewolves. I even offered to keep their existence a secret from the knights if they helped me capture you and your friends. My geas doesn't care if a bunch of vampires keep humans prisoner as long as they stay hidden...not if they're no threat to the Pax."

Dvornik released me and I took in several ragged gulps of air.

"And do you know what?" he said with a calm that was like a thin layer of ice over very dark waters. "Their senses are as good as yours. They believed me because I mostly told them the truth."

"So what was all that with the attack in daylight?" I gasped.

He made a dismissive noise. "They are animals. They tried to betray me and kill us all. Once we subdued Sig's friends, though, it was easy for Andrej and me to drag you back into the light and leave the rest of them there as an offering."

Dvornik's focus wavered again.

"That was a good shot," he repeated. "Andro's dead, you know. That prick hound Cahill shot him when things went to hell in the tunnel. But I shot Cahill."

"He had a remote detonator, didn't he?" I asked. "Andro."

Dvornik reached down and picked the blowtorch up again. "You were supposed to wait until Andrej and I were down there with him. He set off the bomb and shot Sig in the back of the head while she was running to see where you landed. Cahill shot him."

"Andro shot Sig?" I asked. My voice was sinking into a lower register. It didn't sound entirely like a human voice should have.

"She has hard bones," Dvornik said. "Shooting her in the back of the skull is the best way to knock her out."

The words were spoken with something like fondness. Then Dvornik's face twisted. There was anger there, and sour amusement, and despair. He lit the blowtorch and looked down at me. There were tears streaming from his eyes, but his eyes didn't seem to feel them.

"Here's what I don't get." It was an effort to get the words out, to think. "I smelled where a vampire got shot outside the tunnel. And it wasn't Anne Marie."

He made a sound that was almost a laugh. "Now that's clever. You think if my geas forces me to leave and investigate your lies, I'll have to kill you quickly."

That would have been clever, but that wasn't it at all. The powerful, concentrated stench that I'd smelled definitely hadn't been essence of Anne Marie.

I growled.

Knight, wolf, and geas were all in one accord.

The table seemed to turn into a stretch rack. I stared at Dvornik's face through the pain as my head began to split open, my field of vision shrinking. Darkness closed in, and I screamed a welcome. The last recollection I have of Dvornik is the startled look of horrified comprehension coming over his face.

The next thing I remember is staring down at my hands on the floor. I was crouching on all fours, but not because I was hurt. All my pain was gone. I had never healed so thoroughly so quickly before, but I wasn't thinking about that. My hands were covered with blood. The floor was covered with blood and shed fur. There was blood on the desk beside me. There was blood in my mouth. None of the blood was mine. In some way I didn't know how to define, it tasted like Dvornik smelled. I held my hand up and gazed at it, the hand that was too big to have ever slipped out of that manacle, the manacle attached to chains built to restrain vampires. Even if I'd broken my thumb at the joint, the hand still would have been too big. But a paw wouldn't have been.

Not a paw.

I dragged my body over to a corner and vomited, threw up

until it felt like I was spitting toenails and bits of colon, until my stomach was wrung out like a washcloth being twisted in on itself and my throat was scraped raw. I didn't care. I welcomed it. The thought that there might be some of Dvornik in there kept me heaving.

I should have known. All that drivel about being healthy, about finding my balance and believing I might actually be able to be happy. The wolf had been chasing me my entire life, and it had finally caught me and eaten me whole.

Was I still me? I tried to examine myself as if my soul were a sore tooth and my mind were my tongue. I ran through my memories, my feelings, my fears, my desires. Was I crueler? Darker? Does an insane person know he's insane? Does an evil person know he's evil?

Could I still... Sig.

I remembered Sig. I would write down every sign I could think of that a werewolf was losing control. I would make a checklist like a pilot on a preflight, and if I found myself violating any of the rules or exhibiting any of the warning signs, I would kill myself. I would. The thought calmed me down.

My soul was mine. Not anyone or anything else's.

But before I did anything else I had to save Sig.

∾34∾

THE SHORTEST CHAPTER
IN THE BOOK

Andrej opened the door.

"Guess what?" I said.

∽35∾

ONCE MORE WITH FEELING

Hunting monsters isn't that much different from hunting anything else. Patience and good aim and the ability to be quiet are all good things, but what separates an excellent hunter from a competent one is the ability to put yourself in your target's place.

For example, pretend you're leading a vampire hive. Most of your members have been destroyed, and there are only a few of you left. Some burnout you don't trust delivered your enemies into your hands because, he says, he wants them to suffer, but you tried to turn on him and kill him because, after all, where's the advantage in having some backstabbing wack job running around knowing who and where you are? Only the wack job got away, and he took a sniper and the enemy you were most concerned about with him, back into the sunlight where you couldn't follow.

How secure are you going to feel? Not very.

Now fast-forward a few hours.

You've been stuck in your lair all day with a few human prisoners, and you're planning on getting the hell out of there as soon as darkness falls. Maybe you'll start making another lair somewhere else, or maybe you'll try something different, or maybe you'll concentrate on locating the blood bag who's been causing you problems before you make any more long-term plans, but either way your first priority is going to be finding a new crib because you're a planner, and the one thing that's for sure is that you're going to need shelter in twelve hours. Are you going to kill the prisoners? Not yet. You might play with them and drink from them and take your frustrations out on them and maybe even begin the process of turning them, but you don't know what's going to happen or which one of them is the most important to the people who might be coming after you, and they're the only leverage you've got.

Take it a step further.

Now the sun has set. It's dark and you can go outside now, but you don't know what's waiting out there for you. You're a merciless predator and you're not naturally suited to feeling like prey and it pisses you off. What are you going to do?

You're going to send out some scouts, that's what.

That's why I was driving a stolen white pickup truck around in circles in a clearing at night, a beer in my hand, a baseball cap pulled over my head, and my CD player blaring. I wasn't surprised when two vampires came walking toward me out of the darkness. One of them was a female with long stringy black hair and the other was a tall thin male with yellow peach fuzz on the top of his head. Both of them were dressed like vampire stereotypes, the male in a black trench coat and leather pants, the female in a sleeveless red top and black jeans and long dangling earrings that caught the truck's headlights.

Two of Anne Marie's Internet recruits.

What did surprise me was that I could feel something shifting behind my eyes. It felt like a puzzle was being pieced

Elliott James

together out of my optic nerves, or the world's most complicated muscle spasm. And suddenly everything changed. I
could still see colors, but the world wasn't only distinguished
by them anymore. A red glow suffused everything, but to varying degrees of brightness and intensity. The two vampires were
lit up like a hand covering a flashlight bulb.

I was seeing in infrared. My God, I really was a full werewolf. I started to panic, but I reined it in. There were two predators right the hell there; I didn't have time to freak out again.
More than half a century of clamping a lid down on emotions
that were threatening to boil over came to my aid then.

One thought in particular focused me: I had used infrared
gear before, and the only time vampires show up in infrared is
when they've been feeding on humans recently; otherwise their
body temperature is corpse-cold. I had to struggle to let the
surge of rage that followed that realization pass through me.

I turned as if I were going to slowly pull my pickup truck
next to the vampires, then readjusted the steering wheel at the
last moment and gunned the accelerator, aiming right toward
them. There was no way I was going to hit them—their reflexes
were way too fast for that—but I did scatter them. The tall
male leaped over the pickup, pulling a rifle out from under his
trench coat. He fired continuously and one-handed while in
midair, but I don't know where his shots went. I'm sure he had
human memories of slow-motion Hollywood sequences in his
mind, but trying to shoot a rifle one-handed while you're jumping around like a kangaroo on crack takes practice, vampire
or not.

The female simply stepped to the side of the truck like a
matador dodging a bull, but I had been expecting this and
opened the driver's side door, putting my shoulder and the
truck's speed behind it. The door slammed into the vampire

and sent her rolling backward on the ground. Something went flying out of her hand, a gun probably, but I didn't stop to see. I pressed the accelerator and saw the male vampire coming up behind me in my rearview mirror, first trying to aim his rifle at me with both hands while running and then tossing it aside. He'd probably used up his ammo and didn't want to stop to reload.

I was only going forty miles an hour, and as soon as the male vampire caught up and jumped for the truck bed, I slammed on the brakes. The truck stopped and the vampire continued forward through the air. The lower half of his body smashed into the back of the truck cab and he flipped over it, tumbling onto the hood.

The vampire kept himself from falling off the truck by actually driving his fingers through the hood and stopping his skid. The last thing he saw when he looked up to snarl at me was the sawed-off shotgun I'd picked up off the passenger seat. I blew his head off through the windshield.

I threw the truck door open and jumped out, but I could see in the side-view mirror that I wasn't going to make it. The female vampire hadn't bothered trying to find her weapon but was coming straight at my back, fast. I pivoted, and her hands were still reaching to stop or grab the shotgun barrels she thought I was bringing around to point at her when the shotgun's butt slammed into the side of her jaw. She was knocked sideways and went charging past me, rebounding off the truck door behind me and half tearing it off its hinges. She fell to the ground. She wasn't knocked out, but she was disoriented enough that I was able to point the sawed-off at the back of her skull and end her right there. There wasn't enough left of her head to send regeneration signals down her spinal column.

I tossed the shotgun back in the truck and climbed behind

the wheel. Then I drove to the edge of the clearing, where I would at least have the cover of trees while I prepared for the next step. Stepping out of the truck again, I pushed the front of the seat up enough to get to the secret weapon I had stashed behind the truck seats.

The huge canvas carryall was still thrashing and rocking when I unzipped it. Andrej was inside, battered and concussed, bound and gagged in one of the half dozen straitjackets I had found while surveying Dvornik's storage room for useful supplies. The hatred in the eye that wasn't swollen shut was so tangible that it felt like he was trying to push me back with a giant physical hand. I could smell his rage on the pheromones he was dumping out of his pores, and it made me want to snap his neck right there. He and his were to blame for what I'd become.

"Let's go, sugarplum," I told him.

∾36∾

END WITH A FANG, NOT
A WHIMPER

Tracking the vampires' scent trail back to their new escape tunnel wasn't difficult. They hadn't even bothered to disguise the exit point. Unfortunately the tunnel wasn't as wide or high as the others had been. There wouldn't be room to swing a sword if it came to that, or to throw myself anywhere but down.

A gentle air current pushed a multitude of smells my way—Sig, undead stink, decaying Cahill, the perfume I'd smelled at Steve Ellison's, cigarette smoke, motor oil, deodorant, bleach, blood, infection, pus, urine, and fainter traces that I associated with Molly and Choo. One of the vampires I smelled was Anne Marie.

I slapped a pair of night-vision goggles on Andrej and pulled my own on over my head. His mouth was sealed with duct tape and he was still bound in a straitjacket, carrying a beige knapsack strapped on his shoulders.

For my part I had my wakizashi strapped to my back, one of Choo's Glocks in my hand, and a silver steel knife sheathed on my left hip. There was also a silver cross pendant hanging beneath my shirt.

I had been tempted to use Andrej as a human shield, but I needed him for later, so he was shuffling behind me. His feet were chained together just far enough apart that he could scuttle but not run, and while an escape artist could have gotten out of the straitjacket he was wearing, he or she couldn't have done it without me hearing. I had told Andrej that I wasn't leaving him behind—not alive, anyhow—and he had believed me enough that I wasn't having to slow down.

There weren't any traps, or if there were, I didn't find them and they didn't work. It was still maddening, forcing myself to move slowly in spite of the urgency that was making my blood surge. The cramped passage was lit in an eerie green, and it felt like I was forcing myself down some kind of bodily tract or canal so that I could be shit out or given birth to in hell.

Eventually I made my way to a bend where I could hear occasional shuffling movements. Dim multicolored pinpricks of light were cast on the tunnel wall before me as if a rainbow had vomited on it.

The moment I stopped and pulled Andrej toward me, a female voice echoed from around the bend. It was young and female and slightly nasal, with a North Carolina accent. "YOU'RE THE WEREWOLF WHO HUNTS VAMPIRES, RIGHT?"

I guess there were crosscurrents carrying my smell forward as well.

"I hunt a lot of things," I said. "But I'm not the one who shot one of your vampires outside the tunnel a few days ago. You know the old guy who looks like he's on steroids? He made that up so you'd go along with him."

At the sound of my voice there was a slurred sound. It could have been vague recognition or protest, but it was Sig.

"SO YOU'RE JUST A BIG OLD PEACE-LOVING VAMPIRE FAN, I GUESS." The voice reverberated with sarcasm. "THIS MORNING YOU SLIPPED WHILE YOU WERE SHAVING AND CUT THREE VAMPIRES' HEADS OFF."

"No, when I kill you, it'll be on purpose," I promised. "But I'm not a liar, and I'm not a maniac, and unless you made a very stupid mistake, you've got some people I want."

"SO I GUESS YOU KILLED THAT OLD SON OF A BITCH WHO HATED YOU SO MUCH." The voice was encouraging and amused. "I CAN SMELL HIS BLOOD ON YOU."

Oh good. We were going to be friends after all.

"I'm going to send you something," I said, readjusting the straps on Andrej's straitjacket. "The guy carrying it is one of the other people who betrayed us, so I really don't care if you shoot him or kill him or what, but you're going to want to see what he's got first."

"MEET HIM HALFWAY, JANICE," the voice commanded, then resumed addressing me. "AND I'LL HAVE YOU KNOW, MR. WEREWOLF, THAT MY TEETH ARE RIGHT NEXT TO YOUR GIRLFRIEND'S NECK, AND IF ANYTHING HAPPENS THAT I DON'T LIKE, I'M TEARING IT UP."

"What's wrong with her?" I asked. It wasn't like Sig to keep her mouth shut this long.

"THAT OLD MAN GAVE JANICE SOME STUFF TO KEEP HER DOPED UP." The voice was full of that fake sugary friendliness again. "SHE HASN'T COME DOWN OFF OF IT YET. TO TELL YOU THE TRUTH, I'M JEALOUS."

"Go ahead and try some," I said. "I'll wait."

"I DID," the voice said flatly. "IT DIDN'T DO ANY-THING. I'VE TRIED BEER, METH, COKE, HEROIN, HASH, SHROOMS...NOTHING DOES ANYTHING. EXCEPT BLOOD."

"Yeah, that's tough. Can we get on with this?" I said, and shoved Andrej forward so hard he almost fell.

"THAT DEPENDS ON WHAT WE'RE GETTING ON WITH."

"We can try to kill each other later," I said.

Andrej halted. I pointed the Glock at him. "You're useful or you're dead, Andrej."

He waited two seconds before deciding not to test me. He shambled forward.

When he disappeared around the bend, I heard a different female voice say, "Stop right there." Then I heard the sound of Andrej being shoved about, the backpack being unzipped, and then silence. Dead silence. No pun intended.

"WHAT IS IT, JANICE?" The voice that was probably Anne Marie's was sharp.

"It's some kind of bomb!" Janice snarled. "There's all kinds of dynamite and some kind of plastic explosive and a timer with a bunch of red numbers on it. It only has ten minutes left on it."

"Relax," I said. "If I wanted to blow us all up, I could have done it from here. That's no little bomb. These tunnels will channel the blast and blow everything in a half-mile radius apart before they bury whatever's left."

"I THINK YOU AND I MUST HAVE VERY DIFFER-ENT WAYS OF RELAXING." The voice sounded playful again, but distracted.

"I just brought it so you won't do something stupid when I

come in to talk," I said, and walked around the bend with my Glock in one hand and the remote device in the other.

Janice was standing in front of me, holding a TEC-9 and using Andrej as a human shield. She was about five foot six and a little on the stocky side, with broad shoulders and a broad face. Her red hair was pulled back into a tight knot at the back of her skull, and she was wearing nothing but a pair of cotton pants and a bulletproof vest.

We weren't in a cavern... it was more a space the size of a large living room. The dim illumination was coming from Christmas lights strung around the walls, hung up on metal rods slammed into the mud. I suppose that was practical if you didn't have an electrician in your group. Christmas lights are cheap and easy to string up around tunnel bends, and they don't use a lot of electricity, so you can run them off a battery for a long time. The lights reminded me of Molly and her holiday fixation, and suddenly I got angry in a way that I hadn't been allowing myself to get angry. What had Molly thought when she'd seen those lights?

There were air mattresses and coolers and unfolding canvas chairs stacked up on the east wall and two dead bodies lying against the west one. The corpses had been recently killed. One of them was a middle-aged woman dressed like a jogger, and one of them was a teenage boy dressed like a gangbanger. Now I knew why Janice was so full of fresh blood that she was glowing, just as the scouts had been.

When you're getting ready to move, you clean out the fridge.

There were a pile of discarded chains and two folding cots and plastic tubes and three footlockers that were full of blood bags and ice. Sig's spear and shield were leaning against the wall along with a bolt-action rifle and a bulletproof vest.

Anne Marie was not in the room. She was around the bend

of another tunnel opposite me, watching me through one of those large sloping circular mirrors that you see mounted in the upper corners of stores—the kind that are supposed to let the clerks at the counters see around bends in all directions. The mirror was embedded in the wall at the mouth of the tunnel, but I couldn't see what was reflected in it. My goggles' light amplification was messing up the refraction somehow, so I took the goggles off and peered again. There were two silhouettes in the mirror, crouched behind at least twelve feet of solid packed clay. Anne Marie and Sig.

I couldn't get a clear shot.

"Should I start shooting him?" Janice asked tensely.

"I don't think so," Anne Marie said reflectively. She wasn't pitching her voice so loudly now that I was in sight. "He might be full of shit...but that old guy had explosives, and he killed the old guy. I'm picking up all kinds of weird chemical smells too."

"Let's talk," I said.

"OK," Anne Marie said unenthusiastically.

"Where are my other friends?"

"They're not here." Her voice became steely. "You can ask for them all you want, but I can't get them for you."

"How is that?" I asked, my voice as dead as hers.

"That priest bitch was smart," Anne Marie said flatly. "We had her and her friend all bound up and she managed to use her hands to draw a cross on his chest with mud. I couldn't even lift a gun to shoot them while she was holding on to him. They shuffled off down a dead-end tunnel trying to escape, and now they can't leave and we can't get in."

"Give me a second." I tilted my head and yelled, "MOLLY? CHOO?"

From somewhere down the second tunnel across the way, I heard Molly's voice reply faintly. *"John?"*

"OK," I said. "Let's talk about how we're going to do this, Anne Marie."

"How do you know my name?" she demanded.

"Steve Ellison told us all kinds of things about you before we ended him," I lied.

Anne Marie began to curse bitterly and creatively.

"It's why that sniper was trying to kill you," I continued. "How come he didn't, anyway?"

"He shot my cousin, Sarah," she said, her voice an odd combination of irritation and smugness. "I wasn't even here. Me and Janice were in . . . somewhere else."

The picture we'd had of Anne Marie was two years old, from when she'd first gone into the juvie system, and adolescents change a lot in two years. People with Anne Marie's background tended to have a lot of half siblings and cousins and nieces and nephews floating around unofficially, and Andro could have mistaken a cousin for her.

My imagination began to fill in a narrative about Anne Marie's relative who looked like her. Anne Marie had gone into the foster system, so the cousin's family hadn't taken Anne Marie in, but maybe that family was the only semi-stable point in Anne Marie's landslide of a childhood, a place where she wound up sometimes when her mom was on a tear. Maybe this cousin was the only person in the whole world Anne Marie trusted, or maybe she had always been easily dominated. Either way, after all her problems with Steve Ellison, when Anne Marie needed a vampire she could trust to have her back, she had turned her cousin into one of the undead.

Maybe that wasn't the way it had happened exactly, but I'd

bet it was close enough. And Anne Marie had left her cousin behind to keep an eye on things while Anne Marie went out scouting and collecting new recruits from among her Internet connections. That was why Stanislav hadn't seen Anne Marie while he was roaming around the tunnels in his spirit form.

"Mistress? That bomb is on a timer," Janice reminded her.

Mistress? Really?

Anne Marie stopped cursing and addressed me without any pretense of friendliness. "If you want to talk seriously, the first thing you need to do is get rid of that gun."

"I don't think so," I said.

"We can't hurt you because you've got your thumb on a bomb trigger," Anne Marie said. "So why do you need that gun to protect yourself?"

"I'm very insecure," I said.

"The only reason you need that gun is you want to keep your options open," Anne Marie went on relentlessly. "But if you're really gonna let me go in exchange for Busty the Vampire Slayer here, you need to prove it. Toss that gun away so I know you won't shoot me the first time you get the chance."

"Fine," I said, and shot Janice in the forehead. She was fast, but surprise can momentarily paralyze the supernaturally quick too. Before she had a chance to react, Janice was dropping to the ground in a convulsion of limbs.

Andrej threw himself sideways to the ground and then scrambled frantically toward the nearest wall on his knees, trying to regain his feet without using his arms. His eyes were wild and frantic. I ignored him.

"WHAT ARE YOU DOING!" Anne Marie screamed. "I'LL KILL HER! I'LL KILL HER RIGHT NOW!"

"I know you will," I said, and threw my Glock across the

room, down the tunnel where I'd heard Molly's voice from. "But not for Janice's sake."

"THAT IS IT!" Anne Marie raged. "THAT IS IT! YOU DO ANYTHING ELSE LIKE THAT AND I'M KILLING THIS BITCH! I DON'T CARE WHAT YOU DO AFTER THAT!"

"Calm down." As if my own heart weren't thudding frantically. "Janice isn't dead, she's just out of it for a while. If she really means that much to you, you can carry her out of here. Fair's fair. I gave up my weapon. You had to give up yours. That's the only way this is going to work."

"No, this is the only way," Anne Marie corrected. "I'm going to walk out of here with your cheerleader, and you're going to let me."

"You're going to make me kill you both," I said.

"I don't care as much about that as you think I do." Anne Marie's voice oozed venom. "Do you know what it's like being me? I'm a damned corpse! I can't feel anything except cold, and I'm cold all the time!"

Then her voice went soft and hollow and hungry for a moment. "Except when I'm drinking blood."

I moved sideways to place myself squarely between her and the exit in case she did start moving. "You died, Anne Marie. You never did come all the way back to life."

She laughed bitterly. "You think I don't know that? I smashed a hammer down on my hand by accident when I was putting some wooden beams together, and I barely felt it! I can hardly taste anything, or if I can, it's because it's so spicy or salty that it tastes like shit anyway, and then I can't digest it."

Her voice took on a plaintive quality. "I tried to go see a live band in Knoxville, just to try to have a life. Just to see if maybe

I could make this be a good thing. My hearing is fuckin' awesome, I ought to still be able to like music, right? And everything was too loud and bright and all I could think about was the blood I kept smelling all around me."

"So what's the point?" I asked, gesturing around me with my empty hand. "Why do all this?"

"There is no point!" she shot back. "Shit just happens. Some people are born rich with nice parents and good looks, and some people are born poor and stupid and ugly and their parents are morons who beat the shit out of them or rape them. Some people who have everything get hit by cars and some people who spend their whole lives trying to kill themselves die in nursing homes."

"I don't believe that." My tone was even and measured. "Even as a vampire, you're smart enough to get by without keeping people in captivity and torturing them to get what you need. That didn't just happen. That was a choice."

"And why the hell not?" she seethed. "It doesn't mean anything. Nothing's good. Nothing's bad. Whatever happens happens. Whatever we do, in a hundred years it's gone. Time wipes it all away like a rag swiping our windows clean. Or it used to."

"That's what you say," I said. "But I'll bet that dead soccer mom over there looks a lot like the mom you wish you'd had when you were growing up. The kind of mom you wound up hating because they made you feel like you weren't good enough to have one."

"Oh fuck you," she said, and for the first time she sounded like a teenager, not like someone trying to sound like a cool and controlled vampire, or the way they thought a teenager was expected to sound to be charming.

"I'll bet that boy next to her is a lot like the kind of guy you used to sneer at, deep down wishing you could date one," I continued. "You're not going out of your way to hurt people because they don't mean anything. They mean so much to you that you can't stand it."

In the mirror, Anne Marie hoisted Sig violently to her feet and began to drag her along, walking sideways down the tunnel toward me with her chin above Sig's shoulder. Sig was limp, but Anne Marie supported her weight effortlessly.

"Why do you need so much blood, Anne Marie?" I asked. "Why are you making plans to support a large number of vampires in a small area?"

Anne Marie ignored me, dragging Sig into the room. I could see now that Sig's arms and hands were bound behind her back with thick chains and that her ankles were manacled together. She was otherwise down to her brassiere and panties.

"I'm walking out of here with her," Anne Marie said more calmly as she scooted Sig toward the tunnel I'd come from. "And if you don't move out of the way, I'm tearing her throat out."

"Sig would rather I kill her than let you keep her," I told her.

"But you won't," Anne Marie hissed. It's always bizarre seeing someone who was turned into a vampire young: Anne Marie's expression was a disturbing combination of an adolescent's disdain and a vampire's predatory menace. "You know what I just learned about you while you were doing your guidance counselor bullshit?"

"Not enough," I said.

"You think this means something. You think God still cares what you do and what happens to you."

Anne Marie's mouth was never more than two inches away from Sig's throat, her fangs bared while she talked. "You're not going to make me kill her because you think you're going to ride away from here on a white horse with your blonde bitch."

"I stopped believing in 'happily ever after' a long time ago, Anne Marie," I said. "You have no idea what I'm capable of."

"Oh, I get it all right. You won't let me go no matter what." Anne Marie placed her fangs against Sig's throat experimentally, staring at me as she pressed them tightly enough to draw pinpricks of blood from the flesh. I froze.

Anne Marie relaxed her mouth so that she could grin and talk to me again, her lips brushing against Sig's neck as she talked, in a mockery of eroticism. "You won't let her die no matter what either. But one of those things is going to happen, and you have to choose now."

Then two things happened in rapid succession.

Sig headbutted the back of her skull into Anne Marie's mouth, hard, and actually broke off Anne Marie's top fangs. I'd never seen anyone do that to a vampire before. I'd never even heard of anyone doing that before. Anne Marie's head snapped back, her right hand going to her mouth while her left hand stayed around Sig. Sig took advantage of that moment and turned so that her mouth was now against Anne Marie's neck, right above her carotid artery. She bit down on Anne Marie's throat with all her might.

The surprise on Anne Marie's face was not comical—the intensity of her shock and rage was horrifying. Anne Marie tried to angle her head so that she could get her remaining fangs under Sig's neck, but the back of Sig's head was nestled under her jaw so that Anne Marie's bottom teeth could find no purchase. Anne Marie shook her head violently to dislodge Sig, but Sig held on to Anne Marie's throat with her teeth like a pit bull, her feet actually being dragged off the ground. Then Sig planted her heels and straightened up, using her greater height and leg muscles to rip Anne Marie's throat out with a violent sideways thrust of her neck.

Anne Marie staggered backward and Sig threw herself down on the ground.

At the same moment, Andrej shot Anne Marie in the back of her skull.

∾37∾

FALLING ACTION

Yeah, I know. When I mentioned making minor readjustments to Andrej's straitjacket, I didn't specify that these included stuffing a Glock down his sleeve and loosening the straps.

And I totally skipped over the conversation we'd had after I'd bounced him off some furniture for a while. The one where I'd explained to him that Anne Marie was still alive and that his uncle's entire life—the one where he'd been a proud and respected vampire hunter—was about to go to waste in one bad day. The one where I'd informed him that his and his brother's legacy among vampire hunters was going to be going down in history as the two incompetent screwups who let personal issues get in the way of stopping a new vampire queen before she got started. The one where I'd pointed out that his gun would only have one bullet, and not a silver bullet either, and that if he tried to shoot me while I was watching for it and he was bound up in a straitjacket, he would either waste his shot, or miraculously disable me and leave himself at the tender mercy of Anne Marie. The one where I'd told him that there was just enough plastic explosive in his backpack to tear out his spine, and that I'd trigger it to cause a distraction if he didn't take a shot when he had it. The one where I promised to give him a twenty-four-hour head start if he shot Anne Marie after I maneuvered her into a vulnerable position right in front of him. The one where I then assured him that I already had an entire secret society of hard-core monster hunters after my ass, and that the thought of a relative lightweight like him being added to the mix didn't exactly scare me enough to make me break something as important as my word.

He wouldn't have been much of a secret weapon if I'd gone around blabbing about all that, now would he?

After Andrej shot her, Anne Marie went still for one long, tense moment while her eyes fluttered and her mouth dropped open, and then she collapsed.

"What were you waiting for?" I demanded, glaring at Andrej. "You had a shot at her when she came into the room."

"She could have killed me with one backhand from that close!" Andrej spat the words. He was still backed against the wall, a smoking hole in his right straitjacket sleeve.

Andrej began thrashing his way out of the straitjacket, pressing against the wall as I approached him as if he could sink into it and disappear. "YOU SAID YOU WOULDN'T HURT ME!" he yelled.

"I said I'd let you go," I reminded him, and I landed a left uppercut under his jaw. Even if his arm had possessed the range of motion to stop it, he wouldn't have been fast enough. Andrej slammed against the wall and then toppled sideways and stayed still. "I never said I'd let you leave first."

I winced while refastening his straitjacket. That punch hadn't had any art to it and my fourth finger had a dislocated knuckle, but it had been worth it.

"Tha' was your big plan?" Sig croaked from behind me. "Giving Andrej a gun?"

"It only had one bullet in it," I said, turning toward her. "How long have you been awake?"

"Since before you got'ere." Sig didn't make any effort to crane her neck to look at me. Her face was slack and her voice was mildly dreamy.

I knelt down beside her and propped her up in my arms.

"If you kiss me I'll kill you," she said faintly. "I've thrown up like eight or nine times and that bitch is still in my mouth."

"I really don't care," I said.

"I do," she said. So I kissed her on the forehead.

"What about the bomb?" she asked.

"It's just some road flares and sculpting clay wrapped around a digital alarm clock," I told her. I had also broken open a shotgun shell and sprinkled some gunpowder into my knapsack, and splashed a few household cleaners and some mercury from a broken thermometer onto the lining just to confuse the vampires' sense of smell.

Unsheathing my wakizashi, I walked toward Anne Marie.

"Wait a minute." Sig forced herself to her feet, swaying awkwardly. "Give me that thing."

You don't give someone else your katana or wakizashi. Not ever.

I looked at Sig's face and gave her my wakizashi.

Her hands were still manacled in a way that impaired how far she could lift her arms, but Sig sank down to her knees and began to work on removing Anne Marie's head from her body.

"Is Stanislav really dead?" Sig asked while she sawed.

"Yes," I muttered, turning to watch Janice, who was still twitching like an epileptic in the middle of a seizure. This was one conversation I wasn't looking forward to having.

"I guessat's good," Sig said, and stood unsteadily. I took the blade from her hands and kicked Anne Marie's head away before turning to finish Janice. At some point my knuckle popped back into place with an audible click.

The padlock on Sig's chains was too massive for my tension pick—it had probably been designed for restraining elephants or something—but too small for my knife. While I was rummaging around for the key or something I could use as an improvised pick, Molly and Choo came shuffling and hopping out of the far tunnel, both bound and chained like Sig. They were both covered with swellings and bruises and blood. Choo's nose hadn't just been broken—it had been shattered, and Molly was missing several teeth.

Eventually I freed all three of them. Their clothes were in shreds—the vampires had simply ripped their garments off rather than bother with buttons or snaps—and none of them wanted to wear the vampires' clothes or any belonging to their victims. Molly managed to wrap herself up in the remnants, and I wound up giving Choo Andrej's pants and Sig my shirt.

As for Andrej, he was still out cold. I'd released a lot of tension with that punch. If I'd released any more I would have killed him.

None of us talked much. Sig still seemed disoriented and only semiconscious, and Molly and Choo could barely speak—it had been less than twenty-four hours, but they hadn't had a drink and they'd been under a lot of stress. I let them all have small sips from my canteen. Choo wouldn't let go of the Glock I'd tossed down their tunnel...he had stooped down and picked it up with his palms even when his hands were bound and swollen behind his back. Molly had her back against a wall and was holding two knives over her chest to make a cross.

"How could you trust Andrej?" Molly asked when she was

reasonably composed. "He was going to let us get tortured to death just because his uncle doesn't like getting dumped!"

"He's spent his whole life worshipping vampire hunters," I said. "The only reason they made their move when they did was because they thought Anne Marie was out of the picture. And he knew there was a chance I would keep my word too. Some chance of living to get revenge for his family is better than none."

"Is that right?" Choo asked softly.

Molly looked at Sig, who was sitting on the ground with her arms around her knees, hands clutching her spear as if it were a guardrail. She still seemed to be having trouble focusing. I could see that Molly had something to say that involved Dvornik, but was tactfully refraining.

Choo got up and staggered over to where Andrej was still lying on the ground. Choo's circulation and balance still weren't a hundred percent. He stared down, his Glock pointed at Andrej's forehead.

"Choo," I said. I could have probably leaped across the room and overpowered him before he had a chance to do anything, but I didn't. I honestly can't say why not. It might have been respect for Choo—it was his decision, whatever the consequences, and one that might define his life or divide it into before and after. Or I might have just been that emotionally exhausted and ambivalent.

"I'm not saying you shouldn't do it, Chauncey," Molly rasped. "But this is getting out of hand. At least give yourself time to think about this."

"I have," he muttered, and pulled the trigger.

Sig looked up as the sound of the Glock filled the cavern. Molly looked down. Neither of them protested.

"I think you'd better get out of the monster-hunting business, Choo," I told him when the reverb had died down. "For your own sake."

"It might be all right for you. You're leaving. But he would've come after Sig," Choo said defensively. "He would've come after all of us."

"Maybe," I said. "And maybe you did the right thing. But that's not why you shot him." And it wasn't. Not when he did. Not the way he did.

Choo was silent for a time. "No, it's not," he admitted finally.

"Let's get out of here," Sig said quietly. Her words were still slightly slurred.

"Yes," Molly said, sitting up. "Let's. We can figure out how we're going to clean this up later."

I picked up a gym bag that I'd found while searching for the key to Sig's manacles. It held a little over eighty thousand dollars: money left over from Anne Marie's disciples and their entrance fees. Even split four ways it would make good traveling money.

There was one last surprise on the way out.

We were making an ungainly parade toward the exit when Sig stopped and stared uncertainly at the bodies stacked against the wall. "I can see Ted," she said. "He's just standing there looking at us."

Molly thought Sig was hallucinating, but I realized that I'd been smelling Cahill's scent mingled with the corpses all along. I walked over to where the bodies were stacked and moved the woman and the boy aside. There were signs where the ground had been disturbed beneath them, and I pulled one of the steel rods that were suspending the Christmas lights out of the wall and began jabbing it into the earth to loosen it up. Natural burrowers or not, the vampires had to have kept some digging tools around, lots of them, but I didn't feel like exploring the tunnels.

I already knew what I was going to find. Why else would Anne Marie have buried Cahill's body when she hadn't buried anyone else's? When I uncovered him, Ted was lying there with two bloody bullet holes in his shirt, one in the center of his chest and one in his stomach. After what felt like an entire minute, I heard a heartbeat. Well, a heart twitch anyway.

Ted didn't just have two puncture holes in his throat...he had blood on his lips. Black blood, dark and thick and alien. Vampire blood.

Anne Marie had begun the process of turning him.

～38～

ALL'S WELL THAT DOESN'T...
WELL...END.

We wound up breaking into a hunting cabin that belonged to some fairly affluent retirees from Molly's old church. They had moved to Texas five years ago but still kept the cabin to stay in whenever they wanted to come back and do some hunting in the mountains or visit friends and relatives. This cabin, you understand, was more like a lake house in the middle of the woods than a bunch of planks thrown together around some cots and a card table. There were no bunk beds or outhouses. There were guest rooms and hot water and lots of plaid. The coffeemaker made gourmet brands a cup at a time out of little foil-covered plastic packages, and the television had a satellite feed, although it didn't work very well.

"What do you think will happen to Ted?" Sig wondered. The question was asked with concern but not much urgency. Sig and I were sitting on quilt-covered rocking chairs on the porch outside the cabin, drinking cider. She had just run God knows how many miles trying to burn off some emotional pressure and whatever sedative was still inside her. I had been trying to meditate while periodically nodding off.

"I don't know," I said. Ted was lying on a bed inside the cabin like a wax statue, draped in crosses and smothered in blankets while Molly force-fed him chicken broth made from holy water, his pulse still fluttering every minute or so. Choo and Ted had the same blood type, and Molly was a universal donor, so we'd taken some of the transfusion equipment from the tunnels and were pumping blood in and out of Cahill as fast as we could.

If Cahill survived, he might remain a normal human with uncommonly sharp incisors, or become an albino who could see in the dark, or some variation of a zombie, or a dhampir, or even a vampire. Supernatural transformations aren't clean or tidy or predictable any more than any other aspect of life is clean or tidy or predictable. I had called Ted's wife pretending to be the police, and Molly had called the police pretending to be Ted's wife, and between us we had bought Ted's body a few days to figure out what it was going to do with itself.

If Ted remained too human, the bullet wounds would kill him. If he became too vampiric, I would, and I would deal with whatever grief my geas gave me afterward.

Settling back in the rocking chair, I propped my feet up on the porch rail. "The odds are he's probably going to die. I have a feeling he's going to beat the odds, though. I think he's going to become something hard to categorize."

"That's how I feel," Sig agreed. "I think whoever's in charge upstairs listens to Molly a little more than the rest of us."

"Maybe she should pray for you and me," I said. That sounded a little like self-pity, but I meant it.

"You mean pray for you and pray for me?" Sig asked. "Or pray for *us*?"

She made air quotes around the last word.

"Is there an us?" I asked. We hadn't really talked about it. Hadn't talked about much of anything. We were all still a little shell-shocked.

"I'm the reason you're a full-blooded werewolf." Sig said this as if she expected me to argue the point. "You tried to warn me about Stanislav. I know you're angry about that."

"Thinking about it does piss me off," I admitted. "I'm scared. I don't like being scared."

"I know," Sig said. "You're all calm on the outside, but it feels like I'm sitting next to a volcano. It makes me want to hit you."

"Go ahead," I told her. "I can take it."

She shot me a complex look full of exasperation and fondness and lust and anger.

"You're mad too," I asserted. "I can smell it."

"You think?" Sig blew a huge breath out, vibrating her lips like a horse's. "You killed the man I want to kill right now."

I wasn't going to offer to role-play Stanislav so she could have some closure.

"I have real regret for a relationship that was bullshit," Sig went on. "That really sucks."

"I know," I said.

Sig ignored me, thumping her upper thigh hard with a clenched fist. "It's humiliating. Then I get angry. Then I get sad. Then I get angry at myself for getting sad."

I took a too-large gulp of cider. It burned my mouth. I barely noticed. "I don't know what's going to happen the next full moon, Sig."

It took her a moment to follow the shift in topic. I was sort of interrupting her, but I couldn't hold it in any longer. Yeah, her dead boyfriend had been a sociopath and nobody had liked him and she should have dealt with it a long time ago and it was some heavy stuff and me killing the guy she had confused feelings about was all tangled up right there in the middle of it and by the way I WAS A FREAKING WEREWOLF!

"You don't have to deal with it alone, you know," she said, her voice softening.

"Yes, I do." I had never been so certain of anything in my life. It was partly fear of hurting anyone close to me if I lost control, and partly irrational, unreasoning shame.

Sig shot me another one of those looks. It wasn't hard to read, exactly, but there were a lot of things going on under the surface all at once. "You're going to be OK, John."

"And you know this how?" That came out a little confrontational, but Sig let it pass.

"Kresniks work with some werewolves," Sig reminded me. "And some kresniks are really powerful psychics, a lot more powerful than Stanislav or me. Kresniks wouldn't work with werewolves if some werewolves weren't able to deal with their gift."

I bit down on a snide comment about Sig's track record with knowing kresniks so well and tried to concentrate on what she was saying. It was difficult.

"You were close to coming to terms with what you are," Sig said. "Don't let this set you back."

"That's just it," I snarled. "I thought I finally had it figured out. And then the wolf took over. I can't remember what I did while I was a wolf. I can't remember a damn thing. That's messing with me."

"I've had blackouts before," Sig said quietly. "And I didn't have nearly as good an excuse as you do. You are the wolf. The wolf is you. You're not being possessed."

I jumped out of the chair and threw the cup of cider far off into the woods. It shattered against a tree somewhere in the distance. It didn't make me feel better. "I hope you're right."

"I think for most people becoming a werewolf must be like finding themselves on a motorcycle going ninety miles an hour, and they've never even ridden a bike." Sig's voice was calm and steadying. "That's why they lose control and crash and burn. But you've had a lot of practice riding the bike, John. You've had training wheels."

I rolled my eyes. I wasn't in the mood for metaphors.

"You're just freaking out," Sig said. "But it's the freaking out that's the problem, not the werewolf thing."

I sat down again and the chair rocked back with my weight. "Like I said, I hope you're right."

"I am," she assured me, reaching out to squeeze my knee.

"If you're wrong, I want you to kill me," I said.

Sig removed her hand. "What?"

"If I become something that thinks it's me but isn't me," I said seriously. "If I start killing for my own gain, or start enjoying it, or hurting the weak, or doing things you know I would never do, I want you to kill me. Or contact someone who will. Would you promise me that?"

"John . . ." she said.

"I know what your word means to you," I said. "It will make me feel better if you promise. It really will."

"All right," she said quietly. "I promise."

"Thank you," I said.

It turns out that asking someone to kill you creates a bit of a lull in a conversation.

After a while Sig said, "I want a beer."

She spoke casually, like she was about to get up and go get one from the fridge. Still preoccupied as I was with my own problems, it took a moment for the full import of those words to register.

"What?" I said brilliantly.

"I've spent the last forty-eight hours drugged off my ass," Sig said. "A vampire was abusing my friends and holding my life in her hands, and the truth is, I still kind of liked it."

I stayed quiet. It was a lot to take in.

"I would really love to just take all these messed-up feelings and get completely obliterated," Sig continued. "I don't know if it's from having drugs in my system again or if things going down with Stanislav the way they did hit some kind of reset button or something. This voice I haven't listened to in a long time is telling me that it's time to come back home."

"You didn't quit drinking because of Stanislav," I said slowly.

"No," Sig admitted. "If anything I quit drinking in spite of Stanislav. It's not like that asshole ever quit drinking to support me. But this isn't about logic."

No, it wasn't. Those little voices don't really get hung up on technicalities like truth.

"So if you really want to talk about being afraid of losing control of yourself..." Sig said.

"Do you have to get competitive about everything?" I complained.

Sig choked and spluttered cider over the edge of her cup.

I draped my hand over the side of my chair and held it out, offering my palm to her. After a moment Sig took my hand in hers. We stayed like that for a while.

"God, we're a couple of train wrecks, Charming," Sig said.

It had been a long time since anyone had called me by my last name. I kind of liked it.

"This week has been...eventful," I said.

"I heard what you told that vampire." Sig hadn't said Anne

Marie's name since we left the tunnels, and she had yet to speak about what had gone on down there. "About not believing in happily ever after."

I let go of Sig's hand and leaned forward so that I could put my forearms on my knees. "Let me tell you a story I heard when I was in India. A man climbed up to a mountain where a wise monk lived and told him that he was desperate and about to kill himself. His wife had left him, he'd lost his job, and his life was in ruins. So the monk looked at this man and said, 'Just remember, this will pass.' And the monk said it with such absolute certainty that the man went away oddly comforted."

"Those monks have it easy," Sig remarked bitterly.

"Be quiet, I'm being profound," I admonished her.

"Sorry," she said, and made a zipping motion over her mouth.

"So five years later the man came back and found the monk again," I continued. "He thanked the monk over and over for talking him out of committing suicide. The man told the monk that the monk had been right, that now the man had a new wife who was the love of his life and a better job than the one he'd lost. The man told the monk that he was happier than he'd ever been. And the monk looked at the man and said, 'Just remember, this will pass.'"

Sig smiled faintly.

"It's not so much that I don't believe in happy endings, Sig," I told her honestly, looking over at her. Some powerful emotion was tightening my chest and my shoulders and my neck muscles. "I just don't believe in endings."

"You don't really know who I am, John Charming," Sig said. "I don't really know who you are. We've only known each other a few days."

I didn't look away. "I know enough to want to know more."

Sig made a shrugging motion. "You know this kick-ass Norse warrior-maid persona I constructed. She was just a scarecrow I made to frighten bad feelings away, and now the scarecrow has had all its straw pulled out and the bad feelings are back."

"That's just self-doubt doing your thinking for you," I said. "The person you're talking about wasn't a scarecrow. She was the parts of you that you were comfortable expressing. I'm glad you're more complicated than that, but it wasn't a fake who ripped a vampire's throat out with her teeth."

"I hate that you rescued me," Sig admitted. "I hate it."

"Well, I am a Charming," I said. "By the way, traditionally, this is the part where you're supposed to give up your virginity to me."

Sig put a hand over her lips. "Oops."

I smiled.

"I guess I did save your life in the alley," Sig said reflectively. "So technically we're tied."

My throat got a little tight again. It made my voice sound choked. "Listen to me. When I finally became a knight after fighting for it my whole life, I had some guys save my life a few times. They knew I'd do the same for them too. It was the closest thing to a family I'd ever had, and it meant everything to me. It defined me. Then I lost it. It wasn't even any choice I made . . . I lost it because of what I was."

Sig reached out and offered her hand again. I took it.

"Then I tried to make a life with Alison, and she died because of what I was. I got to the point where I was so lonely and tired of running that I was just looking for a proud way to die," I said. "And then you came along and saved me. And I'm not talking about throwing that spear in that alley either. Me saving you from a vampire . . . that doesn't even come close to what you've done for me. If this werewolf thing had happened a week ago I wouldn't be struggling with it right now. It would have broken me."

Sig squeezed my hand tighter.

"Speaking of me owing you, are kresniks going to be coming after you or the others?" I asked. "Because of Stanislav and his nephews?"

"I don't think so," Sig reflected. "No matter how you look at it, Stanislav and Andrej and Andro sided with heat-seeking vampires against humans. And they did it because Stanislav was a weak-ass bitch who couldn't handle a little heartbreak. And the kresniks have some really powerful psychics who will be able to get to the truth without torturing anyone."

And the kresniks' secret society started out hunting vampires in particular. Stanislav's betrayal would seem even worse to them than it would have to the knights. On the other hand, secret societies like to cover up messes once disgraced members are safely dead and buried.

And Sig had a history of giving kresniks too much credit.

"Tough guys," Sig went on scornfully, caught up with her theme. "When it comes to dealing with emotions that women deal with every single day of their lives, big strong he-men are the biggest pussies on the planet."

Staying quiet seemed prudent.

"What about you?" Sig asked. "Do you know what you're going to do next?"

"I can't tell you much about my plans for the knights if you're going to be questioned by mind readers and clairvoyants soon," I said. "But one thing I'm going to do is find a place to hole up and write all of this down while it's still fresh."

"Why?" Sig wondered.

So I told her. The truth is, the Pax Arcana is breaking down. Technology has made communication too fast and the world too small. Meanwhile the supernatural population has been growing exponentially, untroubled by mankind, its greatest natural predator. Already humans' subconscious minds are trying to prepare them for the truth—that's why there are so many movies, books, television shows, Web sites, action figures, and pictures about the supernatural being produced right now. The Pax Arcana used to be a wall; now it's a permeable membrane, and an increasing mutual awareness is seeping between the world of mankind and magickind.

I'm not writing this for Sig, or the knights, or even myself. I'm writing this for you. That's why I've larded this book with background lore and survival tips. I'm a Charming. Dealing with enchantments is what we do, and if my geas won't let me participate in the destruction of the Pax, I can at least plant a few seeds and make preparations against that day. I don't know if the Pax will finally break tomorrow, or in a decade, or in a century, and I will do everything I can to preserve it as long as possible, but the truth is that magical nap time is almost over. *Pucker up, princess.*

"Are you going to write about me too?" Sig asked.

"Yes," I said.

She shook her head. "Do you think I'll ever read it?"

"I hope not," I said. "I'll probably lie and say we had sex."

She did punch me then. Not too hard, though.

Anyway, this is the story I wrote. It doesn't end "And they lived happily ever after." This is the way it ends:

Once upon a time there was a . . . well, call him a knight. He used to be one, and he still kills monsters. And he met a . . . well . . . call her a princess. After all, in the old sagas, a lot of Valkyries were the daughters of kings. All kinds of crazy and dangerous things occurred that should have killed the knight and the princess or made them hate each other, but that didn't happen. And they lived.

ACKNOWLEDGMENTS

I want to acknowledge my family, some of whom may be scandalized by this book. I love you guys. Keep praying for me.

A lot of people read this book while I was writing it, and their feedback and support helped me keep going when the rejection slips built up. Bless you all.

I'd like to acknowledge my agent, Michelle Johnson, in something other than clichés, but that is unexpectedly difficult. She believed in me, she works hard for me, she is a wonderful human being. It is all true.

I'd also like to acknowledge my editor, Devi Pillai, whose judgment I trust and whose acquaintance I value. You're awesome.

And Susan Barnes...I don't know if being an assistant editor is a thankless job or not, but just in case it is, thank you.

extras

orbit

interview

What made you want to become an author?
The same things that make anyone want to become an author, really. A combination of crippling loneliness, habitual lying, greed, and delusions of grandeur. I mean, I could slather it on about how the imagination is the key to freeing the mind and all that, but let's face it, ultimately it all comes down to the wild parties, the women, and the limos full of cash. Speaking of which, when are those getting here anyway? [Looks at watch.] Plus I like to read.

When did you start writing?
At the age of five. It was kindergarten, and I penned an opus about a backward planet where cows gave chocolate milk (I'm not sure how that's backward, but it made sense at the time) and grown-ups went to school to get away from their jobs and learn how to play from kids. The thing I still think is kind of cool about that story is that every word was spelled backward. Or misspelled backward in many cases. After that I flirted around with writing. I had a minor fling with journalism, briefly got involved with advertising, and lived with teaching English. But I didn't really get serious about writing until a few years ago, and then writing rejected my first proposal. Rejected quite a few of my proposals, actually.

But I persisted, and now I'm ready to settle down and start having kids. Or maybe writing is. OK, I kind of lost track of the half-assed metaphor I had going there.

What do you like to do when you aren't writing?
Well, I'm constantly processing oxygen into carbon dioxide so that plants can live, and buying perishable goods to keep currency circulating through the economy. It's exhausting. I also like running, hiking, live music, movies, used books, coffee, and worrying my family. The usual.

Who are some of your biggest influences?
Well, as far as urban fantasy goes, I've read everything I could get my hands on by Patricia Briggs, Jim Butcher, and Ilona Andrews, so it's hard to imagine that they haven't influenced me. I guess the authors who I've heard echoes of when I reread my stuff are Lawrence Block, Carrie Fisher, Ross Thomas, Dorothy Sayers, Robert B. Parker, Nelson DeMille, David Wong, Jeffrey Thomas, Roger Zelazny, and Robert Heinlein. I'm not claiming to write as well as those individuals, it's just that every now and again I can see parallels or hear similarities in tone. I do an understatement thing that's very Zelazny-like sometimes, and a sarcastic overstatement thing that's very DeMille-ish. I have a weakness for wordplay that's Carrie Fishery? Carrie Fishy? And so on.

That said, my personal favorite writer is Jim Munroe, and *Flyboy Action Figure Comes with Gasmask* is also about a loner who finds himself fascinated by a strong and mysterious blonde. I never planned that; in fact, I just noticed it for the first time. I don't think the two books are really all that similar, though—I wish they were. There are probably all kinds of authors who I imitate without even being aware that I'm doing it, and authors I wish I wrote like, and authors that I would blatantly rip off if I could.

On the visual-media side of things, I love *Supernatural* and *Buffy the Vampire Slayer* and those shows obviously had a big impact on me. Eric Kripke, Ben Edlund, and Joss Whedon rule. I would say that *Grimm* obviously influenced me, but I had already started sending my complete manuscript out months before its premise was announced.

What inspired you to write Charming?

My grandmother. She was an English teacher, and I don't think she ever threw away a book that she liked. She had this incredible house full of books about fables and myths and folktales. I'm not just talking about the Brothers Grimm collections, although she had those. I'm talking the Jack tales, the Petit Jean stories, Richard Burton's translation of the *Arabian Nights*, Kipling's *Jungle Book* stories, Hans Christian Andersen, mythology collections like those of Thomas Bullfinch and Edith Hamilton, Chinese fables about the Eight Immortals, and so on. All of these beat-to-hell books with ripped or missing covers, but inside they smelled great and had gorgeous illustrations.

Which character is your favorite and why?

John's voice is in my comfort zone, but the character who was the most fun to write was Molly. That might be because she's an amalgam of two real people who I'm very fond of.

Why did you decide to mix John with a werewolf versus other various supernatural beings?

I actually wanted to make John an ordinary person, at least genetically. Urban fantasy isn't really a comedy routine, but

I think normal protagonists can function like straight men, providing a backdrop and basis for comparison against the wild and crazy creatures that authors throw their way. Sometimes this really is done to comedic effect, as with Thorne Smith, and sometimes it is done to induce near-mindless terror as in the works of H. P. Lovecraft (or Caitlín Kiernan). Sometimes the normal protagonist kind of gives the reader someone to identify with, provides a foundation and a window simultaneously. I think that's why Stephen King is so wonderful—he mixes the mundane and the otherworldly in a way that bypasses your defenses and goes straight to your gut.

But the world in my novel is in a state of schism: it's actually two worlds that have been unnaturally divided and are coexisting side by side in an uneasy state of truce. It's kind of like the world in China Miéville's amazing book *The City and the City*, although it's also nothing like it. I reluctantly decided that I needed a character who was going to have a foot in both worlds while ultimately belonging to neither because I have plans. Twisted, evil, mad-scientist-type plans. Whether those plans will come to fruition, I honestly don't know. It still amazes me how different the book I plotted out and the book I finished turned out to be from each other. It's kind of like that saying "Man plans and God laughs." I think authors plot and novels wind up going wherever they want.

I chose to make John a werewolf because werewolves are one of the weakest monsters individually, and also one of the most familiar. I love exotic and little-known supernatural creatures: almost all of my short stories feature them, and I have loved writing those short stories. But if I couldn't have an ordinary human protagonist for my novel, I at least wanted to make his abilities familiar so that I could use him as a starting point to explore this world I want to have fun with. I made my first antagonist a vampire for similar reasons.

Where did the idea for the Pax Arcana come from?

Basically it was an intellectual exercise. I sat down and tried to come up with a way that the supernatural could actually exist. I came up with the following: (1) Some sort of mass compulsion/illusion/hypnosis. (2) Some sort of organized conspiracy or system in place to handle "incidents." (3) Some vague physics principle in action that would make technology unable to function or record the supernatural. (4) Some sort of mental conditioning or fail-safe that would make it impossible for people in the know to turn traitor or go public or just babble insanely in the middle of a breakdown.

That said, the idea of worlds within the world concealed by mass illusions and mind control are nothing new. My first memory of reading about something like that was the illusion that protected the Land of Oz from mundane eyes in L. Frank Baum's books, but there are all sorts of fairy tales where people are suddenly able to see through the illusions concealing reality. More recently, there's "Eight O'Clock in the Morning" by Ray Nelson, *Singer of Souls* by Adam Stemple, Dean R. Koontz's Odd Thomas books, the false "Gods" in Edgar Rice Burroughs's Barsoom stories, the Spiderwick Chronicles, the *Matrix* movies, and so on.

What was the most difficult part about building the world of **Charming?**

Trimming it down. I had something like ten interludes full of background information. I wrote speculations about the

Nephilim in Genesis, theories about the Fae, the hidden history of the fourteenth century, background information on the Knights Templar, different theories of how magic works, and so on. I came up with what I think is a logical explanation on why staking vampires destroys them, why werewolves were created, and so on. And I yanked all of that and more because I thought it was ultimately getting in the way of the story. It hurt. It still hurts.

What is next for John and Sig?

Well, John finds out that Sig is centuries old and really the one who ordered the werewolves to kill his parents. Sig sleeps with John, but it turns out to be his evil twin brother that nobody knew about. John loses control the next full moon and eats Molly. Sig and John meet with all of this stuff going on and try to kill each other but instead wind up beginning a violent sexual relationship marked by self-loathing and dominance games. This lasts until Sig catches some unknown Valkyrie disease that makes her really long-winded and eloquent on her deathbed, and John tearfully vows to get a sex change and take her name in order to make sure that no one forgets her. Then John wakes up at the end of my next novel and there's a sexy vampire in the shower and he realizes that the first two books were all a dream. Or were they?

Actually, the premise of the next book goes something like this: John needs to somehow come to terms with the Knights Templar if he and Sig are ever going to sort things out. The Knights Templar are having problems with a huge werewolf clan in the Midwest that is absorbing smaller werewolf packs, kind of the way Genghis Khan absorbed smaller Mongol tribes into a larger clan and organized these supposedly untamable groups into an army. It looks like the

Knights Templar are about to be pulled into another large-scale open conflict like the one they got into with vampires, and the organization is still recovering from that one. They can't get any reliable inside intelligence on what's going on with this werewolf clan because werewolves can sniff out non-werewolves and technology doesn't work around places where magic is concentrated. And here's John Charming, now a full-fledged werewolf with knight training who wants to reach some kind of truce. Those are the elements I'm working with.

meet the author

Elliott James

An army brat and gypsy scholar, ELLIOTT JAMES is currently living in the Blue Ridge Mountains of southwest Virginia. An avid reader since the age of three (or that's what his family swears, anyhow), he has an abiding interest in mythology, martial arts, live music, hiking, and used bookstores. Irrationally convinced that cell phone technology was inserted into human culture by aliens who want to turn us into easily tracked herd beasts, Elliott has one anyway but keeps it in a locked tinfoil covered box that he will sometimes watch mistrustfully for hours. OK, that was a lie. Elliott lies a lot and, in fact, decided to become a writer so he could get paid for doing it.

introducing

STRANGE FATES

Nyx Fortuna: Book 1

by Marlene Perez

Brooding, leather jacket–wearing Nyx Fortuna looks like a twentysomething, and has for centuries now. As the son of the forgotten fourth Fate, Lady Fortuna, he has been hunted his entire life by the three Sisters of Fate who murdered his mother.

Fed up and out for revenge, Nyx comes to Minneapolis following a tip that his aunts have set up a business there. His goal—to bring down his mother's killers and retrieve the thread of fate that has trapped him in the body of a twenty-year-old unable to age or die.

But when a chance meeting with the mysterious, dangerous, and very mortal Elizabeth Abernathy throws off his plans, he must reconcile his humanity and his immortality.

CHAPTER ONE

The dank bathroom smelled, the stench thinly disguised by a lonely pine-scented air freshener that had probably been there since the club first opened.

I'd been at the bar nursing a beer since six, waiting for somebody who had information I needed. After I figured out my guy wasn't going to show, I'd drowned my disappointment with several shots of the Red Dragon's cheap whiskey, and now I was paying for it.

I started to push open the stall door, but a couple stumbled in, obviously looking for more privacy. The Red Dragon men's loo wasn't my idea of a romantic interlude, but whatever rocked their boats. I peered through the crack in the door to make sure they were decent.

The guy, a hipster-looking dude with a supercilious attitude, said something I didn't catch, but I heard the girl loud and clear.

She was tall and curvy, with ice-blond hair, the rare shade of white blond that nowadays almost always came out of a bottle. Her eyes were probably blue, I speculated.

A glimpse of her heart-shaped face propelled me forward, but I forgot the door in front of me and banged my shin in the process.

"There's someone in here," she said.

I took another peek. God, she was gorgeous, but I'd met plenty of gorgeous girls. The spark of mischief in her eyes called to me. I'd bet the last hundred in my wallet that trouble followed her like a cat after cream. I wanted to get to know a girl like that.

Apparently, so did her date. "It's just some drunk," the guy said. "He won't even know we're here."

"I changed my mind," she said. "Let me go."

The guy smacked his lips a couple of times, which grossed me out no end. It was a good thing my stomach was empty, especially when I heard his sales pitch.

"C'mon, baby," he said. "You know you want to." Charming.

The girl pushed him away. "I said no, Brad."

"And I said yes," Brad replied.

I stepped out of the stall, unwilling to be witness to Brad's borderline attempted date rape any longer. Besides, I kind of liked the idea of playing knight errant for a change.

"She's not interested," I said. I crossed to the sink, washed my hands, and splashed cold water on my face. There was something about the girl that bothered me, but I couldn't get a fix on it.

When Brad looked away, the girl kneed him in the groin so hard he fell on the floor, gasping.

Evidently, no knight in shining armor was needed. I liked her even more. I stepped over Brad's prone form and extended my hand to the girl. "Hi, I'm Nyx."

She took it and a tingle went through my hand and a few other places. I was wrong. Her eyes were green, not blue. Even better.

"I'm Meadow," she said. The lilting sound of her voice sent the vibrations through me again.

"Hippie mom?" I asked.

"No, lunatic," she told me.

It must have been clear I wasn't following, so she elaborated. "Lunatic mom, not hippie mom. My mom's way too young to be part of the peace generation. She did go through a grunge phase, though."

I ignored Brad's bitching and moaning and concentrated on Meadow. "Wanna get out of here?"

You'd be surprised how many times that line actually has worked, but I wasn't really counting on it to work on Meadow. Despite the fact that she'd been playing grab-ass with a creep like Brad, she seemed intelligent enough.

She smiled at me. "I don't think so."

"Listen, Nyx," Brad blustered from the floor. "Meadow is mine."

I raised an eyebrow. "She doesn't seem to think so."

"Wanna dance?" She gave me a smile so dazzling that my head spun.

I nodded and grabbed her hand and we exited the bathroom, ignoring Brad as we went.

The music hit my bloodstream as potently as any alcohol. I lost myself to the rhythm as Meadow swayed in front of me. Heads turned to enjoy the view. I couldn't blame them.

The tap on my shoulder wasn't completely unexpected. I knew Brad would come looking for us eventually. His hurt pride wouldn't allow him to slink off, no matter how much the kick to the balls had made him want to.

I took my time turning around. Brad would probably take a swing the minute I did and he didn't disappoint me. Mortals were so predictable.

I ducked and his fist slammed into the dancer behind me.

Dancer-dude shoved a burly-looking guy, who flew into a couple making out. That guy moved his girlfriend out of the way and shoved the burly guy. Burly guy flew into a group of girls and they shoved him back into the crowd. Burly guy bounced around like the ball in a giant pinball machine. Pretty soon there were punches being thrown wherever I looked. Two girls rolled around on the floor, pulling each other's hair. That's when it became a serious bar fight.

I looked around for Meadow but couldn't see her in the brawling crowd. I finally spotted her as she made her way to the bar, but then I lost sight of her when Brad took another swing at me. That punch connected to my jaw. I bit my tongue hard, and blood spurted into my mouth.

I grinned at him and hit him in the gut. I was no longer a tear-stained child, drenched in my mother's blood. Blood didn't frighten me any longer. Time had hardened me. I wasn't just a survivor. I was a fighter. There was a knife hidden in my boot, but I didn't need it to fight a mortal.

Someone slammed into me and I lost my balance, but I was holding my own. I'd learned to fight a long time ago and I'd learned to fight dirty. Things were going well, too well, it turned out. Someone behind me hit me over the head with what felt like an anvil, but was probably just a barstool. I went limp as the world exploded behind my eyes. I shook it off and tried to stand, but that douche bag Brad put a knife in my heart.

And I'm not exaggerating the excellence of his aim. His blow went straight to my heart. It should have been a killing blow, but instead it felt like my heart was being squeezed by a giant fist. I stood there staring at him like an idiot as my blood dripped onto the floor. My aunts always said that I'd come to a bad end, but that was more of a promise than a prophecy.

"Was she worth dying over?" Brad stood over me. "I guess you'll never know." Ah, there it was. Although luck was always on my left shoulder, calamity kept her company on the right.

The world wasn't any better or any worse today than it was two hundred years ago. Mortals still killed each other in the name of their god, money, or sex.

Some things never changed.

"That hurt," I finally said, right before I passed out.

I bet you're wondering what kind of phony asshole I was or if I was crazy or high or both. I have been those things at one time or another, but that was the old me. The new me was one thing and that is truthful. I couldn't die, no matter how much I wanted to.

When I came to, I heard Meadow and Brad talking—arguing actually. I opened my eyes and saw two of everything, so I closed my eyes while I listened to their conversation.

"We can't just leave him," Meadow protested.

"I'm outta here," Brad said. "My dad will kill me if this hits the papers."

"I'm staying," Meadow said.

"Suit yourself," Brad said. "It's your life, what you have left of it."

If I ever saw that Brad guy again, I was going to curse him with an STD he'd never forget. I passed out again.

When I came to again, I was on the floor, but there was a guy taking my pulse.

"I'm an EMT," he said. I detected a slight slur to his words. He'd been drinking.

"Sure you are," I said.

"I'm off-duty," he said. Like I'd let a drunk corpse chaser work on me.

Meadow was kneeling there beside me, but there was only one of her this time. She was holding my other hand.

I sat up and almost gave the EMT a coronary. Brad was gone, which wasn't surprising. There were a bunch of people standing around me, but they didn't concern me. Meadow and the EMT had hopefully blocked me from the crowd's curious eyes—and if not, the dark bar and substantial amounts of alcohol that had been consumed would do the rest.

My jacket was on but my shirt had been ripped open, probably to get to the wound, but I didn't care about that. My rib cage ached and my jeans were smeared with blood. I touched a hand to my chest to make sure my mother's chain was there. It was made of such fine silver that most of the time I forgot I even had it on. I relaxed a fraction when I felt its weight, like a breath, light and warm, at the back of my neck.

"Your wound," the EMT said. "It's gone." I'd been skewered like a pig and would have another scar to add to my collection, but he didn't see that. I'd used a little magic to convince him otherwise.

"My jacket must have taken the worst of it," I lied quickly.

"Yeah, his motorcycle jacket is practically in tatters," Meadow said. "But he's barely scratched." It hurt to look into her green eyes. I realized what was familiar about her. She looked just like Amalie, but Amalie had been dead for a hundred years. I shook off the feeling of déjà vu.

I liked a girl who knew how to ad-lib. She had to see the gaping hole in my chest. I didn't have the strength to glamour both of them. I was intrigued by the matter-of-fact way she was handling my near-death. If I were a normal guy, that is. There was no way she could have known about me.

"It's not a motorcycle jacket," I replied. "It's a World War Two fighter pilot jacket." There were healing amulets sewn into it. I needed the amulets before I passed out from the pain.

"I'll take him home," she said. "He'll be fine."

"Meadow's right," I said. Her momentary lack of recognition of the name confirmed what I'd already suspected. Meadow was definitely not her real name. Probably something she told losers like Brad.

"A scratch?" The EMT was dumbfounded. "But there's blood all over the floor, all over him, all over everything."

"Yeah, I bleed a lot," I said.

"He's a hemophiliac," Meadow said. For a minute, I thought she'd oversold it, but the EMT bought it. The crowd dispersed after they all realized there was nothing exciting to see.

I scrambled to my feet and grabbed my jacket. "It's been fun, but I've gotta go." The sharp pain to my heart reminded me how stupid it had been to make a sudden movement, but I needed to make my exit before the cops got there. Or someone much much worse.

On the way out, I didn't see any surveillance cameras, which was a relief and another reason I gave holes like the Red Dragon my business.

The street was deserted, but it wouldn't stay that way long. Bar fights brought the cops, usually with sirens blaring, so I took it as a good sign that it was quiet.

I looked younger than my driver's license indicated, but that was to throw off the Wyrd Sisters or anyone else they sent looking for me. They'd managed to garner quite a bit of information about me, including the fact that I liked a lager now and then. My current driver's license said I was twenty-five, but I wasn't sure it would stand up to official scrutiny.

I'd grabbed a handful of cocktail napkins, but I had a feeling they wouldn't be nearly enough to stem the blood flowing down my chest. Though I'd made it out of the bar without any problems, the girl caught up with me two blocks away.

"Wait up," she called out. I kept walking, hunched over from the pain.

The original goal of the night was to meet my contact and get wasted, but now I just wanted to get the hell out of Dodge. Or Minneapolis. At least long enough to lick my wounds. I'd need every bit of strength for what I had planned. Meadow, or whatever her real name was, stayed close on my heels.

"I don't know how to say this politely," I said. "But get lost." A strange girl who looked like my dead ex? That smelled like trouble.

I kept one hand firmly on my wound and tried not to think about how my blood was slowly soaking a cheap bar napkin. It had started to snow and I blew on my other hand to try to warm it. Minneapolis was cold as Hades, but I didn't think my aunts would expect me here.

"I know a safe place," she said, panting a little as she caught up with me. "You're fast. It took me a few blocks to find you."

I swayed and stumbled and she grabbed me to help me stay upright. I moved away from her. "I can walk on my own," I croaked.

"Suit yourself."

We walked in silence for a moment.

She was so close that our arms brushed and I could smell her fresh citrusy scent. It didn't seem like her. I had expected her perfume to be something that suggested smooth whiskey and rumpled sheets.

"My car's this way," she said.

I wasn't sure I could trust her, but I was definitely attracted to her. It had been a long time since I'd felt anything that strongly. I shook my head to clear it.

It was the floral barrette that decided it for me. It looked like it belonged on a third-grader. I went along with her, even though my instinct warned me against it. I could pick up my Caddy in the morning. I'd made sure no one would spot it and if anyone tried to touch it, they'd regret it.

"What makes you think I need a safe place to stay?"

"The fact that you only had fifty dollars, no credit card, fake ID," she replied. She handed me my worn leather wallet.

I shot her a look. "I had a hundred in my wallet, not fifty."

"I wasn't going to keep it," she said, offended. "I wanted to see if Nyx was your real name."

I hesitated. She was cute, more than cute really, and I barely had enough money on me for a bus ticket out of there.

"So what's your real name?" I asked.

"What gave it away?"

I'd surprised her. Good. "You aren't as clever as you think you are," I said. What gave it away was that she waited a beat too long before she answered to Meadow. "What's the con?"

"It's not a con," she replied. "I'll explain in the car."

The distant wail of sirens made my decision easy. The scenery would be better with Meadow than where the cops would take me. I seriously doubted I'd find out her real name. I didn't really blame her. Names had power.

For instance, Nyx wasn't my real name, either, but I had taken it after the last time Gaston had found me, and I'd grown fond of it. I'd found myself reaching for that name more than any other, giving it out as easily as normal people did their given names. Regular Joes handed out their true names like verbal party favors instead of what they really were, secrets they should guard with their lives.

We came alongside a cherry-red Lexus with a license plate that read ZOOM-ZMM.

Meadow opened the passenger door and gestured for me to get in. I slid in cautiously.

"*I* don't give people phony names," I told her. A lie, but she didn't have to know that. "You were Meadow earlier. What's your story?"

She shrugged. "My name is Elizabeth. My real name." She looked me up and down. "You should see a doctor."

"No doctors," I said. She didn't seem surprised. Was she a poor little rich girl who picked up criminals for kicks? Not that

I was a criminal, but I wasn't the kind of boy you brought home to meet the folks, either.

"I'll take you to the cottage." She started the car and pulled out without bothering to look in the mirror. I winced, but it didn't slow her down. She gripped the wheel tightly, and I noticed her long slender fingers had nails that were bitten to the quick.

She drove without fear, taking the turns on the icy road with cavalier abandon. I didn't find it appealing, especially after she took a speed bump at fifty and my head went all fuzzy.

"Elizabeth, do you mind slowing down?" I said. I didn't believe that she'd given me her real name this time, either, but I liked the name Elizabeth.

She didn't answer, but she did slow down. When she turned a corner, though, jarring pain radiated out from my heart to my head. That was the last thing I remembered before I passed out.

VISIT THE ORBIT BLOG AT

www.orbitbooks.net

FEATURING

BREAKING NEWS
FORTHCOMING RELEASES
LINKS TO AUTHOR SITES
EXCLUSIVE INTERVIEWS
EARLY EXTRACTS

AND COMMENTARY FROM OUR EDITORS

WITH REGULAR UPDATES FROM OUR TEAM,
ORBITBOOKS.NET IS YOUR SOURCE
FOR ALL THINGS ORBITAL.

WHILE YOU'RE THERE, JOIN OUR E-MAIL LIST
TO RECEIVE INFORMATION ON SPECIAL OFFERS,
GIVEAWAYS, AND MORE.

imagine. explore. engage.